CHARLOTTE GRAY

It is 1942. London is blacked out, but France is under a greater darkness, as the Vichy regime clings ever closer to the Nazi occupier. From Edinburgh, Charlotte Gray, a volatile but determined young woman, travels south. In London she conceives a dangerous passion for an English airman. Charlotte goes to France on an errand for a British organisation helping the Resistance, and for her own private purposes. Unknown to her, she is also being manipulated by people with no regard for her safety. As the weeks go by, Charlotte finds that the struggle for France's soul is intimately linked to her battle to take control of her own life.

Books by Sebastian Faulks
Published by The House of Ulverscroft

THE GIRL AT THE LION d'OR

SEBASTIAN FAULKS

---◆---

CHARLOTTE GRAY

Complete and Unabridged

CHARNWOOD
Leicester

First published in Great Britain in 1998 by
Hutchinson
London

First Charnwood Edition
published 1999
by arrangement with
Hutchinson
Random House (UK) Limited
London
and
Random House Inc
New York

British Library CIP Data

Faulks, Sebastian, 1953 –
Charlotte Gray.—Large print ed.—
Charnwood library series
1. World War, 1939 – 1945—Underground
movements—France—Fiction
2. Love stories
3. Large type books
I. Title
823.9'14 [F]

ISBN 0–7089–9078–9

Published by
F. A. Thorpe (Publishing) Ltd.
Anstey, Leicestershire
Set by Words & Graphics Ltd.
Anstey, Leicestershire
Printed and bound in Great Britain by
T. J. International Ltd., Padstow, Cornwall

This book is printed on acid-free paper

In memory of my father
PETER FAULKS
1917 – 1998
With love and gratitude

Part One

Early 1942

1

Peter Gregory kicked the door of the dispersal hut closed behind him with the heel of his boot. He sensed the iciness of the air outside but was too well wrapped to feel it on his skin. He looked up and saw a big moon hanging still, while ragged clouds flew past and broke up like smoke in the darkness. He began to waddle across the grass, each step won from the limits of movement permitted by the parachute that hung down behind as he bucked and tossed his way forward. He heard the clank of the corporal fitter's bicycle where it juddered over the ground to his right. The chain needed oiling, he noted; the man was in the wrong gear and a metal mudguard was catching on the tyre with a rhythmic slur as the wheel turned.

He could see the bulk of his plane ahead, large in the night, with the three-bladed propeller stopped at a poised diagonal, the convex sweep of the upper fuselage looking sleeker in the darkness than by day. The fitter dropped his bicycle to the ground. He made his way over in the light of a feeble torch which he gripped between his teeth as he helped, with both hands braced against his parachute, to push Gregory up on to the wing. Then he clambered up himself as Gregory hoisted a leg over the side of the cockpit and slithered down inside.

'God, it's cold,' said the fitter. 'My hands can't feel a thing. This north wind.'

Gregory switched on the instrument lighting and settled on to the sculpted metal seat, trying to make himself comfortable on his parachute.

The fitter was talking as Gregory's eyes went over the lit dials. 'My boy's got this cough. I don't know

3

what I can do about it, stuck down here. Oxygen?'

The engine was started and the man was off the wing. He bobbed about underneath, then stood clear as Gregory ran up the engine before signalling him to pull out the chocks that held the plane against the wind. Gregory saw him hold up the torch when at last he straightened and picked up his fallen bicycle; he gave him a minute to pedal his way back to the fug of the blacked-out mess, to sweet tea and cigarettes. Then he opened the throttle and let the little plane creep forward across the grass, bouncing on plump wheels.

When he had taxied to the end of the strip, he turned the plane into the wind and waited. He shivered. With his bare fingers he was able to check the fixture of the oxygen and radio-transmitter leads in his headset. He inhaled the intoxicating smell of rotting rubber from his mask, then pulled the glove back on to his hand and grasped the stick between his knees.

The R/T barked in his ear — someone impatient to get to the barrel of beer he had seen being wheeled in that afternoon. The wind veered a little, due north, between the lines of hooded lamps on either side of the strip; it was making the plane toss like a small boat at anchor. Gregory checked the propeller was in fine pitch and opened the throttle. He moved forward.

Almost at once the tail lifted and he felt the controls firm up in his hand. The engine moaned, and the plane bumped its way down the strip, where the forces of wind and speed first lifted it, then dropped it back to earth. He sensed the wheels come clear, then felt the ground once more banging through his spine as a down-draught forced him back. He began to mutter through clenched jaws, cursing; then with a small inward movement of his fingers eased the stick and felt the earth gone as the plane rose up greedily on the air.

4

Two red lights showed that the wheels were up and locked away. Watching the compass with one eye, he set the plane in a gentle climbing turn to the left. At about ten thousand feet he ran into moist and choppy cloud, thicker and more turbulent than he had seen about the moon. He feared the plane's jolting movement as he nosed it upward: there was the sense of something else up there with them, another element bearing down on the clean lines of his flight. His eyes ran along the rows of instruments. Flying by night was a violation of instinct; there were no steeples or bridges from which to take a bearing, no flash of wingtip or underbelly to show the vital presence of other aircraft. The Spitfire pilots' speed and daytime coordination were of no use: there were needles in glass jars and you had to trust them. Even when you swore you could feel the brush of treetops on the undercarriage, you must believe the altimeter's finger pointing at 10,000 feet.

As the thudding airscrew churned up the night, Gregory stretched inside his clothes. His feet were cold, despite the flying boots and two pairs of thick socks; he lifted them momentarily off the rudder bars and stamped them on the floor of the plane. Kilpatrick and Simmons had laughed when they came to fetch him to the mess after a flight one day and found him with his feet in a basin of hot water.

He was crossing the coast of England: chalk cliffs, sailing dinghies moored for better days, seaside towns with their whitewashed houses along the narrow streets that trickled down to wind-whipped fronts. When as a boy from India he had been sent to school by the English coast he had hated that wind and the blank sea with its baggy grey horizon.

This was the third time he had undertaken a similar flight, but it had taken him months to persuade his superiors that it was worth the risk. First there was the squadron commander, Landon, to convince; then there was Group HQ to be won over. The Senior Air Staff Officer told Landon he could not possibly risk losing a plane, let alone an experienced pilot, in such circumstances. Gregory was never quite sure what Landon had finally said to convince him.

He shook his head and rubbed his thighs with his hands. Beneath the furlined flying suit he wore a serge battledress, roll-necked sweater, pyjamas and a thick wool and silk aircrew vest. If at least his feet had been warm, that might have stopped his body heat from leaking out on to the frozen rudder bars. As the little plane ploughed onwards, the instruments telling their unexcited story, Gregory felt a frisson of unearned responsibility: alone, entrusted, above the world. Then he moved the stick forwards to begin his descent.

He had been to the town before the Germans came. A French pilot took him to a bar called the Guillaume Tell, where they drank champagne, then to another where they ordered beer. The evening ended at La Lune, which was a brothel, but the French pilot didn't seem to care about the girls. From Le Havre the squadron moved up the coast to Deauville and played golf.

When he dropped into the cloud, Gregory began to feel the familiar, unwanted sensation of such moments: someone would soon try to kill him. In Le Havre an anti-aircraft gunner, though he didn't yet know it himself, would concentrate only on this murder. When Gregory had experienced ground-fire from British and French batteries, who had wrongly identified his aircraft as German, it had made him aware that the plane was nothing more than a few pieces of airborne metal and wood. Anti-aircraft fire was different from fighter fire, though one thing was the same: a few inches from his eyes was a fuel tank waiting to explode.

Now he could make out the shape of docks, so far, the terrestrial world, beneath his boots; there were minimal lights, evidence of some defensive caution, but he could remember from his study of photographs where the oil tanks were. He put the plane into a leftward banking turn, wanting to gain height and gather himself for the dive. He reached the top of his shallow climb and checked his position, hanging in the icy air.

He was laughing, though he heard nothing above the engine; for one more moment he held the plane level, then opened the throttle and pushed the stick forward. He watched the airspeed indicator moving up: 340, 360. He was coming in too steep: he was nose-heavy, he felt he would go over. Then, when he could see the ground — industrial shadows, bulky darkness — he could gauge where his horizon was. He held the stick steady. Gravity was starting to push his eyes back into their sockets and he began to swear. He could see what he took to be the oil depot and twitched the rudder to align himself. At last there was some response from the ground: he saw red balls of tracer curving through the air like boiling fruit, lazy until they reached him, then whipping past at the speed of light. Nothing was coming close to him. His thumb stroked the gun button, and when the ground was so near he could almost sense it through his seat, he let the cannon go.

He heard their sound, like ripping cloth, as he pulled the stick back violently to climb. He craned his neck, but could see no gratifying holocaust beneath him, not even isolated fires. When he thought he was out of range of ground defences, he slowed the rate of climb, and felt the pressure slip from his neck and shoulders. He throttled back a little as he headed out northwest towards the sea; there was sweat running down his spine.

He breathed in and dropped the speed again, safe above the Channel waters. He let the plane drift in a circle while he gathered himself and listened, but there was only the chugging engine and the slight whistle of wind through the airframe. His Hurricane carried four 20 mm Hispano cannons, known to their admirers as 'tank-busters', and four 250 lb bombs in place of its regular machine guns. He calculated that he had about half his ammunition left; he could not return to base with it and he could not fire it into the empty sky as he flew back.

He went round once more, making certain of his position, then began to lose height slowly. He pushed through the light cloud and picked up the outlines of the port below: he would flatten out along the harbour wall and fire as he turned to climb.

This time, the tracer started coming up at once, along the path of a weak searchlight. Gregory opened the throttle wider and closed his ears to the engine's screaming. The plane was juddering as he straightened out. He was so low that he could see the ground, and there were no oil tanks in view. He switched the button to fire and emptied the cannon at random in the direction of some parked lorries. Then he pulled back the stick and climbed as fast as he could. He saw the tracer again on his port wing; then the rudder kicked his feet and he knew he had been shot in the tail.

The tracer stopped coming for him. He looked down and saw a foaming black sea of welcome cloud. He started to level out, then breathed in deeply and blew the air towards the windscreen. He tested the rudder, one way, then the other; it seemed to react quite normally — the blow to the tail had apparently done no damage.

The southern shore of England was ahead. At the airfield, there would be someone waiting for him at dispersal, with whisky if he wanted it. Nothing could hurt him. The others were dead, but he was untouchable.

It had become suddenly brighter. A mixture of elation

and indifference to his own safety made him want to roll the plane upward, and he opened the throttle again: 320, 350, the needle said. He adjusted the tail trim: it responded. He pulled the stick back, gently, then harder till he felt the plane was vertical, hanging on the propeller. He pushed the stick over to the right and felt the aircraft go round. He stopped and pushed the stick back. The horizon was upside down in the night. He could see nothing, but he knew how the plane was flying. He pushed the stick forward, then over to the left, and rolled out.

He felt sick. Then he felt worse than sick: he felt disorientated. He did not know which way up he was; sudden clouds were covering up the light of the moon. He pulled the stick back to climb, but felt he was spinning; he was aware of the vastness of space around him and the little box in which he was plummeting.

Bloody Isaac, he was saying into his mouthpiece. Unless he could get a fix by a light or by some static point he did not know which way to push the stick. The tail must be more damaged than he had thought.

The plane bumped as it went into the cloud, and through the floor, though it must have been the canopy, Gregory briefly saw the moon. Craning his neck to keep the light in view, he brought the plane up and round on its axis. His back was aching with the pull and from the effort of keeping the moon in sight as he hauled the invisible horizon to where it should have been, the moon above, the ground below.

He dropped the speed and reset the altitude instruments, whose gyroscopes had been toppled by his roll. Something was wrong; although the rudder seemed to work, the weight did not feel right. He set his course for the airfield and hoped the wind would let him land. Eventually he picked out the flarepath and brought his speed down to 150, then lowered the wheels. He slowed again for the flaps, turned in steeply and felt the crosswind hammering the plane as he reached up to open the hood. The rudder bars were shivering as the wind ran through the damaged tail; below him, Gregory could see the pale runway lamps as they lurched from side to side. He sank the plane down gently, but it kicked and rose on the wind, out towards the edge of the field. He pushed open the throttle and began to climb again. This time he came in from a different angle and hit the ground hard. He held it down and braked.

He taxied to dispersal, ran the petrol out of the carburettor and switched off. He unstrapped himself and climbed out of the cockpit. As he stood on the wing he felt his legs tremble.

He walked over to the hut, pulling off his headset, running a hand back through his hair. There was the smell of a coke brazier; there was an anxious red face in the light.

'How was it, Greg?'

'It was cold.'

2

It was six o'clock at Waverley Station. The mist that had stolen down off Princes Street was hanging beneath the iron vaults of the ceiling, where it mingled with the exhaled steam of the London train. The lights on the platform, dimmed for the blackout, were blue and unhealthy. In addition to the usual passengers there was a squadron of airmen moving south from one of the Scottish airfields: not just pilots, but ground staff as well — fitters, riggers, modest men who called themselves 'erks' and carried kit-bags over their shoulders.

Up on Princes Street, a young woman was kissing her mother goodbye and handing her two suitcases to a porter.

'Have to run, lassie. It leaves in two minutes.' The porter moved down the broad ramp, weighed and balanced by the cases. The young woman hurried after him, the tightness of her skirt about the knee preventing her from running properly. She turned and waved to her mother, who held a handkerchief to her eyes; then she glanced up, panting, at the platform clock, whose black Roman numerals were still just visible in the vaporous light.

The train was five minutes out of Waverley Station and the blinds were down by the time she saw a spare seat through the glass door of a compartment. Inside there were only two people: a pair of young Englishmen with golf clubs. As he saw the woman tugging fruitlessly at the door, her two suitcases wedged in the corridor, one of them lifted an eyebrow to his friend as though to register his irritation, but smiled politely when he hauled back the door and offered to help with the suitcases.

'I hope I'm not intruding. The train's very full. I . . . '

'Not at all, not at all. Do come and sit down.' The other man rose unsteadily from his seat and helped to hoist the cases on to the luggage rack, where their brass-bound corners bulged through the string reticule.

The young woman thanked them for their help, then withdrew into herself by folding her hands on the lap of her grey suit and looking through the glass door into the corridor. The suit was well tailored, with a short jacket of military cut beneath which she wore a cream blouse and a pearl necklace. There was a small spot of black beneath her right eye where her mascara had run; her fair hair was pinned up beneath a small hat.

I do hope they're not going to talk to me, she thought.

Everything about her attitude discouraged conversation. She opened a book and began to read with obvious concentration. There was a slight flush on her cheek, though it was not at once possible to say if this was her usual colour or whether exertion or embarrassment had raised this mild pink beneath the pale skin. There was a scattering of freckles beneath her eyes, and her eyebrows were the colour of the darkest of the different shades in her hair.

They were almost at Berwick when the man who had first opened the door suddenly began to talk. He began by introducing himself. 'Richard Cannerley. But my friends, like Morris here, all call me Dick.'

'Charlotte Gray,' she conceded, briefly shaking his proffered hand.

'What takes you south?' said Cannerley.

'I'm going to work in London.' She had a slight Scottish accent. 'I wanted to do something to help.'

'The good old war effort.' Cannerley laughed, and a lock of fair hair fell down over his forehead.

Charlotte crossed her legs and turned a little into the compartment. It was a long journey and her book was not that interesting.

'And are you from Edinburgh?' said Cannerley.

'Not originally.'

'I thought not. Your voice is not as . . . precise.'

'No. Not an Edinburgh Mary.' Charlotte smiled, 'I was brought up in the Highlands. My parents moved to Edinburgh about ten years ago when my father took up a position in a hospital there.'

'I see. Morris and I have been playing golf. Do you play?'

She shook her head.

'I expect we'll go along for dinner in a bit. Would you like to join us?'

'No, thank you. I had some high tea with my mother before I left.'

'Well, just come and have a glass of wine with us. They have an awfully good list. I know from previous journeys. My treat.'

Charlotte looked at Cannerley with rapidly appraising eyes. 'All right,' she said. 'Thank you. Excuse me for a minute.'

She stood up and reached to the luggage rack for her handbag. The button on the cuff of her jacket became entangled in the string mesh and it was difficult for her to stretch up with the other hand to free it. The jacket rose up to reveal the creases of her blouse tucked into the waistband of her skirt. The skirt had also ridden up a little, showing the fine little bones of her knee. For a moment she was trapped and unwilling to stretch up further in case of some immodesty. Just as Cannerley rose to help, she managed to free her wrist and take down the bag. She disappeared through the sliding doors and down the corridor.

'What's an Edinburgh Mary?' said Morris.

'I'm not entirely sure. I presume it's someone from

13

Morningside with that prim accent.'

'You're a fast worker.'

'It's the war, Robin. *Autres temps, autres moeurs.* She understands.'

'What about Celia?'

'Celia?' Cannerley looked vague as he pulled out a cigarette. 'Now what do you think for a cold evening on the train? I remember last time they had a rather good Crozes Hermitage. Perhaps she's more of a Burgundy girl. Something full but not too heavy . . . '

Cannerley settled back in his seat and rubbed his hand over the scarlet plush. Above him was a small rectangular mirror with bevelled edges in which Morris could see the top of his own head, where the dark, almost black hair was receding either side of a tongue-shaped peninsula. Morris had a dark, close-shaven face, small hands and a cautious, candid manner intensified by the way he so seldom blinked.

'Will you be at the departmental meeting tomorrow?'

Morris nodded. 'I wish I didn't have to go, but Sir Oliver insists.'

'I suppose it's the French question.' Cannerley brushed some cigarette ash from his knee.

'It's always the French question.'

'I've almost completed my paper. I imagine you'll get a copy in due course. It's B-listed.'

'I hope so. I'd like to know how you pass your time. Do you think you'll be able to get down to Woking at the week-end?'

'It's hard to see what further national emergency could arise.' Cannerley's voice took on a signalled languor.

Morris did not blink. 'I haven't played there since the spring. The wind was terrible. On one of the par threes I had to take a wood.'

The spoken assumption was that their games were as important as their work. Each thought he held some

14

part of Britain in his hands. They lunched in clubs that flanked St James's Street; they talked to politicians, serving officers and newspapermen — not reporters, but editors or proprietors. Cannerley had been put up for membership of two clubs by his father when he was still at Cambridge and had moved over their dim parquet and threadbare rugs with ease since he came down; he was bilingual at his father's insistence, having studied with a French tutor in the holidays from school and spent a year at university in Poitiers.

At some stage in his education he had grasped, without exactly being taught it, the knowledge of what was right for his country. In the meetings of his department and in its dealings with other departments there was never any need to spell things out. Cannerley knew. Morris knew. Sir Oliver Cresswell, the head of the service, certainly knew.

Morris had had to work harder than Cannerley to acquire this understanding. In his last year at Oxford he was surprised at his books by the Chaplain of the college, a gaunt man with grizzled silver hair. Despite his ascetic manner, the Chaplain was reputed to know 'people' in London; he had a collection of avant-garde French paintings and a bronze by Archipenko. In a college where publication by the fellows was viewed as vulgar, he had been in print three times: on Saint Augustine, on Jacob Epstein and on Greek ceramics. He had held the position of Chaplain at the British Embassy in Athens and had been briefly in Teheran. Morris at first believed the Chaplain was trying to recruit him to a homosexual prayer camp, but the Chaplain's meaning gradually became clear, by way of digressions into European political history and the integrity of British institutions. He talked about a time of coming national emergency and left Morris with a telephone number in Whitehall. This was fourteen years ago.

'By the way,' said Cannerley. 'We've finally got a man into G Section.'

'That's marvellous. Who is it?'

'It's some little Midlands crook called Fowler. He's not one of ours, he's one of theirs. He's already been in France twice, blundering about, blowing up trains, recruiting a lot of reluctant villains to the noble cause of Resistance.'

' 'Setting Europe ablaze', as the PM would have it.' The drawling manner was not quite as natural to Morris as to Cannerley.

'Exactly so. And completely buggering up our operations. Anyway, a little research by our chaps has shown that several of his Brummie businesses have serious Revenue failings. He was called in for a chat last week. We pointed out that the tax man might be very interested in a closer inspection of his books.'

'I see.'

'At this point he became most anxious to co-operate.'

'What's he going to do for us?'

'Sir Oliver hasn't decided yet. Something simple but destructive. In France.'

'Destructive of what?'

'I don't know yet.' Cannerley looked suddenly worried. His manner became urgent. 'Listen, Robin, I entered this business to do some good. That may sound awfully quaint to you. I don't want . . . complications. Compromises. Do you know what I mean? Sometimes I think Sir Oliver — '

But there was a noise as the door was slid back and Charlotte Gray reappeared. They went down the corridor — Cannerley in front, Morris behind, like her bodyguards. The other compartments were all full: overhead lamps in their glass shades illuminated the laps on which books were held, many face-down as

16

their owners' heads began to loll and jerk against the antimacassars. They had crossed the unseen Tyne and were in the frozen fields of the North Riding; there was a flash of Yorkshire ground beneath their feet as they stepped over the coupling.

'Have you found a job in London?' Morris asked Charlotte at the table.

'Yes. I'm working for a doctor's practice, as a receptionist and general helper.'

'What sort of practice?' asked Cannerley, looking up from the wine list.

'He's a plastic surgeon. He treats amputees and people whose limbs don't work. He helps restore movement.'

'I see. And these are war-wounded, are they?'

'Yes, they're sent on to him from various hospitals.'

The spot of mascara had vanished from Charlotte's cheek. While she was tidying herself, she had also changed her mind about dinner. She sipped at the cream of asparagus soup, which tasted like most of the soup they had all eaten in the last year or so, of clammy green flour.

Charlotte smiled with sudden candour. 'It's what my mother calls billsticker's paste.'

There was no fish course and no choice of meat. It was advertised as steak and kidney pie and had derived from an animal rich in kidneys. Cannerley had chosen a Chambertin and started to pour. Charlotte held up her hand when her glass was half full, saying she was not used to wine, but Cannerley poured on.

'You could have joined the WAAF, if you wanted to do something for the war. Or the FANYS.'

'Maybe.' Charlotte felt vulnerable on this point. It was one of the reasons why she was travelling south. She drank some wine. 'But what about you? Why are you not in the services? Or are you on leave?'

17

'They also serve,' said Cannerley, 'who only stand and wait.'

'What do you mean?'

'Reserved occupation,' said Morris. 'Strategy has to be coherent. I can assure you that what we do is no less exacting and no less patriotic than any pilot, any midshipman in the Atlantic, any poor old pongo plodding through — '

'I didn't mean to doubt it.'

Cannerley looked amused. 'And you're patriotic, too?'

'Of course.' Charlotte was surprised. 'Isn't everyone? Particularly at the moment.'

'But what does it mean?' Cannerley laid down his knife and fork, apparently defeated by the pie. 'What exactly do you love?'

'I know what we're fighting. The Nazis. I hate them with a sort of personal bitterness.'

'That's not what I asked. What are we protecting? What is it that's so valuable? A tradition of tolerance? Great achievements? Science, exploration?'

The pink patch beneath Charlotte's pale skin grew a little more intense. 'I don't know. It's not something you can easily put into words.'

'Do you think if you'd been born in another country you would feel the same way? Or is it just something about British tolerance, British science, British exploration?'

'I think so, yes. It's the countryside where you grow up, the towns and villages, the people. The people more than anything. The buildings that make up your home.'

'You must be very fond of stone or brick to think them worth dying for.'

'I am. I worked for a picture gallery in Edinburgh. If you don't protect buildings and paintings and so on then you have nothing left to honour the lives of previous generations.'

'So we go to war, kill more people, to honour those already dead?'

'I don't think that's what I meant. But what about you? You told me you were patriotic. What are you defending?'

'Oh, the same as you, I'm sure.' Cannerley's offhand tone signalled an end to the discussion.

The waiter was standing by the table, braced like a bosun in a gale, as he gathered their plates.

Irritated by Cannerley's dismissive manner, Charlotte opened her mouth to continue, then thought better of it. The waiter brought a brown mousse made with powdered eggs and Cannerley poured the remains of the wine to take the taste away.

Charlotte insisted on paying her part of the bill, and on the back of the receipt Cannerley wrote a telephone number before handing her the piece of paper.

'This is the number of my flat in Ormonde Gate. I thought you might like to have it in case you ever got bored with your doctor's waiting room. I'm sure I could find you something a little more . . . stimulating. We're always very much on the lookout for bright girls. Do you speak any languages?'

Charlotte stared incredulously at the telephone number in her hand, then rallied.

'Yes. I speak French.'

'Fluently?'

'God, you sound like an interview, Dick!'

Charlotte looked steadily at Cannerley. 'Yes. My father fought in France in the last war. He used to take us back to where he had been. To visit the graves. He was . . . obsessed by it, you might say.'

'And is that how you learned?'

'I also went on exchanges to a French family during the summer holidays. Then I read French and Italian at university.'

Cannerley pushed back his chair. 'It sounds perfect.

Do bear it in mind, won't you?'

They went back down the swaying corridors. There was nothing to see through the blinds; even the stations were only grudgingly illuminated, and passengers stumbled as they alighted. For some reason they talked in lowered voices, as though the German bomber crews might hear them. England was blacked out and afraid.

3

Charlotte had been to London only twice before in her life and had recollections of nothing much more than the moving staircases in the Underground. She had been frightened as a girl that she would not get off in time and had made a little hop as the stairs collapsed and slithered back beneath the floor. Her mother had taken her to a department store where she had bought fabric for curtains and some school shoes for Charlotte. Then they had been to an Edwardian hotel somewhere near Piccadilly Circus where a waiter with shiny hair wheeled a great chariot of hors d'oeuvre to the side of the table. On a second visit there had been a theatre in Shaftesbury Avenue whose rococo decorations interested Charlotte more than the winsome drama. When the famous actress sauntered on to the stage with an expectant modesty the whole audience applauded, which Charlotte thought was silly. That was almost all she remembered, apart from the names — Cambridge Circus, Oxford Circus, Bakerloo.

She spent the night of her arrival from Edinburgh in the station hotel, and the next day through her taxi window she saw the undamaged mansions of Harley Street as they sped west along the Euston Road. Caught by a blockage in Sussex Gardens, the driver diverted through the burrows of Paddington, and Charlotte looked up to see what at first she thought was slum clearance. Two of the little terrace houses had been excised from the row; while the bricks and structural supports had been blown out by the blast, tenacious bits of stucco made a tidy proscenium arch. A fireplace and a sofa were suspended intact on the first floor like cut-out scenery in a children's theatre.

21

The driver told her that parts of London were obliterated and parts of it untouched; there seemed to be no reason why the German bombers should have been so vengeful towards Battersea and Chelsea and so lenient on neighbouring Victoria. The taxi pulled up in a small street behind Old Brompton Road; it was an area that was neither safe nor specially targeted, but in any event the bombing of London had, for the time being, come to an end.

The driver helped Charlotte out with her suitcases and left her looking up the steps to the front door. She felt anxious to get inside. Any misgivings or unassimilated fears she might have felt were buried and sealed with the efficiency of long habit. There were four bells by the front door and she could see a white two-core flex run up from the one named FORESTER over the ledge below the first floor and in through a hole drilled in the front windowsill.

The window was pushed up in answer to her ring and a young woman's head poked out.

'Charlotte? I'm on the telephone. Let yourself in and come up to the first floor. Catch!'

A single key on a piece of pink ribbon came spinning down and landed on the step. Charlotte let herself into a dark hallway. There were two bicycles and a pram on the lino floor as well as an old walnut dresser. When she had heaved her suitcases past the obstacles she paused at the bottom of the stairs and looked up: a narrow strip of worn orange carpet wound up past a windowed half-landing; she breathed in, expecting the boarding-house smells of cooking, cats and gas geysers, but found it smelled only of hyacinths.

The door of the first floor flat was open and Charlotte put her luggage down in the tiny hall. Above a table with a bowl of bulbs and numerous magazines was a small gilt mirror. She unpinned her hat and shook down her hair before replacing the tortoiseshell comb;

22

she could see the young woman who had opened the window waving theatrically to her to come into the sitting room. As Charlotte entered, she put down the receiver and came across the room.

'I'm Daisy. That was Ralph on the phone. I thought I'd never get rid of the little pest. Sorry about the mess. It's — well, it's just a mess. Sorry.'

Charlotte looked around. There was a tea tray on a low table in front of the fireplace; it was laden with crockery she could tell was yesterday's by the way the milk had separated from the cold leavings of tea. There were newspapers and magazines all over the floor and women's clothes draped across the various chairs. The room was very cold.

'How was your journey? Bloody awful, I expect. I hate trains, don't you?'

'It wasn't too bad. There were two men in my compartment and we had dinner together. The food wasn't up to much, but — '

'You *are* a quick worker! Did they ask for your telephone number?'

'No, but one of them gave me his.'

'What a beast! What a horribly ungentlemanly thing to do — to make you do the ringing. Don't you dare. Was he gorgeous?'

'It wasn't really like that. It was a question of him perhaps being able to help me with a job.'

Daisy Forester laughed, and her round, guileless face broke open. 'Darling, don't be naive.' She looked at Charlotte more closely. 'You're awfully smart, aren't you?' She went up and felt the lapel of Charlotte's suit. 'It's lovely. Is it Jaeger? I do love their clothes, but Mummy gives me such a piffling allowance I really can't afford anything nice. Look at me.'

Charlotte did. She wore a tight fawn sweater that made her breasts bulge, a single rope of pearls, a brown tweed skirt, woollen stockings and battered brown court shoes. Actually, Charlotte thought, she didn't look too bad. She began to say so, but Daisy interrupted her.

'I'd better show you your bedroom. It's tiny, I'm afraid, but you know we're jolly lucky to have anywhere at all. There's such a scrum for flats at the moment.'

'Why?' asked Charlotte, thinking of the spacious Georgian houses of the New Town. Why on earth would people fight over a cramped and icy little place like this?

Daisy looked at her in surprise. 'Because of the Germans, dear. They've knocked down most of the houses in London. Hadn't you noticed?'

Charlotte's room was at right angles to the end of the hall. It had been sliced from the adjacent room by the addition of a plasterboard partition that bisected the ceiling rose of the original, larger room. It had a small chest of drawers with tear-drop brass handles and a glass top pressing on a kind of lace doily. There was a bed with a damson-coloured candlewick counterpane, one upright chair and a grimed single window over the street. It was flanked by lime-green curtains, unlined, on metal runners in a rusty track.

It was difficult for both women to be in the room at the same time, and impossible when Charlotte tried to introduce the suitcases as well.

'I think I'll unpack in the hall, if you don't mind,' she said, 'and carry the clothes in.'

'Good idea. You've got quite a lot of clothes, haven't you?' Charlotte could tell what Daisy was thinking before she said, 'Do you think we're about the same size?'

Charlotte began, 'I think maybe I'm a bit — '

'More or less, I'd say. Perhaps I'm a bit bustier.' Daisy looked at Charlotte with her head on one side. 'Mind you, you're not exactly flat, are you?'

Charlotte laughed, not knowing what else to do, and said, 'I'll just make a start on this one,' as she undid

24

the larger of the two cases.

Daisy had taken the morning off work and did not leave until almost midday. 'It's frightfully dreary,' she said. 'I work for the Red Cross. It's grisly work, but the office is in St James's so there's lots going on. I've convinced Mummy that my work there is absolutely vital for the war effort and that's why she lets me stay on in London. She'd be much happier if I went down to dreary old Gloucestershire really.'

'Does she worry about you?'

'Oh yes. All the time. I'm not frightened, though. If there's a bomb with my name on it then that's just bad luck. I must fly. I'll be back about six. There's a spare key on the hall table. Sally'll probably be back before me.'

'Sally?'

'The other girl who lives here. Didn't you know? She's got this ghastly boyfriend called Terence. I'll tell you about him later. He's very high up in the Navy. Make yourself at home.'

The first thing Charlotte did when she was alone was to clear the tea things. The kitchen looked out over a small garden and the back of the terrace beyond; there were some tins of food in the glass-fronted cupboards and a part-eaten loaf of bread on a wooden board. The room had an only half-inhabited quality.

The rest of the flat did not take long to explore. Next to Charlotte's room, the other side of the partition, was another bedroom. It was slightly larger, but equally cold; it had a hanging rail on wheels with a number of women's clothes. It also looked over the street, though it had a greyish lace curtain over the window; on the bedside table was a book called *Love in a Harem*, and tucked in beneath the counterpane was an eyeless teddy bear. Sally's room, Charlotte presumed.

The largest of the three bedrooms had a photograph of Daisy on the chest of drawers; next to it was one of what Charlotte took to be Daisy's parents — the man in spectacles, baldish, moustached, vaguely medical or academic-looking; the woman dark, round-faced with pretty eyes, a slightly more spiritual but perhaps also more vacuous version of Daisy — and, tucked between the mirror and its wooden frame, a young man with crinkly hair in army uniform. Daisy's silver hairbrushes were laid out among the pots of cream and powder. An open lipstick stuck up between them, and Charlotte had to restrain herself from winding it back into its base. The bed, unlike Sally's, was not properly made; the eiderdown had been hastily straightened over the tangle of blankets beneath. There was a volume of Swinburne's poems on the bedside table and a copy of *The Great Gatsby*. This room, unlike the others, had a built-in clothes cupboard, and Charlotte could see a sliver of purple chiffon caught in its door. The walls were painted an indulgent crimson; there was a French couronne above the bed, from which hung some scarlet patterned fabric. On the wall was a reproduction of a Burne-Jones painting, all muscular breastplates and knightly, coiled desire.

Charlotte went to change her clothes. Because she had been living with her parents for the last two months, her mother had supervised her packing and had insisted on a sheet of tissue paper between each layer. Her mother, Charlotte knew, had dreaded her departure, yet was aware that in some way it would simplify her own life.

★ ★ ★

Amelia Gray was amazed by her daughter, proud, and shocked by her. There seemed no limit to what the girl thought she could accomplish by herself. She had swallowed all the education she was offered without apparent effort, though it was five times what had been available in the suburban ladies' establishment she had herself attended thirty years before. Charlotte seemed impatient of the values of her mother's generation, yet she retained a personal delicacy in her dealings with other people, an almost excessive reticence, a lack of trust, from whose likely cause her mother turned her gaze away. Charlotte had sprung from most unpromising beginnings.

In the autumn of 1916 Amelia Gray's husband returned on leave from the Western Front to visit his wife and their three-year-old son Roderick. In his quizzical, doctor's eye his wife saw some exquisite pain. He prowled the house, unamused by books or conversation, silently tearing at himself. She thought of Nessus and his shirt of flame. He went for walks along the edge of the moor, then retired to the inn by the river. He would have stayed all evening, but the landlord was a proper Christian man who would not stay open late to serve a soldier on leave, even if he was an officer.

Amelia Gray at first feared that during his time away he had found another woman. He appeared to feel guilty towards his own wife; it was as though he was anxious to be back in France. When she tried to search his mind, approaching him gently with oblique questions, he tossed his head and muttered some short phrase to cut her off. He had always been stoical, but his emotional state was now close to nullity. It seemed to his wife that he was oppressed by some unbearable secret, yet it was something that was not of his own making. She herself occasionally had a dream — common, her husband professionally told her, to many people — in which she found she had committed a murder, of which she had no recollection: all she had was the knowledge of her guilt and the fact of being hunted. Her husband wore the look of someone who had made the same discovery about himself; he

27

seemed unable to cope with the knowledge he had unwillingly acquired, but his intellectual pride and medical detachment made him unable to confide.

When he made love to her it was with a disinterested passion. She was aware of his eyes examining her, him, both of them, as their bodies went through the attitudes of surrender and possession. This natural act held for him no healing or forgetfulness; in the animal but tender moments he could not shed himself. His wife looked up and saw his eyes wide open, as though his consciousness of what he did would not leave him.

From these leave-time couplings a second child was conceived: Charlotte, a child of the war years, as her father frighteningly reminded her. He seemed to think it curious that she could have chosen to be born at that time of universal death; he sometimes looked at her as though she were insensitive, or perverse.

He had survived, but did not seem to feel himself lucky. Deprived of the daily emergencies of war, he had lost his framework of denial. The medical authorities took an enlightened view of returning veterans and he was allowed a short sabbatical before resuming his work. Soon afterwards his wife persuaded him that Roderick would be better off at boarding school. As her husband's struggle developed, Amelia Gray was aware that the main casualty was Charlotte. No motherly fussing over tissue paper, no last minute indulgences from Princes Street, could take away the knowledge that she had failed her daughter.

The War had ended for ever Europe's centuries-long dream of itself as a continent chosen or blessed. Amelia Gray felt that her failure with Charlotte lay in her inability to protect the child from the aftershocks of the cataclysm.

★ ★ ★

Daisy Forester arrived home that evening with exciting news. Sally's ghastly boyfriend Terence had got them all invited to a literary party and the place would be swarming with delectable poets.

Charlotte felt she had not earned the right to an invitation.

'Don't worry, half the people there'll be gatecrashers. What are you going to wear?'

'I don't know. I'm a bit tired, really. Maybe I'll just — '

'Don't be silly. You can borrow something of mine if you like. You look nice in that skirt. You suit navy.'

Charlotte could not resist Daisy, though she tried. She found herself shepherded into the bathroom and told to have first bath. 'Leave the water, won't you?' Daisy called through the door.

Charlotte saw why when she turned on the tap. The big cylinder above the bath roared like a bomber on take-off, but the scalding water came only at a trickle down its narrow pipe. The room was draped in underclothes in all conditions, from the still damp to the almost desiccated. Charlotte wiped a swathe through the misting mirror on the cabinet and washed her face in cold water while she waited for the bath to fill. She did not want to go to this party, any party, but she would do it to please Daisy: if she seemed too aloof, Daisy might complain to her mother in Gloucestershire, who in turn might tell Charlotte's mother in Edinburgh. It was through the ancient friendship of the two women, though they never saw each other any more, that her place in the flat had been arranged; and even if it was not much of a flat, she owed Daisy something.

Charlotte undressed and folded her clothes on top of the linen basket. As she lay back in the bath she wondered how Sally would compare to Daisy. The teddy bear in bed, the 'high-up' naval officer, the literary party . . . perhaps the gathering would be in honour of the author of *Love in a Harem*. Charlotte felt her face adopt what her mother called her minister of the kirk expression and stopped herself.

She climbed reluctantly from the bath to let Daisy have a turn before the water lost its heat and stood on the cork mat to dry herself.

'Jolly good, you're out already,' said Daisy, who was suddenly in the room.

Charlotte presumed Daisy would back out when she saw that she had interrupted, but Daisy merely started to undress, pulling her jumper over her head to reveal the top of a much-worn slip beneath. Wrapped in a towel, Charlotte gathered up her clothes and made her way down the icy hall.

The party was in a flat in Redcliffe Square, only ten minutes' walk along unlit streets. Daisy wore a blue silk dress; Charlotte wore a skirt and a jacket with a velvet collar and a narrow belt. Arriving at the party was like walking into a scene from the *Inferno*; it was what Doré might have etched if only he had known. Under the low, settled cloud of cigarette smoke Charlotte could see nothing but bodies pressed together, shouting. She could not make out the shape of the room, though the scale of the building and the double doors through which they had entered suggested something spacious, and the intensity of noise could not have been generated by fewer than 150 people. By the door, a little bald man with a bow-tie and exophthalmic eyes was addressing a tense and occasionally stammering soldier.

'Of course,' the small man was saying, 'the hope was that Laval would turn his duplicity to the defeat of the Germans. But that Auvergnat dishonesty is only ever self-serving. They should have read La Rochefoucauld.'

'Of c-c-course.'

'There's Sally,' said Daisy. 'Come with me.'

Charlotte sidestepped her way through the press, her

face aching with the number of mouthed apologies she made as she followed in Daisy's powerful slipstream. Sally was standing by a marble fireplace; she had brown, glistening hair and wide-set eyes. Her voice was high and childlike as she introduced Charlotte to a man called Terence, presumably the ghastly Terence, standing next to her.

'Let me get you girls a drink,' he said. 'Gin or whisky? I think the sherry's all gone.' He was a big man with a frizz of fair hair retreating from a fleshy, shining face.

'Have you seen anyone you know?' said Daisy.

'The man we met at the Ring of Bells — the one who told us he was a trumpeter. There's that famous poet. I can't remember his name.'

'Give me a clue, darling.'

'You remember,' said Sally, 'the one who wrote those poems.'

'Is the party for anything in particular?' said Charlotte.

Sally reached into her bag and pulled out an invitation.

'How clever of you,' said Daisy. 'I didn't think you'd actually got a card.'

Charlotte looked at it: The Directors of the Flagstaff Press invite you to celebrate the publication of *The Frontier Pass & Other Poems* by W.S. Melrose. 'Which one's Melrose?' she asked.

'No idea,' said Sally. 'He's not very famous, is he?'

Terence pushed back with two glasses of warm gin and French, and a whisky for himself. He raised his glass to them, then drank with thirsty sucking noises.

A lugubrious-looking man with a beard was trying to climb on to a table. Charlotte looked on with some surprise as he established his footing, helped by two laughing women. He was too cumbersome and too paunchily middle-aged to be trying such tricks, but

31

from the jacket of a tweed suit he extracted a bunch of papers which he waved in the air.

He called for silence in a bass voice whose natural resonance was muffled by the heaving room. Next to Charlotte a short and voluble man with grey-streaked sandy hair was squeezing the arm of a young woman in a black velvet dress. 'I thought we might try to do something on old W.S. in next week's paper,' he loudly confided, to the woman's evident satisfaction. Charlotte watched as the man looked up, registered her presence, smiled at her in a candidly lubricious way, then suddenly looked troubled as he saw someone making for him through the throng. 'Excuse me, darling,' Charlotte heard him whisper to the woman in the black dress as he moved off: 'bore-raid warning.'

The party extended a conditional silence to the table-top speaker as conversation died to a grudging simmer. The bearded man, clearly feeling he needed no introduction, offered none, but appeared to be Melrose's publisher. From the papers clasped in his fist, he constructed a speech about the importance of Melrose's poetry. His appreciative remarks about the poems were interspersed with frequent references to the Government's printing restrictions so Melrose emerged less as a powerful voice against Fascism than as a peevish critic of rationing. Before the publisher had finished his remarks the conversation had resumed a level that rendered him inaudible; his generous wish that everyone recharge their glasses had been widely anticipated.

Charlotte looked round to find that Daisy had disappeared from her side. Terence was leaning over Sally and tickling her beneath the chin while Sally looked bashfully entranced.

Charlotte saw Daisy — a few feet away, but unreachably far in the crowd — talking to two young men, one in army uniform, the other in a corduroy jacket; Daisy looked happy and poised between them. Charlotte did not feel she could impose herself on them, even if she could have barged her way that far.

She drifted from the edge of the group where she had been standing and moved deliberately round the rim of the party. Her mother had told her as an anxious teenager that the way to find someone to talk to was to be quite candid about her solitude: if she could be brave enough to let people see that she was alone, then soon enough someone would take pity. Charlotte went slowly round the edge of various groups, pausing to sip her drink, looking as honestly alone as she could in such a confined space. She elicited an occasional glance, a half-smile, but no offer of conversation. She found that she was back by the double doors by which she and Daisy had come in: the temptation was obvious.

She stepped out on to the landing and was on the point of tripping quickly down the stairs when she remembered her coat, which had been taken to a bedroom. As she turned, she saw a table with a pile of books. They were all copies of *The Frontier Pass & Other Poems* by W.S. Melrose. On the back was a photograph of the author: a man with a face like a rare-breed sheep in giant black spectacles. She picked up a book and opened it at random.

> We are not any more the waiting-to-be-judged,
> Barbarous refugees in the cold waiting rooms of
> The six o'clock express. We are gathered in the
> Soft sigh of History, where others have dissolved
> But are not dead. We are sleeping, but our bodies
> Do not sleep amid the howling of the greatest Lie.

'What are they like?'

'Not bad,' said Charlotte, looking up towards the clipped English voice. It was the man from the train.

'Dick Cannerley. You remember, we met yesterday and — '

'Yes, I do. What a coincidence. Are you a friend of Mr Melrose?'

'God, no.' Cannerley laughed. 'Is anyone? I'm a friend of Michael Waterslow's. It's his flat. Come on, I'll introduce you.'

For the second time Charlotte plunged into a Red Sea that was reluctant to part. Another glass of warm gin was pressed into her hand, and she drank it quickly in the hope that it would transform the scene from a smoky rush-hour to a starlit bacchanal. It sat in her stomach, acidly, and seemed to do nothing at all. Cannerley insinuated them into a group near the closed window; it included the little pop-eyed man who had been in the doorway, the woman in the black velvet dress, who presumably worked for the Flagstaff Press, Cannerley's friend Michael, who looked like a civil servant, shiny and correct, and a tall man in RAF uniform with tie aslant and an expression of confused detachment.

'In my view,' Michael was saying, 'the anti-Semitism of the French would have found its way to the surface with or without a Nazi invasion. Pétain's government is merely the expression of a long-felt national wish.'

The little man with the bow tie was having none of this. He began to rattle off the opinions of various writers, puffing at his cigarette as he went along, so the names of the authors he quoted came out each in its own smoky bubble. 'Anyway,' he said, holding out his glass to a passing whisky bottle, 'it's all in Benjamin Constant.'

'How are you on Benjamin Constant?'

Charlotte found herself addressed by the RAF man. His face was drawn into a smile. As she looked up at him Charlotte noticed a small patch just beneath his chin where he had not shaved properly. His voice was

34

quizzical, but not threatening.

She smiled. 'Not quite up to date, I'm afraid. What about you?'

'I've never heard of him. Saint-Exupéry I've heard of. He's a pilot, like me. Not Benjamin Constant, though.' He coughed. 'I suppose it's not really my sort of party.'

'What is your sort of party?'

'I like dancing, or night-clubs. Otherwise I'd rather be outside.'

'Flying?'

'Yes. Or walking. But not standing around. You look like a literary girl, though.'

'Do I really?' Charlotte laughed. She thought of saying, 'What makes you say that?', but caught herself. Having eliminated the arch, she was obliged to settle for the literal. 'I've just arrived in London. I wasn't invited to the party myself.'

She was aware of a gramophone starting up. Some tinny jazz tune was cutting through the burble of talk; Daisy was at her elbow, still flanked by her two men. She wanted to be introduced to Charlotte's pilot. Names went round; his was Peter Gregory.

Charlotte found Daisy's back between her and Gregory and felt a twist of irritation. She saw his head bend down in polite attention to Daisy's chatter; his hair was so untidy she wondered if he could have combed it at all before coming out.

There was a slow leakage of guests from the party. Through the double doors and down the stairs a continuous trickle of people made its way to other flats and houses, where more gin and whisky would be drunk. Those who remained began to dance. Michael Waterslow, the host, had drifted away from Charlotte's group and helped to roll back the rug in one half of the room. Half a dozen couples were swaying to the beat on the revealed wooden floor. Among them, weaving

35

a solitary pattern, was one who bore the unmistakably sheepish look of the author.

With Gregory's hand lightly on her back, Charlotte tried to remember the quickstep movements learned at Mrs Heaton's dancing class; as one of the taller girls she had usually taken the boy's part, and now the backward movements seemed elusive. In any event, Gregory was what might politely have been called an instinctive mover; he did not seem to be following any particular step, though there was a vague rhythm in his shambling movement and a certainty of touch on her hand and back. He talked to her a little, but his voice seemed to come from too great a height to be able to compete with the hopping tenor saxophones. Charlotte briefly closed her eyes as she swept about the floor. This was a mistake, she recognised at once, when not just her body but the whole of Redcliffe Square seemed to spin within Gregory's retaining grasp. She opened her eyes, gripped his hand a fraction tighter and was aware of a tiny line of damp along her upper lip.

After the song had finished she went to the top of the stairs, where she hoped the air would be fresher. Dick Cannerley emerged from the flat and asked if she would dance with him. The thought filled Charlotte with a disproportionate revulsion. She wondered where Gregory had gone. She had not excused herself from him but hurried off rudely. She went back into the flat to apologise to him, to find Daisy and tell her she was leaving, to thank Michael for the party, to escape from Cannerley . . . She was not sure why she went back across the dance floor, which had become, in her short absence, like some ruleless rugby game of lurching communal contact. She reached the other side and found the woman from the Flagstaff Press in a deep embrace with the sandy-haired editor: whatever he might do for Melrose 'next week' did not seem to be, in the view of the publishing woman, soon enough.

Seeing no one else she knew, Charlotte decided that all she could do was leave. She set off to fetch her coat and bag from the bedroom and was almost knocked over by a man being roughly ejected from a group of people by the door. Swearing and muttering, he staggered to the landing and plunged down the stairs at an involuntary run, bouncing heavily off the wall. In the bedroom Charlotte found a couple lying on top of her coat: the woman's dress had ridden up round her thighs, and she was laughing in an enthusiastic, horsey way. Charlotte wrenched her coat clear and made for the landing. She threw one last look behind her as she went downstairs and out into the night, where the cold wind drove the air from her chest. By the railings in front of the house a man was being sick into the basement area; he turned his anguished, sweating face up to her. Even in the blackout, she could recognise beneath the giant spectacles a particular sheeplike quality. 'Baa,' he said.

4

Peter Gregory was sitting in a wooden barrack-room in southern England. A lecture was being given and he was not listening. The Germans were putting into the sky a terrifying machine with a BMW engine of 1800 horsepower and with a speed of over 400 miles per hour. It could fly faster and turn quicker than even the nimble Spitfire. There seemed no hope for Fighter Command unless someone could think up something miraculous and quick . . .

Gregory was thinking only of a suburban road in India. It was not like the metalled roads with paved edges that crawled through England's deadening suburbia: it was flanked by palm trees, deep ditches, and was filled with running, bare-backed children. There was a house at the end, which was his house, and in its cool rooms he would shortly be given tea with samosas, jellies, gulabjamuns and cucumber sandwiches. Then he would go on to the verandah at the back of the house and his mother would read to him. He would want to see his friends but she would insist that books were important for his education.

But what good were books? They had not saved anyone. The lecturer was frightened by the Focke-Wulf 190. Gregory heard his awed description of the German plane and looked at the faces of his fellow-pilots, intent and yellow in the low gleam of the overhead bulbs. He was probably the oldest amongst them and the thought made him weary. There was a time when the inexperienced daring of those who sat next to him seemed in itself worth fighting for; but these young faces looked not so much innocent as vacant. They had absorbed some myth, some pattern of behaviour to which they believed they should aspire.

The lecture over, Gregory wandered outside, hands in pockets. Borowski, a Polish pilot of daring but erratic skill whose survival was a cause of constant wonder, offered him a cigarette, and they went over to the mess for a game of billiards.

Borowski told Gregory about the RAF's new wonder-plane: the Typhoon. It had 24 cylinders set in an H section, and sleeve valves. Borowski's solemn pronunciation of 'sleeve valves' made Gregory smile as he lined up a gentle cannon off the top cushion. It 'belts out', as Borowski had it, more than 2000 horsepower and had a top speed of well over 400 mph — 'easily enough to match those Fockes'. Borowski spoke fluent English, but to compensate for his accent he lost no opportunity to display his knowledge of RAF slang.

Gregory slid the red into the middle pocket and went to replace it on the spot. He thought he would like to try one of these Typhoons. The fighter squadron to which he was attached was not doing much these days. The Hurricane was an admirable plane in its way, but its best days were past: having flown Spitfires in the summer of 1940, he was not roused by anything the Hurricane could offer. He had been careful in his report to Group HQ of his lone flight to Le Havre. He knew other squadrons were also running experimental flights, testing new ideas and equipment, but Landon had told him it was very unlikely his exercises would ever become part of the squadron's activities. He had almost certainly flown his last such mission.

Borowski had seen a photograph of the Typhoon. 'It's gigantic. You don't get a leg-up from the fitter, you have to be a mountaineer to reach the cockpit. Then you don't just slide in, you go in through a door like a Daimler. It has a four-bladed propeller of about twenty feet across, four cannon mounted in the wing and eight rockets too. Hell of a crate.'

Gregory and Borowski went to the bar for a bottle of beer before lunch. The other thing that Gregory had been contemplating, he told Borowski, was a switch to night fighters. You had a navigator, who read the radar for you and told you where the blips were coming; you couldn't see anything until you were right behind the enemy. It was all quite different from the fast-reaction daytime flying he had been taught, where you took your bearings from the ground or from other planes that you could see. But they said night flight required a special kind of skill, or at least a kind of calm, because the process of reading instruments was not an art, but a form of trust.

Gregory was good at trust, at least where his own safety was concerned. He had come to think he was inviolable. He thought he was the last survivor; and of certain small groups he was. He knew that other pilots from the first days of the war were still flying, and that even of those who had fought in the Battle of Britain there were many who were still alive. His friends, however, were all dead. Those with whom he had joined and those he met in the first months, who became in the strain of mutual reliance even closer to him than his original friends, were all gone. He had been to their funerals, one after the other, or sent his commiserations to their grieving parents when he could not go, and he felt that now he was alone, the guardian of what they had all once been.

Borowski had been on leave and wanted to know what Gregory had been doing lately. Gregory told him he had motored up to town for a book party.

'A party for a book?' Borowski was curious. 'What kind of party? Was it a birthday party?'

'No, more like a christening.'

'And did the book enjoy it?'

'More than the author, by the look of things.'

'And were there some spiffing WAAFs?'

'I didn't see any. Though there were some good-looking women. I even danced with one, her name was Charlotte, but I didn't stay late.'

'You didn't take the girl on to a nightclub? You're losing your touch, Greg.'

Gregory poured the last of his beer from the bottle. 'I was tired.'

That afternoon he went to see Landon, the squadron commander, to ask if there was any chance of a transfer; he had heard that, now the testing was over, some new Typhoon squadrons were being formed. Landon sighed and picked up a paperknife from his desk.

'That little mosquito-sting we sent you on, Gregory. The day trip to Le Havre. Wasn't that excitement enough? Because I can tell you, it was bloody hard to organise. We are an enlightened service, as you know, but we draw the line at throwing planes away.'

'I understand.'

'You know what I told them in the end? I told them it was just a clapped-out Hurricane that nobody wanted to fly and that the pilot was a flak-happy bloody nuisance.'

Gregory said nothing. He never knew if Landon was telling the truth.

'Anyway, you don't want to test Typhoons. They're death traps from what I've heard. They're all going arse over tip when they dive. Something called 'compressibility'. Also you can't see a bloody thing at the back.'

Gregory shrugged.

Landon swung his polished shoes up on to the desk. He was pressing down some tobacco into a pipe, which he occasionally settled between his teeth, then removed, then, to Gregory's irritation, began to repack. He never seemed to light it.

'I could probably arrange for you to have some leave,

if that would help. I'm sure you're due some.'

'I don't want leave. What would I do? Hang around with those idiots at the Cavendish or the Bag o' Nails?'

'You could go on a walking tour of Scotland.'

'I could.'

Landon took a heavy petrol lighter from the desk and rolled the wheel slowly on the flint. A blue flame almost engulfed his hand. When it had settled, he lifted it towards his pipe, held it horizontal, then snapped the lid shut on the flame and put his pipe back on the desk. Next to it was a letter from the Air Ministry he had received that morning. He pulled it towards him.

'There is one other option. Something I've just heard about. But I don't really think it would suit you. It means flying at night. In bombers.'

'In bombers? I couldn't do that.'

'You don't actually drop bombs. Let me explain.'

★ ★ ★

Charlotte Gray was drinking tea in the kitchen. In the week she had been in the flat she had pushed back the tide of chaos. Not too much — she didn't want to seem obtrusive; but there was now a small impetus towards order: at least the bath was clean and the bread was put back in the bin.

She was a dreamy starter of the day, didn't like to talk for the first hour of wakefulness. Her sleeps were like death. She was sunk many levels down below the light of everyday and her waking was like being drawn from the bottom of a fathomless well. The odd thing was that while she found it hard to speak and therefore avoided company, her brain worked at its fastest, so she could anticipate at once what people meant and was frustrated by their inability to express it.

Her fear that she would have to be bright in breakfast

42

conversation had proved groundless. Daisy left the flat by eight to be early at her desk; whatever the excesses of the previous evening, she would be pounding down the stairs, toast in hand, to be at work before the others. The first half-hour could not be fun: Charlotte saw the level of the aspirin bottle in the bathroom, heard the early-hours returns and Daisy's whispered cautions counterpointed by a deeper voice. But her resilience seemed limitless, and the storm-force of her evening return was anticipated by telephone calls forecasting parties.

Sally departed ten minutes after Daisy, leaving sometimes a grinning Terence to clog the bathroom basin with his sticky shaving soap and his moulting badger brush. Sally was a secretary at the headquarters of a charity who were particular about punctuality.

Dr Wolf did not begin his consultations until ten; he liked Charlotte to be there by nine-thirty so he could go through the post with her and settle her with things to do while he consulted. Even allowing for Charlotte's morning slowness, it was not an early start.

The news in the paper was gloomy. The Russians were in retreat, as the Germans drove them back from town to town; the Japanese were threatening Singapore; the Americans had in theory joined the war, but for all the popular belief that this meant the Allies must win, it seemed to Charlotte they had as yet made little difference.

She resented the anguish that reading the newspaper brought and felt the news of deaths keenly; the war had aroused in her a feeling that surprised her. When she was a girl her father had taken the family to France and pointed out the million-acre graveyards of the British dead; Charlotte did not take in all he said about the war, but even at the age of seven understood that such a thing could never be endured again. An unthinking allegiance to a national cause seemed to have been the motive that led ten million men to die, and the danger of such thinking had been alive in the calculations of all the people she had known.

Yet something had changed. She had come to see the enemy as not one competing cause whose selfish aims were as defensible as any other's, but as a plain manifestation of evil. When she told Cannerley on the train that she was patriotic, she was not saying quite what his easy smile suggested he thought; she was saying that, despite the implicit danger, and against her former judgement, she had come to feel this way. What she meant was that she had unwittingly developed an almost motherly identification with the men being killed. She despised their killers. There was no doubt in her mind; and although she was not particularly pleased to have been driven to this conviction, she saw no possibility of its changing.

There was news from France, a country she saw through the eyes of her sixteen-year-old self. The Loiseau family in their house near Chartres had an innocent severity in their approach to learning. Monsieur Loiseau worked in an engineering business and was patriotic to the point of chauvinism; it seemed natural to him that an English — Scottish, he corrected himself with heavy humour — girl should want to learn the language of Racine and Voltaire. It was natural, too, for him to insist that no English be spoken in his house and that his sons help Mlle Gray in every way they could. An unconcealed horror of 'English' customs made both Monsieur Loiseau and his wife anxious that Charlotte should also learn about French manners, wine, restaurants, theatre, the niceties of conversation. They were able to recreate in their ample bourgeois house a placid version of a better age, as though Verdun had never happened and as though the panic-stricken coalitions of the actual government might yet avert disaster. Madame Loiseau took Charlotte to

Paris, negotiated a number of green-and-white-flanked buses, and showed her the Sainte Chapelle and the Panthéon. Afterwards Monsieur Loiseau joined them for dinner at a restaurant in the rue de Tournon. It was Charlotte's first proper dinner, with four courses and wine from Bordeaux, accompanied by a lecture from Monsieur Loiseau on the viticultural regions of France.

Now, at the edge of the Jardin du Luxembourg, where Charlotte had walked along the brown paths with their light dusting of gravel, beside those stately railings, the Senate House was draped with an outsize Nazi flag. At the top of the rue de Tournon the Luftwaffe had its headquarters: blank-eyed Nazi sentries kept guard in front of white hoardings they had erected against hurled incendiaries or suicidal acts of civilian defiance. They need hardly have bothered. In Paris the worry was about food. The papers talked of the black market and something called the 'grey' market, which, from what Charlotte could gather, was no more than a morally acceptable version of the black.

She was not interested in eating; she was thinking of the Jardin du Luxembourg and what it meant. In its shade, behind its small pavilions, she had imagined Gilberte and Madame Swann. Impressed by her progress in his language, Monsieur Loiseau had ceremoniously presented her with a copy of the first volume of Proust's novel, and in the long, quiet afternoons she had read the whole sequence with incredulous pleasure. Some of it had become a little confused in her mind and, amid the shadow of the young girls among flowers, an amorous wrestle had been transported from the Champs Elysées to the Jardin du Luxembourg. Her teenage years were not so long ago, so there was no forcing of remembrance. She could still taste the red wine from the rue de Tournon, but what she felt about this country was connected to a low responding note that the book had sounded in her. It had fused ideas of love and national honour to the memory of a kind of earthly paradise — a bell ringing on the garden gate, a little phrase in a sonata — that had been betrayed from the inside. And this betrayal was bound to happen, always — in her own life and in the life of a country.

Charlotte found she was close to tears. She gathered herself and tried to smile at her foolishness. The memory of happiness was never lost; the difficulty was to re-establish the connection when the thread appeared to have been broken. France was not quite given up to the destroyers; her own life, too, was not beyond redemption.

5

'We're going to Ralph's house this evening. Would you like to come? Should be fun.' It was Daisy's early evening forecast, telephoned in from St James's just before she left for home.

'I thought you didn't like Ralph,' Charlotte said when Daisy came home.

'I can't stand him,' said Daisy, kicking off her shoes. 'Have you got a sixpence for the gas?'

Blue and orange flames crept up the cracked honeycomb of the fire. Daisy sat on the floor and put her feet up on the low brass fender.

'But he does know some nice people. Painters and so on. They're hideously dirty, some of them, but they're quite fun.'

'Is Ralph a painter?'

'No, darling, he's a poet. Didn't you know? That's how we got invited to that party. Ralph wangled it. He's awfully clever like that.'

At the mention of the Melrose party Charlotte was aware of a moment of acute anxiety.

'I think Sally wants to come too. The ghastly Terence is having to do something naval and she'll be all moony without him.'

'Has he gone to sea?'

Daisy laughed. 'Terence? I doubt whether he's ever set foot in a mackerel boat. He's just got to be in Dartmouth for a week. I think he's instructing some young recruits on the hardships of the North Atlantic.'

'Poor Sally.'

'What she really hates is that Terence then has to go and see his wife in the New Forest. What are you going to wear?'

Charlotte thought. 'Perhaps that skirt and jacket I had on at the party the other day when — '

'Oh, I wouldn't wear that,' said Daisy quickly.

'Why?'

'There might be some of the same people from the other night. Anyway, tonight's not at all smart. I'll probably just stay as I am. Unless . . . '

'Unless what?'

'Well, you know your tartan skirt . . . '

'It's at the cleaners.'

'But you've only worn it once! My God, Charlotte, don't you know there's a war on? Ever heard of Make-do and Mend?'

Sally was tearful when she came home and it took all Daisy's persuasive force to make her go with them. Ralph lived in an attic flat in a house on the Fulham Road; the blacked-out ground floor was by day a flower shop, and a bare wooden staircase took them up three flights before they arrived at Ralph's open door.

'Hello, girls. All three of you. My God. What a little collection.'

Ralph was a pale young man with a nose like a fox terrier, reddish hair and a wheedling, ironic voice. Charlotte stepped into what was effectively a one-room flat, with a double mattress on the floor in one corner, a kitchen area with sink and gas ring in another, and in the middle of the room a long maroon-covered sofa. Sitting on it, drink in hand, was a man she recognised, with an appalled pang as she struggled to regain the composure lost to Ralph's greeting, as Peter Gregory.

He unfolded himself from his low seat and rose to greet them. He appeared to have no difficulty in remembering Charlotte and seemed pleased to see her again. Charlotte gained time by elaborately re-introducing Sally and Daisy, despite Gregory's protests that he remembered them quite well.

A third man emerged through a door in the corner,

followed by the sound of a flushing lavatory, and was introduced as Miles. He gave a general wave to the room and sat down heavily on the sofa. He leaned over the arm, apparently studying Ralph's unremarkable rug.

'Beer all right for you?' said Ralph, handing Charlotte a glass with the word Worthington stamped on the side and pouring light ale from a bottle.

An air-raid siren was whining in the distance. 'Bugger that,' said Ralph. 'I'm not going down into Mrs Porter's cellar. I thought I might try and cook some dinner. Anyone like to help me?'

'Sally's the best cook,' said Daisy firmly. 'She'll help.'

'What have you got in your larder, Ralph?' said Sally, whose temporary bereavement made her sound more than usually like a lost child.

'Why aren't you up in the sky shooting down Germans?' Daisy asked Gregory.

'I'm on leave. We have a rota. They think it's bad for you to be on standby for more than a certain number of days.' He made to resume his seat at the end of the sofa, but gestured that one of the women should sit down first. There was room for both of them between him, at one end, and the threateningly silent Miles at the other. Charlotte felt Daisy's hand in the small of her back, while Daisy herself turned towards the kitchen area.

When Charlotte had settled herself, Gregory crossed his legs and turned inwards to face her. He was wearing civilian clothes, an open-necked viyella shirt, a battered jacket. He asked her about her work and how she was enjoying living in London.

She wanted him to tell her about his life on the station. Was he afraid? Did they sleep in barracks or in houses? Was it true they were sometimes drunk when they went up? Which was his favourite of the planes he had flown?

His answers, even though these were questions he must have been asked many times before, were detailed and humorous enough; but the more he talked, the more Charlotte saw in him a sense of absence: at some level he was not willing to engage either with her or with his own experience. With a trickle of fear that grew almost to alarm, Charlotte detected that at the centre of him, where there might have been hope, bravado, even fear, there was a void.

The first form her passion for Gregory took was a desire to feed him and encourage him, to trace out the elements of his deep fatigue and restore him to fitness. It was almost pity that she felt as she spoke to him on the sofa in Ralph's unheated, chattering room, but she did not see how pity could coexist with the sense of vulnerability he induced in her. If she was to mother and heal him she would need to be the controlling and superior force, yet his slow, deep speech made her sense submissive danger. She felt disconcerted by her inability to find a word that expressed the nature of her response to him. Compassion, longing, gentleness, a wish to lose herself in him, to purge the conflicts of her life in the solution of his troubled weariness . . . These seemed to be aspects of what she felt, though she experienced them not as separate factors but as a single, precipitous anguish.

★ ★ ★

A young man, perhaps a year or so younger even than Charlotte, sat on one of the hard chairs in Dr Wolf's waiting room, clutching a magazine in his clawed hand. With the good fingers of the other hand he turned the pages, searching for something to detain his interest. Charlotte was behind the desk, filing patients' notes, preparing to type a letter from Dr Wolf to a station medical officer. She consulted the scribbled notes she had taken in dictation; Dr Wolf spoke too fast for her aching fingers. She worried that she would make a crucial error — left leg for right, grams instead of grains — and begged Dr Wolf to read the typed letters carefully before signing them.

When Charlotte rose from the desk to reach up for a file the young man's gaze ran over the swell of her hip in its navy blue skirt. When she sat and crossed her legs he let a sideways glance still linger in the hope of some momentary glimpse of hem or shadow. He was unrewarded, and ploughed his eyes back down the columns of *Horizon*.

'Miss Gray? One moment please.' Dr Wolf's head came round the door.

Charlotte followed him in. It was a cold and cavernous room with old leather furniture; it smelled of gas, which the fire emitted in greater quantities than heat. Brown leather screens surrounded a couch covered with a sterilised white sheet; this was the only touch of the medical in the room. Dr Wolf in his heavy grey suit, a thin-linked watch chain roping one side of his belly to the other, looked like a doubtful financier. He had abundant woolly grey hair and dense eyebrows over gold-rimmed glasses; he characteristically held one hand in his jacket pocket while he carved words with the other in what seemed to Charlotte an exaggeratedly unEnglish way.

His patient, a man whose leg had been amputated below the knee, sat in one of the big armchairs, his crutches on the faded Wilton carpet beside him. He and Dr Wolf looked very small in the empty room, Charlotte thought, like two figures from de Chirico lost in a giant piazza.

'We need to arrange an operation for Lieutenant Dawson,' Dr Wolf said. 'Would you be kind enough to confer with my diary and see which day suits the Lieutenant. He will need to be in hospital for two days.' He pronounced it Lootenant, the American way. Charlotte suspected his pronunciations were sometimes less a matter of accent than of predilection.

'Lieutenant Dawson was wounded in France. A matter of sabotage which unfortunately . . . misfired.'

' 'fraid so.' Dawson gave a schoolboy grin. 'One of our very own devices.'

'What were you doing in France?' said Charlotte.

'Oh terribly hush-hush, I'm afraid. There are quite a few of us over there. I was hiding out in a little village in the Loire valley and the first person I bumped into in the local café was a fellow from Manchester!'

Charlotte helped Dawson to his feet and held his crutches till he balanced himself and made his way to the waiting room. Dr Wolf had put one of his two weekly operating sessions at the disposal of the Ministry of Defence; the reduced payment was to be deferred until the end of the War. Wolf had been a refugee from earlier displacements in Eastern Europe and viewed the new disasters in a fatalistic way.

At lunch-time Charlotte walked up to Regent's Park. There was a coffee stall near the Outer Circle where they had sugarless bath buns of a lumpen consistency that nevertheless did a job of kinds by occupying the stomach for two or three hours. The coffee itself was best avoided. Charlotte walked briskly in the park, threw the end of the bun to some pigeons, and tried to clear her mind.

Ten days had passed since the evening in Ralph's flat. She saw this interval in retrospect as confused and incomprehensible. She viewed life as narrative, because that was how she experienced it. There was the time before an event, and then, the world changed, there was the time after it. When someone died suddenly or young she always thought: who could have known, who could have foreseen this, on the day of her wedding or when we last met, when no one even knew she was ill; yet the cells were already silently about their fatal work? This violent unknowability of life was central to her experience of it, and it was pointless to pretend that it was 'mere chance' or that subtler philosophies were not concerned with anything so vulgar as incident or 'story': any interpretation that was not concerned with random changes had, in her view, begged the biggest question.

This was what made the days of uncertainty in retrospect so baffling. Once her feelings for Peter Gregory had crystallised, she found it hard to picture herself in a previous epoch, while the days of transition themselves seemed lacking in self-awareness, almost comically confused. She loved him. How could she once not have loved him?

The night before she had lain in bed and wept. She could not stop crying. She wrapped a pillow over her head so the noise could not be heard outside her room. She dreaded Daisy coming in and offering some salacious, short advice. In her confusion she heard the word 'inconsolable' and knew that it was apt because she did not wish to be consoled: it was more important to have him than to save herself. Was that 'love'? Was that what it meant? She struggled with the question because she needed to find a word for the feeling that had overpowered her. In identifying it, by whatever surprising word, she might bring it within bounds. Love had never felt like this to her before: not in the tough little loyalty with her brother, not in the resentful affection for her mother, not in the liberating fondness of friends.

In the morning she saw that whatever name she gave the feeling, it had, in any case, become a given of her life: an incident, a narrative development that changed everything. The relief of recognising a new fixed point was qualified by her knowledge of how inconvenient it was. The last thing she needed was some uncontrolled romance. She wanted to be helpful, she wanted to lead a serious life, not to lie sobbing in her bed for a disembodied yearning. Still less did she wish to see it embodied, with the complication and the fear that all that would entail.

As she walked through Regent's Park she looked at the old people, children, women, non-combatants, but felt no sense of kinship with their cold walks, their individual ties and errands. She felt as though she had stepped outside the normal scope of daily life. Perhaps drug addicts felt this separation from reality, this powerful dissociation that made them both superior and helpless. She wanted to return, to reinhabit a life in which normal forces mediated, yet was unable to quieten in any way the volume of her ecstasy.

When Dr Wolf returned to his consulting rooms after lunch he failed to offer his usual greeting. Charlotte looked up anxiously from her desk.

'Did you have a good lunch?' she said.

'Perfectly acceptable, thank you, though alas not in the place of my choosing.'

'Why was that?'

'Because, Miss Gray, you failed to book my table.'

'Oh my God, I'm sorry. It completely slipped my mind.'

'In the normal way I could have eaten at the long table with the other members, but since I had a guest to whom I wanted to talk in private, we were obliged to go elsewhere.'

'I'm very sorry, Dr Wolf. I just forgot.'

'Is there something on your mind, Miss Gray?'

'No, not particularly.'

'You've appeared somewhat distracted over the last two or three days. I wondered if something was troubling you.'

'No, no, I . . . don't think so. I was thinking about the situation in France. It's very sad, isn't it? I used to

54

go there a good deal. I'm worried about some people I know. A family I used to stay with.'

'Are they in the Occupied Zone?'

'Yes, they live near Chartres.'

'Then I share your concern. Are they Jewish?'

'No. Not that I'm aware of. I suppose it's possible that they have Jewish blood somewhere in the past. But they're ordinary Catholics now.'

'I daresay they've made what accommodation they feel is necessary with the occupying power.' Wolf's tone was ambiguous.

Charlotte said, 'I suppose so. They're quite elderly. I doubt whether they can have much choice.'

'At least in the Occupied Zone they can comfort themselves with that knowledge. One can't help feeling that in the Free Zone one would feel more uneasy.'

'In what way?'

'Even by doing nothing you would be making a pact with the devil. I think one would feel compelled to take action against the Government.'

'One?'

Dr Wolf smiled. 'I am probably as old as your friends. But you are a young woman of spirit, Miss Gray.'

Charlotte said, 'Perhaps you're right. I think maybe I would try to do something. It's hard to know what, because it isn't easy to discover what's going on.'

'They have sold the honour of the country.' Wolf's doubtful tone resolved itself into tetchy certainty. 'That exquisite civilisation that took so long to bring to flower. They're not just Nazis, they're worse than the Nazis, because they're French.'

Charlotte looked down at the desk. 'Perhaps.'

Wolf had gone half way through the door to his room when he stopped. 'I almost forgot. After you had gone out to lunch there was a telephone call for you. A gentleman. I've written his name down somewhere.'

Charlotte watched him disappear into the gloom,

then return with a piece of paper. 'A Mr Cannerley. He says he'll telephone again later.'

'Thank you,' said Charlotte. Her mouth felt dusty. 'I'm sorry about the table.'

★ ★ ★

Cannerley, thought Charlotte, as the bus jolted along the Bayswater Road. What do I want with Cannerley? Among other things, she resented the way that someone like him who knew 'people' had been able to discover her telephone number. She looked down on to the railings of the park. Across the road the big hotels looked bulky and deserted, their glimmering windows darkened.

She was numb and cold when she reached the flat and squeezed past the walnut dresser in the hall. Her plan was to have a bath, then retire to her room with a book. Cannerley. For heaven's sake.

★ ★ ★

It took all Gregory's willpower not to telephone.

Luckily, the prospect of a change of job occupied his mind for much of the day; it was liberating, if not quite reviving. He would need to retrain to fly bigger planes, some of which required plain muscular strength: the fabled lightness of touch, sometimes having only to stretch your toes inside your boots to feel the tail twitch . . . that wouldn't work. Gregory was happy to leave it all behind and start again. There was something comic about the handling of big planes and something pedestrian about flying with a navigator, but he felt the change was timely, almost decorous.

It was still difficult not to telephone this woman. It had been hard enough not to invite her to go with him when he left Ralph's flat. He had been led to expect that the invitation emanated from his friend Michael Waterslow. He kept expecting Michael to appear and felt deceived when it became apparent that this Ralph and the drunk, Miles, were the only other men. They produced some food at about ten o'clock, then Ralph played the guitar. They had made a sort of bolognaise out of tinned meat and spongy carrots to go with some spaghetti the girl with the dark hair had found in Ralph's cupboard. It was repulsive, but by that time Gregory, who had been instructed to bring whisky but found himself the only person drinking it, was too drunk to care.

And the girl, the woman, Charlotte. She had an astonishing nervous intensity. They talked for three hours on the sofa, at the end of which he felt as though he had been subjected to a violent electrical charge. Her force seemed to him magnificent, particularly as it was filtered by such a diffident manner. A roué's reflex in him swiftly calculated factors of propriety and emotion, passion and control, and what the amorous consequences might be; but, intrigued though he was by the idea, he was more charmed by a solemn sweetness in her. She did believe in things, and said so, then seemed to find her superior education mocking her desire for earnestness. She did laugh too, sometimes at the traps she inadvertently set for herself and sometimes at the things he told her.

He found himself becoming confidential. He was able to check this tendency, though only with difficulty; and when he heard himself talking to her in intimate terms about his childhood in India he thought he had better leave.

There was an awkward exchange on the landing outside the flat. In the light of the shadeless stairwell bulb he could see the even brown colour of her eyes as she determinedly held his gaze.

'I have enjoyed talking to you. I have to go back to

the squadron tomorrow. I'll . . . Perhaps we'll meet again at Michael's or . . . '

He had not meant to get in touch again.

★ ★ ★

Charlotte was sitting on the sofa of the sitting room, her shoes off, her arms round her thighs, her chin on her shiny knees. The flame was flickering up the cracked filaments of the fire, turning them from white to blue to glowing orange. She was staring at the colours, trying to feel some warmth through her feet. Fires always reduced her to the condition of childhood. It was five o'clock and she was back from school; she was allowed to set a match to half a dozen corners of the newspaper and watch it curl into the spliced kindling. The draught of the nursery fireplace sucked the flame up into the pyramid of coal, where it smoked and faltered, momentarily defeated. Before this there was a time when the flames were making bridges from one part to another and Charlotte, like other schoolgirls, saw the different fires within the fire, the struggles, extinctions, gathering blazes, as emblems of her life. Then her mother arrived with a teapot and put it on the table behind her; the catching coal was starting to give a uniform red glow. Charlotte turned away.

The gas fire in the flat had raised a patch of pink in her cheek. She ran a hand through her hair, pushing it back from her high forehead. She was confused.

The telephone rang. Dick Cannerley wondered if she'd care to join him for dinner one evening this week. To decline the invitation Charlotte would have to claim to be busy every night, so she decided to make a strategic concession. It was better to accept straight away than to be bullied into it: if she went once, she needn't go again.

Charlotte replaced the receiver and went back to

the sofa. She was already doubting the wisdom of her acceptance. On the other hand, what did she have to lose?

There was a pattern in her thinking which had become irksomely familiar to her over the years. She felt herself now entering this sequence, which began with a sense of powerlessness, then gathered into a positive despair from which she could not be roused for days and sometimes weeks.

She stood up and went to her bedroom. She must do something to save herself.

6

One of the hardest drinkers in Gregory's squadron was a man called Leslie Brind. The high point of his evening came when he reached up to the beam in the lounge bar of the Rose and Crown and took down the glass yard. Walter, the beaming barman, was happy to fill it with the ale of his choice and watched admiringly as Brind lifted it to his lips. Since he liked as many people as possible to place bets on his ability to drain it, he usually waited till just before closing time to perform this feat. By this stage he would have been drinking steadily for three or four hours, yet the sudden 'boost-override', as he called it, after an emergency function on the Hurricane, had no apparent effect on his behaviour: he simply became a little more bonhomous as he collected his winnings.

His income from drinking was not, however, enough to balance his expenditure on drinking, and he was forced to sell his little open-top car to pay off some of his more persistent creditors. The buyer was Borowski, who paid only a few pounds for it on the grounds that, as he pointed out to Brind, it did not actually go. To a man of Borowski's mechanical ability, however, this was no more than a challenge: after two week-ends under the bonnet he coaxed out signs of life. He enlisted the help of his fitter to cut down and weld a part from another car when the manufacturer could not supply the spare he needed. On the third week-end he arrived outside the cottage in which Gregory was billeted.

'We're going for a spin,' he said, as Gregory's head appeared from an upstairs window.

'For God's sake, Borowski, I didn't get to bed till six.'

Borowski merely hooted the horn until Gregory's unshaven figure appeared from the cottage, pulling a scarf round his open neck and kicking his feet down into flying boots as he crossed the gravel.

'Hmm. That fuel smells suspiciously high octane to me,' he said as he climbed in.

'Don't ask.'

'I wouldn't let Landon get down-wind of it.'

'I thought we might go up to town,' said Borowski.

'It's far too bloody cold for that. Haven't you got a hood?'

'Poor old Greg. Always the bad circulation problem.'

'Always.'

Borowski put the car into gear, revved up and dropped the clutch, so that a hail of gravel pattered into the leaded lights of a downstairs window of the cottage.

After half an hour, Gregory persuaded Borowski to pull in at a pub off the Hog's Back. They were the first customers of the morning, and a thin fire in the grate had not begun to warm the empty bar. They sat on either side of the mantelpiece, holding whisky and ginger ale in chilly hands.

'I don't know why you want to give up fighters,' said Borowski.

'It isn't really the planes themselves, it's this work over France that sounds interesting. It's different. They're forming a little group of pilots to be attached permanently. Sometimes you have to drop people and stores, sometimes you just have to fly over and make a noise.'

'Why on earth?'

'So the Germans think that explosions were caused by bombs, not by saboteurs on the ground. Then they don't take out reprisals on the local population. It's a question of split-second timing.'

Borowski looked unconvinced. 'Why don't they just

get the bomber boys to do it?'

'If something actually needs to be bombed, they do. But I can learn that, too.'

'But to begin with you're just transport. Oh dear.' Borowski smiled. 'What a fate for a Spitfire man.'

'That was a long time ago. It was a different world. Anyway, I might move on to Lysanders later. You have to land in a field by the light of a drunk French peasant's torch. It's not that easy.'

'Why should they want to retrain you?'

'Because I've made Landon's life so difficult. And you know what they're like. They'll let you do anything if you just keep on at them long enough. In the meantime I've got to learn French.'

'Why?'

'In case of accidents. I'm supposed to be able to get out of France on my own and find my way home. They're going to give me some sort of exam before they'll let me go. I've got to have conversation lessons from some old dame they've put me on to.'

Borowski was laughing. 'It doesn't sound like you at all, Greg. Who is this French mistress?'

'*French* mistress, Borowski. In English we say *French* mistress. A French *mistress* is something else.'

★ ★ ★

Daisy Forester returned later than usual from work and sprinted upstairs to the flat, calling out her greetings as she turned the key. She was due to meet a new admirer later that evening and wanted to hear any news from her flat-mates first. Her expression of innocent enthusiasm faltered when she heard no answering voice and saw no light on in the sitting room.

She went and knocked on Charlotte's door at the end of the hall. Charlotte's voice softly and reluctantly answered, and Daisy turned the handle.

'What's the matter? Are you ill?'

'No. I just thought I'd have an early night.'

Daisy sat down on the edge of the bed. 'Have you got a cold? You look a bit bleary-eyed.'

Charlotte breathed in tightly. Her situation had seemed to require something drastic and she had decided to take Daisy into her confidence; but she had forgotten what Daisy was like — she could not possibly confide in this woman.

'It's him, isn't it?' said Daisy.

'What?'

'The pilot. Oh God, I knew it. It's all my fault.'

'What are you talking about?'

'Oh God, Charlotte, I'm sorry. I should never have interfered.'

'Daisy, will you please tell me what on earth you're talking about.'

'No, I won't. You must tell me first.' Daisy stood up and walked over to a little boarded-up fireplace where she rested her elbow on the mantelpiece. 'You have to trust people, Charlotte. Come on.'

Charlotte had to grind the words out through her learned discretion. 'I think . . . I think I've gone a bit mad.'

Daisy silently raised her eyebrows.

'I've developed this feeling for . . . ' Charlotte nodded, 'this man, Peter Gregory. And it's quite absurd. It's quite out of proportion.'

Daisy's sympathetic manner could not conceal the light of intrigue in her eyes. 'Go on.'

'I feel completely out of control.'

Daisy smiled. 'I could tell from the moment I saw you swooning on the dance floor.'

'What are you talking about? I don't swoon.'

'Believe me, darling. You closed your eyes as though — '

'I was trying to keep the smoke out.'

Daisy laughed, and Charlotte felt a small, unwilling smile.

'That's why I rang up and asked Ralph if he could get hold of him through Michael Waterslow. I could see you weren't going to do anything. Don't look so shocked. They were quite happy to play along.'

'It's awful, Daisy. I don't understand how I can feel like this. It's not reasonable, it's like an illness. No sane human being should feel like this, so soon, before anything has happened — if ever.' There were tears along the rims of her eyes.

Daisy walked back across the room and sat down on the bed again. 'What we have to do now is decide on our plan of action. We just have to lay out all the alternatives and examine them. When I was at Oxford there was a girl in my college who fell in love with one of the dons. We used to spend hours plotting how she could seduce him. Is something the matter?'

'No, no. I just didn't realise you'd been to Oxford.'

'Try not to look so amazed, Charlotte. It's not polite.'

'What did you read?'

'Greats. Anyway, we got her sorted out in the end. She used to call me Aunt Daisy afterwards. I really hated that.'

'And what did you do?'

'It's not relevant to your case. Tell me, have you had boyfriends before?'

'Yes, I've had what I suppose you'd call admirers.'

'But have you had a really big, passionate affair?'

Charlotte felt Daisy's question masked a more intimate curiosity. She was evasive. 'Never a great love, perhaps.'

'Don't think I'm prying. I just need to know what makes you tick.'

'You're sounding like a psychiatrist.'

'What do you know about psychiatry?'

'My father worked as a psychiatrist for a long time. That's all.'

'Shall I be honest with you, Charlotte?'

'Yes.' Charlotte did not sound enthusiastic.

'I think you might do better to have a few little flings rather than jump straight in at the deep end. I like your Mr Gregory, but I wouldn't trust him. Actually I find him a bit frightening.' She looked at Charlotte's doubtful face, the eyes clouded. 'Though I suppose that's the part you've fallen for.'

Charlotte sighed. 'I hadn't thought of it like that at all — the way you describe, the practical details and so on. I just felt impelled to him. I felt it would be a betrayal of something if I didn't go to him. It was like a call that it would be wrong to ignore. It feels very deep inside me.'

'Well, you jolly well ought to think about the practical details, I assure you. You don't want to feel 'impelled' to someone who isn't there or who's got half a dozen other girl-friends.'

'What would you do?'

'Well, I've told you. I think I'd play the field, go out with lots of different men and see if he came after me. Then I'd play it jolly carefully. Don't look at me like that, Charlotte. You make me feel the most awful tart. You don't have to sleep with all of them.'

'No.'

'I do, but that's my choice. You can have fun just going out with them and maybe just a kiss at the end of the evening.'

Charlotte didn't look convinced.

They went round the problem two or three more times, but no new vantage point was gained. By the time Daisy left Charlotte's room she had agreed, against her better judgement, to help Charlotte make contact again with Gregory.

Cannerley took her to the Ritz.

'I hope you don't think it's too corny,' he said, his hand lightly on the small of her back as they stepped into the bar. 'It's about the only place I know where you can still be sure of a reasonable choice on the menu.'

Without consulting Charlotte, he ordered champagne. Their table was at the side and gave a good view across the room, which had a foreign, elderly air. Grey-haired men were accompanied by young women; the waiters spoke accented English. There was an unreal, and in Charlotte's eyes, slightly sinister feeling to the place. She wondered where the people ordering trays loaded with drinks had made their money; to be in this golden mockery of the Belle Epoque while from Chelsea to Poplar the streets were darkened seemed either defiant or dishonest. Perhaps it was always so with big hotels; perhaps the Ritz's ornate Parisian sister had equally camouflaged the indiscretions of Swann or the Baron de Charlus.

In the dining room Cannerley ordered knowingly from the Bordeaux section of the wine list and settled his attention on Charlotte. She wore a dark emerald brooch at the collar of her blouse and a jacket with green velvet cuffs. She was not intimidated by his show of confidence with the waiters or by his descriptions of the muscular qualities of the wines of St Julien.

'How's your doctor? Are you happy with him? Not much of a challenge for a girl like you, surely?' Cannerley gave her a conspiratorial smile. He was a good-looking man, Charlotte thought, with his clear skin and wide-apart blue eyes, and his fair hair that occasionally disrupted his neatness by flopping on to his forehead. She found him completely unattractive.

'Shouldn't you be putting that fluent French to more use?'

'I don't know quite what as.'

'There's always a need for bilingual people, interpreters and so on. Your gift is a rare one.'

'So is yours presumably.'

'I suppose so.' Cannerley smiled. 'I do use mine, as I think I may have mentioned on the train. France and the French colonies are part of my brief. I know there are other organisations which urgently need French speakers. You're concerned about what's happening over there, aren't you?'

Charlotte looked up from her plate. They were both eating jugged hare and carrots; the menu had not been as full as Cannerley had imagined. 'Yes, of course I am. I almost feel as strongly about France as about Britain. The thought of Nazi uniforms in French streets and villages makes me feel quite ill.'

'Quite a lot of English people are working there. They drop them in by parachute.'

Charlotte laughed. 'Is that what you're suggesting I should do?'

'Not quite.' Cannerley smiled and leaned forward. 'I don't think those pretty ankles are quite sturdy enough for that sort of thing.'

Charlotte said nothing.

Cannerley sat back again. 'All right. It's none of my business. In any case, we hardly ever speak to other organisations. If ever you did think you'd like a change of job, though, I could probably put you in touch with someone.'

Charlotte nodded. She found the idea of herself as some sort of secret agent both alarming and ridiculous. She was not sure of the extent to which Cannerley was playing with her merely to amuse himself: perhaps he found some erotic charge in portraying himself as a dispenser of dangerous assignments to young women; perhaps he thought it would make him seem glamorous.

'Lots of smart young women are doing their bit, you know,' he said. 'The FANYS are as posh as Queen Charlotte's ball. You needn't think it infra dig.'

'That isn't what I thought at all. I'm not a snob. I just thought it didn't seem realistic for someone like me who's had such a quiet life.'

Cannerley poured the last of the wine into her glass. 'Nothing seems realistic these days, does it? The world's upside down. Anyway, I shan't bully you. There's just one other thing.'

He didn't have time to tell Charlotte what it was, as a couple approached their table. The man wore a dinner jacket, the woman a dress with beads and tassels across the bust.

'Hello, Dick, you old devil. Fancy finding you here. I thought you chaps never left the office. You remember Sylvia, don't you?' The man stood grinning by the side of the table. He had grey hair and a sweaty, indoor complexion; a scarlet cummerbund had been pushed down to an angle of forty-five degrees by the belly it restrained.

Cannerley sprang to his feet and embraced the woman with apparent fervour. He introduced Charlotte, and the man shook her hand with a conspiratorial chuckle in Cannerley's direction. His appreciative gurglings prevented Charlotte from hearing what his second name was, but Cannerley addressed him as 'Roly'.

'Are you going on?' he asked.

'Rather,' said Cannerley. 'Shall we team up?'

* * *

Peter Gregory was sleeping badly. He had a narrow bed in a low-ceilinged cottage. The mattress offered sinking reassurance when he was tired, but on bad nights the woollen blankets knotted themselves round him and the lower sheet was drawn up into corrugated ridges by his continual turning. Moonlight glanced through a space in the curtains and spilled a track across the floorboards, prompting his mind to turn at once to visibility, cloud base, instruments.

He was twenty-eight years old, but there were one or two lights of grey in his cropped and uncombed hair. He climbed out of the deep mattress, crossed the room and hauled a packet of cigarettes from the breast pocket of his tunic. He switched on the bedside lamp, which shed a tight glow beneath the circle of its floral shade. In it he could see a green glass ashtray and a book, face-down, broken-spined. So mean was the little pool of light, that when he actually wanted to read he had to balance the lamp on the headboard, behind his right ear. He sat up to smoke, then found he was too cold and had to lie beneath the eiderdown with the cigarette sticking out from his lips like a periscope. He whipped his hand out and knocked the ash off as fast as possible, so he could get his fingers back in the warmth. His feet were iced up from the walk across the room.

His mind was on Charlotte Gray. Once, he had been able to indulge his admiration, his desire for women in such a way that they seemed to expect little from him. There were mild reproaches when an affair ended soon after it began (he had found another woman, he was posted somewhere else, it was only a light-hearted thing); but something in the way he behaved allowed the women to escape intact — with a sentimental letter, briefly brimming eyes, but then smiles and bravado and no feeling of betrayal. He wished he could recapture that lightness, but he felt that it sprang from an innocence of which he had been deprived. It belonged to another time.

He had been farming in Nyasaland when the war broke out. Like many of his contemporaries, he had found it difficult to settle in England and a family friend had spoken seductively of Africa. At that age he regarded his work as provisional; he was still looking, not very urgently, for what he would really do. A fierce South African neighbour called Forster told him they should at once return to England and join up. Forster was unhappy with the way some people in his own country seemed sympathetic to the Nazis and wanted to put every distance he could between them and himself. Since he and Gregory had both flown planes in Africa they should obviously volunteer as pilots. Gregory reluctantly agreed. Another war? What did they want with another war? But he went, and thought he could fight it in a way that suited him.

He reached up from under the eiderdown and stubbed out the cigarette. Forster was the first man in his squadron to shoot down an enemy plane. Gregory confirmed it; he flew round in fascinated circles, watching the German fighter plummet through the air and bury itself in the hillside with a squally blossoming of flame. Forster was also the first man to be killed.

Others quickly followed. Every man to whom he grew close in the desperate intimacy of shared experience was able to return affection and support for only a brief time. Gregory did not feel blessed or lucky; he felt he had in some way let down the others. Perhaps he was not worthy of dying. A woman with whom he had thought himself in love began to make demands of him; she wanted to be married and have children. When he heard himself explaining to her that this was probably not the time and that he was certainly not the man, he saw how much things had changed. He could not risk drawing someone in to this extent, when he viewed his own life with such detachment, when he

70

saw it as impermanent, waiting for a shape. And at this ending there were no tearful smiles, but remorse and bitterness.

A year ago he would have been round at Charlotte's door. He was powerfully drawn to her; she engaged not just some reflexive male desire, but a will towards friendship such as he had known as a child, when he would become besotted with some small friend and grow fractious if denied his company. A year ago it would have been irresistible; there was a pleasure in her conversation which would have seemed a guarantee against a fickle loss of interest and some woundingly short romance.

As he switched off the bedside light and searched once more for sleep, he wondered if these days he was capable of such feeling. For Charlotte's sake, it was much better not to risk it.

★ ★ ★

Charlotte was in Dick Cannerley's arms. His face was smooth, his left palm moist. He was holding her tightly to him, his right hand against her back. Their feet were in a pool of light, one of several thrown on to the floor by the low-shaded lights at the small tables round the room. The singer was wearing a white tuxedo; he put his head on one side and closed his eyes while his voice sidled up to the melody. Charlotte looked over Cannerley's shoulder and saw the clarinettist lick his lips as he raised the reed for his unctuous solo. Between the tables went a stout woman in a low-cut plum satin dress, her mouth a glistening cherry bow of lipstick; against a narrow bar with shaded violet lights were two other women, equally made-up, and unattached. The barman set out a silver tray with a bottle of champagne he had just taken from the shelf behind, and two glasses. Although the shelves were full of other bottles, champagne was the only thing that anyone was drinking. The wire brushes made a circular pattern of sound over the cymbal and the papery drum, while the pianist's muted minor chords descended in ersatz tenderness. Charlotte blinked through the smoke and tried to loosen Cannerley's grip. He was murmuring something inaudible, perhaps seductive, perhaps an offer to make further introductions.

Maybe she should take him up: anything would be better than this nightclub, or her icy little room without Gregory.

★ ★ ★

All through lunch on Saturday Charlotte was afraid. She kept looking at Gregory and she knew it was going to happen. When he stood up to go to the bar she imagined what his legs would look like: thin, naked. When he was lighting a cigarette she wondered what the skin of his hands would feel like, not twitching the ribbed metal of the lighter wheel, but on her back. While he talked, she was thinking of what he would say to her when they were alone. How much of this public person would he shed? Would he remain considerate and controlled, or was it such a different game that she would not recognise the creature he became? Was she supposed to do everything he wanted, or did she invite and guide him?

It was a curious lunch. Michael Waterslow had brought Gregory at Daisy's instruction, even though he had to be back at the airfield that evening. Charlotte was required for an extra surgery with Dr Wolf at six. There was a hasty, organised atmosphere because they knew they all ought to be somewhere else. Daisy had chosen this hotel at Streatley-on-Thames because she remembered being taken there before the war; there was a view of the river through the window of the lounge where Charlotte could see a swan bending its neck into the reeds by the far bank. With the speared cherries in the drinks, the menus bound like illuminated manuscripts and the corridors of unoccupied bedrooms upstairs, it felt, for all its half-timbered exterior, like a place of assignation.

Gregory was drinking beer from a dimpled mug; Michael, above his gin and tonic, was expressing correct but surprisingly forceful opinions about the conduct of the war. Charlotte had absent-mindedly accepted some yellow, cloying drink in a schooner. She was looking at Gregory and thinking how much she loved him. She felt as though the organs of her stomach had mysteriously liquefied. There was fear in the exquisite anticipation because she was not in control of herself.

She was embarrassed that all of them must know why they were there, but she did not really care. Since she had conceded a single name to the violent mixture of feelings that assaulted her she had felt better about it. Properly speaking, this probably wasn't love, she understood; but love was part of it. There were only perhaps two dozen words in English to describe two thousand mixed emotions people felt; but if she called it love, then that at least suggested both the gentleness — like an extreme opposite of wanting to do harm — and the obsessional longing for his presence. She remembered a character in a book who measured his feeling for some cruel girl by the anguish of his anticipation at seeing her, and by his grief at her departure, because he actually enjoyed her company so little. With Charlotte it was the opposite: Gregory's presence was an enchantment greater even than his absence.

As they moved into the dining room she felt him watching her. She smiled at him and saw a light of understanding in his eyes. It was all right. He had overcome his own reservations, though she had no

73

idea what they might have been. She would be able to know him properly, to understand and pacify. The violent change that was necessary to her life would now be made. It would be all right.

* * *

'Goodbye, Peter. You don't mind running Charlotte back, do you?'

'Not at all. Goodbye.'

Gregory pulled on his silk inner- and his leather outer-gloves and banged the passenger door of Borowski's two-seater. 'Don't worry,' he said to Charlotte, 'it'll soon warm up.'

On the steps of her house, he said, 'Do you mind if I come in for a moment?'; and, once inside the flat, he said, 'You look freezing. Let me feel your hand.'

Once Charlotte's hand was in his, it was not difficult for him to wrap both arms round her.

Charlotte allowed her head to rest for a moment on his shoulder, then lifted her face to his. He kissed her quite gently, while his hands rubbed her back, between her shoulder blades; she felt his tongue on the inside of her lips. His hands moved beneath her jacket and pulled her more closely to him. He moved his mouth from hers and lowered his head to the base of her neck, opening the top button of her blouse to find more skin for his lips. Charlotte sighed a little and ran a hand through his hair.

He pulled back from her and held her face in his hands. Charlotte opened her eyes and smiled at him. She felt an overpowering relief. She had not been imagining it all. Now that it was acknowledged between them, they would be able to drop the falsity of reserve and move into a new and honest world, where they could be happy. She saw suddenly how much she had feared that he didn't care, that perhaps she had misinterpreted the signs, the small flirtations. What a burden was lifted from her by his complicity; she loved him for having felt the same thing she had felt.

His eyes seemed to be searching for consent before going on. She answered by kissing him again, and rubbing the palms of her hands down the side of his hips. He moved both his hands to the front of her blouse and undid the buttons. His hands had been kept warm by the gloves, she noticed, as she felt them stroke her. Somehow he managed to work his fingers beneath the layers of her underclothes and she sighed again as she felt them on her skin.

'Which is your room?'

She led him by the hand, her clothes disarrayed, down the narrow hall. Once in her bedroom she pressed close to him again, to lose herself. He whispered flattering, encouraging words to her, which she barely heard; though she did hear it when he said, 'I think we should get undressed.'

She had somehow not foreseen anything so mechanical; she had imagined that their clothes would just cease to matter. This access of self-awareness made her turn her back to him as she undressed, hurriedly for fear of losing the momentum of his desire. She yearned for invisibility: she wanted to be with him but she didn't wish to feel his gaze on her private flesh. She felt excruciated by all its imperfection, so known to her, so long concealed. She turned to face him as she slipped off the last of her clothes and awkwardly walked the three or four paces to the bed.

He smiled with reassurance, encouraging, admiring her. Now she felt his warm hands everywhere, over the small of her back, stroking the rise of her hips, gently trailing along the skin inside her thighs. For fear of doing the wrong thing, she did little in return. Eventually, when she thought perhaps he never would, he let his hand drift up between her legs and she felt herself separated by his touch.

Charlotte was beginning to slide, as though she were about to slough off an old identity and take on something more direct and powerful. She wriggled against the bed, her legs widening a little. She put both arms round his neck so that there could be no ambiguity, no sense that she was holding back. She felt him roll over within her circular grasp and push one of her knees with his, wider still. She closed her eyes tight as his body lowered itself on to hers.

After a few moments she heard him say, 'I can't do this, Charlotte.'

She opened her eyes. 'What do you mean?'

'I'm sorry. You're . . . you've never done this before, have you?'

'No. But it's all right.'

He had rolled off her and was lying on his back. She propped herself on one elbow and looked earnestly into his face. 'It's all right. I want you to. I want you to do it.'

He shook his head. 'It's too much. I should never have come this far. I was carried away. You're irresistible, Charlotte. You know that?'

'It doesn't seem like it.'

'I'm sorry. You'll be grateful in the end. I'm a useless case. You don't want me.'

'I do want you.' She leaned over him and kissed his face all over. 'I do want you, I do.'

He pulled himself away from her and rolled off the bed. He walked over to where he had left his jacket on the floor and took a packet of cigarettes from the pocket. In her embarrassment Charlotte had not noticed that he had managed to keep his shirt on. The tails hung down almost to his bony knees; his legs were as she had expected, bare, thin, slightly bowed.

He offered her a cigarette, she shook her head, and he leaned against the mantelpiece of the little boarded-up fireplace as he lit one. Charlotte was struggling not to sob.

'I know what you're thinking.' He blew out some smoke. 'I just didn't realise that you hadn't done it before. It made me stop. I should never have done it anyway. I'm so sorry. All I can say is it's better this way. You can hate me for a little while — you *should* hate me for a little while. Then it'll be over. You'll have hundreds of men, real men, decent men, to choose from.'

Charlotte quelled her urge to weaken. She would not let him go. She climbed out of bed, naked and cold, and went and stood by him. He was facing the wall, to flick some ash off his cigarette, and she circled his waist with her arms as she laid her cheek against his back. Her arms slid down a little so her hands were over his abdomen.

She held on to him tightly, and, as she stroked him, her hand brushed against something; she heard him suck in his breath and felt his body tense as he gripped the mantelpiece. Although she moved her hand away he took it in his own and put it back. His flesh was warm and inflated, almost pneumatic, in her hand as she moved her fingers up and down; she was amazed by the softness of his skin. He was gripping the mantelpiece, so there was only one point at which their bodies touched. She heard him panting and she felt exultant as she quickened the imprisoning movement of her hand. When she heard him gasp, 'No', she knew that it was the last thing he meant as the flesh inside her fingers swelled and seized. He turned round and kissed her, but she held on to him for a moment with her hand.

Back on the bed she fixed her eyes on his as he lay beside her, then climbed back beneath the blankets. He looked shame-faced. He shook his head. 'You're a very determined woman, Charlotte.'

77

When Gregory awoke it was dark. He looked at his watch: he was due back at the station at eight and it was now a quarter past five. He glanced down at Charlotte's head and stroked her hair.

He said, 'What time are you due at your doctor's?'

'Six.'

'I think you'd better get going.'

Charlotte sat up with a start when he told her the time. 'God. You're right.' She caught him looking at her breasts, which were flushed and rosy against the white of the sheet. Gregory wanted to take the soft, filmy tips and pull them gently with his lips, but he could see that Charlotte's modesty had been restored by sleep. She covered her breasts with her arm. 'Aren't you getting up?' she said. He shook his head.

She got off the bed and crossed the room stiffly. He saw how much she resented the intimacy of his eyes, but could not bring himself to turn them away. She pulled her underclothes on quickly, standing sideways to him in the narrow room. Her face was pink from sleep and her cold fingers fumbled on the tricky fastenings.

'You haven't got a spare pair of those, have you?'

'What?'

'The stockings. My feet get so cold when I'm flying.'

Charlotte, without looking round, said, 'I might have an old pair. I'll have a look. My mother sent these from Edinburgh.'

To spare her his scrutiny, Gregory reluctantly got out of bed to dress.

'I haven't even got time to make you a cup of tea,' she said. 'I'm sorry.'

'Don't be sorry. Would you like me to drive you to your doctor's?'

'I'd rather take the bus. People would notice that car.'

They took their coats from the hall and went downstairs. Inside the front door he kissed her; then they stepped outside and he watched her disappear down the blacked-out street. She didn't turn to look back at the corner, and Gregory felt in his stomach an unexpected surge of anguish.

7

Gregory's French mistress set him to read from *Le Petit Prince* by Antoine de Saint Exupéry. She would go through a sentence first, then ask him to repeat it. A woeful expression passed across her face; sometimes she could barely wait for him to reach the end of the phrase before she remonstrated.

'No, no, you are still saying *roue*. The word is *rue*. Like this. *Rue*.' Her lips puckered and whistled.

Gregory repeated the sound he heard, but not to Madame Fanon's satisfaction. '*Rue*,' she barked.

'*Rue*,' he replied.

'*Non, non, non. Rue.*'

'*Rue.*'

'*Mais non! RUE!*'

'*Rue.*'

Gregory inspected the unconvincing hairline on her neck. He thought she wore a wig, yet there was no doubt that at the front the hairs sprang naturally enough from her rounded forehead: rooted, chestnut, salted with realistic grey.

'I'm sorry, Madame Fanon, I'm afraid I'm a very poor student. Do you mind if I have a cigarette?'

She pushed a little brass ashtray across the tablecloth. 'You should say 'Madame', not 'Madame Fanon'.'

'There's so much to learn. Which part of France do you come from?'

'From Montauban.' Madame Fanon seemed relieved to put Saint Exupéry aside for a moment. 'It's in the south-west, not far from Toulouse. It was the birthplace of Ingres.'

'And is there any sort of resistance going on there?'

'Oh yes.' Madame Fanon's face worked beneath its

powdery creases. 'From the beginning there has been activity in the south-west. These men and women are of independent spirit. It has always been the case in our part of the world.' She stopped and looked at Gregory, as though deciding whether or not to trust him. She sighed. 'But for many people the Occupation is the opportunity they have waited for all their lives. For as long as I can remember there have been people who wanted a revolution because they believed the Republic had failed. Now with Marshal Pétain they think they are achieving it. The presence of the Germans is necessary because it allows the Vichy government to act without a democratic process. No Germans, no revolution. They only wish the Germans would be more helpful.'

'I see. I just imagined they were under the invader's thumb.' Gregory had never considered French politics, least of all the possibility that, for whatever circuitous reason, the Germans might be welcome. Perhaps Madame Fanon had got it wrong.

He looked about the cluttered sitting room. Madame Fanon had come hastily to join her husband in London, and the stratum of her snatched possessions lay thinly over the long-accumulated furnishings of the absent English owners. A glass photograph frame from which a boy in uniform with his hair cut *en brosse* grinned out manfully sat on a shelf packed with the novels of Warwick Deeping and Hugh Walpole.

'You need to practise your French. It's no use coming to me three times a week if you're not talking the language in between. Don't you have any friends who speak French?'

Gregory stroked his jaw with the tips of his fingers. 'I'll have to think about that.'

When he got back to the station that night he found that his transfer papers had come through. He went to the Rose and Crown with Borowski for a farewell drink; or, in the end, to drink enough to make them incapable

81

of remembering where anyone was going. Gregory was suddenly fired by the idea of France: if the situation was as hopeless as Madame Fanon portrayed it, then the people who cared about it, those independent spirits she described, would need the help of the big British planes ploughing through the night. It would be good, it would be purposeful, it would be . . .

Beer was cascading down the front of Borowski's uniform as the glass yard slopped its contents from his full mouth and desperately working throat. Gregory watched Borowski's Adam's apple shuttle up and down until it stuck at the top of its run and the beer splashed out over his cheeks and blinking eyes, forcing him to lower the yard with spluttering regret.

After the Rose and Crown they went back to the mess, where Gregory bought a bottle of whisky to mark the occasion. In another room the younger pilots began to play a game in which the furniture was piled into the middle of the floor and they had to make a circuit without letting their feet touch the ground. The winner was a sullen Norwegian whose prize was to have his trousers pulled down and his genitals smeared with boot polish. Someone told a joke about the King's African Rifles.

Gregory tried to climb the stairs of his cottage, but he could not seem to gather enough momentum; each time he reached the fourth or fifth stair he found his body halt, balance and tip back again. At the third attempt he took a long run-up and managed, at the crucial stair, to keep his weight moving forward. He climbed the rest on hands and knees, like a child. He undressed roughly and dropped his clothes on the heaving floor.

Often he had found that the first few minutes after sleeping with a woman were what determined how long the affair would last. Sometimes he experienced a Darwinian urge to leave at once, the pollination done.

Only the advice of some expatriate African roué — that it was the height of bad manners to sleep with someone less than twice — had prevented him from doing so more often. On other occasions he had felt a sense of patient curiosity that he was happy to let time satisfy.

Now when he laid his head on the surfing pillow he had a momentary recollection of the imprisoning pressure of Charlotte's hand. It was wonderful. This desire of women, it was so overmastering, so deep in the genes. Oh God, he thought, it has an almost moral force . . . And yet, he must not lead her on, he must not let her down. But why not risk it? Why should he care so much about her feelings? Only, of course, because he was falling in love with her. When he thought about her he felt a desperate exhilaration, a feeling so joyful it threatened to sweep away all judgement. It was destiny, it was what he was born for . . . but sleep was overwhelming him.

★ ★ ★

All day at work Charlotte felt the weight of expectation. She had made a move and consequences would surely flow; the only thing that could not conceivably happen was nothing.

She wrote Dr Wolf's letters and answered his telephone; she smiled politely at the young men who stepped, or limped, from the lift on to the marble-floored landing and into his consulting rooms. She endured their stares, their silence and their flirtation.

Her fear was that Gregory did not take her seriously. She wished she had somehow, forgettably, disposed of her inconvenient virginity: she hoped it had not disqualified her in his eyes. Yet such a loss could not have been borne lightly; there was fear there, too.

'Miss Gray. Those letters I gave you. Have you finished them yet?'

'No. I'm sorry. I was just coming round to it.'

Nothing could at first disturb her waiting. She had behaved well, if 'well' could be the adverb in the circumstances of her bedroom. At least she had been decided and resourceful; she had not let him go. Now all she had to do was wait for the dividend of her initiative.

Three days passed and there was no word from him. What she had forgotten in her cautious waiting was the imperative of seeing him: the enchantment of his presence. This need began to wear away her better judgement until by the fourth day she could no longer be sure even of what it was she had known with such calm certainty a short time ago. The desire for him merely to be there now so occupied her thoughts that it left no room for planning or manoeuvre. She laid her head on her arms: I just want to *see* him, that's all.

★ ★ ★

Charlotte was sitting in the flat. *The Times* had a report from Paris that the former foreign minister Pierre Laval had returned from political exile to became 'head of government', leaving Marshal Pétain as head of state. Charlotte did not know how to interpret this news; her views were coloured by the memory of how Monsieur Loiseau used to spit out the name of Laval. Her recollection was that he was some sort of socialist, yet that hardly seemed any longer to be the case. It was perplexing, and the *Times* article did not illuminate the situation; it merely contributed to Charlotte's impression that the news was somehow sinister.

She put down the paper and went to open a window. It was the moment of spring when she found herself constantly wearing the wrong clothes; she took off her powder-blue cardigan and carried it through to her

84

bedroom where she opened the window and looked down on to the street. It was the first time since she had been in the flat that it had been warm enough to let the air in, though even now the skin of her bare arms showed a moment of contraction in the breeze.

'You're a very determined woman.' That's what Gregory had said to her. All right, she thought, then that's what I will be. I'm not going to wait any longer for things to happen, and the first thing I'm going to do is find a proper job. I will resign from Dr Wolf's and take up Cannerley's offer, whatever it entails. Because what matters most to me is Peter Gregory, I will concentrate on other things: by indirections find directions out.

She heard the sound of a latch key. She hoped it was Sally, who was too absorbed in her own life to ask Charlotte questions about hers. There had been for once no early evening telephone call from St James's.

'Charlotte!' Daisy's voice rang cheerfully down the passage. Charlotte emerged from her room.

'Isn't it a lovely evening?' said Daisy. 'Do you think we might persuade someone to take us for a drink on the river?'

Before Charlotte could answer, the telephone rang. Both women moved into the sitting room doorway to answer it, but Charlotte was quicker.

Her concentration was not helped by Daisy's frantic mime from the doorway: her body had become a question mark, her lips italic capitals forming the word *HIM*? Charlotte turned her back and laid the cool bakelite against her cheek. She twisted the furry, fraying cord between her fingers. She didn't see the comic details of domestic life because she was so engulfed by joy.

★ ★ ★

Charlotte had her hands on Gregory's bare shoulders and could feel the blade bones jut beneath her palms. The physical sensations of sex were so bound up with her apprehension of Gregory as an individual that she could not reach any separate conclusions about the acts themselves. She had not needed to seduce him or assure him; from the moment of their reunion he had made it clear what he had in mind.

When they had come back into the house he could not even wait till they had climbed the stairs. His hands were running over her clothes as he pressed her against the wall, kicking the front door shut with his heel. He had lifted her skirt as they stood there, put his palm against the skin of her inner thigh and teased a hem with his lifting finger. She removed his hand, then took it in her own as she led him upstairs.

He seemed to know so many things to do, so many ways of touching her. She had to dispose of any sense of modesty as he undressed her, kissed her, but the unspoken condition of her doing so was trust: the more freedom she allowed him, the more he must be bound to appreciate what it meant to her, and what she expected from him in return. How odd, she thought, that all the things she imagined made her and other women attractive to men — their hair, their eyes, the things they said, their elegant clothes — were surrendered in this undignified spreading of arms and legs; yet far from resenting this change, he seemed excited by it.

There was some pain at first, but it did not last, and his murmured consolations were not what she was interested to hear. She wanted him to release himself in her, as soon as possible. The urgency of his physical passion seemed an emblem of the loss of trust she sensed in him. She moved against his rhythm and held him tightly inside. He seemed to want to continue, but she made it impossible for him to hold back.

She took her hands off his shoulder blades and ran them down to his haunches to pull him further into her, squeezing him as she did so till he emitted a surrendering, despairing sigh. Now she had him; and she had started a cycle of desire in herself at the moment he finished. Gregory seemed to sense this, and Charlotte wondered how he could. How many women must he have done this with? What tricks of their breathing had he learned? What half-caught exhalations told him when to stop and when to carry on? She felt his searching hand and his mouth against her ear. Quickly she was again on the brink of some decisive moment, and again she saw no choice but to let herself go.

It seemed incredible that this bodily feeling was so specific, when her purpose in it all was to use the act only as a means to some vague, profounder union, far removed from flesh and sheets and physical sensation. Meanwhile her ears were filled with the sound of a soft but frantic gasping, and it was some time before she identified it as her own.

★ ★ ★

When she got out of the bed to make tea for herself, to fetch whisky for him, Charlotte felt the old self-consciousness come back. She wrapped a dressing gown round her with a swiftness that made the flaps and cord flail. Gregory had lit a cigarette and balanced an ashtray on the bed by the time she returned.

He pushed back the hair from her forehead and face and kissed her cheek. 'You've got beautiful skin,' he said. He ran his finger down the side of her neck and over her throat. He kissed her ear.

'You speak French, don't you?'

'Yes. Why?'

'I'm having a difficult time with my Madame Fanon.

It's a hell of a language, isn't it?'

'Yes. But why do you need it?'

'In case I crash. I at least need to be able to ask for help. They'd rather I was able to pass myself off as French so that I could make my own way back over the Pyrenees, but they accept that that's not possible.'

'Are you so valuable to them?'

'I'm afraid so. All pilots are. The training is long and expensive. They hate losing us.'

'You won't crash, will you?'

'Charlotte, I must tell you that I seem completely incapable of crashing. I've been straight through a squadron of Messerschmitts after my ammunition had run out and wasn't even scratched. I've flown upside down a hundred feet from the ground to give the impression of being out of control and somehow managed not to touch a tree. Even when my plane's been damaged it's seemed to fly normally.'

'You sound disappointed.'

When he did not answer, she said, 'When will you be going to France?'

'In a few weeks' time. Provided I'm passed fit to fly Halifaxes.'

'A few weeks . . . It's not long, is it?'

'It's long enough. They're easy to fly. I'm more worried about the French.'

'I meant it's not long . . . not long to go if you didn't come back.'

'Of course I'll come back. I'm indestructible.'

Charlotte touched his cheek with the tips of her fingers.

'Why did you change your mind about me?'

Gregory shifted his weight on the pillow. 'Perhaps I shouldn't have done. Do you mind?'

'Mind? Oh no . . . Don't frown so much. It's all right.'

He seemed unable to change his anxious expression.

'I wanted to help you,' she said. 'I wanted to make you feel better.'

When Gregory had gone for his train Charlotte coaxed the bathroom geyser into noisy take-off. She supposed she would now have to pay attention to Daisy's contraceptive lectures: she had managed to avert her eye when Daisy hoisted her skirt, planted her foot on the edge of the bath and demonstrated the art of douching; she had discreetly thrown away an unsolicited gift of something called Volpar Gels.

Charlotte did not bother to straighten the bed, but, bathed and in a clean nightdress, slipped beneath the still-warm covers and felt her body plunging towards sleep. There was hardly a moment to think about what she had done or how it had differed from her long-held apprehension.

Why was I so fearful? She had time only to phrase the question to herself before sleep unpicked its grammar.

* * *

In her brief bodily paradise Charlotte did not hear Daisy and Sally noisily attack the bathroom in the morning, nor their clattering departure for work, nor even Terence's bumbling from room to room. Her own alarm clock had remained unset in the preoccupying pleasures of her going to bed.

She awoke when the noise of a car horn in the street penetrated her still-open bedroom window.

She had been profoundly happy in her healing sleep, and was disorientated when she sat up. It was almost half past ten. She flew across the room and pulled on her clothes in an ecstasy of fumbled fastenings. Smoothing her skirt, pushing a comb into her hair, she rushed out of the flat with her toothbrush still in her mouth. She hailed a taxi and swallowed the toothpaste as she sat in the back of the cab, dabbing on some powder and checking the results in the mirror of her compact.

She let herself into Dr Wolf's building and ran up the stairs. His consulting room door was closed, so Charlotte settled at her desk and began to open the letters.

After about twenty minutes Dr Wolf's door opened and a young man in army uniform came out, smiled at Charlotte and made his way towards the stairs.

'Ah. Miss Gray.' Dr Wolf's head appeared from his room. 'How nice to see you. Is everything all right?'

Charlotte began to apologise. She had forgotten to set the alarm, she told him; but without the crucial events that preceded this amnesia, the story did not sound good.

Dr Wolf said, 'I see.'

'I'm sure I can catch up. I won't go out at lunchtime. I'll make sure everything's up to date. I'm very sorry.'

In the course of the morning, Charlotte came to see that this was the ideal moment to resign. When lunchtime came, Dr Wolf took his coat and hat from the pegs in the outer office.

Charlotte said, 'There's something I've been meaning to tell you for some time. I've very much enjoyed working for you, but I feel that the time has come now for me to — '

Without listening to Charlotte, Dr Wolf had begun speaking at the same time. 'Miss Gray, I need a receptionist I can rely on. I don't require her to show initiative or to be an original thinker.' There was a sarcastic weariness in his voice. 'There were those letters I had to ask you about the other day. There was the problem with the table at my club. And now you seem unable to get up in the morning . . . '

Charlotte, who found it embarrassing to have to break her news to Dr Wolf, was ploughing on with her own speech, looking down at her hands as she spoke: ' . . . And it's not that I don't appreciate the work, it's just that I feel could contribute more to our effort in this war if I . . . '

'I have no doubt that you are a young woman of many parts, Miss Gray, but you are not suited to being a doctor's receptionist. I think we would both be happier if you looked for some other employment.'

When Charlotte understood that Wolf was dismissing her, she was so surprised that she began to laugh. It was preposterous: she was only doing the job out of a willingness to help; it was not as if she couldn't have found something more interesting to do; and then apparently not to be up to the task of answering the telephone or writing a few letters . . .

She stood up. 'You're right. You ought to have a proper receptionist and I ought to do something else. I hope you don't feel I've wasted your time. Of course I'll stay till you find a replacement.'

Charlotte was aware of an incoherent excitement starting to seethe inside her. It was edged by the cool clarity of relief: only by solving the problem had she finally brought it into full view.

8

Depression — though that seemed a limp word for the storm of black panic and half-demented malfunction — had over the years worked itself out in Charlotte's life in a curious pattern. Its onset was often imperceptible: like an assiduous housekeeper locking up a rambling mansion, it noiselessly went about and turned off, one by one, the mind's thousand small accesses to pleasure. So gradual was its beginning, so quick her mind's ability to adjust, that she never saw what was happening: an unwillingness to admit that anything was wrong compounded the stealth of the disease. Sometimes the first moment she admitted to herself that she was suffering was when it started to get better. For several weeks the effort of speech had made her jaw ache; the tricks and self-delusions by which people avoided confronting the tragic lineaments of the world were an unforgivable frivolity: the air about her limbs felt solid.

Then suddenly, one morning, she heard the post fall on to the mat and felt a minute shock of anticipation. She heard a song on the wireless and felt a stir of response. What was this strange, unknown throb? Ah yes, she remembered now: it was what you felt a thousand times a day; it was what impelled you and made living bearable. It was what she had not felt in her sealed darkness since . . . since . . . She would then weep with bitterness at how long the world had been withheld from her.

The process by which the problem was fully revealed only when its lessening became apparent seemed parallel to what had happened with Gregory and Dr Wolf. As soon as she had left the consulting rooms, her anguish over Gregory seemed less. But this was only a beginning: in her bag was a bill for dinner on the train, and on the back was a telephone number in Ormonde Gate.

They met again at the Ritz, where Cannerley talked a virile code of numbers and initials. The chaps in Nine might be interested, though he had a hunch that G section was the answer.

He slid an olive off its toothpick between his front teeth and twirled the little stick in the viscous surface of his pale Martini. He was wearing, Charlotte had to admit, a beautiful charcoal suit, which shimmered and dripped from his folded body in the little gilt chair. One leg was crossed over the other and the trousers rode up just far enough to show the fine black woollen socks, the bench-made shoes and a slit of pale leg.

Although Cannerley attempted his usual playful languor, Charlotte had the impression that he was nervous.

'Who are all these people?' she said. She wondered if they really existed or whether Cannerley was playing some game of his own devising. Perhaps he was not the glad-handing boulevardier he affected to be; perhaps he too was trapped or limited in his manoeuvre.

Cannerley laughed, but his eyes remained still.

'Leave it to me, dear girl. I'm having lunch with Bobby at his club next week. I'll drop a word in that great big ear of his. Now can I perhaps tempt you to a bite of dinner?'

'I'm afraid I already have an appointment.' It was true. She had offered, at any rate, to cook Gregory something at the flat.

★ ★ ★

Ten days later Charlotte received a brown foolscap envelope in the post. Inside it was a smaller white

93

envelope. Inside that was a letter headed WAR OFFICE, with the official address in Whitehall. A heavyweight typewriter had punched its inky message into the low-grade paper. It invited Charlotte to present herself to a room on the third floor of a West End hotel. It requested her to bring the letter with her on Wednesday at 2 pm.

'I've got an appointment to see Mr Jackson,' Charlotte told a large man in a stained tunic behind the Reception desk. As she said the name, she saw for the first time how much it sounded like an alias, chosen for the way it was unlikely to be garbled on the telephone. The porter said nothing, but allowed his eyes to travel slowly down Charlotte's figure. When his inspection had reached her knees, he nodded and called over a youth in braided uniform who took Charlotte across the lobby to a lift.

He rotated a lever inside the cage and they moved heavily upwards. They stopped at the third floor with a juddering suddenness and the boy hauled back the metal doors; Charlotte stepped out into a dim corridor. The youth set off ahead of her, dragging his feet soundlessly along the strip of carpet. Charlotte saw the tired acquiescence in his bobbing shoulders as the room numbers rose into the high three hundreds on her right; every now and then they passed a fire extinguisher and a notice pointing the direction of the air-raid shelter. There was the distant clank of a tea trolley, as though life were sustainable in these twilit corridors without reference to the world outside.

The bell-boy deposited her at a door with no number and knocked. Charlotte put a florin in his hand to hasten his departure; she did not want the youth to see her meet this Mr Jackson. He moved off quickly as the door opened and Charlotte found herself looking at a slightly built man of about forty with buck teeth and thick glasses. He had a pale, froggy look, a damp handshake and a broad, nervous smile.

'Have you brought that letter with you?'

'Yes.' Charlotte pulled it out of her bag and handed it over. Jackson held it close to his face to read it, then visibly relaxed.

'Jolly good. Now come and sit down. Frightfully uncomfortable, I'm afraid, but we just have to make do with what we're given.'

There was a trestle table in the middle of the room covered by a green baize cloth. The washbasin in the corner had been partly concealed by a board on which a pile of papers was dangerously balanced; the hard little chair on which Charlotte sat down was also of the willingly collapsible type. She noticed that Jackson lowered himself very gently on to his, as though he had learned from hard experience. Provisionally poised, he gave her another welcoming smile, like the headmaster at a boarding school inexpertly trying to reassure his new pupils. He slipped Charlotte's letter into the jacket of his suit, and it occurred to her that there was no longer any evidence of who had asked her or of where she had been.

'Now then, Miss Gray. I think the best thing is if I try and put you in the picture a little bit. Then I shall ask you one or two questions about yourself. Does that sound agreeable? Jolly good. I'm not going to give you a lot of technical stuff. All you need to know is that I work for something called G Section. We answer to a parent group which in turn answers to the Chiefs of Staff Committee and ultimately of course to the War Cabinet. What we're concerned with, quite simply, is France.' He gave a short tenor laugh.

'I understand that you're a fluent French speaker and of course that's jolly handy. It's a great shame that our two languages are so incompatible. At least, I mean the accents are. We've had a few awfully good people we've had to turn away because although they speak fluent

French they couldn't pass themselves off as French for a minute because of the accent. Anyway. Our work in France comes broadly under two headings. The first of these is organisation. We try to help local Resistance people to set up reliable networks. The other thing we do is sabotage.'

Jackson's cheery manner had a frightening effect on Charlotte; it made her think nostalgically of the gassy comfort of Dr Wolf's rooms.

'Now most of the people who work for us are volunteers from the services. My job is to take a look at them and see what they're made of. People sometimes have funny reasons for volunteering. One of the most common, you know,' he said, pausing and looking humorously but straight into Charlotte's eyes, 'is that they're crossed in love.'

Charlotte raised an eyebrow and smiled politely at this absurdity as Jackson chortled to himself.

He became serious again. 'We need brute strength sometimes — quick, athletic types who are not afraid. We also need patient, crafty people who are discreet and good at organisation. Then of course we need various bods at home, though they mostly have a special technical skill with documents or some such — forgers, cipher people and so on. We recruit from all sorts of unlikely places.'

Charlotte, thinking of her inability to keep up with Dr Wolf's letters as well as her deficiencies as a saboteur, began to explain to Jackson that perhaps they had better leave it there; but he seemed not to hear her protests and rode over her interruptions as though in the middle of a prepared speech.

'Discretion is in fact the absolute keystone of the whole thing. Of course one gets tied up in a tremendous amount of red tape with the War Office, who insist on making lists all the time. In a way that makes it all the more important for us to be utterly and totally discreet.

Are you good at that sort of thing?'

This time he was looking away, towards the lace curtains that covered the window, but Charlotte had the feeling that he was still somehow able to take in her response.

'Yes,' she said. 'I think that's one thing I probably am good at. But, listen, I don't think I'm very suitable for — '

'Let me finish, Miss Gray.' Jackson gave an extra little laugh to palliate any rudeness. 'I'd like to tell you one other thing about us. Most of our cipher clerks are teenage girls — jolly good they are too. Many of our staff are women — not just clerks and telephonists, but wireless operators and linguists who run the training schools. We also have women agents in the field. I'm just telling you this in case you were thinking your sex is a disqualification. It most certainly isn't. However, I must tell you that women who do go to France are subject to particular danger. No woman is allowed to go without being fully put in the picture.' He looked benignly at Charlotte.

'I see. What sort of work do you think I might do?'

'That entirely depends on what we find out about you. I would think the most likely thing at the moment is that we might find a use for you in one of our training schools. But you never know. Did you have anything particular in mind?'

'I thought I'd like to go to France. It's a country I feel very strongly about. But I can see from what you've just told me that I'd be quite unsuited to the sort of things you need. The thought of me planting a bomb or something . . . '

Jackson smiled. His eyes, like the hall porter's, took in her tailored suit, her hands folded in her lap. 'My view is always to keep an open mind on these things. Training brings out extraordinary qualities — things

97

people never expected. First of all, though, I think we should establish whether or not we should even go that far. I want you to tell me about yourself.'

Jackson stood up carefully, pushing himself up slowly with his hands. Although this should have put her at a disadvantage Charlotte did not feel intimidated. As she answered his questions about her family background she thought his humorous face acquired a reassuring quality; he seemed pleased by her father's war service and asked her to tell him more about it. He was particularly interested by the fact that Charlotte had also read Italian at university: the Italians, he told her, were expected at some stage to occupy the part of France east of the Rhone, and the thought of someone trilingual excited him.

'I'm not fluent, I'm afraid,' said Charlotte. 'Not in Italian.'

'But you are in French?'

'Yes.'

'And do you understand the political situation?'

'Does anyone?'

'Ha. I doubt it. What do you make of the return of our friend Monsieur Laval?'

'I don't feel qualified to say. Instinctively I feel it's somehow sinister.'

Jackson nodded his head in a brisk, approving way. 'Of course, it's hard to say . . . I encourage our people not to worry about the complications, but just to keep one thing clear in their minds and that is that the fight for France is not lost. In that respect the Vichy government is quite wrong. For two years they have taken defeat as a *fait accompli* and tried to manoeuvre for a place in the new German Europe. They have viewed British resistance as perverse and likely to collapse at any moment. Even with America in the war they still think a German victory is inevitable. That is what the whole Vichy philosophy, what I think they would call their *Realpolitik*, is founded on, and I must tell you, Miss Gray, that it is a fatal error. We are not finished. We are going to win.'

Charlotte smiled. 'Yes, I hope so. I think so.'

'Now tell me, if you will, a little about your feelings for the country.'

Charlotte spoke slowly, trying not to sound sentimental, though she was aware that none of the words she used seemed to have much practical bearing on what she might actually do. Jackson walked slowly round the room, occasionally nodding his head as she talked.

'I have a feeling,' she said, 'that some almost perfect pattern has been lost . . . not just in the obvious fact of the Occupation but in the way that it has been dealt with. I think that even when I first went to France as a schoolgirl one could sense that something was unravelling. That was ten years ago. There seemed to be a feeling that people were fed up with politicians and wanted somehow to take the law into their own hands. It was very difficult for a foreigner to understand because to me it looked such a beautiful place, both Paris and the provinces. It seemed untouched by modern developments, as though it had hardly changed since the nineteenth century. Of course I could understand that the politicians were not exactly great statesmen — people like Daladier and Laval and Reynaud and all these characters who seemed to crop up in one another's governments. I don't think even they themselves imagined they were men of great vision. But the contempt people seemed to feel for them was almost anti-democratic. I had the feeling that most French people wanted to do away with parliament and get back to something more straightforward, more dictatorial.'

'And now they have that wish. Marshal Pétain saved them once before, in 1916. He was the hero of the Great War.'

'Yes, and I'm sure he's a good man. But there's something wrong, isn't there? I doubt whether someone who saved you once, in his youth, can do it a second time, in his old age. It's as though the French have turned their backs on the problems of the present and run back to Grandpa and told him to take the modern world away.'

'And presumably you know what our aim is in France?'

'Well, you've told me, haven't you?'

'Yes. But in practical terms what this means is that we are encouraging the French to disobey their government — though I use the word 'government' reluctantly, since one must doubt its real legitimacy. The means at our disposal are also what you might call 'anti-democratic'. We aren't going round organising meetings at which we air the anti-Vichy point of view; we're using guns and explosives. Even the organisational side of our work is only a prelude to violence. The trouble is, Miss Gray, that this message is still falling on fairly stony ground. A large number of people welcome the Vichy government and deeply respect the Marshal, but an even greater number are motivated by a fear of something worse — of civil disorder. They fear that the Resistance, such as it is, would be the prelude to a full-scale Communist revolution. So they cling to the idea of stability, of law and order, and turn their face away from the actual shape it takes.'

'Obviously you know much more about this than I do. I haven't been to France for five years.'

Jackson stopped circling the room and resumed his position on the opposite side of the table from Charlotte. 'That's quite enough politics, Miss Gray. What I'd like to do, if you're agreeable, is recommend you to the people who run our preliminary course. You can have a look round, and see what you make of them.

Then we can go ahead with some training if you're still keen.'

'So you're going to take me on?'

'I'm bound to say that I'm jolly impressed. Before you begin in earnest you'll have to see the old trick-cyclist.'

'I'm sorry?'

'The psychiatrist. It's absolutely routine. All the chaps do it. He asks a few questions about your family and then shows you some funny squiggles and asks if they remind you of a baby's cradle or a house on fire or some such thing. A lot of mumbo-jumbo, really, but the nature of the work, as I'm sure you'll appreciate, does attract the occasional misfit. You don't look very sure. It's nothing personal, Miss Gray.'

'No, no it's fine. I quite understand.'

'Jolly good. Well, you'll be hearing from us. Don't try to reach me, just wait till you hear. Do you think you can find your way back to the lift?'

Charlotte found herself being politely but swiftly ushered out of the room. She made her way back down the long corridors, the falling numbers on the bedroom doors her simple thread back from the minotaur. She felt exhilarated by her meeting with 'Mr Jackson' and by the thought of going over to France.

It would be easier for her to understand herself there; away from the doleful influence of her parents she might be able to see how things had gone wrong in her life. This was the chance she had long wanted — to escape through action, and in her absence from the world she had known to reassemble the fragments of her life into a harmonious whole. This would be accomplished, she felt sure, by the light of the passion that she had for Gregory.

The thought of him filled her with light and expectation as she strode across the lobby, unconscious of the porter's sullen stare.

9

Charlotte's hunger for happiness led her to ascribe to her brief and infrequent meetings with Gregory the status of routine.

There were a few repeated elements. First of these was his unreliability, or at least his uncertainty until a very late stage that he would be able to come at all. This seemed to her natural for a pilot in a war; and if not, she had no wish to inquire further. Once he had confirmed, she would make sure Daisy and Sally were both out for the evening, which was easy enough to achieve: Terence's new job with the Admiralty required him to be in London four nights a week, on each one of which Sally required to be taken out, and Daisy's desire for company showed no sign of weakening. Then there was the question of dinner, which Charlotte would cook to the accompaniment of records Gregory pulled out from what looked like an old plate rack next to Daisy's gramophone in the sitting room. Of the limited selection Charlotte preferred Ravel and Beethoven, but she came to like the dance music Gregory invariably selected. He brought gin from the mess, which they drank with vermouth and ice; she cooked whatever she could find in the shops. Gregory was not much interested in food and never objected to the recurrence of various forms of pilaff in which Charlotte as artfully as possible disguised the odds and leavings of exhausted rations. She insisted on a proper tablecloth — white linen damask, worn in places, that she had found in a second-hand shop in the Earl's Court Road — flowers and candlelight; when dinner was finally served she always raised her glass to his and drank his health with playful sincerity. By stressing the repeated elements in all the few evenings they spent together she convinced them both that there were more of them.

Gregory made his first successful sortie over France, a drop of ammunition, supplies and cash to a G section network near Brive. His navigator was a Londoner called Brierley, whose patient voice guided him over the curfewed blackness of the Occupied Zone down towards the plateau of the Limousin. Arriving twelve minutes early at the drop zone, they circled while Brierley counted off the minutes before directing Gregory back towards the thin torchlight of the waiting men. It was simple; and as he eased back the stick Gregory had to fight the inclination to indulge some exuberant display of relief.

'Don't tell me,' said Charlotte, when she saw his modestly smiling face. 'Does the word 'cake' come into it?'

He laughed. 'No. Even easier than that.'

'And how would I find out if anything happened to you? I'm not the next of kin. And if the job you're doing is so secret they wouldn't list you missing in the paper, would they?'

'You can always find out from Borowski. Or you can get in touch with the Halifax people — McGrath or Wetherby, the squadron leader. I'll tell him to let you know. But listen, Charlotte, nothing's going to happen. These are very safe operations. If you can survive in fighters with Messerschmitts swarming all around you, you can drop a few boxes in an undefended field.'

★ ★ ★

Charlotte received another letter, asking her to present herself at a country house in Surrey the following Friday evening. She decided to say nothing about it to Gregory until such time as she could confront him

103

with something complete; she did not know why, but she wanted to startle him. At some stage she would have to join the absurdly named FANYs, whose members, Daisy excitedly told her, were issued with silk stockings and the most flattering uniforms. She feared Gregory's reaction; it would be no use explaining that few of these well-bred women had much to do with the first aid, the nursing or the yeomanry of the organisation's name, but were chiefly being trained in the use of explosives; in fact, that might provoke his anxiety as well as his teasing. For the time being all he knew was that she had a compelling need to be in France.

Charlotte told Daisy she was going to see some old friends for the weekend and took a train from Waterloo after lunch. The taxi dropped her at the end of a long gravel drive flanked by laurels. She had been told to arrive at 'tea-time', but feared that, at ten past four, she was likely to be the first. She lingered in the driveway and was on the point of finding a quiet place in the neighbouring woods to read her book for half an hour when a fat yellow labrador appeared from behind the bushes, waggling its back half, and emitting the soft, unthreatening bark, part warning to the owner, part greeting to the stranger, that was, unknown to Charlotte, the indigenous call of wet Surrey lawns. The dog waddled up and thrust its broad, flat head up her skirt. As Charlotte struggled to disengage it, she heard heavy footsteps on the gravel and a male voice calling to the dog.

'Don't worry. He's quite friendly.'

'Yes, I can see that.'

'Tony Sibley. Here, let me take your bag. A couple of girls are here already. Are you Nancy Lee?'

'No. Charlotte Gray.'

'Ah, the Scots lass. Of course. Well, ye're reet welcome and no mistake. Get down, Sandy.'

At the bend in the drive a squat Edwardian house

came into view. The coloured glass panels in the front door and the stone pots of pink geraniums could not disguise a burly, utilitarian look.

'I hope you don't mind sharing a room,' said Sibley, pausing in the tiled hall to consult a noticeboard. Charlotte caught a smell reminiscent of Roderick's boarding school — prayer books, cottage pie, floor polish. 'You're in with Freeburg and Lee. I'll show you up, then you can come and join us for tea in the drawing room.' He motioned with his hand to an open door as they began to mount the uncarpeted stairs.

Sibley was a fit man in his late forties with fair hair and the beginnings of surprising side-whiskers, wispy and grey. He wore a tweed jacket and pale grey flannel trousers which slid up and down his swiftly climbing legs to show maroon socks above his thick-soled shoes. They went down a long landing flanked by mahogany banisters on one side and windows over the garden on the other; although Sibley carried her bag, Charlotte had to hurry to keep up. A threadbare rug made the polished floorboards treacherous where she followed Sibley up a second flight of stairs. He threw open a white door to reveal a plain little room with three wooden beds and a washstand.

'You're the first. If I were you I'd bag the place by the window,' said Sibley genially, dropping Charlotte's canvas and leather grip on to the bed. 'Bathroom's at the end of the corridor. See you downstairs in five minutes.'

Charlotte smiled to herself as she laid her nightdress on the bed and, by so doing, presumably 'bagged' it.

Tea in the main drawing room was served by an imposing woman introduced as Mrs Mitchell, whose role seemed to be somewhere between headmistress and chaperone, as though the dozen young women who eventually assembled could not quite be trusted in Sibley's raffish company alone. Tea included sponge cake of almost pre-war yellow and peppery tomato sandwiches whose white bread was saturated with pink juice. Afterwards they were instructed to look over the grounds and get to know one another. Sherry and an introductory talk would be at seven, followed by dinner and an early night before the rigours of the dawn. Charlotte smoked a cigarette on the terrace with her room-mates and wondered what on earth she was doing.

She had never shared a bedroom with anyone before and briefly recoiled from the intimacy of it before reminding herself that saboteurs needed to prepare for worse hardships. Dinner was less good than tea: mushroom soup, cottage pie and steamed pudding all needed something more than the jugs of tap-water provided to wash them down. Gloria Freeburg, forewarned by friends, had brought a flask of brandy in her suitcase, which she shared afterwards with Charlotte and Nancy Lee, but nothing of what Charlotte imagined to be the dormitory spirit developed as a result: both the others seemed anxious about the next day as they discussed the trials of daring that awaited them.

After breakfast, Sibley took them down the gardens to a paddock, a small roped-off area of which, he explained, was a lake of sulphuric acid. He invited them to split into two teams, elect a leader, and cross the lake with the help of an empty oil drum, two cleft sticks and a length of frayed rope. Other obstacles were set up around the paddock, which looked set for an austerity gymkhana. The women, in issued trousers and plimsolls, responded to Sibley's encouraging cries and made their way, with only two fatalities, through a small but densely laid minefield and a factory ventilation shaft. Charlotte incurred some time penalties and an acid burn to her left foot but was otherwise unharmed. She sat, flushed and breathless, at

106

the edge of the final obstacle, watching the last three women struggle through. She thought how glad she was, for once, that Gregory wasn't there.

* * *

He was taking a few practice swings beside the first tee while Ian Watson prepared to let rip.

'Short par four, this,' said Watson. 'Green's just out of sight below the dip, but it's straight down.'

'Don't worry, I'll follow you.'

'Christ, I wouldn't do that, old boy.'

Watson planted the ball, stood back a few paces, swished his driver a couple of times, then waddled up to the ball and smacked it down the middle. 'Settle for that,' he said.

Gregory tentatively mounted the tee with a three iron. 'I told you I haven't played since — '

'Just get on with it, Gregory.'

Gregory swung the club back slowly, concentrating on keeping his head preternaturally still, stamped his left heel down at the top of the backswing, kept the club-head accelerating through impact and raised his thumbs, as recommended by a grizzled African caddie to counteract his natural slice. A shock like that from an electric socket jarred his fingers, and the ball fizzed flat and low for fifty yards before burrowing like a homing rodent into the wiry heather.

'Hard cheese,' said Watson, striding off towards his own shot, which was a short chip from the green.

The next time they were close enough together to talk was on the fourth fairway, where Watson said, 'Word is you've got a new lady friend. Anyone I know?'

'I don't think so, Ian. I met her at a literary party in London. Not your sort of circle, I think.'

'Not really yours, either, Greg.'

Gregory laughed. 'She's a remarkable girl. Somehow

she's got it into her head that she ought to get dropped into France. Don't ask me why. Something to do with her romantic feeling for the place.'

'What? France?'

'Yes. And the French.'

'Christ,' said Watson. 'What a bloody shower.'

'I know.' Gregory looked at his wretched lie in the damp sand. 'Stand clear.'

After a few holes Gregory began to play better. His irons, instead of burrowing deep into the Surrey earth, merely clipped out a ragged oval of sandy topsoil. They began to fly straighter, or at worst with an allowable fade. His putting was still approximate. He imagined the hole to be the size of a dustbin lid; he pictured the ball on a piece of string; he conceived of a follow-through so straight as to coerce the ball by the discipline of his forearms into the hole. Still it slid by to the right, drooped left or smacked into the back of the cup and leapt off with frisky topspin.

Ian Watson had been brought up in Scotland and had played golf since the age of five; the irritation of the game and all its frivolous trickery were natural to him. In front of the sixth green was a magnetic little brook, but he found it easy enough to land his second on the welcoming green beyond. It was good for him to be better than Gregory at golf: having joined the squadron in the winter of 1940 he felt at a disadvantage with men like Borowski and Gregory who had flown in August and September, in what had seemed like pure chaos at the time but had later become glamorously known as the Battle of Britain. Like most of the younger pilots Watson was an assiduous pursuer of women, but news of Gregory's romance came to them as a surprise. They presumed he had become inactive.

'Tell me more about this girl.'

'I don't think so. I don't want any competition.' Gregory thought briefly of Charlotte's brown eyes fixed on him with their eager intensity, of the way he would stroke her cheek with his fingers and make her laugh at her own earnestness. He thought of the sensation he sometimes had when she focused on him of being in the spotlight of an alarming intelligence. When he thought about her he felt an awful weakening; there was an impulse to admit some feeling — to give in, and, by submitting, to intensify it. It would be like coming home; it would be like finding an end to his bereaved uncertainty, and he was aware of the effort of will it took to crush the weakening impulse.

'All square,' said Ian Watson, through narrow lips, as they walked to the sixteenth.

Gregory looked over a weedy pond to the long, thin green behind it. Although the flag was at the back, it still looked no more than a six iron to him. Watson had stopped offering advice on club selection as the score became closer.

Gregory swung through the shot, but seemed to make more contact with the wooden tee than with the ball itself.

'WG, I fancy,' said Watson, watching its tinny, steep parabola. 'Watery grave.'

The ball fell among weeds on the far edge of the hazard. Watson took no chance with his shot, and battered his ball low to a bank at the back of the green.

At the seventeenth tee they turned for the final approach to the clubhouse. Watson spent a long time, tee-ing and re-teeing his ball, then stiffly carved it high away to the right, where it clattered through branches and disappeared from view. Gregory, relaxed beyond caring, watched his slowly hit drive make its own straight way, bouncing over a dog-walkers' path that crossed the fairway and running on towards the distant flag.

When they stood on the last tee the match was level.

Watson clearly felt that this was not a fair reflection of the game and that somehow he had been defrauded. The last green was set between the clubhouse on one side and a large lake on the other; it was a short par four, almost reachable, like the first hole, in one.

Gregory hit a three iron to the left, a short, safe shot, that opened the green to his second. Watson controlled his nerve well enough to take a wood, which he hit to within thirty yards of the green. There was a little bounce in his step as he led the way forward.

'Now you want to be careful not to hit the clubhouse from there,' he said. 'That window on the end is the ladies' powder room. Very expensive nineteenth-century glass. I believe that when the Varsity match was played here the Cambridge captain salvaged a half by climbing on to the clubhouse roof, where his partner had put him, and laying the ball dead.'

With these pictures in his mind — a young man in a pale blue scarf crouched among roof tiles with a niblick; half-dressed ladies at their powdering startled by exploding glass — Gregory stood over his ball. It was a straightforward eight iron. His natural fade would keep him from the clubhouse or the tree that stood sentinel beside it. He glanced up the fairway and saw Ian Watson, waiting for him to play.

He looked at Watson's eager face, its expression of friendly anticipation drawn sharper by his will to win. He thought of the similar expression on the face of Bill Dexter, climbing into his Spitfire for the last time; of Forster's modest, colonial smile as he explained to an enraptured mess how he had made his first kill; of the rubbery grin of the Canadian, Jimmy Somers; of Borowski's sharp-featured Polish friend whose plane had made such a crater in the Sussex Downs. Gregory felt a surge of anxious pity for poor Watson. As he stood over the ball he shifted his feet so that they were at forty-five degrees to the line of the shot; on the backswing he snapped his left elbow-joint open so that the club veered down from far outside the line, across the ball, and sent it, with all his strength, soaring, slicing high across the green, hanging still for a moment on the air, then plummeting down into the lake. Watson turned, his face lit up with incredulous delight.

★ ★ ★

Charlotte Gray was sitting in a leather armchair, sunk so deep that she could barely make her elbows reach up over the arms. Her eyes were following a line of book spines on a shelf: Gray's *Anatomy; Child Psycho-Analysis* by Melanie Klein; *Psycho-Analysis of the War Neuroses*, Introduction by Sigmund Freud. Her eyes moved over the letters of the titles again and again, though she read without taking in the meaning of the words. Beneath the shelf was the head of the surprisingly young psychiatrist, Dr Burch; it was a head sleek with hair oil, with a bespectacled face of impassive curiosity. He occasionally tapped the end of his pen against the pages in the open folder on his lap. He wrote nothing.

'Let's talk about your parents. Are they happy?'

'As far as I know.' She thought of the windswept house, her father's long absences at work, his awful wordless days, her mother's nervously chattering complicity.

Dr Burch said nothing. Charlotte said nothing. She knew he expected her to be motivated, embarrassed even, by the silence into giving more details, and that the spontaneous first rush of information would be, by the nature of its self-selection, significant — either in what it chose to include or by what it chose to suppress.

So she said nothing.

Dr Burch smiled, a humourless, slightly reproving smile, as though to suggest that Charlotte was being difficult, or impolite. 'Would you like to tell me a little more about them?'

'It depends what you need to know. They've been married for a long time. They have two children of whom they're fond. They have enough money. My father still works. They're healthy. They certainly have every reason to be happy.'

'But you're not sure. Is that because you don't see them much?'

'Some rift, you mean? Not at all.'

'And what about your childhood? Was your home life happy?'

Charlotte sighed. 'We were a very ordinary family. I had an elder brother called Roderick. We had a dog and a couple of cats. My mother was a nice woman, a good wife and mother. My father was a serious man. He worked very hard. He was a doctor, a physician to begin with, but he became interested in psychiatry, I think perhaps partly as a result of his experiences in the Great War, though I'm not sure about the timing. He was very well read and would certainly have been aware of Freud and people like that quite early on, though of course they didn't have the kind of acceptance then that they do now. People thought they were pornographic.' She inclined her head in the direction of Dr Burch's bookshelf.

'Did he practise as a psychiatrist?'

'Yes, he did eventually. It was odd, because he really rather despised most other psychiatrists. He thought a lot of it was rubbish. He hated all that talk about dreams. He was happier being a physician.'

Burch said nothing and Charlotte looked at him. He raised an eyebrow, but still did not speak.

Charlotte suddenly sat forward in the chair and gave him her fullest and most charming smile, smoothing her skirt down over her hips as she resettled. 'This must be a thankless job for you, questioning all these young women about their past.'

Burch recoiled a little in the floodlight of her social manner. In reestablishing the artificial basis of their conversation he was impelled into a slight awkwardness. 'We're not here to talk about me, Miss Gray.' Charlotte felt she had won a small victory.

'Though you might make a more interesting subject.'

Her attitude was now bordering on the flirtatious. Burch became firmer. 'You didn't answer my question. Was your home life happy?'

'Whom shall we call happy? It was all right.'

Her eyes travelled once more down the line of books and for the tenth time unreadingly traced the kicking spokes of the K in Klein. She was thinking of another doctor's room: not that of Wolf, or Burch, but a cold first floor sitting room in a granite house in Aberdeen.

She is seventeen years old, on the point of leaving school. Her hair is clipped back off her face in the neat combs of the Academy sixth form; her schoolgirl knees are pressed together. The spaces beneath her eyes are puffed outwards in damp pink swellings; she is gasping and heaving to catch the breath denied her by the repeated sobbing of her chest. She cannot hold the grief any more and bends her swollen, shiny face down into her hands with a great cry. She wants by that noise to blow the pathways clear to her lungs and to loosen, then expunge, the gripping memory of her betrayal.

The doctor to whom she speaks does not believe her.

★ ★ ★

'I'm going to show you some pictures now,' said Burch, 'and I want you to tell me what each one reminds you of.'

113

He slipped his hand into the drawer of the desk and brought out a pile of folded papers. He opened the first one and passed it across to Charlotte, who had moved from the depths of the armchair to sit opposite him.

She looked at the symmetrical shapes made by the paper folded in on itself across a blob of black ink.

'Tarantula.'

'Are you frightened of insects?'

'Averagely.'

'This one?'

'Ink on paper.'

'This one?'

'Wine on paper, paint on paper, black water on paper.'

'This one?'

'Castle in a forest.'

'This one?'

'Scrambled egg with truffles.'

'All right. This one.'

'Nothing really. Insects. Brambles. Patterns in the sand.'

'This one.'

'It's like an archipelago, somewhere in the southern seas. Here's the governor-general's house with its shady verandah overlooking the sea.'

'Charming. This one.'

'Is a face. A gargoyle on a church.'

'This one.'

'Is another blot. We're back to blots, I'm afraid. Ink on paper.'

'This one.'

'Blot.'

'This one.'

'Blot. Vaguely canine, but still a blot. I have a feeling they're all going to be blots from now on.'

Eventually Burch slipped the papers back into his desk. 'All right. Now I'm going to say a word and I want you to say the first word your mind associates with it. I do want you to take this seriously. You must relax. Let your mind just take its own course. Go and sit back in the armchair and close your eyes.'

Charlotte sank down into the cushions, leaned her head back and closed her eyes. The room had a churchy smell; she relaxed more than she expected. Burch squatted on the hard chair with a list on his lap. His eyes ran down the words.

'Drink.' 'Water.'

'House.' 'Garden.'

'Mother.' 'Hair.'

'Dog.' 'Legs.'

'Apple.' 'Eve.'

'Stick.' 'Beat.'

'Father.' 'Sad look.'

'One word, please. Try again. Father.' 'Waistcoat.'

'Home.' 'Cold.'

'Friend.' 'Girl.'

'War.' 'Peace.'

'War.' 'Planes.'

'London.' 'Flat.'

'Kiss.' 'Lips.'

'Floor.' 'Board.'

'Ceiling.' 'White.'

'Bed.' 'Lie.'

'Red.' 'Lips.'

'Blue.' 'Uniform.'

'Flowers.' 'Roses.'

'France.' 'Roads.'

'Sex.' 'Female.'

'All right. You can open your eyes.'

Charlotte blinked. Burch laid the folder on his desk. On a low shelf was a rectangular basket containing some wooden blocks, like a child's building bricks. Burch started to move his hand towards them, then saw Charlotte watching him. Something in her expression appeared to make him think better of it.

'All right, Miss Gray,' he said, standing up. 'I think we've probably finished. Will you ask the next girl to come in, please.'

'Have I passed? Are you going to recommend me for further training?'

'I think so.'

As she passed the desk Charlotte glimpsed the notes he had made on a page headed 'Ensign Charlotte Gray'. The only thing he had written was: 'T.C. by 1/2'.

10

Gregory took the stairs two at a time, one hand clamped against the bottle of gin in his coat pocket. He had stopped worrying about his motives; he only knew how anxious he was to see the door of the flat swing open. Charlotte was waiting, leaning against the door frame, wearing a floral summer dress with bare arms and legs. Gregory inhaled the scent of lily of the valley as he kissed her warm neck.

'Is the coast clear?'

'Yes. I don't think anyone'll be back before eleven.'

Gregory ran his hands through Charlotte's hair. She pushed him away and resettled the tortoiseshell comb he had dislodged.

Gregory poured drinks. 'I'm off to France again any day,' he said. 'As soon as the weather's clear.'

'Another drop?' said Charlotte, sitting down next to him on the sofa.

'That sort of thing. They've given me an address in Clermont-Ferrand.'

'Why?'

'It's a Citroën garage in the middle of town. The owner's a part of the local network. He's called Chollet, I believe, but he goes under the name of Hercule. I'm supposed to get in touch if something goes wrong.'

'Like what?'

'I . . . I don't know. I'm sure it'll be all right.'

'You told me nothing could go wrong in those big Halifaxes.'

Gregory seemed distracted, then made a sudden effort. 'I just discovered today what the G section codeword for the moon is. Guess. It's a girl's name.'

'I don't know,' said Charlotte. 'Phoebe? Selena?'

'No, it's Charlotte! I've been reading all these messages about 'Charlotte Unsatisfactory', 'Charlotte Impeccable', 'Regret Operation impossible, state of Charlotte'. Charlotte and Isaac, the two most important people in my life.'

'Who's Isaac?'

'Isaac Newton. The black knight.'

'What are you talking about?'

'Isaac is what pilots call gravity.'

'I see.' Charlotte smiled and laid her hand on his knee. 'And how's your French coming on? Would you like to practise?'

'Not today. I'm just not as clever as you, Charlotte, that's the trouble.'

'You don't have to be clever to learn a language. Children can do it.'

'Well, I suppose I can just about make myself understood but as soon as I open my mouth they'll know I'm not French.'

'You'll just have to be careful. Don't look so sad. I hate it when you go all remote like this.'

Gregory lit two cigarettes and gave one to Charlotte. He sighed. 'You're worth ten of me, old thing. That's the trouble.'

Charlotte raised a finger. 'No RAF talk.'

'What?'

'Isn't that what you call your planes, 'old girl' and 'old thing'?'

Gregory smiled tiredly. 'I'm not like that, you know, Charlotte. All that balls about 'wizard prangs'. I don't really like those sort of people.'

'I know. I know you're not really like that.' She had taken his hand as she began to speak in the voice of a soothing and indulgent mother, which Gregory found shamefully affecting. He laid his head on the cotton fabric of Charlotte's dress while she stroked his hair.

'I sometimes talk like that because I grew fond of

those men. That's the trouble. They probably all seem absurd to you, and in some ways they do to me. But they were very young. They hadn't even begun their lives. You must forgive them a few silly phrases.'

'You talk of them with such devotion.' said Charlotte. 'I sometimes think you're fonder of them than you are of me.'

Gregory stood up. 'Come on. Don't let's waste these evenings together being morbid. Let's have dinner. What is it? Spam?'

'No. It's a *pot au feu à la mode de Ministère de Guerre.*'

'Sounds interesting. I want you to tell me more about your training. You're not really going ahead with this, are you?'

Charlotte drew the curtains of the kitchen and lit the candles on the laid table. She told him about Dr Burch and of how she would shortly have to go on a course in Scotland.

Gregory watched her as she spoke. Sometimes, when he heard her talk, he felt that he had merely stumbled from one thing to another without ever properly thinking about it: India, England, Nyasaland, farming, friends, women, war . . . He must have made decisions, some based on quick gratification, some on what was sensible, but he had never thought it through in the dimension Charlotte inhabited. It was almost as though he had never grown up at all, but had just trusted to luck and to a childish belief that things would probably work out. Perhaps if he had undergone her self-scrutiny he would not have been so shaken by the experience of war. He liked to watch the nervous intensity of her narratives, as she described her interviews and experiences. He shuddered at the completeness of her trust in him and felt unworthy of its intensity. He was, in fact, though he did not admit it, a little frightened of her; and the only way to subdue that

119

fear was by indulging the violently erotic feeling that her fierce attention to his well-being aroused in him.

At ten o'clock he had to leave. Charlotte was asleep on the bed, her face pink and untroubled, her breathing steady. Gregory picked up his service shirt and flannel trousers from the floor and pulled them on. He ran his hand back through his hair, then sat on the hard little chair at the end of Charlotte's bedroom and looked at her in the unlit gloom of the summer evening.

He had not told her of the true nature of his flight. Perhaps he would never see her again.

She was lying on her side with one leg raised as though running. There were tiny dry lines where the skin of her upper foot met the sole. Her toenails were painted scarlet. Gregory's eyes ran over the sharp ankle bone, up the straight shin to the pocket enclosed by the stretched sinews of her raised knee, the thin pink creases behind the other, straightened, knee, then up the sweep of her thigh, whose packed flesh was of the same firm consistency as that of her lower leg. At the top of the hip-bones were two soft folds, which, to her intense embarrassment, he referred to as love-handles. Gregory's lips twitched as he recalled her indignation. He explained to her that it was necessary to have some flaw to balance what might otherwise have been too orthodox a figure, but Charlotte was ashamed of them, as she was of the small roundness of her belly that made her tighter skirts swell a little at the front, not fall in the perpendicular line of a fashion drawing. This too Gregory liked, though the way she lay made it invisible to his gaze, which could make out only the bottom of her ribs and her upper arm with its pale freckles trickling over on to the shoulder where her fair hair lay disarrayed, a single darker strand of it stuck to the side of her face by sweat.

When he had finished dressing he stood by the bed and gave her body one last glance, straining in the almost-full darkness, as she lay deep in one of her death-like sleeps. He was moved by a paradoxical sense that there lay like an invisible film over the practical volume of her rib cage and the bumpy spinal cord with its vital wiring, something personal, something essentially hers, that transcended the facts of her physical incorporation. He wanted very much to stroke the line of her thigh and hip, to kiss the mandolin-shaped cheeks, childishly bare; but he feared to wake her, so instead drew the sheet carefully over her and tiptoed from the room.

He found himself inexplicably reluctant to walk the few steps down the passage to the front door; he wished he had told her what he was really going to do. He took a piece of paper from the hall table and scribbled a note on it. 'Charlotte Satisfactory. 10.21 pm. A bientôt. XX' He went back to her room and left it on the bedside table.

★ ★ ★

Gregory had been driving for three quarters of an hour through the night when he felt a sudden pressure rising in his ribs. For a minute he thought he was going to vomit, and he pulled the car over to the side of the unlit country road. He climbed out and stood by the door. Something was struggling to come out of his chest and was making his arms and hands shake.

He held on hard to the top of the open door, fighting to control himself. A volume of packed air erupted from his mouth in a cry. He bent over the bonnet of the car to steady himself and found that other wild exhalations were struggling to follow the first. Soon he was sobbing like a child.

While he knelt on the ground and held his face in his hands he had the curious feeling of standing simultaneously outside himself. In a detached way he could picture the strange figure he made, weeping for no apparent reason in his uniform. His vision was detached, but it was not dispassionate, because he felt a dreadful pity for this second person.

The reflexes of his body had shown him what his mind had refused to admit. He had not been able to absorb as well as he had thought the things the last two years had shown him. He was still young, and he had seen in that short time things that normally only old men knew. And then there had come this woman.

When he thought of Charlotte, Gregory felt a terrible exhilaration. Out of all the death had come this redeeming chance. When he thought of the passion she had so transparently conceived for him, he felt singled out by an extraordinary fortune. The chance that of all the women in the world, the one he loved (and with relief he admitted that this was what he felt) — the thought that she should actually reciprocate his feeling seemed a possibility of incalculably long odds. His incredulous joy at his good luck was almost as exhilarating as the emotion itself.

He slumped down in the seat of the car. The most terrible aspect of it was the timing. It was only when it was too late to tell her that he had finally understood. In a few days he would be gone, and he might never come back.

★ ★ ★

Charlotte wrote to Gregory from Scotland. She pictured him taking the letter to his billet and lying down on his hard bed to read it. It pleased her to think of his fingers where hers had been; she imagined the cigarette smoke that would curl from his hand and billow from his lips, sardonically smiling at her letter.

My Darling Peter,

I expect this is against all the rules and I will be shot as a spy if anyone knows I've written, so don't leave this letter lying around. How are you? I do miss you. I think about you in your horrid cold plane and your poor feet freezing. I miss you.

I arrived at the end of a course at Inverie Bay. The others have been shown how to use Bren guns and Sten guns and how to creep up on the enemy at night and kill silently with their bare hands. I look at those hands with their manicured nails holding cocktails in the evening and have to suppress a giggle. I wonder if the Germans know what's coming. I seem to have missed all the violent stuff, for which I'm grateful. I have been taught by a man with whisky breath how to transmit by morse; some of this I remembered from the Girl Guides. Don't laugh. Yesterday an old trawlerman took us out in a rowing boat. The idea is that we should be able to pick up parachutes or stores that have landed in the water. You know how careless those wretched RAF boys are with their drops . . . Anyway, this old chap was very flattering and told me I had a natural feeling for a boat, which was surprising. It was extremely hard work, as the wind was whipping across the bay and the waves were smacking into the side of the boat. My poor arms.

Every night we have to put on our uniforms for dinner. They're not nearly as flattering as Daisy believed: they are rather scratchy and my skirt is too tight round the middle — no rude remarks, please. The food is variable, often quite good — fresh herring and mackerel, home-made bread, but a bit heavy and too reminiscent of 'home' for my liking. The others on the course are mostly English girls from the Home Counties. There is a girl called Marigold with whom I have become quite friendly. She is very good at the cross-country runs and the obstacle courses. It is perfectly clear to me, and I imagine to the instructors, that I am no good at all at these things. However, since I've started the course I have to finish it. They will then decide what job, if any, to offer me. Driving the Brigadier's car, I imagine, will be just about all they will think me up to. This is a pity, because I do very much want to go to France and do something worthwhile.

Next week we are going to Manchester, where we will be trained in parachute jumping. Even I can manage to fall out of a plane, I should think. Before that, however, there are two important dates: first, the 36-hour cross-country trek, which is famous for being very, very tough indeed ('Believe me, lassie, ye'll be lucky if ye can get yer wee shoes on fer a week afterwards' — a good deal of that rather gloating talk from the whisky-breathing wireless instructor), and the day after that: tea with mother. I tried to explain that I had no free time, everything very hush-hush and so on, but she had insisted we meet in Fort William and is making a special journey from Edinburgh to come and see me. We do in fact have two days off before Manchester, so I can't very well say no.

Some of the girls have apparently been given instruction in how to resist interrogation. For some reason this involved two of them being told to take their clothes off while they were questioned by two 'Gestapo' officers. So that there was no question of impropriety the large woman who runs the dormitories was present as a sort of chaperone. Marigold said she thought this woman's interest was rather more unhealthy than that of the men!

I will be back in London at the beginning of the week after Manchester where I will wait to hear my fate. Will you be able to come up to town? Probably you will have done your trip to France by then, 'Charlotte' permitting. I do hope you can come up and we can start to have our evening routine again. I miss your sad old face and the horrid things you say and do when there are just the two of us. You can't write to me here, but you could write a letter to the flat in London to wait for my return.

Do you love me just a little bit?

I send you my biggest, biggest kisses. Charlotte.

One of the reasons Charlotte had wanted to come on the course was somehow to shock Gregory into an increase of feeling: perhaps if he felt she were demonstrating her independence of him he might recognise the true extent of his dependence on her. She had not been sure that she would ever, really, go to France; but, now she had seen the other women who had volunteered and recognised that they were not much different from her — no stronger, no braver, no better at the language — the prospect of her actually going had become real.

Meanwhile, she needed reassurance. She wanted to be told by him, not once but many times, that he needed her; she wanted him to tell her that the compromises she had made with her modesty for the sake of his desires were understood; more than anything, she wanted him to tell her that he valued her.

All this, she thought, as she sat on the stopping train to Fort William, without seeming weak or clinging. It was a hot afternoon, and from the carriage window she saw a fisherman on a stool by a narrow river. While his right hand gripped the rod, he was waving his left back and forth by his neck to drive off the midges. It was strange to see this placid scene: Scotland, France . . . Were men now fishing off the banks of the Seine near Monet's house at Giverny? Why were they not fighting? How many citizens did it take to wage a war, and what was the responsibility of the ones who did not? Someone must carry on with the ordinary business of working, eating, going to bed: somebody must fish. Could you in all conscience play your line across the seething waters of the Garonne at Toulouse, knowing that where it met the sea at Bordeaux the docks were patrolled by German soldiers? You voted for a government, then did what you were told: no one could really ask for more. And what right had she, a foreigner, to interfere?

Charlotte waited at the station for the Edinburgh train and saw her mother's familiar but ever stouter figure step down on to the platform. She waved from the ticket barrier, then turned away so she would not have to hold her mother's gaze while she walked the length of the train. Amelia Gray's powdery cheek dabbed against her daughter's unmade-up skin and, nominal contact made, recoiled. Charlotte took one of her bags, which bulged with her unvarying baggage of knitting, library books and presents wrapped in tissue paper.

For Charlotte there were vests, handkerchiefs and chocolates, which she unwrapped in the hotel lounge while they waited for the waitress to bring tea. Amelia, satisfied by Charlotte's gratitude, settled back in the floral-covered armchair. She was a big, handsome woman, run to fat, whose waved brown hair was shot with grey. Her fussing indulgence worked hard to compensate for her natural reticence and her fear of scenes, storms or emotions.

The waitress wore a frilled apron and a white cap clipped to her hair with pins that Charlotte noticed as she laid the heavy tray down on the low walnut table. Wisps of cress trailed from the sides of bulging egg sandwiches; three different kinds of cake were fanned about a willow-patterned plate.

'Tell me how you're getting on with this course.'

'We've finished. Tomorrow I'm off to Manchester, then back to London.'

'What's it for, though?'

'The FANYS. You know, the First Aid — '

'I know what the FANYS are. Mary McKechnie's daughter is a FANY too. Are you going to be a driver?'

'I expect so, yes.'

'So why do you need to go on a course?'

'I'm not really supposed to say. You never know who's listening.'

'Really, Charlotte.' Amelia laughed. 'I'm your mother.'

There was a pause in which Charlotte could have said more, but after a moment's awkwardness she could tell that her mother was relieved not to know: her curiosity was formal.

'How's father?'

'Ooh, you know. He's just . . . father.'

'Busy?'

'Of course. Very busy. They're making a lot of changes at the hospital and he wants to be involved in the reorganisation.'

'Are you seeing much of him?'

'He's getting back very late.'

'And have you heard from Roderick?'

'Yes, I have. I had a nice letter from him the other day. His battalion's still in Lincolnshire, but they're hoping to go overseas soon. They don't know where yet. He says he's very fed up with all the training. He wants to get out there and do something.'

'Typical Roderick.'

'Yes.'

'Are you worried?'

'No. He knows how to look after himself.'

Amelia poured some more tea for both of them. She

127

took a piece of cake, her third, then put it down again. Something effortful was clearly going on, Charlotte thought.

'Of course I do worry about you — both of you.' She was looking down at the table. 'I wish you'd get married, Charlotte. Have you got a young man?'

'Not really.'

'It's none of my business, of course. I just . . . '

'Go on.' Charlotte felt embarrassed by her mother's obvious discomfort but thought that, having come unusually close to frankness, she should be encouraged.

'I sometimes ask myself whether I really did enough for you when you were a child.' Amelia's face was tense with effort. Charlotte said nothing. 'Perhaps I was not a very good mother.'

'In what way?'

Amelia could go no further, and Charlotte, who could see the effort she had made, took pity on her. 'It's all right,' she said, and patted her arm. She felt her mother's instinctive flinch at being touched.

'You say that, Charlotte, you say it's all right. But I don't really know what you think. I never have.'

'It's all right, Mama. It's all right.'

Eventually Amelia said, 'I didn't know you smoked.'

'I don't. Not usually.' Charlotte had not even been aware of lighting a cigarette. It was Gregory's fault.

★ ★ ★

'Remember what your mother told you,' the parachute instructor called leeringly to the women as they queued up to do their preliminary jumps from a fourteen-foot tower. 'Legs together.'

'I wonder how many times he's said that,' said Marigold, standing with Charlotte in the queue.

The next day they jumped from a plane. Charlotte was grateful for the dispatcher's uncompromising shove;

short moments of terror were followed by a feeling of powerless ecstasy as the canopy jerked open. The hardships of Inverie Bay seemed to have been worthwhile, and with the exception of one man who turned his ankle, they were all eager to go up again. Marigold told Charlotte that the final part of their training, in the New Forest, was arduous and dull, but in the exhilaration of jumping they treated this as a typical service rumour.

The next day Charlotte said goodbye to Marigold at Euston and took a taxi. The driver jerked and twisted sickeningly through narrow back streets to bring them out into Trafalgar Square; perhaps with her uniform and her suitcase at the station he had taken her for a stranger to the city, Charlotte thought, as they accelerated down the Mall. Office workers on their lunch break sat in striped deck chairs on the grass of Green Park where they threw bread to the scraggy ducks. London still functioned.

Would there be a letter from Gregory when she got back to the flat? He was not much of a writer. Apart from the occasional note left on her bedside table (what did he think when he looked at her vulnerable and asleep?), she had very little by which to recognise his handwriting. Surely, however, he would have the simple politeness to have answered her letter, even if it was just in a few lines.

When they arrived at the house Charlotte felt her fingers tremble slightly on the key. Perhaps it was merely from the exertion of hoisting her heavy case up the steps. Inside the hall she went rapidly through the letters for the first floor flat on the old walnut dresser: there was nothing for her. Up in the flat, she sorted the papers, previous post and magazines on the hall table. She had an invitation to a gallery, a bank statement, a postcard from Roderick in Lincolnshire and a clothes catalogue.

129

She felt a descending bitterness and loss of hope that were out of proportion to the lack of a letter. She went into the sitting room and sat down on the sofa. This is a war, an historic emergency, she told herself, and he is flying dangerous machines; how high in the list of priorities does my self-righteously expected letter come? That was the logic of the situation; but, as her professor of French at university occasionally used to remark, what use is logic when faced with the power of truth?

Charlotte went to the kitchen to make some tea. It had relapsed in her absence, though not quite to the pure state of chaos that had once existed. Charlotte warmed the pot, set the cup ready, and poured the boiling water on the leaves before discovering to her extreme irritation that there was no milk.

She took her black tea through to the sitting room and looked through a day-old newspaper on the sofa. If he hadn't rung by seven, she would get in touch with Marigold Davies, who was staying in some kind of hostel, and go out with her for the evening. *The Times* reported no good news from the Eastern Front, where Hitler's armies continued to move into Russia. Charlotte put down the paper and went to the hall to get a book from her suitcase. It was cool and quiet in the flat, the noise of the turning pages loud in the gloomy sitting room. Charlotte had the sense of life happening elsewhere, while the carriage clock on the mantelpiece ticked off the passage of unfilled minutes. Occasionally she glanced up from her book to the black telephone on the table in the window; once she went over to it and checked that the receiver had been properly replaced. She laid down the book and closed her eyes.

The days had been very full: the psychiatrist, the obstacle courses, the throwing herself from the hold of a slowly chugging plane . . . The extraordinary had become normal, or, if not normal, everyday. Some aspect of the past few weeks had stirred something unwelcome in her thoughts, though it remained just beyond the reach of conscious memory. With her head tilted back against the pimply nap of the sofa, Charlotte probed into the reaches of her mind.

She is in her childhood bedroom. There is the fender that wraps its iron mesh about the coal fire; there is the scarlet rug with its faded golden curlicues. There is a row of dolls propped up along the wall beneath the window. There is a blue-painted wooden bookshelf with a row of stories about witches, schools and ponies. There is the battered bed, beneath the deep and comforting eiderdown. It is night-time and she is playing in her dressing gown on the floor — puzzles or a book in the few minutes before bed. It is a fragile paradise.

She hears an awful noise. It is half shouting, half crying. She goes along the landing, through an open door. Her father is kneeling by a bed. He turns to her, and she is frightened by the tears on his masculine and warlike face. She is aware that at some invisibly remote level she may pity him, but in her child's mind all she experiences is fear.

She goes to him. He has some agonising need. Then the picture, quite clear until this point, explodes and fragments: there is the sensation of betrayal and violation. It is physical pain to an extent, but stranger than that is the sense of borders crossed, a world tilted out of its true orbit.

What really happened she could never fully recall. The harder she tried, the more remote it grew, until it seemed to have happened at another time, in another life, in an existence where different rules applied. All she could be certain of was the intense reality of the incident; it was more real than any clear or normal recollection.

Charlotte opened her eyes again. She had lived for so long with this half-memory that it was part of the scenery of her mind. It had become assimilated, albeit in faint outline, into the person she was; and in long, uncomplicated passages of her life it was as unregarded as any other fragment of the past. What had presumably moved it back into the centre of her awareness were Dr Burch's questions; but she was confident that she could let it drift away, that this most fully real experience could be successfully relegated once more to the shadows.

She took her teacup back to the kitchen. She just had time for a bath before the others came home from work, so she took her suitcase down the corridor to her bedroom and had squeezed it half-way through the door when her eye was caught by a piece of paper on the bed. It was a note from Daisy. 'Dear C, Welcome back — I think it's today you're coming back. Someone called Borowski (?) rang and left this number. Could you ring him back? Love, Daisy.'

Charlotte took the piece of paper back into the sitting room. For two hours she had been sitting in the flat and never even thought to look in her bedroom. She lifted the receiver and waited for the operator. Her voice sounded distant but remarkably calm as she read out the number from Daisy's note. It's probably an invitation to a squadron dance, she told herself. It's probably to ask if Gregory and I will make up a four at bridge or tennis; Borowski hasn't been able to reach Gregory himself since he moved, so I'm the only way to get in touch. He's probably just looking for Gregory, nothing to do with me at all ... He's ringing to say he's dead, they've heard, they tried to reach me ... In a curious way, the question of whether she became hysterical was almost a conscious choice.

The number was of the pilots' mess, where a steward

answered. 'Flight-Lieutenant Borowski? You're in luck, Madam. I've seen him around this afternoon. It may take some time to find him, though. Do you want to hang on?'

'Yes, please.'

'All right, I'll send someone.'

In the excruciating silence Charlotte heard each crackle on the line as the sound of Borowski's happy step/funereal pace, as he strode cheerfully/plodded mournfully to the telephone; she framed offers of religious devotion in the event of Gregory's escape — good works, church attendance . . . She made herself smile at the extravagance of her nunnish vows, because at root she was sure that such terrible things as she envisaged didn't really happen to her. She needed just to concentrate and not give way to premature jubilation, not to tempt providence, until the all-clear sounded.

'Hello?'

'Hello. Is that Borowski?' She didn't know his first name. 'It's Charlotte Gray. I think you rang.'

'Yes, yes, that's right.' Something church-like, decent, solemn, already sympathetic, in Borowski's voice made Charlotte sit down suddenly on the hard chair next to the telephone.

'Yes, Peter Gregory asked me to give you a call if . . . if, you know, if there were any mishaps or what-have-you. And, I just thought I'd — '

'What is it? What's happened?'

'It's not very good news, I'm afraid. He's gone missing. It's a bit unclear. As you know, he's with the Halifax chaps and I've only got this second-hand, but I gather he went down last week. They haven't heard a squeak since.'

'But . . . he told me you couldn't crash a Halifax.'

'He wasn't in a Halifax. Apparently he was in a Lysander, which is a little single-engined monoplane. He'd been training on the quiet to do some pick-up. I don't know the details. They're tiny things. They can land on about five hundred yards of grass. They use them to pick up personnel. Agents, I suppose. He was a natural, having been in fighters.'

'Do you know any more? Is he alive?'

'I'm afraid I really don't know. As I say, it's all second-hand. What you should do is try and talk to the people where he's based. It's a bit tricky because the work they're doing is all so hush-hush, but they're perfectly nice chaps. The squadron leader's someone called Wetherby, I think Greg told me.'

'If he hadn't crashed, then he would have come back, wouldn't he?'

'Not necessarily. I don't suppose he'd have enough fuel. I doubt whether the range is much more than four hundred and fifty miles, even if you strip off the arms and armour and whack on another tank. So if for some reason his man didn't turn up and he couldn't refuel, then he'd be stuck.'

'No wonder they wanted him to learn French,' murmured Charlotte. 'He never told me he was doing this.'

'You must try not to worry. He's a hell of a good pilot. Got the luck of the devil, too. I should think he's most likely drinking too much local wine with some farmer waiting to be picked up tomorrow by another plane. They'll do everything they can to get him back, you know. They won't want to leave a pilot of his experience over there.'

'But what if he's crashed?'

'Well, that's a different matter. I wish there was more I could do to help. I'll try and get in touch with his people, if you like. Who's his next of kin?'

'He hasn't got any. He's an only child.'

Charlotte tried to say goodbye to Borowski, but the words would not pass her throat; she put the receiver down, but in her blurred vision missed the cradle, so it slipped from the table and dangled by its plaited brown cord with Borowski's anxious voice twirling in the bakelite earpiece as Charlotte sank to her knees and laid her head on the floor.

★ ★ ★

Half an hour later Daisy Forester let herself into the flat and called out to see if anyone was there. She had had a long day at St James's and was looking forward to a bath, a change out of her hot clothes and whatever the evening might offer. When there was no answer, she turned on the water in the tub, then went to her bedroom and undressed. A minute later she emerged in her dressing gown and was on her way into the bathroom when she noticed a suitcase sticking out of the door of Charlotte's room at the end of the corridor.

'Charlotte?' She padded down to the open door. 'Charlotte? My God, what's the matter? Tell me.'

'He's . . . ' The words were squeezed singly through the air-lock of her throat. 'Dead. He's . . . crashed . . . Oh, Daisy . . . it's not fair.'

'Take it easy, Charlotte. It's all right. Calm down, now. Calm down.'

Charlotte clung to Daisy's shoulders while Daisy stroked her hair. 'Gently now, gently.'

Charlotte looked up again and Daisy saw the passivity of grief yielding in her expression to something more violent. 'It's not . . . *fair*. I so loved him . . . '

Although Daisy found her eyes damp with the depth of her sympathy, she simultaneously felt detached. Perhaps it was to do with having Charlotte's body in her arms: her failings seemed enclosed by Daisy's grasp. Fond though she was of Charlotte, she had always viewed her as unstable: the way she had fixed herself on this obviously damaged man, the way her unquestioned

135

education afforded her so little protection. She was a little intimidated by Charlotte's self-possession, but she felt sorry for her because she was so vulnerable.

Charlotte began to wail again, and Daisy was reminded of a poem she could not place . . . A woman wailing. It was frightening because it was so elemental; the noise she made as she pulled herself away from Daisy's embrace and threw herself back on the bed was atavistic.

'Now, come on, Charlotte,' she said. 'You've got to stop this, you've got to calm down. Now come on.' She lifted her up again and held her jaw quite firmly so Charlotte had to look at her. When Charlotte tried to wrench her head away, Daisy shouted at her. 'Stop it!'

Charlotte's face for a moment filled with hatred, then softened. 'I can't,' she sobbed, but did then seem to drift off the pitch of her emotion, back into a more manageable grief.

Over the minutes, stroking her hair, holding her hands, Daisy elicited the story as far as Charlotte could tell it. As soon as she could see that there were some grounds for hope, however unsteady, Daisy switched all her efforts into encouraging Charlotte to believe that Gregory was alive. She proposed practical ways of finding out: telephone calls they could make, letters they could write, friends they could ask to contact other friends.

After a quarter of an hour she coaxed from Charlotte the first twitch of a timid, bloated smile and felt a great relief that this hurdle was behind them, followed by a guilty foreboding of the qualities of patient friendship that the long weeks would demand.

'Now I'm going to make us both a nice big drink,' said Daisy. 'You stay here. I won't be a minute.'

On the way to the kitchen, she felt a sogginess in the carpet under her bare feet where the water had trickled from the forgotten bath.

11

Richard Cannerley was late for his meeting with Sir Oliver Cresswell, and this worried him considerably as he hurried up the steps of the Travellers Club. Cannerley's father was dying, and he had lingered too long by his bedside at the Westminster Hospital. Every day when he said goodbye he presumed it would be for the last time, and he tried to fix the moment — the moment of his father living — in his mind, as though in this way he might preserve him. It was a routine that varied only slightly from one he had used as a child on the last day of the holidays, when he would impress on his memory the final sight of his parents to last him through the boarding school term ahead.

In the taxi he wondered if he might use the excuse of his father's illness to mollify Sir Oliver for his lateness. It was his father, after all, who had instilled in Cannerley his sense of national pride and honour, these things of which he presumed Sir Oliver was the inheritor. Unfortunately his father had also bequeathed a code of conduct which would view the pleading of personal emotion as an excuse for professional inadequacy to be quite improper.

Cannerley found Sir Oliver on a sofa in the back window of the drawing room. Breathlessly, keeping his excuses vague, he accepted the waved offer of a seat.

Sir Oliver's physical appearance was a little disappointing to Cannerley. He took no care when he sat down, so that his suit jacket was always creased at the back. There was nothing so glaring as an egg or gravy stain on the lapel, but the fabric never had the soft or laundered look of something absolutely clean.

His uncropped eyebrows overhung a pair of thick and greasy spectacles.

'This Charlotte Gray woman,' said Sir Oliver, when Cannerley had settled down. 'I gather you know her.'

'Yes,' said Cannerley eagerly. 'I put her on to G Section.'

'Have you kept in touch?' It was a favourite phrase.

'Certainly.'

Sir Oliver nodded. 'You remember Fowler, the crooked little businessman I told you about?'

'The chap who's our way into G Section?'

'Exactly. Well, he's managed to get me a copy of their psychological reports on this Gray female. They're rather good. Some suspicion of childhood upsets. Otherwise clear-thinking, resourceful. Determined.'

'Oh, yes,' said Cannerley. 'She's determined all right, but she's set on the wrong thing. She's got some fixation about France.'

Sir Oliver nodded. 'What do you know about her boyfriend?'

'He's an ex-Spitfire pilot,' said Cannerley. 'Like a lot of those Battle of Britain chaps he's a pretty useless case. He was on some ludicrous suicide mission over Dieppe or Le Havre in the spring. The RAF really are incredible.'

'But the girl's keen?'

'Absolutely besotted, according to my inquiries. She was certainly resistant to other forms of male charm.'

'I see.' Sir Oliver inhaled deeply and Cannerley heard the rattle of mucus behind his nose. 'He's gone missing over France. He was in a Lysander. He appears to have had an accident.'

'Is he alive?' said Cannerley.

'We don't know. The point is that this Gray woman is likely to be sent over to Fowler's section. That's the rumour, anyway.'

'From Fowler?'

Sir Oliver nodded.

'But surely she's not up to being an agent?' said Cannerley.

'God, no, she'll go as what G Section charmingly calls a 'courier'. She has to deliver an agent to his destination, then run a little errand of her own.'

'Rather like a FANY at home.'

'Exactly. Be alert. Keep her seams straight. Not stall the car. Apparently the agent needs an escort because his French isn't up to it.'

'Can't they find enough French speakers?'

'Apparently not. Remarkable, isn't it? They say it's all right when he's among friends, but they don't want to risk him talking to security and so on.'

Sir Oliver paused as a Spanish waiter came over and refilled his after-lunch coffee cup. 'Anyway,' he said, when the waiter had disappeared, 'I wondered if this missing airman might work to our advantage.'

'I'm not quite with you.'

Sir Oliver spooned some of the gritty coffee sugar into his small white cup and stirred it briskly. 'I'm not sure there's anything to be 'with' yet.'

'I see.' Cannerley felt flattered to have been privy, at such an early stage, to Sir Oliver's famously intricate thought processes. 'But is there anything you'd like me to do?'

'Yes. The usual thing.'

'Keep in touch.'

'Exactly.'

Cannerley, seeing that Sir Oliver could not be bothered to extend the conversation with smaller talk, made his way out into Pall Mall. As he stood waiting for a taxi, he felt an oppressive melancholy descend. Something was not right. Was it the girl? He envied the airman, but he did not feel unduly concerned for her. No, it was something to do with Sir Oliver that had unsettled him.

A taxi stopped. 'Ormonde Gate,' said Cannerley through the window, but once inside he leaned forward and tapped the glass. 'I'm sorry. I've changed my mind. Westminster Hospital.'

★ ★ ★

Charlotte set off for the New Forest on the train with Marigold Davies. In her handbag was the note Gregory had left by her bed on the last night she had seen him, and a letter from his squadron leader.

Dear Miss Gray,

Further to our telephone conversation today I am writing to confirm that while we have received no news of Flt Lt Gregory since he left on a mission some time ago we have no reason to believe the worst. Although we are a standard RAF squadron independent of other organisations albeit working in liaison with other services you will no doubt appreciate that I am not at liberty to disclose details of the flight, either with regard to its destination or in respect of its operational purpose. I can tell you that Flt Lt Gregory is an extremely able pilot and a patriotic officer with a proper sense of duty. My own belief is that for any one of a number of possible operational reasons he was unable to execute the full purpose of his mission but that he will make every endeavour to contact us when it is safe and prudent for him to do so.

He will be officially posted 'Missing' but I'm sure you have every faith in him, as most assuredly do his colleagues.

Yours sincerely,
Allan Wetherby, Squadron Leader

On the telephone, Wetherby had told her 'strictly between ourselves' that the most likely explanation was that the man Gregory was supposed to pick up had not been there. Without the agent or the support of his network, Gregory would have been unable to refuel and therefore obliged to 'make his own arrangements'. Charlotte pictured him begging petrol from a farmer in his dreadful French and finding himself reported to the Vichy authorities; she tried to develop this picture in her mind because the only alternative was to believe that he was already dead.

She told Marigold nothing of her worries as the train headed out into Surrey. She had confided in Daisy, and that was enough. Now she would complete her training with the greatest assiduity, and when it was finished she would go to France and find him.

Security, recognition, interrogation and security. That, the intelligence officer running the course told them with a smirk at his witty repetition, was what Group D was all about. Charlotte and Marigold were among only six women on the course; they sat next to each other and learned to identify every German plane and badge and rank and regiment. Vaguer but more important were the instructions for recognising German counter-intelligence officers, the Abwehr and their colleagues, of whom there were unknown numbers in France — presumed standing at station ticket barriers, sitting in cafés, idly making bogus calls from public telephone boxes. In her state of stunned concentration Charlotte committed every detail to memory and entered mistake-free test papers when required.

A grave, actorish man in his sixties gave them practical hints on looking ordinary and natural. It was no use knowing a cover story and giving away nothing under interrogation, he told them; they had to look at all times like people who didn't even have a cover story.

Charlotte shared a bedroom with Marigold and a young woman called Liliane, whose mother was French. She took the course more lightly than the other two, and claimed that when she first went to Scotland it was in answer to an advertisement for bilingual secretaries; the first time she realised she was not being groomed to be a typist was when they offered to instruct her in silent killing.

The three of them were joined by three men for an exercise in interrogation. They were told to prepare a cover story giving details not only of assumed identities but of the precise way in which they had all passed the four hours of the previous afternoon, in the course of which a local train had been derailed. Each was then to be interrogated separately.

Charlotte was woken at three in the morning by a torch being shone in her face, and was taken down by an orderly to the billiard room at the back of the house, where two officers were waiting, dressed in SS uniform. One was the course commander, one was a man she had never seen before. The presence of a senior uniformed FANY made Charlotte wonder if this was to be a naked interrogation, like the one Marigold had described. The two men had either not heard of or had disregarded the idea that one interrogator should abuse and one cajole: they both attacked her from the start, standing close, using their physical size to intimidate her. Charlotte, drawn from her deep sleep, pale and puffy-eyed, her pink dressing gown drawn tight about her, found all the details of her learned story undisturbed and was able to repeat them with the mental precision that she always had on first waking.

They tried to destabilise her by claiming other members of her group had given different accounts of how they had passed the afternoon, but Charlotte told them they must have been mistaken. She was sure the self-taught mnemonic tricks that had helped her pass

142

school tests as a girl were still working.

After two hours they let her go. She climbed back up the broad shiny staircase and went along the corridor to her room. She turned the door handle, gently, so as not to wake the others, and walked across the lino-covered floor, shedding her dressing gown as she went. The bed springs made no noise as she slipped beneath the blanket and prepared to resume her interrupted sleep.

Her mind was too full. It was a warm night, and the curtain had been drawn back a little to allow any breeze to enter through the open window.

She had found the early parts of her training impossible and absurd, but her attitude had changed: it now seemed urgent and serious, and even the sight of two Englishmen dressed up in Nazi uniform did not strike her as ridiculous. These pantomimes and costumes, these colours of allegiance, were tokens of a deadly moral order. She was not fooled by their superficial absurdity: British people laughed at Hitler and his preposterous acolytes, but, as German philosophers long before the Nazis might have argued, abstract evil did not choose the form in which it emerged in the particular.

She thought of France under darkness. It was hard to imagine how this country which in her first visits was still so harrowingly proud of itself, intoning the word Verdun like a muttered prayer, could so utterly have lost the thread that connected it to the innocent glory of Rheims and Proust's Combray and Louveciennes, the village the Impressionist painters had made seem essential. There was this sense, on a grand scale, of national breakdown, and next to it was the loss of continuity in her own small life. She felt that the outcome of the one depended on the other; that only if France could find itself again, could she hope to reconnect her own future to the lost happiness of her past.

More urgent than this hope was the need to get herself as soon as possible to Clemont Ferrand: to track down Monsieur Chollet in his garage and see if Gregory had called; and, if not, to use whatever method her cunning and determination could devise to go out in the dark and find him.

The curtain blew back a few inches from the window as the hoped-for breeze rustled through; and in the revealed slit of sky she saw a clouded moon. Charlotte crescent, Charlotte full . . . She closed her dry eyes and felt her lips come inwards in a narrow line. She saw his face. Don't worry, my love, don't worry, I'm coming to get you.

Part Two

Summer 1942

1

André Duguay was running down an overgrown alley between two fields. It was a short cut his mother had forbidden him to take for fear of the adders thought to nest in the long grass, but André was in a hurry. The muscles in his fatless thighs slid up and down beneath the rim of his shorts; his calves, on which the baby whiteness of his skin was acquiring a dim honey-coloured gloss in the course of the summer, propelled him bounding over wiry bramble traps, the ruts of long-dried mud, the sleeping serpents.

When he arrived at the road, panting, he hesitated for a moment. Left, right . . . He was still too young to know the difference, but he knew the school was that way, up the hill: his route must therefore be towards the woods. He followed the road for ten minutes, walking to regain his breath, then running a little to make up time. Eventually, he saw the path he recognised and heard the frenzied barking of a German shepherd dog as the sound of his first footfall reached the farmyard. André walked cautiously nearer. Often his father had told him what to do when confronted by dogs, but still he had the urge to stroke them: in the rough diagram of his understanding, animals were with children against an adult world of rules and obligations. He stood still, offered the back of his hand to the dog and made no move to cross its territory until the animal backed off, its hairy tail swishing, its growls diminishing to a provisional acceptance.

André climbed the steps on the outside of one of the neglected outbuildings. A door was open to a gloomy room with a stone sink in one corner. A purple-faced woman in a headscarf, known to André only as Marion's mamie, was pouring fat from a pan over the top of a duck's leg in a glass jar. She looked up as André stood hesitantly in the doorway and let out a greeting in the cracked accent of the region, which André was too shy to return. The old woman continued with her greasy work, sealing the bottle with a rubber washer and a glass top. André looked nervously round the room, in which three ducks in different stages of dismemberment lay on a long dirty table and a row of blackened pans hung from a beam. Marion's mamie wiped her hands down the front of her apron, exchanging the fresh fat for accumulated layers of older lard transferred from the cloth to her sliding palms.

'Have you come for some eggs?' She rolled across the room like an old sailor, the heel of her hand stuck into the flesh above her hip.

'Yes.' André's voice had the clarity of a treble bell, especially when he was unsure of himself. 'Please,' he remembered.

'I can only let you have four. Have you got the money?'

André took a twist of paper from the pocket of his shorts and handed it to her. The old woman opened it and counted the coins inside. She nodded. 'I'll put them in a paper bag for you. Don't drop them, will you?'

André shook his head vigorously, opening his eyes and pulling his lower lip down in a self-mocking grimace. Eggs were vital.

He went gently down the steps, the memory of first negotiating stairs on all fours still fresh in his mind — often, when no one was looking, he still went up the stairs at home like a dog — and moved off across the farmyard, holding the paper bag tight. 'Thank you,' his father's absent tones prompted him to call in his clear voice, setting off a renewed spasm of barking.

The church spire of Lavaurette came into view as André rejoined the road. His mother had told him the whole excursion would take about an hour, and had smiled impatiently when he asked her, 'Is that a long time?' André clutched the eggs by the top of the twisted paper bag: both his parents had brought him to the edge of tears in their eagerness to impress on him how important it was that the goods came home intact.

Lavaurette was a place that would not die. In the waiting room at the hôtel de ville were photographs from the nineteenth century, and there was one that showed the main street in 1910, before the cataclysm. Small enterprises spilled in black and white from the front rooms of almost every house: tobacconist, carpenter, draper, coiffeur, greengrocer. Young and middle-aged men leaned against doorways, smoking; out of the camera's narrow angle they were working — in the fields, in the giant stone quarry a bicycle ride to the south and in the factory just outside the village. And then there were no men any more, there was only a crudely carved Marianne whose chiselled face, designed to show triumph, looked as though it were blinded by the list of names of the dead that rambled on, up and down the stone pedestal at her feet, through families, through streets, through the ribs and lungs of Lavaurette.

In the years since the Great War it had declined from the character and status of a small town to that of an overgrown village. The main structures were still there: the hôtel de ville was an ambitious Second Empire building with fine tiled eaves; there was a cobbled square in front of it with a neo-classical post office and stern municipal buildings. A plane-flanked avenue led to the railway station, a place of captured somnolence with faded lettering on cream plaster walls; there was a goods siding with rusted buffers and two platforms for the passenger trains that eventually connected their handful of travellers to the main lines for Bordeaux and Clermont-Ferrand. The journey to Clermont was the same as it had been since the line opened in 1882, but the trip to Bordeaux now involved crossing the demarcation line into the Occupied Zone. On the train there were inspections of documents, and beneath the great tubular vaults of Bordeaux St Jean there were German troops. How well behaved they were, it was agreed by all the travellers: how disciplined, polite and neatly dressed.

Although there now existed a new generation of twenty-year-old men, Lavaurette had for many years depended on the vigour of its women: Mlle Cariteau, who ran the post office, a tall, strong-jawed woman of forty whose efficiency was marked by a virile manner and a big, white-toothed smile, a natural wife they said, with no men available in her generation to marry; or Madame Galliot, widowed in the war and left with a baby daughter, whose ironmongery served as a meeting place for the other women of Lavaurette who were unwelcome in the male atmosphere of the Café du Centre.

Whatever the dramatic nature of its changes and whatever the violent reasons for them, Lavaurette retained in the eyes of casual visitors a sense of continuity with more innocent days — a time before the holocaust, when such a village might have seemed as close to paradise as anything that humans had contrived. It certainly, at least, looked old-fashioned, with its three squares, its narrow shuttered streets and its hard-retained dignity. Far enough south to have hot summers, it was sufficiently northern to be wholly French, with no trace of Spain, Liguria or the Languedoc. With a shrinking population, there had been no need to build new houses; and while the soil of the surrounding farmland varied in quality, it had, until the Occupier's ravening expropriations, been good enough to supply an ample market on Saturday mornings; the priest was still respected and his church was full. It was impossible to tell if everything was really lost, because so much seemed to carry on unharmed.

André came to the bottom of the Avenue Gambetta, where he received a wave of greeting from the butcher, Monsieur Gastinel, Lavaurette's only self-proclaimed Gaullist, a man whose low-grade sausages, inventive cuts of would-be steak and dishes of prepared offal were available more readily to those who, like him, had been inspired by General de Gaulle's passionate broadcast from London, in which he had claimed that the fight for France went on and that only a battle, not a war, was lost. A scrap of lamb breast or a spoonful of veal muzzle in brine would sometimes find its way into the rationed bags of those who denied the legitimacy of Vichy and believed that the true spirit of the Republic was now in exile overseas.

Whatever the business of the other shops, there were hardly any goods on display; the only thing of which there seemed an abundance was portraits of Marshal Pétain. His wise and kindly face stared out on to the street, mounted, framed, sometimes surrounded by swathes of crimson velvet or perched victorious on a marble plinth. The snowy moustache and the saviour's tolerant eyes said: we went wrong and we are being taught a lesson; we cannot say how long this improving penance must last; we brought this upon ourselves and now we must see the error of our ways. The older villagers remembered that Pétain had once been the hero of France, when he had seen off the Germans at the Battle of Verdun in 1916 and been the first leader to show a concern for his men's lives. His ramshackle government of 1940, which had voted to dissolve the republic and grant itself full powers, was now the only haven in the storm. The Marshal was a good man, they said; and in any case the people of Lavaurette had nowhere else to turn.

André kicked a flinty stone along the edge of the road. When he got home he would go out into the garden with his younger brother Jacob and continue to excavate the small trench beneath the chestnut tree which served as a moat to the castle they were building with old boxes. André was almost seven, Jacob only four, but their mother treated them alike. Having borne them, fed them, cleaned them, she could not break the bond of touch. Though André could easily dress himself she liked to help him, so that she could feel the packed little muscles beneath his skin. She ran her hands through his black hair and felt the soft spokes of it trickle out over the webs between her fingers. Before going to bed herself, she still crept into André's room and kissed every part of him when he slept naked in the summer, his left arm flung back behind his head, his right arm hanging limp, his golden skin tingling soft beneath her lips, his low breathing undisturbed by her self-indulgence.

André pushed open the door to Madame Galliot's ironmongery and went shyly across the scrubbed boards up to the counter. He felt in his pocket for the second twist of paper his mother had given him, with which he was supposed to buy candles. Half a dozen people were standing round the counter, talking loudly, preventing him from catching Madame Galliot's eye.

'I think it's long overdue,' Madame Galliot was saying. 'The Marshal's the first person who's had the courage to grasp the nettle, that's all. For years they've been undermining us, keeping all the best jobs to themselves, swindling proper French people. The day when they said no Jew should be a school teacher any more, that was the best day we've seen round here for a long, long time.'

André waited his turn. The shop smelled of coir

matting, camphor and galvanised buckets. Behind Madame Galliot's indignantly nodding head was a pointed step ladder she used for fetching down the graded boxes of washers and nails from the top shelf. The shaved floorboards led down the interior of the shop into a secondary room, less pungent, stacked with pans, casseroles, stiff yard brooms and long shelves full of crockery with sets of china laid out round cavernous lidded soup tureens.

'I didn't know Duguay was one of them,' said an old man called Roudil. 'He seemed like a nice enough type. He was no trouble to anyone and I don't think his business was dishonest.'

'Oh, but the mother, though. A typical Israelite,' said Madame Galliot. 'They changed their name to Duguay to take us all in.'

Hearing his family name, André found the courage to speak. The group of people at the counter split apart to let him in and he walked forward, holding up his money. 'Have you any candles, please?'

Madame Galliot's rolling eloquence came to a halt. Her hands flew up to the side of her head, where they pushed nervously at the orange hair that was escaping from its net. She settled her spectacles and gave a turkey-like cluck as she bent down to open a cupboard behind her.

There was silence among the other five adults, who anxiously avoided looking at one another, or at the boy. Roudil coughed and ran his hand over André's hair. 'All right, young man? Off to play now, are you?'

'Yes. I'm going home.' Seeing the old man's worried but kind expression, André was bold enough to add: 'I'm building this castle with my brother. From old boxes. My father's helping.'

'That's nice, then,' said Roudil. 'A castle.'

Silence returned, apart from the sound of feet shuffling on the splintery floor. Madame Galliot handed

André the packet of candles and took his coins. She raised them close to her face to count them out.

'You owe me . . . ' She hesitated. 'Tell your parents . . . ' She paused and looked at her feet; then, with a great effort, as though moving into unknown commercial territory, she said, 'You can owe me the rest.'

'Thank you. Goodbye, Madame.'

The adults watched in silence as the boy swung the door closed, causing the bell to jangle briefly, then started to skip up the street.

André had a natural, loose-limbed action. His feet slithered over the ground with a rhythmic rustle, like wire brushes going over a snare drum. Skipping tired him no more than walking; it was his natural means of going up the hill towards his parents' house in the street behind the square. It was time for him to eat and drink, and he knew his mother would have something ready for him. She had tried to explain to him that it was difficult, these days, to give the children enough food, let alone the things they used to like. André didn't understand the reasons for this shortage, and in any case his mother always used to come up with something.

The front door of the house was closed, which was unusual. André stood on tiptoe and reached up for the knocker. As he did so he saw that a star had been painted on the door. Some dribbles of yellow paint ran from the swiftly daubed diagonals.

He banged on the door again, but there was no answer from inside. His mother had often told him that if he should ever return and find no one there he was to go next door to Madame Redon and ask if he could wait in her house.

With the eggs and the candles still clutched in his hand, André went through to the old widow's house and again raised his small fist. He saw a movement through the half-open window on the first floor, but no one came. It was very odd. If Madame Redon was in the house, why would she not answer the door?

André found his happy poise begin to crack. Just as his mother still liked to treat him as a baby, still wanted him physically attached to her, so in a way he felt that the things he could do — the errands, the hesitant reading — were only fragile accomplishments, and that the real bases of his world were still panic and helplessness. He sat on the step of his own family's house and felt tears coming to his eyes.

'You'd better come with me.' The voice seemed to be in his head almost at once; in his loss of control, André had no sense of the passage of time.

He looked up through red eyes and saw a youngish man hold out his hand. He did not know the man, though he had seen him in the village. 'My name is Julien. I'll look after you.'

André reached out his hand and felt the man take it; some order returned to his existence. 'What's happened? Where's my mother?'

The young man did not answer; he looked afraid. André, seeing that something had happened which was beyond the power even of a friendly adult to explain, and seeing that it had happened to his parents, began to sob. 'What is it? Where is she? Where is she?'

★ ★ ★

The waiting room of the hôtel de ville was filled with bewildered people, some sitting on the benches along the wall, some crowding up to the desk behind which a short-tempered clerk was trying to answer their questions. Their inquiries were to do with obtaining permits or papers within the mayor's gift — permission to leave building waste in a disused quarry, access to

155

food coupons, the right to travel. The room had the smell of bodies confined for too long.

Julien Levade held André's hand tightly as he forced his way to the front of the crowd. Resistance to him initially came in the form of looks and closed ranks; then, when it was clear he was paying no attention, three women began to remonstrate with him.

Julien, who was a reasonable man, explained to them that a boy had lost his parents, that his errand was more urgent than theirs. 'I apologise, Madame, please excuse me. It's not for me, you understand, it's for the child. See how upset he is.'

They looked. André had never been in the hôtel de ville before; its vaulted hall, its marble stairs and now its room of bewildering officialdom had frightened him. He held more tightly to the hand of the strange man, hoping he would find a thread of order that would restore things to their proper place. The man seemed to think that the clerk would know where his mother was and André had no reason to think otherwise. Perhaps she was somewhere behind the counter, in a room at the back of the building. Since she was so powerful and had alone explained the world to him, he could not imagine how she might allow anything bad to happen to herself.

'I don't care what the matter is, you can't just push your way to the front.'

'That's right. We've all got problems. You wait your turn like everyone else.'

Julien elbowed the woman to one side and leaned across the counter. He took the clerk by the arm and pulled him forwards. 'This child was sitting in the street outside his house. On the front door they've painted a Star of David and his parents have disappeared. What's going on?'

The clerk tried to pull himself out of Julien's grip. The forms he had been handling fluttered to the floor.

'Let go of me! What do you think you're doing? Let go!'

'You heard what I said.' Julien released André's hand so he could hold on more tightly to the clerk. 'Tell me what's going on. I heard rumours this morning. Extra trains at the station and things like that.'

The clerk was visibly indignant at having both wrists in a stranger's angry grip and anxious to resettle his half-dislodged glasses. 'Let go of me. I don't know anything about it. It's nothing to do with the hôtel de ville. You'd better go and speak to the police.'

Julien pulled the clerk a little closer. Very quietly, he said, 'You do know something, don't you?' Then he pushed him away, as though the feel of the other man's flesh had become repugnant, reached down again for André's hand and pushed his way back through the reproachful crowd.

Julien and André walked through the streets of Lavaurette. It was now late afternoon and the tables outside the Café du Commerce were starting to fill up. Despite the hot weather, the customers were properly dressed, the men in collar and tie, the women in dresses with handbags and polished shoes. Older men and women were making their way back from the baker's shop with their evening bread beneath their arm or poking out from shopping bags. From some of the houses that Julien and André passed the smell of dinner was starting to drift through open windows: not the rich meat-heavy smell of two years ago, but still passably aromatic with combinations of food saved, or extemporised from hidden stores. The church bell in the Place de l'Eglise was striking six emphatically, a few seconds late, as it had done for a hundred and sixty years.

André's panic now precluded thought as he ran and stumbled alongside the striding Julien. The gendarmerie was on the other side of Lavaurette, across a gravelled forecourt, near to a shaded area where the men played boules. Julien pushed open the double doors and pulled André across the hall into an anteroom where a heavy ceiling fan was stirring the clotted air. He rang a bell on the desk and they heard the sound, further back in the building, of a door grinding open.

A gendarme appeared, wiping his mouth on the sleeve of his uniform, as though interrupted in an early evening snack. He shook hands with Julien, who knew him from his frequent rounds in Lavaurette: Bernard, an amiable enough man, who gave the appearance of being bored by his work.

'I'm trying to find out what's happened to this boy's parents.'

Bernard looked over the counter to where André stood, holding the fabric of Julien's trouser leg.

'What's his name?'

'Duguay. They live in the next street to mine.'

Bernard's gaze flickered; then he looked down. He coughed and picked up some papers from the ledge below the counter.

'I think . . . let me see . . . yes . . . Duguay, Duguay, Duguay . . . just a minute . . . Yes, here we are.' His finger came to rest on a typed list.

'Well?' said Julien. 'What's happened to them?'

'Oh well, I don't really know. It's nothing to do with the gendarmerie, you understand. Some sort of order from the Government as far as I know.'

'Yes, but what happened?'

Bernard looked unhappy 'I . . . I think . . . Listen, do you want to come into the office for a moment, leave the boy here?'

Julien looked down at André's hopeless face. To be left for a moment in an anteroom was not the worst problem he was now confronting. He nodded and followed Bernard through a glass door. 'I won't be a minute, André.'

André sat on a rush-seated chair against the wall and swung his legs. He had stopped crying, but his mouth was filled with a peculiar taste. He felt extraordinarily aware of himself: of his breathing, his skin, the room about him. The seconds would not pass: it was as though time had stalled and had somehow wrapped itself around him with this dry flavour of abandonment.

Bernard lit a cigarette in the office. 'It's nothing to do with us,' he said, pulling an ashtray out from beneath some papers on the desk. He sat down at his chair and indicated a seat on the other side.

Julien shook his head and stayed standing. 'Just tell me.'

'We had a visit from the Vichy police. Those bastards, I hate them. Don't get me wrong, I like the Marshal. I respect him. But those men . . . Anyway, this officer comes along and shows his papers and says he's got a list of people in the region.'

'Jews?'

Bernard nodded. 'Well, Lavaurette, you know as well as I do what it's like. No one's been or come since the war, really. Immigrants, I mean. It's not like Paris or Clermont. I didn't know the Duguays were . . . I'm sure I've seen them in church. Anyway, there was a train coming up from the south, Montauban, Agen or somewhere. A special train and they had to be on it. That's what we were told.'

'A special train?'

Bernard flinched at the sound of Julien's voice; there was an incredulous, unforgiving edge to it. He looked up at him, but could not hold his gaze.

Julien said, 'So then what happened? They came and took them?'

Bernard swallowed. 'You probably heard what happened in Paris last month. There was a huge round-up there and they took them to some sports

159

stadium. They had to put it off a bit because they suddenly realised it was the thirteenth, you know, the day before July the fourteenth and they thought it wouldn't be . . . wouldn't be . . . '

'Festive?'

Bernard coughed. Julien could see the sweat beginning to dampen his shirt collar where it dug into his neck. The cigarette had left a single strand of tobacco on his lower lip.

Bernard looked up at him and his eyes were pleading. 'I'm just a gendarme, I do what I'm told, I don't mean any harm. I just go about the town and try to help. I just — '

'You did it yourself, didn't you?'

'What?'

'You arrested them yourself, didn't you?'

Bernard's eyes went back to the desk. He rested his chin in his cupped hands and sighed. The breath came out jerkily. 'If it hadn't been me, they would have got someone else to do it. That family was going on the train one way or another, that's what you have to understand.'

Bernard stood up. He seemed to be rallying: he met Julien's eye again. 'Anyway, I don't have to explain to you. I've told you what I know because . . . well, because I know you. Because you asked. But if you think anyone in Lavaurette is going to blame me for obeying orders, you're mad. This is a law-abiding town. We respect the Government and we do what we're told. That's the only way forward.'

'Where's the train taking them then?'

'That I don't know. There are a number of refugee camps where — '

'The Duguays are not refugees. They're French. They live here.'

Bernard shrugged. 'Well, that's where they'll take them. It's just until the end of the war. Apparently

160

she's a foreigner, and they haven't been here long. All these people pouring in from abroad, they have to be sorted out. I'm sure they'll be all right.'

'Didn't the documents show where the train was going?'

'I dare say they did, but I didn't see them. I was just told to deliver the family to the station.' Bernard looked down. 'Then they were angry because I only brought the parents.'

'Why didn't you take the children?'

'I couldn't find them. The little one you've got, he must have been out in the fields. The other one, I . . . I couldn't find.'

'But he's only three or four. I've seen him often with his mother. She wouldn't have left him on his own.'

'I couldn't find him. That's all I'm saying. We weren't given enough time. I wasn't given the train time until this morning.'

'Not like the gendarmerie to be so slipshod.'

Bernard said nothing. He took another cigarette from the packet, poked the loose tobacco in with his finger and thumped the little tube on the side of his desk. He wiped the back of his hand across his forehead before lighting the cigarette. He offered the packet to Julien who shook his head.

'I wonder where he is,' said Julien. 'The little one. Jacob, I think his name is.'

'It's a mystery. Probably with a neighbour or something. Now, hadn't you better go and look after the other boy? They'll be back, you know.'

'Aren't you going to arrest him? I'm sure they'd put on another train for him.'

'You're a difficult bastard, aren't you? Can't you see, I'm trying to help you? As far as I'm concerned, both boys have vanished. Now for God's sake take him away.'

'Tell me where the other one is. Tell me where the

other one is and I'll never mention your part in this to anyone. This whole interview will be forgotten.'

Bernard's tongue ran out over his lips and this time he found the shred of tobacco. He pulled it back with his front teeth and worked it to the front of his tongue, from which he picked it with his finger and thumb.

'She was sobbing. The mother, she was clinging on to me. She wrapped herself round my feet so I couldn't move.' Bernard turned his back on Julien and looked out of the window. He pushed it open, and from outside came the sandy thud and metal click of boules; they heard deep, laughing male voices, then the peaceful sound of glasses and a bottle of pastis jangling on a tin tray that the waiter was bringing from the café.

'I was worried we were going to be late for the train. The father was weeping too. They begged me. I didn't know what to do. I shouldn't be in these situations . . . It was terrible.' Bernard's voice began to shake. He turned back from the window. He had gone scarlet in the face and his fists were clenched by the side of his uniform.

'They took the child to the door of the cellar. He was screaming. The mother was hysterical. She was lying on the floor. In the end the father had to drag her off. He pushed the child inside and locked the door. I . . . I had to let them do it. Then I got them out and took them by the back streets. We didn't use the avenue. I shouldn't have done it. I'm in trouble now.'

Bernard was shaking. He rubbed the back of his sleeve across his purple cheek, where a tear had run.

Julien said, 'You're not in trouble. I'll take care of it. Where's the key?'

Bernard put his hand into his pocket and silently withdrew a rusted iron key, which he handed to Julien. He opened his mouth to speak, then closed it. Julien, who had remained pale and apparently impassive, looked at him and put his head interrogatively to one side.

Bernard's confusion of feeling resolved itself into fearful anger. 'It's not my fault. I didn't want to do any of this. Don't look at me like that. I have a wife and family, too, you know. They're my first priority, they're the ones I have to think of before anyone else, before any Jews or anyone. You're not married, are you? Well, you wouldn't understand. If this gets out I'm finished. Do you promise me? Do you give me your absolute word?'

'Yes.' Julien laid his hand on Bernard's arm. 'I give you my word. I'll say nothing of what's passed between us. In return, when they ask you about the children, you just stick to your story. They weren't there, and you don't know where they are. All right?'

Bernard nodded. Julien held out his hand and Bernard took it. As Julien was opening the door to leave, Bernard said, 'Why are you so interested in these children? Why have you taken it on yourself?'

Julien sighed. 'It was just a chance. I saw the child and I thought I should help. It was an accident.'

He went back into the anteroom, where André was still sitting on his chair, hoping for time and the world to start again.

★ ★ ★

'I think we're going to have to be very careful now,' said Julien, as they came into the Place de l'Eglise. 'I think it would be a good idea if I went on ahead to make sure everything's all right. You stay . . . ' He looked around and stopped, as though some idea had stirred in his mind. ' . . . in the church. I'll come back and get you in a minute.'

André sat in a dark corner chosen by Julien, looking at a statue of a marble saint, a cloth or handkerchief

163

clasped in her cold fingers. The moment pressed on him with unwanted clarity: the smell of old incense, the wood on his thighs, the statue of a woman who was not his mother, the pile of cloth-covered books on the ledge beside him. It was not real.

'All right. Come on.' Julien was standing in the doorway. 'Do your parents leave a key somewhere?'

André nodded. Along the wall of the house was a narrow alley that led to a side entrance to the garden. Julien followed him over the stony path and André pushed at a wrought-iron gate whose opening caused a sweet-sounding bell to jangle.

The Duguays' small garden had a flowerbed at one end in which a moat was being dug; at the other end, adjoining the house, was a brick-paved terrace with over-arching ironwork twined by prodigal jasmine. André bent down and lifted up a stone from under which he pulled out a key. He opened a door into the kitchen. There was a choking smell from a stockpot on the cooker which had burned dry. Julien turned off the heat beneath the blackened mess. The table was set with four places; there was a carafe of water and six slices of bread in a wicker basket.

'Where's the cellar?'

'This way.'

The Duguays' hall was cool and dark; there were pink glass light fittings on the wall and a large framed sepia photograph of a Duguay forebear in uniform with medals and drooping moustaches. Julien fitted the key into the lock and turned it. He took André's hand as they made their way down the dark stairs.

'Jacob? Jacob? Are you there?'

André called as well, a theatrical note in his high, clear voice. 'Jacob?'

'We need a candle. Do you know where they are?'

'I bought some from the shop. I . . . I've left them somewhere.'

'There must be some other ones in the kitchen. Go and have a look. I've got some matches.'

While André was gone, Julien made his way slowly down the steps, dragging his hand along the cold stone wall. 'Jacob?' he called softly. 'Jacob?'

André's voice hissed at the top of the steps. 'I've found one.' Julien first lit a match to show him the way down, and then the candle André held out to him. The cellar had a beaten earth floor and a row of empty wine bins against one wall. The candle threw shadows up to the thick wooden beams that supported the hallway and kitchen above.

'Look.' André was pointing. There was a heap on the floor in the corner. As they moved closer, the light of the candle showed it to be a small boy, curled up on his side, asleep.

André reached out and touched him. 'Jacob.' His whisper was frightened and urgent. 'Jacob.' He shook his brother's shoulders and the boy stirred and sat up. Then he climbed abruptly to his feet, his eyes wide.

Julien wondered what they would do. In his experience, sisters and brothers at this age did not embrace unless in some demonstration of false sentiment demanded by their parents.

André took Jacob's arm rather formally and kissed his hand. Jacob said nothing, but looked round in bewilderment. The candlelight showed the big, dark eyes, sunk in his face, fogged by sleep and confusion. André held out his arms to him and Jacob went into his embrace, treading on his foot, staggering a little, as though it was an unnatural process they had learned from watching older people.

'Monsieur? What shall we do now?'

'I think you'd better come with me. My house is in the next street. You can stay with me until I find you a better home.'

'Where's my mother?' said André.

'I don't know. She and your father have gone somewhere on the train. They had to leave in a hurry, otherwise they would have said goodbye.' Julien knelt down and held the boys' hands. 'You're going to have to be brave. It may be some time before you see your parents, but you must try not to worry. I'll make sure you are properly looked after. You can trust me. I'll help you.'

He felt four eyes running back and forth across his face in the gloom, then knelt on the beaten earth and clasped the two small, wiry bodies in his arms.

★ ★ ★

Towards ten o'clock that evening Julien Levade went down to the Café du Centre. The streets of Lavaurette were shiny from a sudden summer storm, and he walked carefully over the unlit pavements. Through half-closed shutters and windows re-opened after the rain, he heard the murmur of voices; a harsh kitchen light showed a tired man recorking a bottle of wine while his wife cleared dishes from the oilcloth-covered table. In the dark street there were occasional signboards on the outside of the houses: a dealer in paraffin, an upholsterer, a repairer of electrical goods. Few customers were ever seen to go into these premises, but an afternoon knock on the door with a broken wireless would invariably raise someone, even if it was only a child, who, with lip-licking concentration, would write out thick brown labels and tie them to the goods to await the father's return.

Julien ordered a glass of wine at the bar of the Café du Centre. Monsieur Gayral, the owner, a stooped, defeated man of only sixty who looked twenty years more, pushed it across the zinc-topped bar. His untrimmed eyebrows hung down either side of his face in superfluous emphasis of his despondent manner. Madame Gayral, who was waiting in the dining room, was a fussy, proper, little woman with brightly dyed red hair and all the energy her husband had surrendered. Gayral was nevertheless a popular host because he was so discreet: nothing that was said in the Café du Centre was repeated by him, and his melancholic manner stretched to apparent deafness in the face of extreme opinions or gossip of a prurience (usually speculations of paternity) shocking even by the standards of the bar. Among those who had benefited from his discretion Gayral enjoyed a reputation as a man of great wisdom, albeit guarded, and a startling dry wit, the more legendary for being unexpressed.

Julien had not eaten, but was wary of the dining room. Even in the days of plenty, Madame Gayral's cuisine had been nervous. She disguised her lack of confidence by serving many different courses in the hope, presumably, that one of them at least might please. Following a thin soup might come ham and a piece of melon, some sliced herring in vinegar, then a knob of preserved duck with peas, a damp green salad, then a grilled sausage with purée of potatoes, a trolley of cheeses and various milk-based desserts. It all added up to less than the sum of its parts; the diners typically felt bloated yet unsatisfied. Under the Occupation, by which the Vichy Government agreed that the Germans needed to eat more than the French, and that France, as well as paying 20 million francs a day for the privilege of being occupied, should yield the best part of its produce to the Occupier, dinner at the Café du Centre had become hazardous. It was only Madame Gayral's inspired idea to hire Irène Galliot, the ironmonger's daughter, as dining room waitress that kept the male clientele faithful. Irène was her mother's daughter, they agreed — by which they meant formal, unyielding, almost pitiless — yet strangely more handsome. Roudil gallantly believed that this proved Madame Galliot must herself have been a beauty when young; most people thought it showed only that old Galliot, whom some of them remembered from before his death in the spring slaughters of the Chemin des Dames in 1917, was not the girl's father. Irène had thick, wavy brown hair, slender legs with only a hint — an exciting hint to many of the men in Lavaurette — of peasant heaviness about the hip, a numbingly effective if rare smile, aristocratically (suspiciously) fair skin and a face which, although it was of a kind that might perhaps not wear well, could only fairly be described as beautiful.

It was Irène's day off, and Madame Gayral was clearing the plates in the dining room from those disappointed male clients too slow-witted to have worked out the waitress's weekly time-table. Madame Gayral's absence in turn meant that conversation in the bar was even more unguarded than usual. Even Gayral himself was fired up to speak, and his opinion was granted a surprised but respectful silence.

'Some people say Laval's not to be trusted, but I say he's a very clever man. Every time one of these Communists shot a German soldier in the Occupied Zone the Germans would take ten innocent people and execute them. Now Laval's done a bargain. Now we have French police in the Occupied Zone, and they administer discipline. That's how it should be: France policed by the French, occupied or not.'

There was a pause while the others took time to digest Gayral's opinion. A man called Benech, who was a schoolmaster, said respectfully, 'You may be right there, you may well be right. But you must admit that the Boche soldiers have behaved impeccably — in the face of great provocation, too.'

Gayral nodded.

'Not that great,' said Julien. 'The odd isolated incident, but really hardly any — '

'Oh, those wretched Communists,' said Benech. 'When will they ever learn? They're as bad as the RAF with their bombing. The sooner the English face up to the inevitable the better for all of us.' Benech had only recently started to come to the Café du Centre. He allowed himself only two drinks each evening, yet elicited a certain respect for his vigorous opinions.

Gayral began to speak. 'I heard a story about a big factory in Clermont. I'm not going to say which one.' Two or three heads nodded in approval of his discretion. 'The chief was visited by some Englishman who told him the RAF were going to bomb his factory because it was making machinery the Germans were taking for their war effort. This Englishman said if the chief gave him a copy of the plans of the factory he'd make sure they dropped their bombs on the right targets, just the vital bits that would be impossible to replace, and no one would get hurt. If he refused, they'd just bomb the whole thing. The factory owner told him to prove he was really in touch with the RAF by getting them to fly over the next night and drop a single bomb in a field outside the town. Well, apparently they did. And the chief gave the man his factory blueprints and two nights later they came over and destroyed the vital machinery, exactly according to plan.'

'How did this Englishman come to be in France?' said Roudil.

'They come by parachute. There are hundreds of them.'

'It's that monster Churchill,' said Benech. 'He's the most selfish man in Europe. For the sake of his own glory, he's prolonging this dreadful war. Why can't he accept the inevitable? If the Marshal — the Marshal, the victor of Verdun, if you please — accepts that the Boche have won the war, why can't this foolish man see it? And where were the English when we needed their help in the Great War? They stayed at home.'

169

'I think some did come over,' said Roudil.

'I think not, my friend,' said Benech. 'Anyway, why should this factory owner help the English? It's against the law. The Marshal made that clear when we entered into the 'way of collaboration' with the Occupier. Those were his actual words, and quite right, too. We have to think about our future and our children's future. This war's only going to last a year or so — it's a drop in the ocean — and when it's over we'll be in a position to take our place in the new Europe.'

Roudil creased his ancient face a little as Benech propounded his clear and trusting view. Benech had a thick, straight moustache and grey, pocked skin; he spoke as a man who feels the flow of history is at last vindicating his long-held beliefs.

'I think it's a little more complicated than that,' Roudil said. 'The Marshal's playing a double game. He seems to go along with everything they ask, but he's waiting for his moment. He may be old, but he's shrewd, that one. Look how he's kept the sovereignty of France alive. You tell me another country in Europe which has kept its independence after being occupied. Norway? Sweden? Belgium? Oh, no, he's a canny one, the Marshal, and we've not seen the last of his cunning.'

'What exactly is this sovereignty worth?' said Julien. 'An old man in a hotel room with powers that no one voted him, doing what he's told by the Germans. Is that sovereignty? While Paris is occupied and the Republic is dead?'

'Oh, the Republic, the Republic,' said Benech, sipping at his second glass. 'The Republic killed itself. I'd have thought anyone could see that after the mess Monsieur Blum and his Jews made of things. If it took the Germans to bring us to our senses, then frankly I'm glad of it. And I'll tell you another thing — we need another couple of years to put everything

170

straight. If it takes the presence of the Occupier to give the Marshal time to get the country back on course, then so be it.'

Julien had heard this view so many times before that he was tired of arguing with it. In a way he admired its logic. To believe that being occupied by a well-behaved foreign power enabled you to put in place, peacefully, the conservative internal reforms your country had long needed seemed not only practical but also rather gamely philosophical. Under the influence of this Panglossian strain of thought, you could view the situation as not only convenient but lit up by a sort of providential optimism.

Instead of quarrelling, Julien said to Gayral, 'I hear your son's coming home.'

Gayral smiled. 'Yes, at last. It's taken for ever to get him back from Syria. But I can tell you, there's one boy who'll be glad to see the back of that desert! We expect him home next week.'

'He wasn't tempted to join the winning side, then?' Julien could not resist teasing him.

'Which side?'

'The Free French. The units that defeated him.'

'Free my foot! They're just a few brigands run by the Americans and the English. In my boy's regiment there were just two men who went over to them. That's how popular they are!'

'And the rest have come home?'

'Of course they have!' Benech interrupted enthusiastically. 'There may be work to do here, you know. You've read about the Allied landings, haven't you? They think the English might try and invade in the north. The Marshal says we've got to be ready to see them off. I tell you, it won't be a pretty sight, especially if the Americans join in.'

'The Americans,' said Roudil incredulously. 'What's it got to do with them?'

'They've sent a representative to the Free French,' said Julien.

'Well,' said Benech, 'that shows just how much they know.' He laughed in rich amusement. 'Poor old Americans! They really have got the wrong end of the stick.'

Roudil cackled at the humour of the situation; Gayral gave a grunt. Benech's amusement was so tearfully rich and his beliefs so apparently guileless that Julien also found himself smiling.

2

Charlotte was sitting in a red armchair in a flat in Marylebone, trying to overcome her twists of gastric nervousness sufficiently to concentrate on what Mr Jackson was telling her.

He was prowling round the room, hitching up his trousers, tucking in his shirt more tightly as he talked. She followed him with her eyes until he disappeared behind a standard lamp, when she had to turn in her seat and strain her head to bring him back into view.

'I know it's a bit rushed. We're not really doing it by the book, I'm afraid, but of course there isn't actually a book, as I'm sure you appreciate.'

Jackson stopped by a desk in the window and picked up some papers. 'Your reports are awfully good, I must say. And the French bods said you could pass for a native. They don't say that about many people, you know.'

'Are those the Free French?'

'Heavens, no, they won't talk to us. De Gaulle's running his own little networks and never the twain shall meet. Anyway, my chaps said you were first class.'

'It's very kind of them. I don't think it's quite true.'

Jackson raised a scholarly eyebrow. 'Let me put my little proposition to you. Did you bring the letter by the way?'

Charlotte handed him the envelope containing a brief instruction to present herself at the flat. Jackson slid it into the pocket of his flannel trousers.

'There's a relatively new network not far from Limoges which was started by one of our best chaps. It's called Violinist.'

As he spoke, Charlotte was calculating: Limoges to Clermont . . . Probably not more than 250 kilometres, all in the Free Zone. A three-day bicycle ride; perhaps four days — it was a long time since she used to ride to the Academy in the mornings with a basket full of books.

' . . . so your task is really very simple. First you're to accompany Yves. We wanted to call him Hugues, but he has too much trouble pronouncing the 'u'. He's a Lancastrian, and I'm not going to tell you his real name because there's no need for you to know it. He's an extremely able man and although he does speak the language, our tame Frenchman wasn't too happy with his accent — a little more Burnley than Bourges, if you take my meaning. You will therefore act as his chaperone, keep him from having to talk to anyone, until you're safely arrived at the house near Uzerche, where he'll join forces with a very busy little network and you wish him *bon voyage*. All clear so far?'

Charlotte nodded. 'Yes. Quite clear. You'll give me more details at the time.'

'Of course.' Jackson gave a froggy smile. 'Maps, money, addresses, not to mention the jolly old cover story. They'll be plenty to learn by heart, but they say you've got a memory like an elephant, if you'll forgive the expression.'

'I'll do my best.'

'Jolly good. Now the second part of your job is even simpler. We want you to deliver a set of wireless crystals to one of our operators in the area. These little chaps are very light and easy to carry. The drawbacks are twofold: they're very fragile, and they can't be disguised as anything else. The wireless operator you're going to see has had a little accident — I'm not quite sure how it happened — but anyway, she needs a new set. You'll be given a suggested meeting place and time, naturally, and the rest is up to you. I suppose it's possible they'll ask you to do a drop rather than actually meet the girl. You know: leave them in the ladies' excuse-me or some such thing.' Jackson gave a little laugh.

'And then what do I do?'

'Then? Then, my dear Miss Gray, you come home. The return flight.'

'The same place, the same plane?'

'No, I rather doubt that. I think you're going over in one of the big boys, a Whitley probably. They may want to drop some stores at the same time. You'll come back in a little Lysander, I imagine, something that can actually land. So. What do you think of all that?'

Charlotte licked her lips and tried to generate some saliva over her dry tongue. 'It sounds very straightforward.'

'It is, it is! Now, listen, I don't suppose I could interest you in a bite of lunch, could I? Got to feed you up, you know, food's wretched in France. Can't take you to my club, alas, for obvious reasons, but there's a jolly good little place round the corner. Do you like fish?'

* * *

Everything began to happen swiftly. Jackson gave responsibility for Charlotte to a woman called Valerie Kay, a stern, academic person of the kind Charlotte imagined to have been among the pioneers of women's education at the ancient universities. She had wiry brown hair pulled back tightly and a manner which at every turn seemed to emphasise the seriousness of the undertaking. The cover story was the first and most important aspect of preparation. Charlotte was to be called Dominique Guilbert; she was born in Paris in 1917, married to a clerk in Angoulême who was now a prisoner of war in Germany, and was travelling to see her sick father who lived in Limoges. She had

175

been partly educated in Belgium, to allow for any falsity of accent: the French contempt for 'the little Belgians', she was told, was such that even the most bizarre non-francophone noises could safely be ascribed to a brief period in Brussels. The details of the cover took them two hours to go through, at the end of which Charlotte was given a day to learn them, and the names and addresses of contacts, by heart before reporting to the flat in Marylebone, where she would be tested. In addition to a cover name, she was given a field name, Danièle: good agents, she was told, could manage under interrogation not even to divulge their cover name, and such double security was helpful to other people in the network. From now on she was to be Danièle in all her dealings with them.

Charlotte wrote a letter to her mother saying she would be away on official business and would contact her when she could. She told Daisy she would be away for a fortnight and to let anyone else have her room in the meantime if she wanted. Daisy gave her a long, worried look, then let her go. Valerie Kay took her through the cover story, bit by bit, with added cross-examination from an emaciated Frenchman who fired questions through a slowly gathering cloud of cigarette smoke. Charlotte missed Mr Jackson's cheery presence, but they seemed satisfied by her response.

'Of course, there is one other thing we haven't mentioned,' said Miss Kay. 'Your hair.'

'What about it?'

'It's not a very French colour, is it? I've booked you an appointment for two o'clock with a French hairdresser in Brook Street. The dye should last for several weeks unless your hair grows very quickly.'

Charlotte nodded, wishing she did not think that Miss Kay was taking some unkind pleasure in the idea of turning her hair a dull brown.

At four o'clock, cropped, brunette, Charlotte returned

to the flat for the final preparations. The door was opened by a butlerish figure she had not yet met: he stood aside to let her pass, then took her firmly by the elbow and showed her to a bedroom. 'Wait here, please, Miss. Someone will be in shortly.'

Charlotte looked about the neat room, which had fitted wardrobes and a watery seascape above the bed; there was a dressing table in the window with a floral frilled skirt, but no make-up or hairbrushes. She sensed it had been a long time since anyone had actually slept here. Charlotte felt both calm and excited: what she was doing was not only right but also somehow inevitable. Her life and her education had led her to this point; she was not frightened to be returning to a country that she loved and which in her mind was associated with a completeness of civilization. She was confident she could carry out her simple errand, yet the prospect brought an intoxicating feeling of escape. Unlike so many people caught beneath the bombs in London or trapped by the German army and the French bureaucracy, she had the liberating privilege of action.

The door opened, and Charlotte smiled broadly to see Mr Jackson again. 'Goodness me, what a splendid job they've done. You look as French as Joan of Arc.' He placed a brown paper parcel on the bed. 'These are some clothes I want you to put on. They're of French manufacture or, if not, we've sewn French labels into them. The pockets have a few shreds of French tobacco and some dust from the area you're going to. There'll be one complete change in your suitcase and two spare sets of underthings. Someone'll be along for you in a minute.'

It was with some sadness that Charlotte undid her knee-length, navy-blue skirt and slid it down over the ivory slip. G Section had taken no chances with their idea of what French women wore under the Occupation: woollen knickers, coarse stockings, apparently to be held up with the provided pair of garters, calf-length skirt and poorly knitted pullover. Charlotte laced the clumpy shoes and looked at herself in the mirror of the dressing table. The door opened again. Valerie Kay came into the room to gather up Charlotte's own clothes.

'We'll keep these safe for you until your return,' she said, her expression communicating disapproval as she folded the bundle into a sheet of brown paper. 'In a minute I'll want you to go to the bathroom and take off any make-up, but please wait here until you're called.'

Charlotte sat on the edge of the bed and waited. She could hear several other voices in the flat and a continual opening and closing of doors. Something was going on. The caution and periphrasis that had so far characterised her dealings with these people had suddenly been replaced by short words and quickening steps. Charlotte had the impression that at least three other people like herself were being briefed and prepared, and also, for reasons of security, kept from seeing one another. She could not help smiling at the thought of the butler going to and fro, of false identities being taken up and trousers being dropped behind different doors; but presumably it would be worth it to be incapable of showing any sign of recognition if ever she should meet one of these people at night, at Bordeaux St Jean, beneath the scrutiny of an SS officer.

The butler reappeared and took Charlotte down the corridor to another bedroom, which was fitted with what looked like a dentist's chair. 'Sit there, please, Miss.'

A few minutes later, following more footsteps and banging doors, a short, white-haired man came in and introduced himself as Mr Legge.

'And you are . . . Let me see,' he said, looking at a clipboard hanging from the side of the chair. 'Danièle.'

'That's right.'

'Open wide.'

'I beg your pardon.'

'Open wide, please. I'm going to replace your fillings. Let's have a look. Not too bad. Only six that I can see. You must have had a good dentist when you were young.'

'The Belgians are famous for it.'

Legge seemed too old and frail to be able to pump the drill mechanism hard enough with his foot for the bit to turn to its full effect; the silvery Scottish fillings were thus chiselled out piece by piece, to be replaced by a heavy, gold, and presumably French mixture. As the old man ground on, Charlotte wondered bitterly whether they had assembled the metals from the very area of her intended drop.

After two false starts, one of which involved the butler pushing her back against the wall and covering her eyes with his hands, Charlotte was eventually delivered to the sitting room of the flat, where Jackson had first outlined to her the details of her mission.

'Danièle,' he said. 'Welcome. Do sit down.' As she did so, he gave her his froggiest, most reassuring smile. 'How do you feel?'

'I feel all right,' said Charlotte honestly, calmed by Jackson's manner. 'I could have done without the dentistry.'

'I know, I know. Most of our people think I'm mad, but my view is simply that anything we can do to protect our agents is worth doing. That's all. Now I think we may be in luck. With 'Charlotte', I mean. Does that name mean anything to you?'

'Of course.' She pointed through the window towards the sky, where a crescent moon gleamed white.

'Nothing else?' Jackson grinned.

'Certainly not.'

'Jolly good.' He straightened his face and coughed. 'Now, once you've delivered Yves to Uzerche, you're to leave him there and make no attempt to contact him. Understood? He'll be with friends there and he won't need you. Then you take the crystals to this address, go into the hairdresser's and repeat the lines written here.' He pushed a piece of paper across the desk. The hairdresser's was in a town called Ussel. Charlotte read and memorised the contents. 'Got that? Good.' Jackson took the paper back and tore it up. 'We're pretty much ready for the off now. Sometimes we have to keep people hanging around for ages, either here or in one of our houses in East Anglia. But the weather forecast's first class. Bright as a button all the way to Limoges. As far as your return journey's concerned, you're to do as instructed by the local Frenchman. It's just possible you'll hear from our man there who's running Violinist. He's called Mirabel, but he's very busy and I expect the Frenchman can handle it. I don't have a name for him, but he'll tell you at the drop. There'll be a plane to bring you home in a week or ten days. The local chap'll have the gen from his wireless operator. All clear?'

Charlotte nodded.

Jackson sucked in his breath. 'This is all terribly straightforward, but of course if it all goes well, and I'm sure it will, we might find you something more exciting another time. Do you follow?'

'Of course.' Charlotte nodded.

'Now there's just one more thing I must tell you about.' Jackson settled himself on the edge of the desk. 'Sometimes people get very lonely over there. You can tell no one about yourself, you have very little human contact with anyone at all. You're only going to be there for a week, so I'm sure you'll be fine, but even a week can seem a long time. Be prepared for it and don't let it affect you. Are you subject to feelings of loneliness?'

Not exactly loneliness, thought Charlotte: bereavement, desolation, despair . . . 'Not particularly,' she said. 'Not really.'

'Good. You'll receive your final briefing from one of my staff at the aerodrome. He'll also give you a small package with the crystals in it. I normally like to come myself, but as you've probably noticed we've got a rather busy day. Quite shortly I'm going to introduce you to a young woman who's going to be with you from now until you get on the plane — a sort of a chaperone, really. You can call her Alice. All the girls who do this job are called Alice. She's just there to keep an eye on you, make sure you don't absent-mindedly slip a packet of Craven A into your pocket and so forth. She'll even have to accompany you to the you-know-what. It's all perfectly usual, but before we say goodbye I want to wish you luck. It's an awfully simple little job, but the first time's always a bit tense. I'd like you to have this.'

He held out a small box, tied with an orange bow. Inside was a silver powder compact.

'Thank you,' said Charlotte. 'It's lovely. It's not too expensive for a girl like Danièle?'

'Dear me, no. It's French, too. Look at the maker's name.'

★ ★ ★

Julien Levade's office was on the first floor of one of the larger streets of Lavaurette. A double outer door opened from the street on to a courtyard on the far side of which the main entrance led into a gloomy reception area that smelled of floor polish and caporal tobacco. The receptionist, a plump woman in her thirties called Pauline Bobotte, directed visitors to any of the half-dozen enterprises in the building, and worked the small telephone exchange, parroting the number in her uncompromising accent and prodding in the little plugs with their frayed cords. It was a matter of unquestioned routine for her to listen in on any conversation she chose, and no visitor, however long he had waited in the hall, however urgent his appointment, was allowed to interrupt her deft manoeuvres.

'Mademoiselle Bobotte?'

'Yes?'

'It's Monsieur Levade. I wondered if you had one second . . . not if you're busy, of course.'

'It's not time for coffee already, is it?'

'Very nearly.'

'I'll see what I can do.'

Ten minutes later, Pauline Bobotte entered Julien's office with a small white china cup, slightly out of breath from the slippery climb. Julien thought it better not to ask where she procured the coffee — she was a resourceful woman with good connections among the local shopkeepers as well as a reliable intimacy with a businessman from Toulouse, who frequently stayed in Lavaurette on his way north. Pauline Bobotte was capable of discretion in her turn. For instance, she never asked why various callers referred to Monsieur Levade as 'Octave', nor why it was always these people who seemed to be making urgent assignations. There was a time to keep silent and listen.

The price Julien paid for the coffee was a brief, slightly flirtatious conversation with Mlle Bobotte, in which she asked him about his work, and he questioned her about her home life, implying that she concealed from him the large number of suitors who kept her busy.

Pauline Bobotte went to look at the plans on Julien's

drawing board. 'You haven't made much progress, have you?' she said.

'I'm at the stage of creative thinking. Beautiful shapes are forming in my head. Marble staircases are rising up out of nowhere. Fountains are shimmering. I'm wondering whether there should be peacocks on the lawns.'

'Well, I hope you're going to put some bedrooms in this hotel.'

'Really, Mademoiselle, bedrooms, bedrooms, is that all you think about?'

'You Parisians are all the same,' said Pauline Bobotte sternly to hide the beginnings of a blush. 'Quite impractical. If a traveller stops off for the night he wants a good comfy bed, that's all. He doesn't want peacocks and fountains.'

'I thought we'd keep the cloisters, perhaps put some tubs of flowers along here, geraniums, pansies. What do you think?'

'I think it's a shame to wreck a lovely old building. Why can't it carry on as a monastery?'

'There hasn't been a monk there for years. Everything passes, everything changes.'

'Well, I'm surprised people have got enough money to do things like this nowadays. It's all we can do to keep body and soul together.'

'On the contrary, the Occupation has provided ideal circumstances for the shrewd businessman. Life will resume. There will be full hotels and rich clients. Whether they'll be French or German, of course, I really can't say. But my employers are prepared for all eventualities and they have no doubt taken care to offend no one. Listen. I think I can hear the telephone.'

Pauline took the empty cup, reluctantly, and made her way downstairs. A few seconds later, Julien's telephone rang. 'I'm just putting you through,' he

183

heard Pauline's voice say.

'Octave?' said a man's voice.

'Yes,' said Julien.

'Auguste. It's on. Ten thirty. Understood?'

'Yes.'

The line, to Pauline Bobotte's irritation, went dead.

★ ★ ★

Charlotte waited an hour and twenty minutes, dressed as Dominique Guilbert, sitting on the edge of the bed in yet another room in the flat. There was a short knock at the door and an expensively dressed woman, a little older than Charlotte, came in and introduced herself.

'Danièle? I'm Alice. I'm going to look after you now.'

Charlotte took in the woman's tailored suit, her crocodile handbag, and felt the dowdiness of her own mousey hair, her clothes, the cumbersome shoes.

'The car's waiting downstairs. It's about an hour's drive. Do you need the loo?' 'Alice' had what Charlotte recognised to be a smart — perhaps affectedly so — English accent. Although she was not in uniform, she reminded Charlotte of what Cannerley had said about the FANYs being as posh as Queen Charlotte's Ball.

'No, I'm all right thanks. I went when I took my make-up off.'

'Super. If you're quite ready then, I think we'll make our move.'

Alice opened the door a few inches and received an affirmative nod from the butler at the end of the corridor.

'All right, my dear. Here we go.'

Charlotte followed Alice to the front door of the flat, a brief 'Good luck, Miss' from the butler following her out on to the landing.

A black Riley was waiting at the foot of the steps

184

outside, a uniformed FANY standing chauffeur-like beside the open rear door. She took Charlotte's roughened brown suitcase and stowed it in the boot, while Charlotte sank down on to the red leather seat. It was early evening and a newspaper seller was barking some incomprehensible sound. The driver moved a switch in the walnut dashboard and Charlotte heard the indicating finger slide out from the side of the car as the three women pulled out into the traffic and headed north towards St John's Wood.

* * *

Julien finished the dinner the housekeeper had made earlier and left on top of the cooker. He wiped a piece of bread round the edge of the plate to soak up the remains of the gravy generated by the concoction of meat and vegetable. He never asked what the ingredients were in case it put him off, but tonight's effort had been almost palatable, helped by the half-glass of red wine he had thrown in while reheating it.

He poured the last of the litre of Côtes du Rhône into his glass and lit a cigarette. It was nine thirty. He could not conceal from himself the fact that he was enjoying this very much indeed: he was in perfect time, he was just drunk enough and it was a beautiful, star-packed night. He carried the dishes through to the kitchen and left them by the sink; then he went round the apartment closing the shutters. The high ceilings and the bare floors made it noisy; he left his shoes by the door so as not to disturb the family who lived on the ground floor. He filled a small flask with brandy and slipped it into the pocket of the old leather jacket he took from the row of pegs in the hall. He could not remember when these excursions had taken on such an alcoholic character, but it now seemed indispensable.

185

He checked that the bedroom window was open and noted with pleasure how well the housekeeper had tidied the room: the great wooden-ended bed and its antique canopy looked positively seigneurial, he thought. No one else had wanted this ancient, draughty apartment; only an architect would have been foolish enough to rent it. He put on some heavy boots, patted his pockets to make sure he had cigarettes and took a small rucksack from beside the front door. Inside were four electric torches and some spare batteries.

Julien clattered down the stairs, forgetting as always, until it was too late, that his footsteps would cause a scuffling from behind the concierge's door. He strode across the hall but was not quite fast enough.

'Out again tonight, Monsieur Levade?'

'Absolutely. I'm meeting my fiancée at the station. She's just arrived from Lyon.'

'I thought she was from Paris.'

'Oh, that's a different one,' said Julien, as he slipped through the front door. 'Good night.'

He went round to the side of the building where he kept his bicycle. He connected the dynamo to the wheel and pedalled off, the thin beam of his front lamp expanding to a handsome glow as he accelerated into the village.

On the main road out of Lavaurette, just before the school, was a solid, spacious house that belonged to Mlle Cariteau, the post-mistress. Julien left his bicycle propped against the railings at the side and went cautiously to the back door, where he knocked on the glass.

'Who is it?' A manly figure with a woman's voice moved in silhouette across the lit blind on the door.

Julien smiled. 'It's me. Julien.'

A bolt was slid, the door opened on to a large, untidy kitchen, and Sylvie Cariteau offered one cheek, then the other, in greeting.

'Good evening, Madame.' Julien went to shake hands with Mlle Cariteau's mother, who sat in an easy chair by the vast, blackened fireplace.

'Sit down.' Mlle Cariteau pulled back a chair at the table, which still bore the remnants of the two women's exiguous dinner. She poured Julien a glass of wine and pushed it towards him over the pitted oak surface.

Julien looked at Mlle Cariteau. He needed to do no more than raise an eyebrow. 'All right?'

She nodded. 'All right. They're asleep. My mother looked after them today.'

Mlle Cariteau opened her hands and glanced towards the rafters. Julien followed her gaze. He had never been upstairs, but it was easy enough to imagine from the outside of the house that it had ample unused spaces. 'We have twelve bedrooms,' said Mlle Cariteau.

'How are the children, Madame?'

He always had some difficulty, as a Parisian, understanding exactly what Madame Cariteau said. Although she was probably no more than seventy, a lack of teeth added to the puzzle of her accent.

'They were frightened. The little one, Jacob, wept all morning, then suddenly he seemed to cheer up. I gave them some paper and pencils and they did some drawing. I heard them laughing together in the afternoon. The older one kept asking me when his parents were coming back.' The old woman drew her lower lip up over both gums and shrugged. 'I don't like to let them downstairs, that's the nuisance of it.'

Julien sighed. 'We'll have to try to work something out.'

'Leave them for the time being,' said Mlle Cariteau. 'We can manage.'

Julien looked interrogatively towards the mother, who gave a sour little nod of agreement.

★ ★ ★

The Whitley smelled of raw machinery: oil, tin, rivet. Charlotte felt a pair of hands pushing on her backside, then a shoulder being added to the shove. She sprawled inside, almost unable to move for the bulk of the parachute, and lay down as instructed by an RAF sergeant across the bomb bay with her head and shoulders propped against the side of the fuselage. Somehow, despite the training, she had been expecting seats. 'Yves' followed her into the plane and took up his position opposite. He gave her an encouraging wink. Charlotte was filled with a sudden certainty that she was going to feel sick. The lack of any view, the mechanical smell and her sense of anxiety reminded her of sitting in the back of her father's shooting brake on long drives across the Highlands, with the windows half fogged by rain, the air heavy with pipe smoke, her view bounded by the back of her parents' heads and Roderick's bare knees beside her.

There were several wooden crates stowed at one end of the fuselage with parachutes attached. In addition to Yves and Charlotte, there were two RAF sergeants on board, who would act as dispatchers when they reached the drop zone. The engines started up while the two men checked that everything was securely strapped; then one of them settled himself between Charlotte and the partition that separated them from the nose section, which contained the controls and the flying crew. He patted her on the thigh and grinned. 'All right, my love?' Everyone seemed to be from Lancashire.

The plane came to a halt and the engine noise increased. Gregory would know what this meant: perhaps they were waiting for a signal. Then they had it; and the plane began to roar and shake as it committed itself full-heartedly to the runway. The whole body of it seemed to tremble with the effort of making this unnatural transition; metal, weight, loading, bodies and gravity fought against the bull-like perseverance of the engines until, reluctantly, against nature, the plane hauled itself up off the ground.

Until her training at Manchester Charlotte had only once been in an aeroplane, when she flew to Rome to complete her Italian course; all her journeys to France had started with the boat train at Victoria and finished at the Gare du Nord. The peculiar thing about this plane was that it seemed to be pointing downwards: there was a clear upward slope from nose to tail. After a few minutes she asked the sergeant why this was and he told her it was just a characteristic of the Whitley, nothing to fret about, and that they were in fact climbing steadily. From a cardboard box he produced some cups and a thermos, from which he poured tea. Yves accepted with a smile and Charlotte, thinking her stomach might be happier with something to work on, did likewise.

'I've got something a bit stronger if you'd like it,' said the sergeant, holding up a flask. Charlotte remembered her father telling her how the rum ration would come up to the front in the last war before the men were required to go over the top into the storm of steel.

'What is it?' she said.

'Rum.'

She shook her head: she did not need that kind of courage to drop into an unoccupied field in the country for which she yearned. Yves also declined, and the sergeant replaced his flask in the box.

'We'll be going over the French coast at Cabourg,' he said, 'then down over Tours. We'll have to have the lights off soon. I suggest you try and get some sleep. I'll not let you miss your stop. Oh, and by the way.' He was having to shout to be heard over the engines. 'If you hear gun fire that's probably our lad in the rear turret just testing his equipment. Doesn't mean Jerry's on our tail. All right?'

Charlotte had not known there was a gunner on

board, but it seemed a vaguely comforting thought. Yves smiled and nodded; he seemed to be dropping off already. The dim lighting was extinguished as they crossed the Channel, and in the darkness Charlotte tried to picture Cabourg below them. She thought of how she had sat in Monsieur Loiseau's shady garden with her book. In the shaping of one man's imagination, this Norman seaside town, renamed Balbec and moved a little to the west, had offered a version of unstable paradise. After the journey of the little train and the bewitching sight of the small band of girls on the beach, the furtive grandeur of the hotel itself had been the setting of snobbery, humiliation and the narrator's kiss declined by Albertine, the object of his love. Yet as a teenager, reading Proust's novel for the first time, Charlotte had seen Balbec as a place which had encapsulated some perfectly developed society, where an intense feeling might be properly valued, not dismissed merely because, like all things, it passed. She did not really understand what the jealous narrator meant when he suspected Albertine of enjoying 'hidden pleasures' with Léa and the other women.

Now perhaps there were Nazi officers in the hotel dining room; all the bedrooms where once the wealthy inhabitants of the Faubourg St. Germain had changed from their modest woollen bathing costumes into their evening dresses and white ties were occupied, four at a time, by murderous young men in grey uniforms. Perhaps the gorgeous world of the book was more than just fictional; perhaps it was untrue.

Eventually Charlotte felt the sergeant's hand once more on her thigh. 'We're starting to go down, love. We've passed over Tours and we're coming near Limoges. We're going to drop the stores first, then the two of you. Obviously if we did it the other way round you might get a nasty surprise dropping on top of you. He's going first, then you. Now I'm going to

190

show you the line because I want you to be happy that you're firmly attached.'

He pointed to the connection between the parachute and the static line that would jerk it open as soon as Charlotte was clear of the undercarriage.

'See? Nice and firm. No worries?'

'Fine.'

Both sergeants went forward to the drop hole, which was just behind the cockpit partition. They hauled the two halves of it open and beckoned Yves and Charlotte to come forward. Charlotte peered into the darkness. At first she saw nothing, and then she could make out the twinkle of lights in a small town. She felt a stinging in her eyes.

The other sergeant gestured them back to their places as the plane began to descend, though he himself stayed by the hatch. The pilot seemed to be having difficulty in getting the heavy bomber on line, and it pitched and heaved weightily as he fought to level off at the prescribed height. Charlotte felt sweat erupt on her palms as the engine roared, faded and roared. She swallowed hard and forced out saliva; she saw the sergeant by the hatch mouthing something anxiously, but could not hear for the sound of the engines. Then she saw his thumbs go up and she lip-read the word 'lights': somewhere in the heaving darkness below was a farmer with a torch and Charlotte's heart filled with absurd love for him.

The sergeants began to push out the crates, and they could feel the heavy jerk beneath the fuselage as the strops paid out and ripped open the parachutes. Six crates went down in quick succession, then the plane climbed and began a long banking turn to come in for its second run.

'You lot now,' grinned Charlotte's sergeant as he beckoned them up to the hatch.

Yves offered Charlotte his hand. 'Good luck.' They

squatted by the hole as the heavy plane once more bucked and plunged its way round. Interior lights were switched on in the fuselage and a red lamp appeared on the wall above the hatch. Yves's sergeant pulled him forward, watched the light until it turned green, then heaved him out into the night. They heard a bang and a flap. Charlotte's sergeant pulled her by the arm to the edge of the hole; she sat with her feet dangling in the darkness. She saw his anxious eyes straining up at the red light. Then he kissed her cheek and hurled her through the floor.

She was driven upside down, then sideways, by the blast; she had no breath, no sense, then she felt the straps of the parachute dig into the flesh on the bottom of her thigh-bones as the canopy opened and the straps took her weight. The parts of her body, which seemed to have been dispersed about the sky, head there, legs far behind, stomach somewhere back in the fuselage, began to reassemble themselves about one central point provided by the pull of gravity on the webbing between her legs. The momentum of the plane meant that the parachute was still oscillating in wide, sickening arcs, but beneath the nausea and the fear Charlotte felt the exhilaration of the drop and the safety of knowing, from the pressure of the straps, that she was safe. The ground hit her while she was still swinging, much before she expected, and she cracked her elbow as her legs — irreproachably together — could not stop her hurtling sideways on impact. She felt earth and grass smacking into her face and entering her mouth. For a moment she lay still, unable to move or breathe. Slowly she gathered herself, bit by bit, and climbed to her feet. As she breathlessly took in the solid facts of her arrival, smacking the disc on her belly to release the parachute, looking round at the beams of torchlight in the darkened field, she felt no fear, only the irresistible uprising of happiness.

In the farmyard the three men worked swiftly to unload the crates from the cart while the ribby horse snorted in the moonlight.

'Almost done. Just wait one minute.'

Yves and Charlotte did as they were told; neither could think of anything to say, but they found themselves continually smiling at one another. One of the men produced their suitcases from an opened crate.

They were led into the house and introduced properly to Octave, Auguste and César. Having been trained by a G Section visitor, the men were scrupulous about using only these names, and Charlotte found it difficult to penetrate even this elementary cover to guess what kind of people they were. They did not seem like farmers. The one called Octave was in his late twenties, dark, with a twitchy, humorous face; he spoke quickly and in a markedly Parisian way. César looked like a schoolboy, tall, with big hands and a low voice, but clumsy and deferential in his manner, as though embarrassed by his education. Only Auguste looked like a man of the region: he was solidly made, with a high colour and a shaggy moustache that seemed prematurely grey. He also took charge of the cooking, producing a five-foot length of thick sausage, which he cut into shorter pieces and threw into a frying pan on the range. César fetched a round loaf of heavy bread from a cupboard and Octave filled their glasses with wine.

As they drank each other's health, Charlotte had the impression that it was not the first wine the men had drunk that night. When the sausages were almost ready, Auguste broke half a dozen eggs into the pan, then served the whole lot on two plates.

'But what about you?' said Charlotte as Auguste

joined the other men at the table and sat back with an expectant look to watch his visitors eat.

'We've already had dinner.'

Charlotte calculated that in addition to three fried eggs she had two and a half feet of sausage on her plate.

None of the three men would be available to help them in the morning, so they spent several minutes going over maps and making sure that Charlotte and Yves knew where they were and where they had to go. They admired the false papers that had been made for them in London — in a grey stucco-fronted house on the Kingston by-pass, Mr Jackson had told Charlotte with dry enjoyment. The next day they would walk to the station at Lavaurette, a distance of about five kilometres, and take a train; Octave told them to take what they wanted from their cases for the night, and he would arrange for them to be left at the station: walking across country with suitcases might look suspicious.

When Charlotte could eat no more, she pushed her plate into the middle of the table and over-rode Auguste's exclamations of surprise and disappointment by persuading César, who had been watching with insatiable adolescent hunger, that he might help her out.

The men said goodbye and shook hands warmly. Yves and Charlotte would be quite safe for the night; there was no need for them to worry. Octave wrote down his office telephone number on a piece of paper, showed it to Charlotte, then, when she had memorised it, put it in his pocket.

'There are hardly any Germans in the Free Zone,' he said. 'But you need to watch out for the Vichy police. And be careful with gendarmes, though most of them will turn a blind eye. I'm sure you've been told all this.'

Yves nodded. The more time she spent in his

company, the more Charlotte liked Yves; he was a calm, taciturn little man, but he had the light of a wicked impatience in his eyes.

They found two bedrooms upstairs on either side of the farmhouse. Offered the choice by Yves, Charlotte picked the one whose bed had a bolster. She had kept back from her suitcase one of the G Section French vests, which she wrapped over the part of the bolster on which she intended to lay her face. She had also retained some washing things, though these were less useful since the farmhouse had no running water.

As she pulled the shutters noisily together, Charlotte glimpsed the rear light of a bicycle, wobbling from side to side, as Julien Levade tipsily tried to keep his balance with the weight of Charlotte's suitcase on the metal luggage rack above the rear wheel.

★ ★ ★

Mlle Cariteau's house, despite its open position on the main road and its numerous large windows, seemed incapable of capturing the light. The upstairs room in which André and Jacob were lodged admitted only slats or wedges of summer sun across the window seat and on to the worn floorboards; the long interior corridors, lined with vast wooden-fronted wardrobes, were in perpetual dusk.

As the days went by, Madame Cariteau, thinking it might stop their thoughts from roaming, tried to settle the boys into the semblance of a routine. She had one or two children's books left from the childhood of her own daughter, and she found a doll and some wooden toys in one of the wardrobes. Sylvie had been a good girl, an easy child to bring up, with a naturally hopeful attitude, despite having no father. So many children in Lavaurette were in the same situation that, although Sylvie might have felt it as a sadness, it was never a

195

peculiarity. But, while the relationship between mother and young daughter had been happy and fruitful, it had also been a long time ago. Madame Cariteau found that her touch with small children seemed to have gone; she fought to remember how to talk to them, what they required for entertainment. Luckily, the elder boy seemed to have picked up the rudiments of reading, so, after lunch, when she dispatched Jacob to his bed to rest, she took André on her knee and went through Sylvie's old books with him.

It was a narrow decision as to whether André Duguay or Madame Cariteau was the better reader. Her greater experience of having seen groups of letters clustered on shop fronts or road signs made her able to recognise some long or complex words, as she would have recognised a human face; but André's dogged phonetic technique helped build up the sounds of words that had defeated Madame Cariteau. After some days of resting his head against the old woman's bosom, inhaling her unwashed, ancient but oddly comforting smell, André in any case came to know the story of the crocodile and her missing egg so well that he barely needed to look at the words. Madame Cariteau was impressed by his scholarship and by her own unsuspected aptitude for teaching.

To his question, 'Where is my mother?', she gave her response in the same words: 'They've gone away, but they'll be back. Until then you're quite safe with us.' By never varying this formula she managed to make André feel that the question was less and less worth framing; and from a hundred times a day the frequency with which he asked it declined to half a dozen.

Madame Cariteau enjoyed looking after the children, and saw it as a natural act of female kindness. Although she accepted that Jewish people were dishonest and anti-French, and that the Vichy legislation to restrain their activities and confiscate their businesses was

196

overdue, she didn't see how the little ones were to blame: after all, it was not André or Jacob's fault that they were born Jewish. Her daughter's view was more developed, which was why it was she who had been approached by Julien to look after the children in the first place. That was her business, Madame Cariteau thought: Sylvie was entitled to any opinions she liked, but none of them need affect her own attitude.

André, meanwhile, just wanted to be happy, and, having been happy all his life, was driven naturally towards this regular state of mind. Sylvie Cariteau told her mother she thought he was 'adaptable', and praised him for it, but it was a blinder craving than that. Because he had no power to change his circumstances, his will to survival and his legacy of natural content deceived him into experiencing them as bearable.

Yet something was checked in him. Without his mother's constant touch, he shrank a little; his movements became less fluid; he walked more often than he skipped; he remembered himself more, never any longer forgetting to say please or thank you. Slowly, too, he began to register his father's absence; he missed his physical bulk and the stability it represented; he missed the feeling of bodily release that followed their wrestling matches. And for all the way the observable changes were so small, he also still had fits of misery.

★ ★ ★

'I think we should speak French, don't you?' said Charlotte.

'All right,' said Yves. 'Just as well to get in practice.'

They walked down a cart track until they came to a small country road with high hedgerows and cow pastures on either side. The sun had a midday strength by only ten o'clock; the sound of cattle-bells came from

197

distant fields, in some of which the hay had already been rolled into huge circular bales. Charlotte felt well rested and at home; the events of the previous evening had for once driven tormenting thoughts of Gregory from her mind and she had slept well.

The brightness of the late summer sunlight made the landscape look almost surreally French; the farm buildings and the vegetation were so typical that they verged on exaggeration: everything is safe, they seemed to say, everything is unchanged. Yet Charlotte also felt the fraudulence of her own position and imagined that it would be clear to anyone they met. What else could she and Yves be but two British people who had parachuted in last night, bent on undermining the French government and its German masters?

When they eventually passed a young man on a bicycle and exchanged a brief greeting, Charlotte felt an impulse to declare herself, admit the game was up and ask him to take her to the nearest police station; but neither this man, nor an old woman in a farmyard, nor Bernard, the gendarme, whom they passed on the outskirts of Lavaurette, paid them any attention at all. When she told Yves what she had felt, he admitted to the same sensation, and they agreed to put out of their minds at once the peculiar and infantile idea that their true identities were so apparent.

Even so, when they had retrieved their suitcases from the stationmaster's office and gone to the ticket window, Charlotte could not help feeling surprised at the ease with which the first francs she unrolled from the large bundle provided in London were accepted by the clerk, or at the weary manner in which he went through the routine of issuing their tickets.

The idea of being someone else, of being Dominique Guilbert, born in Paris, married to a clerk, was in fact appealing to Charlotte. The anguish of Peter Gregory's presumed death meant nothing to Dominique Guilbert;

nor was Dominique in the least affected by the lesions and unresolved knots of Charlotte Gray's childhood: she had her husband and her sick father to think about.

The train did not leave till two o'clock, so Charlotte and Yves went into Lavaurette for lunch. The dining room of the Café du Centre was half full, mostly with men. Charlotte's eye raked over the waitress — an attractive, disdainful young woman, too aware, in Charlotte's judgement, of her good looks and the effect they had on men. She brought them a small meal of indifferent quality and afterwards abruptly clipped the coupons from the Kingston by-pass.

They walked back to the station and waited for the train. Before joining the established network in Uzerche, Yves had business to do in Agen, a large town further to the south-west. The slow connections out of Lavaurette meant that they would spend all afternoon on the train, and Charlotte bought some newspapers to pass the time. She gave one to Yves, though she was not sure how much of it he would understand; the French he had talked to her so far had been worse than Mr Jackson had suggested. His other skills must be of a high and unusual quality for G Section to have risked him, Charlotte thought; perhaps one day she would discover what they were.

3

Twenty minutes on foot from Lavaurette was a house with slate-covered towers and a low, rectangular courtyard that included an arched pigeonnier, surrounded by abundant but untended land. It was not quite a château, though it was almost big enough; it was known in the town, to the postman and to its very few visitors, as the Domaine. It was not the sort of house that anyone in Lavaurette wanted to live in: it was too remote, too draughty, too imposing. It was impossible to heat in winter, and in summer impossible to fill, with its echoing salon, immense panelled dining room and numberless bedrooms, none sealed or closed but all kept in a state of suspended life, the beds made, the floors not exactly clean but swept occasionally, the decorations faded but intact.

A family must once have lived here, though even the most fruitful parents could not have filled all the rooms; it would have needed cousins and visitors to justify the half-dozen servants' bedrooms in the attic, and to prevent the long, connected spaces from imposing their silence. For many years the undisturbed volume of the rooms had swelled against the practical limits that contained it; the air seemed to have expanded within the confines of the house until it could spread no further and had instead become thicker, turning back on itself, and cloaking such movement as there was with quietness.

It was early morning in the Domaine; wood pigeons were calling in the trees beyond the long grass, and the climbing sun was already striking deep inside the house through the open shutters on the east side.

In one of the smaller bedrooms the house's single

inhabitant was sitting up in bed and frantically searching his memory; he was trying to remember if he had dreamed. By his bed was a large pad of paper with pencil notes and sketches, put there for the purpose of instant recollection; but one page had taken him three months to fill, and neither the images nor the words seemed to be of any consequence. The man scratched his thick white hair and sighed. Nothing.

In the corner of the room was a small shrine. On a table, a figure of the Virgin was set on a lace cloth, with a missal and some candles. The man climbed out of bed, a little stiffly, rubbed the tendon behind his ankle, and made his way over to the shrine, where he knelt down to pray. As a convert to Catholicism, he was anxious to do everything the right way, but as a Jew he could not quite shake off a more conversational style of dealing with his Maker. He prayed for himself and he prayed for his departed friends, may God have mercy on their souls, whose names he kept in the missal and spoke out loud. His own family name, Rutkowski, had been changed by his father to Levade, in what he believed was a compromise between the phonemes of his adored, adopted country and an acknowledgement of his Hebrew origins.

He said a brief prayer for his son Julien and for the other children he had sired but had not known. He fiercely regretted that he could feel no tie with these scattered people, whose ages varied from forty to ten; he did not even know if there were four or five or six, though he believed there was a daughter in Limoges. Since his ten-year conversion to Christianity, he had felt troubled by this negligence.

The Domaine had only one bathroom, a minimal space whose door was disguised as the last of a series of cupboards, reluctantly conceded its bare existence in the otherwise dry landscape of the upper floor. It was a long and inconvenient walk for a sixty-two year old man to make each morning, but he was unwilling to change to a nearer bedroom because he believed the one he had chosen had particular dreaming qualities.

Levade's tenancy of the Domaine had been the subject of hostile discussion in Lavaurette. He was reviled by Madame Galliot as a lecher and by Monsieur Benech as a Jew; Madame Gayral believed he was a Satanist. At any rate, he was indisputably Parisian and peculiar; although occasional visitors, including priests, had been seen to take the turning to the Domaine, Levade himself had never set foot in the Café du Centre, had never been seen to buy food or tobacco. He had a housekeeper, a girl from another village who was thought to be mentally defective, and his son took him food and wine once a week — a further reason why Julien, though not disliked, was regarded with caution in Lavaurette.

The main bedroom in the Domaine, an airy, high-ceilinged chamber whose floor-length windows granted long clear hours of light, was rumoured to be the centre of whatever unsavoury, un-Christian activities it was that the old man enjoyed. No reliable witness had returned with a description of the bacchanalian squalor to which he had reduced what was once the parents' bedroom, a sacred place at the heart of the family, at the centre of an old, traditional house.

An hour after rising, washed, dressed and dreamless, Levade made his way to the locked door of the principal bedroom.

★ ★ ★

The newspaper Charlotte read on the train was the first indication she had of how greatly the country had changed since her last visit. She had previously found French newspapers arid and charmless. She had been influenced by the way in which they had been introduced to her as a teenager by the father of her exchange family, Monsieur Loiseau, who spoke reverently about *Le Figaro* and its great, murdered editor, a Monsieur Gaston Calmette, who had had the honour of being the dedicatee of *A La Recherche du Temps Perdu*. Dutifully she had persevered through reports of stock exchange movements, foreign policy and structural developments at the Justice Ministry.

The paper she flicked through on the train to Agen seemed less interested in reporting than in propaganda: fatherland, patriotism and the dangers of Bolshevism were invoked in almost every article. She counted eight photographs of Marshal Pétain, who seemed to be presented as a sort of supra-political figure, giving the reader an excuse not to have to think about public affairs. There were cheerful reports of leagues and societies dedicated to the rebirth of traditional folk songs, and pictures of children in a variety of uniforms. To Charlotte they looked like English brownshirts or Hitler youth, though oddly enough there was hardly any mention of the fact that France was partly occupied and wholly subjugated by the Nazis.

The society encouraged by the uncritical articles was one of camp fires, khaki shorts and breeding. A cartoon showed a Spirit of France with its arm round a uniformed child; the figure that embodied this sacred spirit was not a banner-clenching Marianne but a giant Gaul in a skirt, with a blond walrus moustache and shoulder-length fair hair. To Charlotte it was as though England beneath the Blitz had chosen to invoke the spirits of Caratacus and morris dancing.

The tone of the articles was not just stoical or resigned, but extraordinarily cheerful: a new Europe was being built, and the finest brains of France's bureaucratic class — by a natural sequence of logic, therefore, the finest brains in Europe — were at the heart of this process, working from a number of hotels in Vichy. It was accepted that some political power had been temporarily ceded, but this was viewed by the writers of all three articles on the editorial page as a worthwhile manoeuvre. They argued on strategic grounds that the Germans would provide a strong framework within which French interests could best operate after the imminent end of the war. On tactical grounds, they said, the current state of emergency helped hasten through some overdue reforms, such as terminating the democratic excesses of the Third Republic. And on moral grounds they thought that a degree of mortification of the flesh (rationing, curfews) was not only well deserved, but would renew the national vigour that had fallen into a state of flabby, Jewish decadence.

Charlotte offered the newspaper queasily to Yves, who shook his head silently, as though unwilling to risk his French in front of the three other people in the compartment.

After an hour the door slid open and a policeman asked to see their documents. He wore a different uniform from any they had seen before, but the three French people in the carriage seemed unsurprised by his request and meekly offered up their papers. Charlotte looked out of the window while he examined the identity card of Dominique Guilbert, checked its photograph against her averted face and wordlessly handed it back. She noticed that Yves managed to look both resigned and slightly truculent at yet another official's questioning his bona fides; the policeman himself seemed irritated by his task and slid the door closed with a minimal grunt. Charlotte had to check the beginnings of a smile of elation; she turned it into a yawn as she surveyed the passing countryside of south-west France. The phrase that came to her was 'piece of cake.'

At half past six the train eventually slowed beside

a steep, wooded hill in which Charlotte could make out occasional patches of white stone and a couple of houses. Agen, Agen, barked the station tannoy in a jangling south-west accent. Yves and Charlotte descended from the train and walked along the platform to the main concourse, where they found a left-luggage office. Yves carried a small briefcase.

Across the street from the station was a wedge-shaped building painted pale blue, with ridged plasterwork like a wedding cake, called the Café Hôtel Terminus.

'We'll meet there after you've taken me to my address,' said Yves.

Instead of taxis, there were only horse-drawn carts outside the station. In Agen itself there were hardly any cars, and those that there were moved ponderously, powered not by petrol but by charcoal-gas engines — a cumbersome cylinder stuck into the boot. In atmosphere the town was fully southern: the street that took them down to the Boulevard de la République had roof tiles and wrought iron balconies of an almost Italian kind; yet at this time of day, the hour that in Rome or Naples would have seen the chattering *passeggiata,* there were few people on the streets and nothing for them to look at in the shop windows except photographs of Marshal Pétain. There was a sullen, despondent air that the hot evening and the sound of women's voices through open shutters did nothing to dispel. A young man came toiling towards them on a bicycle, pouring sweat from the effort of pulling an adapted trailer in which sat two elderly, self-conscious people in Sunday clothes.

For the first time Charlotte felt frightened. The fear was not of being arrested or deported, but a visceral response to the place itself. There were no Germans, there was no coercion; but this southern town, with many dark-skinned people, not French in the same

205

way as Vichy or Illiers, seemed utterly adrift, in a state close to breakdown.

She hurried Yves down narrower streets towards the address whose location, and the route to which, they had both memorised. They made their way swiftly and unchallenged through the hot, pathetic town; they seemed almost the only people with anywhere to go.

They rang the bell on a door next to an empty café and heard footsteps on the stairs inside. A woman with a headscarf opened the door, and after what seemed to Charlotte an unnecessarily protracted exchange of coded reassurances, took Yves inside the house with her.

'Two hours,' said Yves as he closed the door behind him.

Charlotte walked a long loop back towards the station, as slowly as possible, to pass the time. She found that her lips were moving silently and that she was talking to Gregory, as she often did when she was alone. Her conversations with him served different purposes according to her mood, though the premise on which they all operated was that he was not dead.

★ ★ ★

Not dead, she thought, as she sat in the bar of the Hôtel Terminus; not dead in either sense: still breathing, somewhere in France, and the love she felt for him, which existed between them like some fragile but ferocious third entity, that too was still alive.

Was it only the effort of her memory that sustained it and was that effort bound to be worn down, in the end, by the passage of time? She believed not. The survival of the feeling was in some ways more important to her than the survival of Gregory himself. The existence of that transcendent emotion had allowed her to escape from the confines of her personal history; it had granted value to her life. It did not seem to matter whether it had first flared then, or then, at that, or this, or any other moment, because if it was real and had value, then it existed outside time.

Yet she did miss him. Simply, like a child removed from its mother, like any being taken from its source of love, she yearned for him — now, here, this instant in the bar of the hotel, where she drank foul, dark coffee. With her hands she longed to stroke his hair; the pores of her skin missed his touch; she felt sick and closed-off inside because the natural fluency of her thought had become shaped by conversation only with him. She did not feel the shapeless despondency that had afflicted her at various times before: on the contrary, she felt directed, almost galvanised. But the weight of her anguish over Gregory — this one missing airman, this unreliable, perhaps (she shook her head as her lips moved) unworthy man — filled her whole upper half, diaphragm, lungs, ribs, shoulders, with such crushing gravity that the sighs with which she was obliged to displace it shook her entire body.

She looked up from her table and saw Yves standing above her, looking down a little curiously.

'All right?' she said.

He nodded.

'We should perhaps find somewhere to stay the night,' said Charlotte.

'Here?'

'It's rather gloomy, isn't it?' said Charlotte. 'I'm sure we could find somewhere a bit more cheerful. Shall we go and explore?'

Yves nodded again, and Charlotte left some coins on the table. She forced all thoughts of Gregory from her mind, trying to channel their unwanted energy into a renewed concentration on the assigned task of looking after Yves.

The problem of room-sharing was one that Yves raised diffidently, in English, in the park to which he directed Charlotte to be sure of not being overheard. It was peculiar enough that it should be she, not he, who did the talking in the hotel, he explained, but downright suspicious that she should then book two rooms. Of course, their identity cards would show they were not married, but that in a way made their travelling together far more plausible: a man would only ever take his mistress, never his wife, on a business trip such as his cover story described, and that was one thing, whatever the changes undergone by this traumatised country, that would still be understood by any real hotelier. His intentions, he would like to reassure her, were of course . . .

Yves dozed upright in an armchair in the corner of the room, having absented himself in the passage while Charlotte undressed. The bed was of three-quarter size, guaranteed to compel intimacy between two people but spacious enough for one to stretch out. For all her comparative comfort, Charlotte slept badly. Through the thin walls she could hear a couple making love, she with whinnying abandon, he with dogged grunts and floor-rattling shoves. The single lavatory at the end of the passage flushed on and off throughout the night while unembarrassed footsteps pounded back and forth over the bare boards of the landing.

Charlotte was relieved to be back on the train, heading north, the next morning. There were no seats available and almost no room to stand. Everyone on the train seemed to have at least three large pieces of luggage, and the purpose of most of their journeys, to judge from the smells that came from their suitcases, was to buy and bring home food. Order seemed to have broken down under the burden of numbers; at one of the many halts on the way north she saw young men wriggling on to the train through the windows.

At Uzerche, Charlotte delivered Yves once more to his destination. Here he was in deep cover, according to Mr Jackson, and no longer needed her guiding hand. His further movements were of no concern to Charlotte, and, on the G Section model of minimum information, she was strongly discouraged from inquiring about them. She gained the impression that he would be returning to London, perhaps even on the same flight as her, but did not ask. Until then her only contact with Yves would come as a result of wireless messages from London via the operator in Uzerche; communication between there and the Lavaurette area was unpredictable, though such messages as were received would pass through 'Octave'.

In Uzerche, the connection was established much more quickly than in Agen: the retired schoolmaster at whose suburban house they arrived had been expecting them for some hours and seemed relaxed about the contact. He introduced himself as Gérard and invited Charlotte to have a drink before she made her way. It was mid-afternoon, and Gérard, a tall, courteous man, took a tray of drinks out on to the terrace at the back of his house where two black dachshunds were sleeping fatly on the gravel. He was a widower, he explained, and the dogs were his chief companions; it seemed clear to Charlotte that they were certainly receiving the better part of his meagre food ration. Gérard spoke of his visits to England in the 1920s and of his particular love of the Lake District; his punctilious and enlightened attitude seemed unperturbed by public events, though this civil equilibrium, it seemed to Charlotte, must have required him to avert his eyes.

Their drinks were finished, refilled and finished once again. Gérard's remarks to Charlotte took on a valedictory air. Yves looked at his watch. Reluctantly,

Charlotte stood up to go, and both men escorted her back into the house. She kissed Yves on either cheek as they stood in the hall and shook Gérard's hand.

When she heard the door close behind her and began to walk off down the quiet street, she felt for the first time a panic of loneliness.

* * *

Meanwhile, on a grey London evening, Cannerley was waiting in Sir Oliver Cresswell's outer office, twisting the cufflinks in his shirt beneath the scrutiny of an elderly secretary. He assumed there must be something unusually important behind the summons he had received by telephone that morning. This time he had made sure he was early.

'Come in.' Sir Oliver appeared briefly at the door, which he left slightly ajar. 'Sit down.'

Cannerley perched on the single hard chair that faced the desk. Sir Oliver stood with his elbow resting on the mantelpiece. For such a mentally scrupulous man, he kept a remarkably untidy office, with tottering piles of paper and two or three parched plants. The room was panelled, and above a long table against one wall was a reproduction of the Goya portrait of the Duke of Wellington.

Sir Oliver sat down at the desk and looked out of the window. 'You remember our little chat the other day? Well, I've been thinking about it. And a little notion has occurred to me.'

'Really?' Cannerley tried not to notice how unpolished his superior's shoes were.

Sir Oliver coughed. 'Are you familiar with the pattern of French resistance, such as it is?'

'Certainly. I wrote a paper on it. It was B-listed, but — '

'Of course you did. Well, as you know, the

Communists have been the only active group so far. But our government's not worried about them. They have the whole weight of the Occupant and Vichy and the French populace against them. The problem is that there are now a number of Gaullist outfits starting up.'

Cannerley leaned forward. 'I haven't heard much about them.'

'There's been nothing to hear. Their policy is to wait for the moment to strike. 'Long-term action', I think they call it.'

Cannerley laughed and Sir Oliver wiped the back of his hand swiftly across his own mouth. 'Meanwhile they're in the market for arms drops. Their main network was infiltrated from the beginning by Abwehr agents. But although it's very small beer at the moment, our masters feel the Gaullist movement is something that needs to be watched.'

Sir Oliver had a rolling 'r', which made a phrase like 'arms drops' problematic; it gave it an inappropriate smack of the nursery. Cannerley found that this childishness made the whole enterprise sound paradoxically more frightening.

He tried to concentrate. 'I didn't know anyone took de Gaulle seriously.'

'They don't. But if the war continues to run the Allied way . . . '

'Even so,' said Cannerley. 'Old Joan of Arc with his merry men in Carlton Terrace . . . I mean, for a start, he's been sentenced to death by the French government!'

Sir Oliver sighed. 'Like the French, we have to think of the likely configuration of Europe after the war. We have to consider all alternatives, however preposterous. We want to be the first country in the new Europe, albeit with some American support.'

'What about the Russians?'

'Good God, I can assure you there are plans to shake hands with our Russian friends as far East as possible.' Sir Oliver gave a shudder. 'Meanwhile, the spiking of the Gaullist networks would serve a number of purposes. It would be a setback for the Abwehr. It would clear the way for G Section networks and stop de Gaulle getting too big for his boots. It would help keep French resistance under British control. And of course the Service would come out smelling of roses. It's a happy coincidence of idealism and self-interest.'

Cannerley smiled. 'Is the word we're looking for *Realpolitik*?'

'I do hope not. Anyway, it seems to me quite feasible that Fowler — or 'Mirabel', as they apparently call him over there — should wish to speak to the Gray girl now she's in his area. He asks her to run a little errand for him and she passes on the information — if that's the right word — to the local Gaullists. False times, wrong map references and so on. Gentle havoc ensues. The idea is that the confusion should be as public as possible, to do maximum damage to the General's reputation.'

'How will he persuade her?'

'He'll have information she wants.'

'What about?'

'About what motivates her.'

'Patriotism?'

'Yes,' said Sir Oliver. 'What else?'

'Some love of France?'

'And?'

Cannerley felt sick. He licked his lips. 'The airman.'

Sir Oliver inclined his head slightly.

'I see,' said Cannerley. 'He'll tell her where to find him.'

'Only if she otherwise proves insufficiently . . . ductile.'

'But suppose he's dead.'

Sir Oliver opened his hands in a modest shrug. 'To

be honest, I don't think it terribly matters.'

'I see. So long as she doesn't find out, you mean.' Cannerley drew on a short life-time's habit of self-control. He continued to be businesslike. 'And Fowler's all right, is he?'

'Oh, yes,' said Sir Oliver. 'Most obliging. A small-time rogue, superficially very respectable and thus terrified of having his tax irregularities made public.' He coughed. 'A fairly typical G Section appointment.'

Cannerley smiled briefly. 'And the girl's up to it?'

'It's just a message. Regular FANY work, as you pointed out. And it keeps it all at arm's length from Fowler. We'll need him again.'

'But won't G Section want to claim responsibility?'

'I very much doubt it. They're supposed to be co-ordinating resistance, not misleading other factions. 'Setting Europe ablaze' and so forth.' Sir Oliver subdued another smile. 'In theory.'

'And they'd be embarrassed to admit that they'd got this girl banging round like a loose cannon.'

Sir Oliver nodded. 'And that their local chief's a crook. Of course, if it does backfire, then G Section are in the soup.'

'I see.'

'And you may well think that a consummation even more devoutly to be wished. However, for the time being the discrediting of the Gaullists must remain our first objective. The great thing is that it's all completely risk-free.'

'Except for the girl.'

'Possibly.' Sir Oliver took a cigarette from a silver box and tapped it briefly on the desk.

'She's horribly exposed, isn't she?' said Cannerley. He had a sudden picture in his mind of Charlotte's brown eyes, trusting, slightly bashful, when he had first outlined some possibilities to her at the Ritz. 'And she's not even an agent, she's just running an errand.'

'They say she speaks very good French.'

Cannerley ran a hand over his smoothly shaved chin. He knew he looked doubtful, but he couldn't help it. He had an unpleasant feeling in his stomach. It was like the time as a child when he had tried to show off to his friends on the beach at Polzeath. He had swum far out to sea and waved. It was only at that moment he knew that he could not possibly make it back to dry land without help.

'There's no gain without risk, Cannerley.' Sir Oliver peeled off his smudged spectacles and took some papers from the desk, which he held up almost flat against his face to read.

'Yes, but what would happen if it went wrong?'

'Well.' Sir Oliver looked up. 'Let's think. What would happen to someone who excited the wrath of a group of French guerrillas and of the German security who had penetrated them . . . '

'Quite apart from the German military and the French police.'

'The likely outcome,' said Sir Oliver, 'is not something I feel I could predict with any degree of precision.'

Cannerley pursed his lips.

'But do remember that the nature of this war in France is likely to change. If the Allies are successful in North Africa then the Germans will want to go into Southern France as well. There'll be no more Free Zone. The more things go against them, the harsher they'll be on the countries they occupy. And that means that they will eventually provoke real resistance. Even in France.'

'And we'll be in the best position to run it,' said Cannerley.

'Precisely,' said Sir Oliver. 'This is just a little warning shot. Things will get much rougher. Fowler'll have to get a move on, though, because I think the girl's due to come back soon. Anyway, I just thought you'd like to know. Since you put the girl their way.'

'Absolutely. Thank you.'

'Joan will see you out.'

When Cannerley left the building he went for a walk along the Embankment. The Thames was sluggish and grey as it drifted down from Battersea and Vauxhall. It made him think of fast-flowing French rivers, like the Tarn and the Dordogne, of action and sabotage, and of what Charlotte Gray might be doing.

It was not that he particularly cared about her; that was not the problem. The difficulty was that he was frightened. Everyone he knew had made an accommodation with the War, with the demands on their lives of a national emergency, and it seemed to him that he had been drawn into the wrong compromise.

His father was still living, weakening for consecutive days, then briefly reviving. When he was dead, Cannerley felt that an understanding of the world, a way of dealing that was tactical, discreet, yet based on certain given principles, would die with him. He had believed Sir Oliver and others of an intermediate generation had inherited this unwritten, almost mystical understanding; but now in Sir Oliver he saw only the practical aspect of it: the manoeuvring for position, the promotion of one set of interests over another, regardless of its intrinsic merit and with no thought for the human consequences. When his father died, Cannerley thought, there would be no one in the world whom he could unconditionally admire.

I am a coward, he thought: I'm trapped and I'm too frightened to move.

The nature of his work meant that there was no one with whom he could share his worry. His only choice was to carry on, to act, more than ever, by the book.

4

By the time the train arrived in Limoges, the windows were steamed up with a misty drizzle, which, Charlotte found as she left the station, had wrapped itself about the whole grey town.

She had not had a full stomach since the night of her arrival, but Limoges was the kind of place that should have been able to offer every variety of comfortable, traditional dining — modest enough to draw on the fertile local farms, large enough to support big restaurants with menus of Parisian ambition. Charlotte pictured one of those slightly surprising French dinners, such as the one she had had with the Loiseau family in the rue de Tournon, which seem to be coming to a close only to erupt again with the arrival of a loosely set omelette or a pair of roast quails on fried bread.

It was easier to go shopping alone as a woman than to dine alone, and Charlotte exchanged her bread coupon for six ounces of dusty loaf. Her monthly cheese ration having been exhausted by lunch at the Café du Centre at Lavaurette, she was obliged to buy a small piece of fatless cheese for cash from a conspiratorial and suspiciously well-fed creamery owner. He mentioned the possibility of Bayonne ham and tinned peas as well, but Charlotte told him she would be back another day.

That night she sat down on the bed in her hotel room in Limoges and laid out her possessions. There was a small black velvet package lined with foam rubber that contained the set of wireless crystals; a silver powder compact; French branded toothpaste and brush; sanitary towels (made in Toulouse) discreetly pressed on her by Alice at the aerodrome; a piece of paper with scribbled train times she had copied from the hall of the station at Limoges, carefully using French numerals (the fat nine with its short stalk and little upward tail; the one with its great looping sidepiece; a four with only a minuscule vertical); a detective story of the kind that might interest Dominique Guilbert, purchased in Uzerche; a spare set of Dominique's clothes, two sets of underwear and a folded raincoat. There was also an awkwardly large sum of francs which Dominique was, if asked, obliged to carry for hotel bills and to pay for her father's medical care.

Charlotte was forced to confront the fact that she was now candidly frightened. It was dangerous to be in Limoges, because this was where Dominique's father was supposed to be, and it would be easy to expose her story. It was too complicated, however, to get to Clermont from any other point of departure; it would take too long and might cause her to miss her plane back. For the same reason she had, with some relief, ruled out the possibility of bicycling.

She set out the bread and cheese on the table and took a glass from beside the bed. The only water in the room was in a bidet, concealed behind a greasy curtain, and Charlotte felt her face assume its minister of the kirk expression at the thought of it. In the bathroom at the end of the landing she scrupulously washed, then filled the tumbler and returned to her room to dine.

Oh, Peter, she thought, raising her glass and staring at the faded floral wallpaper ahead of her: there is no point in dinner without you, without gin or candles or your rumbling voice. But when she most wanted his words in her head they would not come. She could choose only between her own, obsessive thoughts and the disapproving tartness of Dominique.

For eight or nine days after the news of Gregory's disappearance his face lay flat against the retina of her memory: exact, complete, an image through which all else was filtered. Then, one morning, she woke up and it had gone. Although she could have described his features pore by pore, even drawn a likeness, the unity, the character itself had disappeared. However she turned the kaleidoscope, the pattern would not come back into focus and she was tormented by its absence.

There was the sound of a church bell striking nine and Charlotte went to look out of the window. She could see over rooftops down a clenched little side street to the angle of a cobbled square; there were a few lights showing behind closed doors, but there was no one outside.

In its peculiar way, this must be what Mr Jackson had warned her against, this haunting loneliness. Jackson could have known nothing of the burden of Gregory's absence, but even without that it was bad enough. There was no one in whom she could confide; no one in whom her real self could find answering warmth; and even this glorious country, where once she had only to breathe to feel accompanied and fulfilled, had so lost touch with its prelapsarian self that it had become a foreign land.

She went back to the table and looked down at the dusty crumbs; she ran her fingertip through them and tried to hold her thoughts together.

★ ★ ★

In Lavaurette, Julien Levade was attempting to find out what had happened to Monsieur and Madame Duguay. For two years there had been great movements of displaced people across France, and the division of the country into zones, one occupied, one nominally free, had made it almost impossible to trace individuals. Although Laval's insistence that the Vichy police be responsible for the maintenance of law in the

Occupied as well as the Free Zone might have given a greater unity to police or town hall records, it had been accompanied by an increased secrecy about the movement of Jews. While people of Benech's opinion viewed policing of the Occupied Zone as a sign of how much French autonomy remained, Julien feared that it simply allowed the Gestapo to let the French police do their interrogation and their killing for them.

He had seen large camps for Jewish refugees being built throughout the Free Zone by the Vichy government, unprompted by the Germans, and could not understand his country's reluctance to take in these refugees; it puzzled him that every new arrival from the East was so furiously resisted. Unwilling to accept them, the Government was still more loth to help the refugees escape, even when it became clear that the Germans had designs on them: instead of encouraging them to leave through the free southern ports, it put them behind barbed wire to await an unspecified disposal.

Most of these people had come from Poland, some from Germany, a few from other European countries. When Julien was told that French Jews were also being rounded up in Paris, he had at first dismissed the rumour as Communist-inspired. His grandfather Max Rutkowski had loved his adopted country with the passion of the immigrant who has found the civil freedoms denied him at home and become embedded in his new society. His admiration of France was increased by emotional gratitude, so that he ascribed even his professional success and family harmony to the beauty and justness of the heavenly civilisation in which he lived. Although Max Rutkowski's own father was Catholic, he was proud of his Jewish blood, and of the religion in which he had been brought up, and felt confident enough to acknowledge it in the Paris suburb where he lived. By the time he became engaged to a French Jewess, Rutkowski had, for administrative

219

convenience and out of love for its French sound, changed his family name to Levade, but he had no hesitation in bringing up his son, Auguste Levade, in the faith. Although, in the third French generation, the question of nationality was less urgent for him, Julien had, through his grandfather Rutkowski and his father Levade, acquired a reflexive admiration for his country, which his patriotic education had enforced.

Julien's mother, with whom he lived when his father left them soon after Julien's tenth birthday, was a French Catholic whose family could trace its bourgeois path back a hundred years or so into respectable obscurity. Julien survived his father's departure apparently unharmed; his naturally even temperament absorbed the shock and helped his mother to do likewise. His work at school continued to earn the praise of his teachers, who thought it easily within his power to realise his ambition to be an architect.

Julien's involvement with resistance activity at first owed as much to high spirits as to political conviction. He was unsure about the lugubrious general in London; although he liked the idea that only a battle, not a war, had been lost and that a pure spirit of France was being kept alive overseas, it was difficult to say with certainty that this untested, slightly comic person was its one true guardian. The Communist Party was banned, since, through its connection with Russia, it theoretically supported the Allies. Julien had attended a secret meeting in Limoges, where they talked of sabotage and armed resistance, but he felt uneasy about the Communist plans for France, their enthusiasm for Stalin and most particularly for the way they had, a few years earlier, helped derail the Popular Front, the one government for which he had ever felt enthusiasm. It took an approach from Mirabel on an earlier mission to force Julien into action. His aims seemed attractively simple: blow up as many trains as possible and set up networks which would eventually help kick out the invader. It was the simple, non-political vigour of his language that attracted Julien.

By running errands, taking calls and helping to dispose of parachuted stores, Julien accepted that his actions, however rustic and drink-assisted, did amount to a political statement of a kind. Although he felt a shiver of unease about showing disrespect towards the Marshal, who had been the national hero of his boyhood, he was unsentimental enough to see the deficiencies of the Government. He was not inspired by its unprincipled haggling over the question of sovereignty, and feared that when the force of Russia and America came to bear, as it surely would, the clinging to the illusion of autonomy would be not a bargaining weapon, but a liability that the Germans would exploit.

The disappearance of Monsieur and Madame Duguay changed everything. The look on Bernard's face provided Julien with an instant of clear and shocking revelation: a chain of compromise and inertia, at no single point perceptible as choice in moral colours, had had in the end a cumulative effect. The complicity of an honest man, thinking only that he wanted to be back with his family for dinner, had closed an evil circle. From that day Julien's flirtatious high spirits concealed a new determination: everyone, he presumed, had his own moment of clarity, but for him the revelation was provided by the look of blameless guilt in a gendarme's eye. His rage, after its first eruption in the hôtel de ville, was concealed from the people of Lavaurette. He thought it would be safer that way; but in his subsequent search for information, Pauline Bobotte's switchboard became a hot blur of activity.

* * *

Charlotte packed with care in the morning, checking that nothing extraneously British could somehow have found its way into her possessions. Only my thoughts, she said aloud, as she made one final sweep through the room and fixed her mind on her destination: Ussel.

The station at Limoges was already full by the time she arrived, forewarned by experience, half an hour early for her train. She had a cup of coffee in the buffet and, with the taste of roasted wheat seeds in her mouth, made her way down the platform.

The scene reminded her of the countryside on the day of her arrival; there was an element of unsettling caricature. Although it was really she who was being deceptive, it seemed to her that it was the other way round: that the travellers going about their business, the traffic of the provincial station, the manners, dress and customs of the people, indistinguishable from those that had entranced her on her first childish visits, were in fact part of a conspiratorial drama.

When the train slid into the platform, however, there was not even the rudimentary attempt at patience that she had learned to accept as the French version of Edinburgh queuing; there was a surge round each door which forced back into the carriages several passengers who were trying to dismount. A few disapproving people, including Charlotte, quickly surrendered to the inevitable force of numbers and joined the press for places.

By force and good luck she found a seat, though there was no room in the rack for her suitcase, which she had to carry on her knees. She could see by the easy way many people threw their bags around that they were empty; when they returned that evening to Limoges from their destinations in the surrounding countryside, the cases would be heavy with eggs, ham, sausage, oil of any kind, and would exude the smells she had noticed on her previous journey with Yves. After the bad temper of boarding had receded and the train had been going for half an hour, Charlotte felt an unmistakably festive air creep into the compartment and found it answered in herself by the double exhilaration of her journey.

It was another hot day. The flashing pastures through which they travelled were radiant with a yellowish-green light; the darker shades of the knotted forests and the glimpsed browns of the trunks and branches of oak trees in the established lines that edged the hills made it possible to believe in a future as well in the past they brightly evoked.

Charlotte took out Dominique's detective story and began to read. A man's body was found by his concierge in the hallway of his apartment of the seventh arrondissement; a silver dagger protruded from between his ribs. The concierge was helping a melancholic inspector with his inquiries; the detective would proceed to interview the occupants of all the other apartments in the block, and the author might or might not give some indication as to which one was the murderer. Charlotte found that the only thing that might have been interesting — the process of detection — had, by a convention of the genre, to be withheld from the story, or there could have been no surprise dénouement. After his first fruitless morning the detective went for lunch in a café in the Place St Sulpice, and Charlotte was horrified to hear her stomach roar its envy of his dish of the day: a sausage and lentil stew with green salad 'anointed with thick oil'. The woman opposite her smiled her sympathy as Charlotte begged her pardon for the noise. The young man next to her, perhaps the woman's son, opened a bag on his lap and offered Charlotte the end of a loaf from which extended the edge of a thick piece of ham. After her protestations and his insistence, she took it, and was drawn into conversation.

Charlotte had provided Dominique with a sister

223

in Clermont-Ferrand to cover her intended visit to Gregory's garage mechanic, and the residual Calvinist in her was shocked by the facility with which she described this Germaine's invented life. The young man looked interested, and Charlotte tried to curb her imagination. She touched on the sober subject of her father's illness, then focused the conversation firmly on the others. Both mother and son, as they turned out to be, seemed friendly enough, but there were five other people in the compartment and two in the doorway who could overhear their conversation. Not all would be as sympathetic; and one thing her training had stressed was that the French far outnumbered the Germans in the number and diversity of their police and security services.

It had been a mistake to accept the sandwich and to talk, but she had been hungry and she had been lonely: she wanted to be addressed by someone, even a stranger and even under a false identity. To extricate herself, she began to yawn, and, when a gap of suitable length occurred in the conversation, she feigned an improbable mid-morning sleep.

★ ★ ★

Ussel in late afternoon, under light rain, was smaller and more pathetic than it had looked on the map. There were garages and squares and shops, but it had the feeling of a trading post, a village that had spread back off the strip of the main road that steeply bisected it. Charlotte sheltered with her suitcase in the bar of a hotel, waiting for the time to pass till she could go to her rendezvous with her hairdresser, Antoinette.

She felt absurdly self-conscious; now that the moment had come for this furtive action her hands seemed heavy, her face a self-advertising confession of guilt. Ussel was much higher than the places she had so far visited; the air was thin, as well as damp, and she felt cut off from the rest of France. The prospect of pursuing her journey still further, to the volcano-ringed heights of Clermont, on a passionate gamble of her own devising, seemed a foolhardy plan that could have been conceived only by someone at sea level and slightly unbalanced.

She ground the heel of Dominique's ugly shoe into the floor of the bar and brought her lips together. She would proceed. At ten to seven she left the hotel and went out into the rain. She walked up the main street and forked left towards the church. She moved briskly, not wishing to catch the eye of anyone in this unvisited town. The streets revealed themselves like photographic prints emerging in solution from her acquired memory. On the Avenue Sémard, near the station, she came to the door of a hairdresser's shop; ignoring the 'Closed' notice she pushed it open and went inside.

The row of chairs was empty and the room had a sweet, steamy smell. At the far end was a bamboo curtain through which emerged a small white dog, barking feebly and wagging its tail. There was the sound of a wireless playing a facetious song by Charles Trenet. Charlotte held the handle of her suitcase tightly and stood her ground; a woman's voice called to the dog to be quiet. Still no one came, and Charlotte had the feeling she was on the edge of a debacle. She had come a long way to this stuffy little room; and, now that she was here, was it all quite real?

The bamboo curtain divided again and a tall, handsome woman in a blue pinafore came down the step into the salon.

'I'm afraid we're closed, Madame.'

'I made a reservation for seven o'clock.'

'What name, Madame?' The woman went over to the appointments book on a table by the door.

'Danièle.'

The hairdresser ran her finger down the page,

225

snapped the page over as though searching further forward in the book, then turned it back. 'Danièle . . . Danièle.'

Charlotte felt a line of sweat run down her spine.

The woman turned and, for the first time, looked Charlotte deep and direct in the eye. 'Bad weather for a wash and set.'

Charlotte smiled broadly. 'They said that whatever the weather I must insist on Antoinette.'

'They were quite right. She's the best.'

Antoinette stepped forward and took Charlotte by the hand. 'Let's go through to the back,' she said, leading the way through the curtain.

They sat at a table in a gloomy kitchen, drinking wine that Antoinette poured from an unlabelled litre bottle.

'You look tired,' she said. 'How long have you been here?'

'Do I?' Charlotte's fingers went to her face and pressed the soft skin beneath her eyes. 'Yes, I suppose I haven't slept much for various reasons. A few days. I'm going back to England soon, as far as I know. I have to have confirmation by wireless.'

Antoinette had a deep voice and a quiet, sympathetic manner; she had large dark brown eyes and thick, slightly tousled hair, cut just above the shoulder. Watching her as she spoke, Charlotte put her age at about thirty-eight; she had a ruby ring on her right hand but nothing on her left. It was impossible to resist the impression that she was too cultivated to be a hairdresser; something in her manner suggested education and experience beyond trimming and drying.

'They've done a good job on your hair,' Antoinette said, taking a cigarette from a packet on the table.

'My God, is it so obvious?'

Antoinette smiled. 'Don't worry. Only to the expert. And your French. It's almost perfect.'

'Almost?'

'Almost.'

'I was educated in Belgium. Would that account for it?'

'I think I could believe that.'

The scratchy wireless, the windows steamed by rain and the odd towel hanging up to dry reminded Charlotte of the Monday afternoons of her childhood, when her mother would begin to iron the wash; there was a starchy torpor that was seductively depressing. Relaxed by the wine, she felt oddly emotional.

'Are you taking a train back tonight?' said Antoinette.

'There is one I can take tonight. But I'm not going back. I'm going on to Clermont.'

'I see. Another errand.'

Looking at this woman's quizzical but kind expression, Charlotte had to fight hard to repress her desire to confide.

'That's right,' she said.

'You can stay here tonight if you like. There are two trains in the morning.'

'Is it safe?'

Antoinette laughed. 'It's completely safe. It's like being in another country. The war and the occupation have passed us by. People are a little irritated to think that there are a lot of Germans tramping round the coast, but that's about all. France is a big country. Our life has barely changed.'

'But what about rationing?'

'We're very self-sufficient. There's a bit less to eat, I suppose, but we manage pretty well. When the garage man mends the farmer's car he gives him a chicken as well as some cash. If I cut someone's hair I sometimes ask for eggs or ham. It's all very friendly.'

'It's not like that in Lavaurette, the place I first went to.'

Antoinette shrugged. 'It depends. Some places have

more food. Some are better at working out a system that suits people. Anyway, if you'd like to, you can stay here above the shop. I'll make you some dinner, put some clean sheets on the bed and bring you breakfast in the morning. Would you like that?'

'I'd love to. Thank you.' Charlotte felt absurdly touched by this offer; she even felt a momentary irritation in her eye. She blinked. Antoinette was right: she must be very tired.

To regain her composure, she asked, 'What drew you to become involved with . . . wirelesses and so on?'

Antoinette sighed. 'Just a feeling. My brother and some friends of mine . . . I don't imagine that we're supposed to talk too much about these things.'

'Perhaps not.' Charlotte, however, wanted to talk about them; she wanted to talk about almost anything: she had been too long with only voices in her head. 'What can you do here, half way up the mountains, with no targets, no soldiers?'

'We wait. I think the time will come. There's a good deal of activity in the mountains just because they are the mountains — because they're a good place to hide. The Massif Central will be the heart of the Resistance when it comes.'

'And when will it come?'

Antoinette smiled. 'Do you want my honest opinion?'

'Of course.'

'I think it will come when the majority of people change their minds about the likely outcome of the war. They'll want to back the winner.'

Charlotte said nothing, but looked at the table, this odd pricking still behind her eyes. Antoinette seemed so weary, her opinion so devoid of idealism or belief, yet what she said had the unexciting contours of a probable truth.

Charlotte stood up. 'I think perhaps I should give you the package now.'

'All right.' Antoinette nodded and Charlotte went to her suitcase, laid it on the floor and carefully extracted the black velvet bag from inside one of Dominique's rolled-up vests.

She watched in fascination as Antoinette's long, tapered fingers gently extracted the foam rubber casing from the bag. Inside were what looked to Charlotte like four porcelain cartridge-fuses, similar to those with which she had seen her father struggle, cursing, by candlelight. She picked one up and turned it over in her hand: a sheath with pronged terminals contained a piece of quartz whose calibration determined the wavelength of the transmission. They seemed to her extraordinarily small and insignificant to have been the object of such astonishing care and effort. She found that her lip was trembling. What possible effect on the freedom of a country could ever be exerted by this small piece of domestic hardware in her hand?

Antoinette reached out and gently took the crystal from Charlotte. She laid it carefully with the others in the foam rubber casing. Then she put her hand back on Charlotte's and squeezed it. 'Thank you,' she said. 'You've done a wonderful job.'

Charlotte felt the air suddenly driven from her lungs as all the conquered feelings of the last few days surged out. Antoinette went over and put her arms around her, and Charlotte stood up, the better to feel the comfort of the other woman's embrace.

★ ★ ★

They both changed before dinner, Charlotte into Dominique's slightly less dowdy skirt and jumper, Antoinette taking off her blue pinafore, tidying her hair and putting on some lipstick. They ate in a living room upstairs, and Charlotte eventually told Antoinette the reason for her visit to Clermont. 'Do you think I'm mad?' she said.

'Not at all.'

'But is it dangerous?'

'A woman's allowed to go to a garage and ask a simple question. The problem, of course, is that there are so many different security forces, and you'll find more of them in a big town like Clermont. There are a lot of unpleasant little men who have solved the problems of their personalities by putting on uniforms and telling tales. Some of them are criminals or Fascists who have seen an opportunity to have their sadistic impulses made legal. There are some very violent men. Then there are just people who like sneaking. So I wouldn't say there is no danger at all, but with you I don't see what they could report. You arrive, you go to your garage and you leave. You don't have time to arouse anyone's suspicion. Nor do you have time to arouse anyone's dislike. Don't forget that a lot of people report their friends or neighbours to the authorities to get even over some domestic quarrel. Weren't you told all these things before you came?'

'Yes, we were. But it's always hard to imagine. I didn't realise both how normal everything would be and yet how strange. It's so odd going into a baker or buying a ticket, and everything seems just as it was, yet you know that if you say the wrong thing you might find yourself being arrested. It's the normality of everything that seems so treacherous.'

Antoinette smiled. 'This man, he must be very remarkable.'

'He is.' Charlotte smiled back. 'Very remarkable.' She felt calm after her tears, and had focused the purpose of her journey with renewed clarity.

'Do you want to tell me about him?'

'Not really. I couldn't make you feel what I feel for him. I can only say that what I'm doing seems quite rational. The education I had was very formal, and although there was a belief that the family was important, and that it was initially held together by love between the parents, no one ever encouraged us to believe in romantic love or any such idea. In fact, most of the women who taught us would have been horrified by the thought. They taught us romantic poetry, but for the language and the metre. And I don't believe in the idea myself — not as an idea, at any rate. But I suppose at some stage you make decisions, you have to decide what seems important to you, what seems valuable. It may be for a practical reason as much as for an idealistic reason, like the people you describe who'll join the Resistance when they think it's going to win. It's a judgement. I don't believe in a general ideal, I just believe in one particular man. I believe in the purity of the feeling that I have for him and that I believe he has for me. I think its force is superior to that of any other guiding force and I can't organise my life until I know whether he's alive.'

'You do love him, don't you?'

'Of course I do. And if that love reflects a susceptibility on my part, if he has somehow exploited a weakness or a wound in me, so be it. There's nothing I can do about it; that's who I am. To behave or believe otherwise would be dishonest.'

Charlotte was not concerned by the indulgent expression in the older woman's eyes. It was sceptical, but it was also compassionate; and, Charlotte guessed that, however objectively Antoinette might view her youthful passion, a part of her was likely to regret that the day when her own life might be guided by such certainty was unlikely to come again.

Under Charlotte's questioning, Antoinette revealed that she had once been married, but that her husband had deceived her so often that even the flexible limits of bourgeois marriage had been violated. He had gone to live with a young girl in Normandy and she had not regretted his leaving, particularly as there were no children who might miss him. She had had lovers, she told Charlotte, but preferred to live alone. Her best friend was her brother, a doctor in a nearby town, who had helped to finance her shop.

'I like it here,' she said. 'The countryside is beautiful, the girl who works for me, Gilberte, is charming. We eat well, we drink well, even now. About once a fortnight there's a man who visits me from Clermont to spend the night.' She smiled and pulled another cigarette from the packet among the empty plates. 'It's enough. I'm fond of him. Then about six months ago my brother asked me if I would help him in a little network of people he was putting together with an Englishman who had dropped out of the sky one day. It didn't take him long to convince me. I love doing it. I love the excitement of the transmissions. I'm a very happy woman.' She blew out smoke through her smiling, lipsticked mouth.

Antoinette insisted Charlotte sleep in her bed while she made up the sofa for herself with a pillow and a rug. There were clean sheets, as she had promised, and Charlotte felt their smooth freshness on her skin. It was a warm night, and since G Section had omitted to provide Dominique with a nightdress she slept naked. Dominique's underclothes she had washed and hung out to dry in the bathroom, bringing back memories of Daisy's flat in London, a place which seemed not just distant but to belong to a different existence.

Antoinette's bedroom was the only room in the apartment over which she had taken much trouble. The rugs and antique furniture had been chosen with care; the bed itself was of the three-quarter size Charlotte had encountered in the hotel with Yves, but fresh and deeply comfortable. Within minutes she was asleep, lying on her back, dragging in deep draughts of even breath.

It was almost three o'clock when she awoke, crying and protesting. She sat up and felt her hair damp around the edges of her forehead. In her dream she had been trapped and tortured; the moment of betrayal was similar to the half-buried memory of her father's sinister misprision, but the violence was done not by him but by Gregory.

For all this time she had lost sight of Gregory's face in her mind, and its absence was like a confirmation of his death. Then suddenly in her dream it had been cruelly restored.

'Are you all right?' Antoinette's voice came from the doorway.

'Yes, I . . . I was dreaming.'

Antoinette came and sat on the edge of the bed. She put her arms round Charlotte to comfort her, and Charlotte laid her face against the broderie anglaise of her nightdress. Antoinette murmured comforting words to her and eventually Charlotte found she was drifting back to sleep.

It was thickly dark behind the closed shutters, and the clouds from the mountain rim obscured the sky. Charlotte held on to Antoinette as she lay down and crossed the borderlines from sleep to vague wakefulness and back again, unwilling quite to let go in case the same dream was waiting. She felt Antoinette's hands gently stroke her hair, found herself calmed and once more drifting. Antoinette kissed her cheek and Charlotte felt her hands caress her shoulders with soothing movements till they both slept.

5

At nine o'clock a bicycle turned up the long, stony track to the Domaine. The young woman who rode it was dressed in simple clothes and had no bag or luggage with her. It was as though she herself, her body, was all that she was bringing.

In Lavaurette it was another bright day and the plane trees that lined the pot-holed path, with their pale leaves and peeling, eczemaic trunks, were noisy with the sound of birds.

When she arrived at the front door the woman propped her bicycle against a pillar and mounted the broad stone steps; she did not sound the iron bell-pull, but pushed open one half of the arched front door with practised familiarity and let herself into the house. A light aroma of coffee from the remote kitchen was just discernible in a heavier atmosphere of old plaster, wood and unmoved air. She turned to the right and walked across the flagged hall to another double door, which led into a dining room. The sprung floor cushioned her swift pace as she crossed the huge, grey-panelled room with its twenty-seater table, at one end of which was a single candlestick, a plate and an empty wine glass. She gathered these on her way through to a pantry where she deposited them in the stone sink: washing up was not her job; that was for the maid, who, as usual, was late.

In the vaulted kitchen she took a coffee pot from the range and filled two small white cups. She took them through a scullery and out to the narrow back staircase which gave her access to the first floor without having to return to the main hall. Up the steps, past the empty servants' bedrooms she climbed, carefully watching the black liquid in her hands. There was a smell of lime from the old wood of the staircase. She breached the frontier into the main part of the house and walked along the sunlit corridor to the principal bedroom, where she paused, put the cups down on the landing window-sill, and knocked.

Levade's voice called her in.

'Good morning, Anne-Marie.'

The room was dominated by a huge bed with a canopy and drapes which had been rolled and pinned back. The rugs on the floor had also been pushed to one side. The floor was littered with canvases, tubes of paint, drawings on pieces of paper, messed palettes, books opened and weighted down at a particular illustration, books closed and piled, glass jars full of brushes, pots of cleaner, chisels, hammers, small boxes of nails brought by Julien from Madame Galliot's top shelf and wooden stretchers in various stages of assembly. The numerous tables in the room were covered by cloths and by more books, candles and religious statues.

Levade was shaved and dressed; he had combed his thick white hair and found a clean shirt which hung down outside his trousers almost to his knees. He stood in front of the window where the north light was clear.

Anne-Marie crossed to a screen in a remote corner of the room, behind which was a paint-spattered chair with a long green silk skirt and a pair of thin-strapped sandals. She took off her own clothes and put on the skirt and sandals; then she emerged from behind the screen.

She stood in the middle of the room, bare-breasted, unself-conscious. 'Did you have a good night?'

Levade shook his head. 'No.' His voice was melancholic but resigned. 'Not a thing.'

'Are we going to carry on from where we were

235

yesterday?' said Anne-Marie.

'I think so.' Levade put down his empty coffee cup and, as Anne-Marie sat down on a chair in front of the window, went over to arrange the fall of the green skirt. He looked at the half-finished canvas on the easel and compared the image of Anne-Marie with the actual woman. He went back and moved her arms a little, settled her hair and fussed over the folds of the skirt.

Anne-Marie had picked up a book from the floor and skimmed through it as Levade arranged her.

'What about you?' said Levade. 'Did you dream?'

'Nothing I can remember. My dreams are so dull compared to the ones you've described, the ones you used to have.'

Levade took up his brush and pushed back his hair. 'I think the last dream I had was about a month ago. Do you know what I dreamed? That I had woken up, that it was morning, that I had got up, washed, come to this room to paint, that you arrived . . . It wasn't really a dream at all. It was more prosaic than being awake.'

Levade shook his head and smiled. Anne-Marie crossed her arms.

★ ★ ★

The telephone was ringing in Julien's office.

'I'm putting you through now,' said Pauline Bobotte.

It was a Communist from Limoges, whom Julien, against his better judgement, had approached for information. He did not want to associate with Communists, but in times of war you sometimes had to be expedient. Even as he explained this to himself he realised that this was exactly the argument employed by Pétain and Laval. The difference was that his position was not merely expedient, it had moral backing; also, his judgement, unlike theirs, was sound. So he hoped.

'There was an enormous round-up in Paris last month. Tens of thousands of Jews, French as well as refugees. Apparently the police took them to a winter sports stadium. But that business a few days ago, that was the first time they've done it in the Free Zone. I'm told they'll take them to Paris and eventually they'll deport them. No one seems to know where to.'

Julien nodded. 'Thank you. Will you telephone again if you hear anything?'

'That depends. We may need some help from you.'

'I understand.'

The line went dead, and Pauline Bobotte removed the plug from her switchboard.

Julien sighed. Tonight he would have to go and see Sylvie Cariteau and her mother. Between them they would decide what to tell André and Jacob, and also what to do with them. It was difficult to make out from the newspapers exactly what was happening; but, from what he had read and what he had seen, it was clear to Julien that there would be no let-up in the persecution of Jews. Whatever the Vichy government believed, the Germans were beginning to lose the war. In Julien's simple analysis this meant that their behaviour in the countries they occupied would become more exacting: they would require more money, more food and more labour. If their armies abroad met with reverses, that was all the more reason why they would be rigorous in pursuing whatever ends they could achieve in Europe. And since, for reasons no one outside Germany could fully understand, the collection of Jews into various camps seemed central to a particular strand of Nazi planning, then life for André and Jacob would in the future become more, not less, hazardous.

It was partly to do with his generally optimistic temperament and partly to do with his ingrained trust in his country that Julien did not pause to consider his own position. Although his father Levade was three-quarters

Jewish, wholly on his mother's side and half on his father Rutkowski's Julien, because Levade married a Catholic, had only one wholly Jewish grandparent, Max Rutkowski's wife, though that could be computed as one and a half if Rutkowski's half-Jewishness were included. The other mathematical way of expressing it would be to say that Julien was three-eights Jewish. Since this ridiculous fraction had never seemed of the slightest importance to him, he could not imagine that it would be of interest to anyone else in France.

Tonight he would go down to the Café du Centre and take the temperature of Lavaurette. He presumed its dismal chorus was at least vaguely representative of what the small towns of France were thinking, if only in the degree of its ignorance.

He was also expecting to hear soon from the English girl who had dropped by parachute. She was surprisingly dark for what he had expected from an English person, but the hazel-husk intensity of her eyes in the lamp-lit farm kitchen was something he could not forget.

★ ★ ★

In the lavatory of the train that was crawling towards Clermont Ferrand Charlotte read the scribbled feelings of previous travellers. 'War has been declared by the City of London,' was one view, accompanied by a caricature of a Fagin-like face with wispy beard. This had drawn agreement from another writer: 'Saxon + Jew + Tartar = the Beast'.

Did these statements, scored in the bold capitals of anonymity, express the true feelings of the French people? Was this what they would really say if they were free to speak? Charlotte chose to think not. Although the passion of anti-British feeling (anti-English as they mistakenly called it) continued to shock her, she did not believe, and could not allow herself to believe, that it was universal. She had only to think, after all, of her reception on the night of her arrival.

She made her way back down the corridor and resumed her seat, which the obliging woman next to her had agreed to keep reserved. Charlotte smiled at her, then looked fixedly out of the window. It had taken her only a few minutes with the Michelin Guide to work out which of the two Citroën garages must be the one she wanted. Gregory had definitely said 'In the middle of Clermont'; the telephone directory confirmed that the owner was 'A. Chollet'. She calculated that she could be back on the train by seven o'clock.

To her right she saw a branch line that wound up through the thermal station of la Bourboule to le Mont-Dore. Clouds were drifting down off the mountain and the summer sun of Lavaurette seemed far away; it was beginning to feel cold in the unheated carriage.

Antoinette had woken her at nine o'clock with a tray on which was bread and jam and something that tasted reasonably like coffee. She sat on the edge of the bed and watched while Charlotte ate; she was wearing her blue pinafore, and Gilberte was already dealing with the first customer downstairs. Charlotte hurried through her farewells and promised to write to Antoinette from England when the war was over. As she was leaving Antoinette pressed a bottle into her hand: it was hair dye. 'Just in case,' said Antoinette as she kissed her goodbye.

Half an hour from Clermont Charlotte began to feel a tightening of fear. A police inspection of identity cards passed with its usual swift indifference, but it reminded her of how alone and uncovered she was, without even the stories prepared for her in London. While she carried out the elementary task for Mr Jackson and lived within the limited identity of Dominique Guilbert, she

239

had felt a degree of protection and attachment: it had been like the moment in the Whitley when the sergeant showed her the firm connection of the static line that would ensure her safety. Now she was in free fall.

The train slunk in beneath the vaulted ironwork, snorting steam. Charlotte gripped her suitcase and fought her way down on to the platform. In the forecourt of the station she studied a map which showed the tram routes. She crossed the street to what she hoped was the appropriate stop. There was the usual confusion of pushing people: respectable men in felt hats with clipped moustaches, small widows with jabbing elbows. Squeezed upright between two people near the entrance to the tramcar, Charlotte lodged her case between her feet and grasped at a hanging strap as the tram jolted off towards the middle of town.

She found her way to the street at the end of the rue Blatin and looked down the broad and cloudy thoroughfare. In this weather it had a faded, monochromatic look, compounded by the fact that there were so few cars; it felt like looking back to before the war, even to before the last war. At the top of a five-storey building on one side was the painted name of Franck Gorce, Tailor. At ground floor level, behind curved railings, was a bar called the Faisan Doré with a few unoccupied chairs on the pavement. Opposite was the curved facade of the Crédit Lyonnais, its name cut in deep italics in the stone above the towering doors.

Charlotte looked down the unhindered vista of the street to the distant bulk of the Massif Central, many miles beyond but framed and set in perspective by the straight lines of the rue Blatin. It seemed typical of how the civilisation had imposed itself on the country and of how it had grown in a harmony that seemed both inevitable and impossible to disturb. The sight released in Charlotte the memory of another such street, one she had seen as a child on her first excursion across the Channel with her father. It was the view that always came to mind when anyone mentioned France to her.

She made her way along the pavement, calculating the likely distance to her destination. It took her ten minutes to see the street name, high up on a corner, and five more to reach the garage itself, which was at the run-down end of the road, where it became commercial and unkempt.

Charlotte went through the double wooden doors into the oily gloom. She was trembling. A woman in widow's black, bespectacled, with a tight, narrow mouth emerged from a partitioned area on the right. Charlotte had somehow not expected a woman. It was very dark.

'Yes, Mademoiselle?'

'I'm looking for Monsieur Chollet.'

'He's working on a car. He's down at the end there.'

'Can I go and see him?'

The old woman looked Charlotte up and down. Her mouth declined at the corners. 'He's busy.'

'I won't keep him.'

The widow shrugged, and Charlotte took it as permission. She made her way over the concrete floor, stained black by countless drained sumps, towards where she could hear some activity in the gloom. A bulky figure was bending over the engine of a large, black, front-wheel-drive Citroën of the kind favoured both by Vichy ministers and the Gestapo.

'Monsieur?'

The man lifted his face from the engine.

'Are you Monsieur Chollet?'

'Yes. That's me.' Chollet was a fat man with a purple face and shiny skin; he looked too old to be the son of the widow at the doorway, but it was possible that red wine and large meals had aged him prematurely.

The stub of an unlit yellow cigarette was wedged in the corner of his mouth.

Charlotte breathed in tightly and spoke again. 'A friend of mine asked me to come and see you if I should need news. He was to contact you if he was in trouble. He said you would answer to the name Hercule.' It was a difficult word to say in French; Charlotte tried to concentrate on its swallowed 'r' and whistling 'u'.

Chollet grunted, 'I don't know what you're talking about.'

In the dim light it was hard to make out his expression, but Charlotte could see just enough to think she had noticed fear in his eyes.

'It's very important,' she said. 'I just need to know if you've heard anything from him. He was due a little time ago and we've heard nothing from him.'

Chollet said nothing, but shook his head slowly from side to side, his whole plump body a refusal to engage.

Charlotte had not foreseen this: so preoccupied had she been by her own safety that it had not occurred to her that Gregory's contact might be suspicious of her. She could not think how she might persuade him that she was not an agent of some oppressive organisation. In fact, she admitted Chollet was probably right not to trust her: he was doing the safe and proper thing.

'Monsieur, I understand your reluctance. I can't offer you the identification I should have because you are not my contact. But I beg you to believe me.'

Chollet bent back over the engine and began to resume his work. Even to herself Charlotte had sounded like the worst kind of informer. The more the conversation went on the more she admired Chollet's response. Yet for her the situation was desperate. She had travelled many miles to find this man, and now it was going to be useless.

Gregory might be alive and in need of help. She could get him out, just as she had got Yves to his destination, but without her Gregory could never make it.

'I'm British,' she said. 'I'm not an informer, I'm not with any Vichy organisation. I can prove it to you. I'm going to speak English.' She said in English: 'Please believe me, Monsieur Chollet, I desperately need your help. I can't say the whole war hinges on it, but my life certainly does. Please take your head out of that car and listen to me. All I want to do is to give you a telephone number. I'll speak more English if you like. Once upon a time there was a girl called Cinderella who had two ugly sisters who went to a ball and poor Cinderella didn't have a dress . . . God, I can't even remember the story. I was never keen on fairy tales.'

She leaned forwards and tapped Chollet on the back. He stood up and turned round to face her again. Charlotte tried to make herself cry, to evoke pity that way, but tears were far away, and in any case some police sneak could presumably fake them as well as she could.

She took his oil-grimed, fleshy hand in hers and said in French: 'Now do you believe me?' She smiled at him, summoning up as she did so every last particle of charm, candour and shameless sexual invitation.

Chollet's eyelids slid down over his protuberant eyes like a reluctant toad and his mouth pursed a minimal affirmative.

'And have you heard?'

His head moved half an inch either way.

Rain was falling on the streets outside, which seemed nevertheless bright after the interior of the garage. Charlotte walked a few yards, then leaned against a lamp-post. The fear of discovery and the exhilaration of penetrating Chollet's defences now gave way to despair. She had come to find her lover, all the way to the volcanoes, in the darkness, and he was not there. She had come and she had failed, and Gregory was dead.

6

Madame Cariteau was slightly loosening the bonds she
had set on André and Jacob Duguay. To begin with,
she never left them; now, she was prepared to shuffle
up to the shops for half an hour if she had impressed
on André with sufficient urgency that he and Jacob
were not to leave the house or answer the door.

In the front room was an old piano that her husband
had occasionally played. On the one occasion André
and Jacob had been allowed into the room they had
opened the lid and begun to pick at the keys. While
Jacob could only hit them with his fist, André could
make melodic runs of single notes and, so far as the
width of his hands would allow, play simple chords.
There was a piano at school, he told Madame Cariteau,
and he had been encouraged by the mistress.

The stationer half way up the hill had some sheet
music which Madame Cariteau had noticed without
interest on previous visits, and when she had bought
some bread she went into the shop to have a look
through it. There was the odd sonata or concerto by
Franck, Fauré or Saint Saëns, but most of the music
was folk songs. She chose what appeared to her to be
the simplest of these — the two with the fewest notes
— and took them home for André.

She went through the back door and into the kitchen,
put down her basket and went to find the boys. The
hall of the house was a spacious area that led to the
barred front door at one end and, at the other, a broad,
handsome staircase that rose for fourteen steps to a
half-landing. Bumping down it as Madame Cariteau
came into the hall was a suitcase in which Jacob
Duguay was letting out terrified screams of pleasure,

as he hurtlingly tobogganed over the polished wood. André stood on the half-landing, where his expression of glee turned to one of doubtful innocence when he saw Madame Cariteau.

Jacob arrived at her feet, whimpering with pleasure. When he looked up and saw her, he had no reflex of guilt but began to explain what they were doing.

'We take the suitcase up and André puts me in and — '

'Yes, I can see what you're doing. You don't have to tell me. André, where did you find the suitcase?'

'It was just there,' said André. 'It was just lying around.'

Madame Cariteau tipped Jacob out of the case and inspected it. 'This lives in my bedroom cupboard. Have you been in my room?'

'No,' said André; 'André got it,' said Jacob simultaneously.

Madame Cariteau scolded them for being noisy and for not staying upstairs, as she had instructed them. When André began to protest, she shouted at him to go to his room and stay there for the rest of the day. He turned on his heel and tried to conceal from her his trembling lip; down the dark corridor he made his damp and noisy way, slamming the door behind him when he reached his room.

★ ★ ★

Julien Levade was sketching a design for the converted cloisters when the telephone rang.

Pauline Bobotte's voice had the slightly affronted edge it always assumed when the caller was female. 'Someone called Danièle to speak to you, Monsieur Levade.'

'Thank you, Mademoiselle Bobotte. Put her through, please. Hello? Danièle? Everything all right?'

'Fine, thank you. I'm back in Lavaurette. I'm outside the station.'

'You must be tired.' Julien looked at his watch. He could leave the office for lunch at twelve thirty and take Danièle to his apartment for the time being. 'Do you know the church? Yes? I'll meet you there at a quarter to one. It's not long.'

Charlotte replaced the receiver and breathed out heavily. She had spent a night of dim waiting rooms and arthritic trains; she wanted to sleep for several days, to restore the speed to her slow limbs, to dispel the fizzing little pain in her temple and to purge the pressing anguish in her chest.

She reckoned it would take her twenty minutes to walk to the church, which left her with about forty to kill. The best place would be the station waiting room, but to sit there would be to invite a document inspection by some uniformed official. She lifted her case and trudged along the avenue until she found a track opening off between the plane trees. After a few yards she came across a fallen tree-trunk. She sat down and pulled out Dominique's detective story. It was a strange and conspicuous thing to do, but she had the confidence of fatigue; she would not need to feign irritation if anyone questioned her.

She was five minutes early at the church and was inspecting one of the stained glass windows when she heard the door grind open.

Julien walked swiftly up the aisle to where she stood and shook her hand. 'I think it would be better if we weren't seen together. I'll go ahead. It's the second street above the church, the third house on the right. I'll leave the street door open so with any luck you can get in without being seen by the concierge. I'm on the first floor.'

Charlotte gave him three minutes, then set off. She found the house easily enough and made her way into the tiled hall. A young woman was emerging from a ground-floor apartment: she had wide-set blue eyes, waved blonde hair and a coquettishly thick application of red lipstick.

She smiled at Charlotte. 'Hello. You must be Monsieur Levade's fiancée.'

'I . . . I'm pleased to meet you,' said Charlotte non-committally.

'He's on the first floor. Well — you know, of course. He's just got in.'

'Thank you.'

The woman went out of the front door. 'See you later,' she said genially as she closed it behind her.

Charlotte climbed the stairs and knocked on the open door of Julien's apartment. He emerged from the sitting room and took her case. 'Come and sit down. I'm making some lunch.'

'I met someone in the hall. A rather beautiful woman who seemed to think I was your fiancée.'

'Oh, that's Pauline Benoit. She's nice, isn't she?' said Julien from the kitchen.

'Who is she?'

'She's the concierge.'

'I thought concierges were supposed to be old and nosey and have their hair in curlers.'

'You've been reading too many detective stories,' said Julien, returning to the sitting room and holding out a chair at the dining table for Charlotte.

'No, I haven't. I hate detective stories,' said Charlotte. To her irritation she found that her denial sounded unconvincing.

Julien laid a place in front of her. 'My life is run by two Paulines,' he said. 'Pauline Benoit at home and Pauline Bobotte at work. Bobotte's actually much nosier than Benoit. She listens to all my telephone calls. Benoit just likes to know about any romance that might be in the air. I have to keep her guessing. She thinks I'm a bigamist.'

He disappeared to the kitchen and returned with a plate of food and a glass of wine, which he set down in front of Charlotte.

'I'm sorry about this,' he said. 'It's all I've got. It's not as bad as it looks. I had it for dinner last night.'

'What is it?'

'It's a stew.'

'What sort of stew?'

'Don't ask. I didn't.'

'Aren't you having any?'

'No. I'll . . . I'll have something later.'

Charlotte put a little of the reheated food in her mouth.

'I understand you'll be going home next week.'

'Has it been confirmed?'

'Yes. Of course, it'll depend on the weather. But it's been very clear recently and I haven't heard that it's likely to change. Will you be glad to be back in England?'

'I suppose so.' Charlotte filled her mouth with the rough wine. 'I've done what I came to do,' she said untruthfully.

'If you'd like to rest after lunch, you'll be quite safe here. You can sleep in my bed if you like.'

'Thank you. Please don't go to any trouble.'

'It's no trouble. I'll lock the front door and tell Pauline no one's to come up.'

When he had cleared her plate, Julien showed Charlotte into his bedroom. He closed the shutters and indicated the large bed with its lordly hangings.

'If anyone knocks at the door, don't answer. I've got the key and I'll let myself in at about seven. Sleep well.' He gave her another of his guileless smiles and Charlotte reciprocated tiredly.

She pushed off Dominique's heavy shoes, but thought

249

she had better stay dressed in case she needed to move in a hurry. When she had heard Julien depart, she closed the double doors into the sitting room and went back to the bed.

She sometimes found that if she lay on her front, the physical weight of her body slightly helped to crush the misery in her abdomen. She pulled the eiderdown over her and tried to sleep. His face had gone again.

★ ★ ★

Peter Gregory was sitting up in bed, anxiously watching as the local veterinary surgeon inspected his leg.

There was a fracture of the tibia, suspected but undiagnosed by the vet, owing to the primitive manner in which he had had to make his examination, by probing with his fingers. His major field of expertise was in the digestive illnesses of sheep, though he was competent with all ruminants and would even give opinions, if asked, on domestic pets.

An English airman posed problems of a different nature, largely because he could not be taken to a surgery. The vet had been contacted by a smallholder who knew that his sympathies were reliable, whereas the local human doctor was an uncomplicated Pétainist, who in his spare time organised youth groups to go camping and sing songs with a marching, militaristic snap.

The vet looked up from Gregory's skinny leg and said something fast, in the regional accent, that Gregory did not understand. The elderly peasant couple who were sheltering him nodded their heads in wise agreement. As the vet explained his thoughts in greater detail, Gregory wished he had paid more attention to Madame Fanon's tedious French lessons or more often accepted Charlotte's offer of instruction. For the rest, he had escaped with bruising and cuts; what seemed to be a broken elbow now gave him no pain and the swelling had gone down. A long gash running from his thigh, over his hip and up into the small of his back had now closed sufficiently for them all to see that its swollen, septic edges had started to subside. The bruises beneath his eyes had gone from shiny purple to a jaundiced yellow, and the puffed skin had resumed its former adhesion to the contours of the skull. What hurt most was his neck and shoulders, where he had hung upside down in his straps, waiting to be cut free.

'You were lucky,' they told him for the hundredth time, and for the hundredth time he said, 'I know.' Gregory the unsinkable, the unkillable: lucky to have survived the crash, lucky that it was so near the landing zone, lucky that he was picked up by sympathetic people . . . There was, as he already knew before taking off from England, no apparent end to his good fortune.

He had asked to be shown on a map exactly where he was, but they had no map. They told him the names of the nearest villages, but these meant nothing to Gregory. From the window of his bedroom he could see fields of wheat divided by dwarf oaks and messy hedgerows; beyond them were woods and spinneys that climbed the undulating land, and on a distant hilltop was a tower. He supposed it was a water-tower, but its grey stone and castellated rim made it look like the remnant of a fortification. There were no houses and no roads within his view. He was lost and he could not move.

What kept him from despair was the admiration that he felt for the couple who had taken him in. They knew nothing about him and could not even converse with him, yet they were risking their lives for his. It was not as though they could have had a sophisticated understanding of the situation; presumably they were as bewildered and scared as anyone else in this occupied

251

country. But every morning the old woman, who had told him by shoving a finger at her breastbone and repeating the word that she was called Béatrice, brought him bread and milk; every evening the old man, whose name was Jacques, sat with him and fed him cigarettes and vinegary wine.

The vet explained that he must stay in bed. With vigorous hand movements — both palms at first pressing down, suggesting gravity and stasis, then becoming fists whose index fingers pointed firmly to the bed — he made himself understood.

'How long?' asked Gregory.

The vet shrugged. 'Fifteen days?'

'And then?'

'We'll see.'

Luckily, he still had some notes left on the roll of francs the RAF had given him before take-off; his hosts had been able to supplement the produce of their field with butter and wine from the black market.

The vet left the room and Gregory sank back against the pillow. He took a cigarette from the packet on the bedside table. There was nothing to do but stare from the window over the vacant fields. He thought of Charlotte, of her eyes, of the life-saving intensity of her passion.

★ ★ ★

It was five o'clock when Charlotte awoke, having slept more deeply than she expected. She lay on her back for a minute, believing herself still to be in Antoinette's bedroom in Ussel. This room was bigger, however, and more bare; there was a glass-fronted bookcase against one wall and a small rush-seated chair with a pair of man's trousers thrown over it. A moment of panic and disorientation subsided as the memory of Julien came back to her: his black hair, receding a little at the

252

temples, but the face still youthful with its dark, active eyes and swiftly changing expression. She remembered lunch, the stew, a conversation about when she would be picked up.

Charlotte stretched beneath the eiderdown and yawned. She felt a sudden need for tea: nothing else would switch her back from her sleepy siding on to the main line of the day. She climbed out of bed and straightened her clothes, then went through into the kitchen. The closest thing she could find to tea was a glass pot with some dried leaves which she thought might be camomile or verveine. She boiled some water and poured it over a handful of leaves in a cup which she took through into the sitting room and left on the table to infuse.

Soon she would be going home. She would return to her flat with Daisy and Sally, she would await further calls from Mr Jackson. They would presumably post her to one of their holding schools, where she could help with the last-minute preparation of other agents, teach French or drive the staff cars. Since G Section had started to pay her a wage there would be no need for her to look for another job, and in the meantime she would be free to explore London, to go to galleries or shops; she could even go up to Scotland and visit her parents. She would resume a life, and men like Cannerley would telephone to ask her out to dinner; it was a privileged and pleasant existence that lay ahead of her: it was normal life, it was what most young women wanted. She should count herself lucky.

Yet, at the thought of it, she trembled in revolt. To leave France at this stage was unthinkable. Although she had efficiently completed both her official and her private errands, she had been drawn into the frightening destiny of the people she had met. She could not leave until she had seen whether Antoinette's prediction of resistance was fulfilled; she wanted to see

253

the big schoolboy César load up another horse-drawn cart with stores; she wanted to understand why the English were so deeply hated. And Julien also intrigued her: what made a man like him buzz round a little town like Lavaurette, alighting for a moment here, then there, in his pollination, while the majority of men of his kind and generation went quietly about their business in the tranquil streets of German-occupied Paris?

She took an end of bread from the remains of lunch on the table, dipped it in the tea and sucked. No gateway of unconscious memory swung gloriously open, but through the dusty crumbs a not unpleasant herbal taste slid across her tongue and encouraged her to take a sip directly from the cup.

She would not go back. She would stay in France until she felt she had done something worthwhile. More urgent even than this was her need to find Gregory. To fly home now would be to admit that he was dead, and this was something that she could not do. She had no idea how she would set about finding him, but merely by being in France she had a better chance. At the very least she could telephone Chollet again. But to return to London was to give up; and if she gave up on Peter Gregory, then she was giving up faith in her own life.

She had identified her own troubles with those of the country in which she found herself. They seemed to her like two long journeys that had lost their way, each struggling now to rediscover the doubtful paradise from which they had set out. Her need to stay in France was probably, she had to admit, neurotic; certainly it seemed more compulsive than rational. But although she had long had the habit of self-analysis, Charlotte found it tiresome. Presumably the link between these public and private worlds was the presence in France of the man she loved, and on whom she depended for the resolution of her life. But if that was the motivation, it was buried too deep to be felt. All that she knew was a compelling urgency of personal and moral force; and she was certain that, whatever its tangled roots, she must obey it.

★ ★ ★

Julien returned at six with a noisy ascent of the stripped staircase. Charlotte heard him calling down some mocking retort to the woman's voice that followed him from the hallway. He was kicking off his shoes as, slightly out of breath, he came into the sitting room.

'How are you? Did you sleep?'

'Yes, thank you.'

'Good. Now, dinner. The housekeeper doesn't come on Wednesday so I have to improvise. We can't go out because I've used all my coupons.'

'I've got some money,' said Charlotte. 'Couldn't we — '

'My dear Danièle, what are you suggesting? Not the black market, surely?'

Charlotte thought of the arrangements Antoinette had described to her in Ussel. 'Certainly not, Monsieur. I was thinking of something a little more grey.'

Julien ground his teeth. 'I think I know the ideal place. The Café du Centre.'

'But I went there with Yves and — '

'But you don't know Madame Gayral, do you?'

'I leave it to you, but I insist on paying.'

'We'll see about that,' said Julien. 'I've got one or two things to do first. Suppose we leave at about half past seven?'

'That's fine. I'll read my detective story.'

Julien was attentive to Charlotte's needs. He was amazed by how much dinner she was able to eat: everything on the menu and at least three dishes that were not, silently furnished by Irène in her black skirt and clean white blouse, the empty plates unsmilingly removed a few minutes later. From somewhere Madame Gayral had found a capon, some brie which had reached the point of liquefaction and some eggs she had made into an omelette with a few mean but pungent shavings of truffle. Julien ordered more wine when the first bottle disappeared and was pleased to see that Charlotte drank what he considered to be the correct amount for a woman: less than half but not less than a third of each bottle.

Back in his apartment he made up the bed with clean sheets and put a carafe of water and a glass on the table. He offered her the freedom of the bookcase, regretting that he was understocked on crime novels. At half past ten he held the door of the bedroom open for her and told her to get a good night's sleep.

Charlotte would not go in. She said, 'Octave, if I stayed here in Lavaurette, if I didn't go home, could I be of any use to you?'

Charlotte could see Julien working out the ramifications of such a decision before he spoke. 'I need all the help I can get. We're expecting a further drop of stores any day. One day perhaps we'll be able to recruit all the young men, but for the moment our job is just to exist. That's what Mirabel told me. And it's easier to exist when there are more of you. But — '

'Good. I've decided to stay. I can't go home with a job half finished.'

'We'll have to tell them not to send the plane. They won't like it.'

'I very much doubt that the plane was for me alone. There'll be other more important people. Yves, for instance.'

'There are a lot of reasons why you shouldn't stay. I do think it's unwise. The danger, for instance, the difficulty of contacting London, the — '

'But it's possible, isn't it? You do have access to the wireless operator.'

'Yes, I do.'

Julien stood looking at Charlotte for a long time, with his head on one side. Perhaps, she thought, he too had some private motivation.

'Danièle, you are an extraordinary woman.' He looked at her fair skin and deep brown eyes. 'What on earth are you doing?' He smiled. 'What are you doing standing in my apartment in Lavaurette, dressed like that, refusing to take a small aeroplane home to safety? What on earth has brought you to this?'

'Love,' she said.

'Love?'

'Yes.'

'But why aren't you at home like all the other English girls, doing your — '

'Scottish.'

'Scottish girls, in your pleasant unoccupied country with your family and your friends?'

'It's too late to explain now. But I do love your country. I wish more of you loved mine, though perhaps one day you will. I have this one chance to change my life, to save my soul, and whether I can do that depends for some reason I don't yet understand on whether you can save your country's soul as well.'

Julien shook his head, clearly baffled, but apparently not thinking it worth his while to say so. 'Anyway,' he said, 'if you're going to stay, you might tell me your name. What is it?'

'Madame Guilbert. Dominique.'

Julien stood up and refilled his glass. 'The other thing is, we'll need to find you something to do — a job. As a matter of fact, I've got an idea. Can you cook?'

7

It was mid-afternoon when Charlotte turned Mlle Cariteau's bicycle off the road and up the track between the scabby plane trees to the Domaine. Her hair was covered by the woollen headscarf that had made Julien smile; it was the only clothes purchase she had allowed herself from G Section funds, and she had bought it because she thought it made her look more like Dominique Guilbert. She caught glimpses of the house between the trees, but it was not until the path turned a right angle and delivered her beneath the arched pigeonnier that she saw it whole for the first time. For all its irregularities, its terracotta-coloured shutters and lopsided front door, she felt as though she had seen it many times before; its design was at root so typical that it seemed to have emerged from some remembered blueprint, some universal plan of French rural peace that no Revolution or genocidal war had quite unsettled.

Charlotte hauled with both hands on the iron bell-pull, and, when no one came, turned the heavy knocker that acted as a handle. The large hallway offered passages right or left as well as a staircase that doubled back above her head into the remote ceiling. For all the uncertainty of her position, the feeling that came to Charlotte as she stood in the hall was one of pure excitement: if she could spend long enough in this house, she seemed to feel, it might reveal to her some lost plan or harmony. Here she might find the missing track that led back to the past.

'Madame Guilbert?'

The voice came from above her head. She looked up and saw bare feet between the banisters as someone descended the staircase. On the half-landing, where the stairs turned, he came into full view: an old man in navy-blue cotton trousers, as though he was going sailing, and a shirt without its collar which hung down almost to his knees.

'Please wait there. I'll come down.'

Charlotte felt some animal reluctance to go too near this man. He offered her his hand when he had walked down to where she was waiting, and she took it as briefly as she could. His grip was warm and dry and his skin was covered in splashes of paint; from his body there rose a clean, strong smell of oils. His eyes were hooded and enclosed by lined, reptilian skin, though the bright blue irises were unclouded.

'I think we'll go into the drawing room.' He led the way down the lefthand passage from the hall, past two or three doors, to a long, lofty room that ran the depth of the house. It was dark inside until he had opened some shutters that gave a view of overgrown garden to the side; the freed rectangle of light revealed a room full of formal furniture of the nineteenth century, fussily scrolled and uncomfortably upholstered. There was a mirror in a gilded frame above the marble mantelpiece and, at the end of the room, still in half-darkness, was what looked like an enormous flat desk with a reading lamp.

'Do sit down. I believe you know my son Julien. He's spoken to me about you.'

Charlotte felt fine old dust rise up as she settled on the edge of a sofa. So that was Octave's real name; at the Café du Centre, despite his warnings, she had only heard him called 'Monsieur'. Julien . . . It was not bad; it had the same Roman ring as Octave, but it had a certain lightness and elegance. 'Yes, I know him a little.'

Levade pushed his hand back through his thick hair, disarranging it into white layers. Charlotte felt the clarity of his gaze, even in the gloom; she noticed the scaly skin on his bare feet.

'He thought it's possible you might need somewhere to live for a time.'

'That's right.' She was eager. She did not want to live in the same place as this man, but she wanted to be in this house. 'My father's in hospital and I want to be near him. My husband is a prisoner of war in Germany, like so many men.'

'I see,' said Levade. 'There's a woman who comes to clean the house, but she has difficulties at home, I think. She's irregular. You could live here for nothing if you were prepared to help with the cooking and cleaning. I would give you food as well. Are you a good cook?'

'Your son asked me that. Not particularly, but I could learn. I can do the simple things.'

Levade sighed and stood up. 'When will your husband come home?'

'I don't know.'

'The government is sending people to work in Germany in return for our prisoners. Had you heard?'

'Yes. Three men for each prisoner. It seems a bit hard.'

'It's worse than that. The Germans only want trained men, so they don't count the farm boys. Laval's latest triumph is to send eight men, four of them trained, in return for each prisoner of war. The man's a fool.'

Charlotte nodded.

'Don't you think?'

'I'm not sure I understand politics.'

Levade nodded briefly, as though this was an acceptable position. He walked over to the fireplace and leaned his arm on the mantelpiece. 'Are you quiet? Do you make a noise in the house?'

'Not particularly. I could be as quiet as you like. Your son told me you're a painter, so I suppose — '

260

'I used to be. Not any more. Now I put oil on canvas, but anyone can do that.' Levade began to walk down into the still-dark end of the drawing room. 'I spend some hours every morning in the studio upstairs. I don't have lunch, so you needn't bother about that. I normally eat at about six, then in the evening I read. I don't want you to work while I'm painting. You'd have to do the cleaning later.'

'I don't mind. Whatever's convenient.'

'I could give you some money if you liked. As well.'

'Yes,' said Charlotte quickly, 'I was going to come to that.' It would have been Dominique's first thought.

'Whatever you think is right,' said Levade. 'Why not ask in the village? Of course, there's nothing to spend it on. Unless you want to buy a photograph of Marshal Pétain.'

'I need to save some money for when my husband comes back,' said Charlotte primly.

'Very well, I'll show you a room. There are two you can choose from.'

Levade walked briskly out of the salon, his movement unaffected in any obvious way by age, and Charlotte followed him to the stairs. They walked along the landing of the first floor, past the locked studio, with Charlotte's eyes swivelling from side to side to take in as much as she could of the rooms revealed by doors left tantalisingly half-open. At the end of the landing there was an enclosed area from which different corridors opened, presumably into the tower, and a narrow, plain staircase up which Levade led the way. At the top were servants' or perhaps children's rooms, with low ceilings beneath the eaves but views over the grounds towards a lake. The best of these had a threadbare rug, a boat bed made up beneath a grey silk cover, and, on the wall behind the bed, a faded toile with Watteau-like figures in the colour of antique rose.

'It's beautiful.' Charlotte was more stirred than she could reasonably explain by this plain room. 'May I have this one?'

'If this is what you like. Do you have any luggage?'

'I have a suitcase, but it's with your son. He said he'd bring it later if everything worked out.'

'I see. There's another thing I should mention.' Levade was standing in the doorway; he was lean and not particularly tall, but his figure almost filled the narrow frame. 'Nothing you see or hear must be repeated. I live a quiet life, but I have certain small habits which I don't want discussed in the bars of Lavaurette. Do you understand?'

'Yes. Of course.'

'If you should ever find me distracted or unresponsive, you must ignore it.'

Charlotte nodded. She felt self-conscious as Levade's eyes ran up and down her figure in its homespun clothes; she had the sensation of having been appraised. Levade's long face softened a little; it was not a smile, but it had some affirmation in it, some acknowledgement of her as a separate being.

'Will you call me at six, when you've made dinner? You'll find food in the kitchen.'

Everything Charlotte saw at the Domaine confirmed her conviction that she was right to stay. She had the peace of mind that came when a difficult decision appeared to be vindicated, and with that a practical energy. It was from this house that she would find Gregory.

★ ★ ★

In the afternoon Julien went to the Domaine to fetch Mlle Cariteau's bicycle in a van he had borrowed from Gastinel, the butcher. Dominique could use one of the old family bicycles in the barn, he explained, but Sylvie

Cariteau needed hers for her daily business.

Julien enjoyed it when Dominique opened the door of his father's house. They had come far enough as friends that it was right for him to offer his cheek to her to kiss, and when she offered hers in return he allowed his lips to linger for a second while he inhaled the faint smell of lily of the valley on her skin. The social contradiction also pleased him: he was intimate with Dominique and with Levade, yet she called Levade 'Monsieur' and was employed by him. What his father made of Dominique he could not imagine.

He thought Levade would like her and presumed he would at once divine that she was not what she claimed to be. Julien himself was excited by the thought of the English girl — Scottish girl, he corrected himself — whose true identity lay like an unplumbed reef below the shallow waters of this Dominique. As he came to know her and to care for her, he was aware that he did not come to know her at all: his growing friendship was with someone who did not exist and was therefore not subject to the limits and cautions of normal relationships. Why was this so exciting?

It was Levade who had told Julien in outrage about the plan to convert the monastery into a hotel. At the beginning of his exile at the Domaine in 1937, he had frequently gone there to pray. When the order had made the decision to sell, he had mentioned it to Julien as a sad development, not as a possible source of income. Levade was distressed, or appeared to be, when Julien's company submitted plans for the conversion. Later, he told Julien it was better that he should do it than that it should fall into the hands of a barbarian; and at least it meant he would see something of his son. To begin with this was not the case, as Julien was able to do most of the work from Paris; then the practice was seized by the Government because its senior partner, a man called Weil, was a Jew.

263

The development company who took over the contract wanted to retain Julien as architect, and he, already uneasy at the supine collaboration of many Parisians, felt it was a good moment to leave the capital and come down to the site. Levade was delighted by the move and encouraged him to settle in Lavaurette.

★ ★ ★

At Julien's suggestion, Charlotte went to visit André and Jacob at the Cariteaus' house on the way back. Julien thought that in the absence of their mother they would appreciate seeing a young woman, and Charlotte was delighted to go, feeling that here was a positive act of resistance.

Sylvie's handsome, smiling face appeared at the back door. It was halfday at the post office and she was looking after the boys while her mother was out. She called up the stairs for André and Jacob, and there was the sound of eager feet before they came tumbling into the room.

Jacob was still at an age when fatigue registered itself as tears, when swift storms burst in clear skies, but André was at the delicate moment when life was ceasing to be a sequence of unrelated sensations and was on the point of becoming something that formed a continuous and more or less coherent whole.

He was fascinated by knights in armour, soldiers, heroes of the Middle Ages, Greeks, Romans and stories from the Bible. Julien had been able to acquire second-hand books by post from a dealer in Clermont-Ferrand, but while he was waiting for a new consignment he told Charlotte she would have to rely on her memory or make up new stories of her own.

The two small boys sat with her on an old sofa in the kitchen. Charlotte felt a little nervous. It had been a long time since she won the junior Academy prize in classical studies. What had been the name of Icarus's father, who had made the wings? She recalled Persephone being carried off by Diss, but how had she finally escaped? The Trojan War she remembered clearly for the most part; in any event, she could easily extemporise battles in which her favourite heroes (Hector, Aias; Achilles was too self-indulgent) defeated others after the intervention of a sponsoring goddess. The return of Odysseus she could spin out over several visits.

André sat with his chin cupped in his hands, staring up at Charlotte with unblinking eyes. His concentration appeared to be tireless, and he would occasionally interrupt or rebuke Charlotte for having skimped some detail of the characters' previous lives; he wanted to have the complete picture, and there were certain details — the motive power of Agamemnon's ships, the wax of Icarus's wings — that were crucial to his satisfaction.

Jacob listened to part of the story, but was more easily distracted; he would light on some comic detail and repeat it several times or walk round the room acting out some private game it had suggested. This was something of a relief to Charlotte, who did not discourage Jacob from wandering off in mid-story.

Mlle Cariteau moved efficiently about the kitchen, taking crockery to the stone sink, sweeping the floor, occasionally lifting the lid of the giant stockpot and shaking her head in disappointment at the thin and meatless aroma she released. Still, her good humour seemed imperturbable.

Jacob eventually asked the question Charlotte feared, about his parents, and she had to stop the story she was telling to André.

'I don't know for sure when you'll see them again. I'm afraid I can't say.'

Although it was Jacob who had asked, it was André's intelligent, reproachful eyes that Charlotte feared.

'Where are they?' said Jacob in his unformed voice.

'I don't exactly know. I believe they may be in Paris. You must try not to worry. One thing we can be absolutely sure of: they'll come home just as soon as they can. I know they wouldn't waste a minute. So you just have to remember that — as soon as they can, they'll be on the train home.'

'But why have they gone away?'

'It's a difficult time. There's a war. People have to go to different places in a war, to places they don't always want to be.'

'Why did they go to Paris?'

'I don't know. I expect they had no choice. Sometimes you just have to do things when you're a grown-up.' Jacob had clearly forgotten about the gendarme's visit to his parents' house.

'And when will we see them?' Jacob was more tenacious than usual.

'I don't know. I can't pretend that I do know. But I hope it'll be soon. We all hope so and every day we hope so more. We never, never stop hoping.'

Although only Jacob conducted the cross-examination, Charlotte felt throughout the pressure of André's fixed and disbelieving eyes.

Sylvie Cariteau leaned across the sofa to pick up the book she had left on the floor. As she did so, Charlotte caught the scent of her clean skin, efficiently scrubbed in wartime as in any other, and saw the waistband of her modest skirt, stretched tight by her solid, mannish figure. When she stood up and turned back towards the table Charlotte also noticed that where the skirt met her plain and tightly tucked-in blouse a strip of her underpants had been caught and was clearly visible across the width of her back. They were of coral satin, embroidered with lace in which was woven the frivolous patterns of daisies and forget-me-nots. Charlotte wondered if Sylvie just liked flowers or whether they were evidence of some private, hopeful fantasy, cherished for twenty years in emasculated Lavaurette.

'Come again, Madame,' said Sylvie Cariteau when Charlotte was leaving. 'They've enjoyed it, haven't you, boys?'

'Yes, yes, come again, come again.'

★ ★ ★

That evening Charlotte had to make dinner for Levade. A stranger in the kitchen, she spent several minutes opening and closing cupboard doors.

Whoever had once owned the Domaine had acquired enough plates and glasses to entertain a hundred people, but it was not until she explored a back annexe that Charlotte found anything that could be eaten. It was a little after six by the time she went in search of Levade to tell him that his dinner was ready. He had told her he worked upstairs but had not said in which room, so she knocked at every door in turn without eliciting an answer until Levade's voice, sounding dim and abstracted, answered her call, and she heard him cross the room. She waited till he opened the door, hoping to catch a glimpse of his studio, but he moved quickly through the opening, leaving her time to see only a huge bed before he turned the key in the lock.

He went silently ahead of her to the dining room, where she had laid a place for him at the head of the table. He muttered grace, then poured wine into a crystal glass and drank quickly while Charlotte went back into the kitchen to bring the food. He tucked a white napkin into his collar, as though anxious to protect his paint-bespattered shirt, and leaned back in his chair as Charlotte placed some fatty terrine in front of him. The bread she had found was as dusty as everyone else's but he tore off a large piece with enthusiasm. He made no comment on the pâté or on the main course, a piece of chicken she had found beneath a wire-mesh cover and reheated with a sauce improvised from what was in the larder. She had found a peach on a tree in the orchard for his dessert, and this, too, he ate without speaking.

'I'm afraid there's no coffee,' she said, when she cleared his plate.

'It doesn't matter. I'm going out for a walk now. I'll be back in about an hour.'

Now that she was standing close to him, Charlotte could see that he was not as old as she had thought: the white hair was misleading, and his skin, though lined, was not shrivelled or shrunk.

'Was the dinner all right?'

'What?' He turned as he was leaving the room. 'Yes. Thank you. Have some yourself.'

It was not exactly the gracious invitation to lay an extra place in future that she had half expected, but it was something. She didn't particularly care whether this man liked her cooking or not; she just wanted to remain in his house.

She was eating what was left of the chicken in the kitchen when she heard a voice calling out in the hall. She hurried over the springy floor of the dining room and found that Julien was paying his second visit of the day.

'Ah, Dominique. Exactly the person I wanted to see. Here's your suitcase. Has my father gone out?'

'Yes. He went for a walk.'

They sat at the end of the cleared dining table, where Julien poured them both a glass of wine and lit a cigarette. Charlotte watched his humorous face begin to settle as he organised what he was going to say. He was wearing a pale blue open-necked shirt and a shabby tweed jacket; he looked more like a week-end painter than a professional architect who had just come from his office.

'Do you like it here at the Domaine?'

'Yes, I do. It's a beautiful house. Rather mysterious, don't you think?'

'Extremely. I wouldn't want to be here on my own in the winter.'

'Your father doesn't mind, though.'

'No. He has ways of keeping himself occupied in the long winter nights.'

'He told me he's not a painter any more, that he just puts oil on canvas. He sounded rather sad.'

Julien laughed. 'Yes. He used to paint wonderful pictures. He can't get used to the fact that it's finished. He ought to feel lucky, he ought to be happy that of all the people who tried to paint he was one of the few who managed to produce something worthwhile, who got inside himself and made it all connect. But he doesn't see it like that. He thinks he's under a curse, that something is being withheld from him by some cruel, arbitrary power.'

'I suppose most people are reluctant to concede that luck has anything to do with their successes.'

'Yes. Particularly when luck isn't the principal element, when ability and effort are the most important things.' Julien smiled. 'Which room have you taken?'

'It's a little one on the second floor with a pretty toile behind the bed. It's charming.'

'Yes, I think I know that one. Presumably it belonged to a servant.'

'Like me.'

'Very like you, I expect, Dominique.' Julien ran his hand back through his hair. 'I'm glad you're staying. I need more people. César is all very well, but he has to bicycle for miles to get here. I shouldn't really tell you this, but he's the head boy of the lycée. You probably guessed.'

'I wasn't sure.'

'And Auguste has left us. He told me that he didn't want to work for the English any more. He's joined some network run by General de Gaulle.'

'I didn't know there were any.'

'Well, that's what he told me. Look, Dominique, I've had a message. From Mirabel, the man in charge. He wants you to meet him. He says it's urgent. He's got important news for you. He's going to ring again and suggest a meeting place.'

'News?'

'That's what he said.'

'I suppose he's going to tell me to go home at once.'

'I didn't get that impression. Perhaps he doesn't know you were supposed to go back with Yves. Minimum information. Isn't that your watchword?'

'Maybe. What's he like, Mirabel?'

'He's fine. This is his third visit. I know him quite well. He's a big broad fellow — very strong, physically and mentally.'

Charlotte went through to the hall with Julien and said goodbye; she felt for a moment bereft as she watched him go down the broad stone steps.

She turned back into the house. What could Mirabel's 'news' be? Presumably it was some admonition from G Section, some order to get herself picked up and brought back. Of course, she thought, there is only one important piece of news as far as I'm concerned, and that is whether Peter Gregory is alive.

And in the light of her belief she allowed herself to hope, and almost to believe in the preposterous idea that Mirabel was going to bring her just such news. There was a dry taste in her mouth as she went upstairs to bed: the taste, she thought bitterly, of fantasy.

8

One way in which the Occupation pleased Claude Benech was that there were fewer things in the shops on which he felt obliged to spend money. Although he was generally self-controlled to the point of paralysis in disposing of his schoolmaster's salary, he did occasionally feel that his position required him to buy a new suit or shoes for work, and even to show himself on the eve of feast days at the wine-merchant to give the appearance of some civic geniality. It was with a reluctant step that he trod the streets back to his plain apartment, the shopping bag heavy with cheese, wine and unwanted madeleines. In these austere times, however, such fripperies were simply not on sale, and he could take a far greater proportion of his salary to the savings bank.

Benech flourished in Marshal Pétain's new world of Work, Family and Fatherland; he would have gone so far as to say that it was the first time in his life he had been happy. Different eras suited different people, and the austerity of the new regime brought out something doughty in him: he was a man of destiny whose fated hour had come.

Work was something of a passion in any case. He had risen to certain heights at school, where the director had given him the task of administering the time-table for all his colleagues. Benech fell on this task enthusiastically; his desire for position and control outweighed any tedium involved. He flourished in the school, became the object of a silent awe among his colleagues and of fear among the pupils he had previously struggled to control. When, at the end of 1940, religious instruction was restored to schools, Benech, though not until that point a devout person, welcomed it: he had read that the Marshal believed the French army had been humiliated by the Germans because its reserve officers had been taught by Socialist teachers. When the next administration allowed religious instruction to become voluntary, Benech successfully lobbied for it to be retained at his school. He had always hated the way his fellow-teachers had supported the Popular Front and various other doomed causes of the Jewish Left, and now he felt vindicated. The Government's removal of all Jews from teaching in 1940 was a move that delighted him in its elegant simplicity, uprooting with one firm pull both distasteful cause and pernicious effect.

At school Benech organised youth groups, more or less affiliated to Catholic and national organisations; they went camping at the week-end, put on uniforms and sang patriotic songs. The fact that these groups were banned in the Occupied Zone, because of their militaristic nature, made Benech proud of them: it showed they were threatening, and that the real France had survived in Vichy.

Fatherland was a subject on which Benech felt secure. What he feared more than anything — far more than German occupation — was a Communist revolution. The Communists had come close to power in Government: they had enabled the Popular Front to come into being. As far as Benech was concerned, that was bad enough; it certainly sufficed to efface the memory of how they had also contributed to the Front's collapse.

His feelings towards the Germans were a little complicated. On one hand, he felt personally humiliated by his country's defeat, and was glad to find internal culprits in the feeble Republicanism of the Jewish Left; on the other hand, he admired the German troops and believed that Laval's longterm plan, to secure France the second seat at the top table of the new Europe, was a sound one.

Meanwhile, the Communists were merely using the Occupier as a rallying point for their revolutionary ends; their real enemy was the traditional France of the centuries, not the temporary German inconvenience. The Vichy government had in Benech's view not only deftly kept the autonomy and spirit of France alive, it had vitally blocked the Communist advance. Vichy was the best — the only — hope of order, the bulwark against Bolshevism, and those who tried to resist it, or to resist the Occupation, were the true and most dangerous enemy. It was not a difficult stretch of logic to conclude that his enemy's enemy — the Occupier — must be his friend. He would not have put it quite so bluntly, but in opposing the Communists and supporting the traditional France of Vichy, the Germans were certainly, Benech believed, on the right lines. Their continued presence was necessary while the Vichy government sorted out the undesirable elements and set the old country back on course.

Family was a less happy area of Benech's life. He had been the middle of three sons who had lost their father on the Marne. They were brought up in Lavaurette by their mother, who indulged her adoration of her eldest son, Charles, a handsome boy who eventually found work with the railways. The youngest, little Louis, was clever and, despite minimal encouragement from his mother, won a scholarship to the lycée, from which he ascended to a different social plane and away, out of their lives. Madame Benech's attitude to the middle son, Claude, was one of frank indifference. She found his coarse looks disappointing: he had wiry black hair, a long moustache from the age of seventeen, pale, mealy skin and a nervous, would-be ingratiating manner. She did not dislike him, she just did not seem to care; she talked to him as though he were a lodger whose parents had forgotten to take him home.

As far as starting a family of his own was concerned, Benech had come close to an agreement a few years earlier with a woman who worked at a bakery, but two weeks before the intended marriage she had disappeared with a farmer. Sylvie Cariteau was probably past child-bearing age, Benech thought; Pauline Bobotte could not be separated — not by him anyway — from her visiting Toulouse businessman; Irène Galliot . . . But he preferred not to remember the hilarious disdain with which Irène had met his hopeful advances. He concentrated his thoughts instead on a young woman he had occasionally seen in the village, a new arrival in Lavaurette who had apparently gone to live at the Domaine to work as housekeeper for the old Jew. There was something suspicious as well as attractive about this woman, and he conjured plans as well as fantasies for her.

In his new, contented life, Claude Benech had begun increasingly to enjoy the company of other people. He allowed himself two drinks an evening in the Café du Centre, where he felt the regulars viewed him with a certain respect. His opinions had been vindicated by events, and he felt confident about the vigour with which he expressed them. As a man for whom the historic tide was running, he felt it was likely to be a matter of time only before the family difficulties of his life also fell into place. As he put on his coat and climbed on to his bicycle to go down to the Café du Centre, he felt certain that the world was spinning his way.

★ ★ ★

That night Charlotte lay down for the first time in her new room. She placed Dominique's spare set of clothes in a drawer and hung her skirt on a rail behind a scarlet curtain. She had so far guarded G Section's funds as though any spending might amount to an act of treason, but now she was staying indefinitely she felt sure the war effort would not fail completely if she bought some new underpants. The dense fabric of Dominique's meant that they often took two days to dry out fully, which had sometimes left her the awkward choice of putting them on damp or wearing the same pair two days running. There seemed to be no clothes at all on sale in Lavaurette, so she thought she might take a train one morning to a bigger town. She wished she had some photographs to put on the bedside table: one of Gregory, and perhaps one of Roderick, even a sufficiently ancient one of her parents.

Dominique's voice was less often present in her head these days; Charlotte found that it was she who talked more often to Dominique, explaining the things she did in her name. The idea of being someone else was attractive to her, and that, she recognised as she turned off the light and pulled up the covers, was what had so drawn her to the Domaine.

She was living someone else's life. This house was suffused with unknown histories, but instead of seeing them as a disenfranchised spectator, she had become a legitimate actor among them. By assuming a new identity, she had somehow rid herself of the restraints imposed by her own and allowed herself to join the flow of a timeless reality more urgent than the one in which she otherwise moved.

As she lay there, she remembered reading Proust's novel at Monsieur Loiseau's house and being thrilled by what the writer seemed to have done. The more you came to know a place, in general, the more it lost its essence and became defined by its quirks and its shortcomings; the suggestion of something numinous or meaningful was usually available with full force only to the first-time visitor and gradually decreased with familiarity. Yet in his book Proust seemed to have worked the paradoxical trick of making his places universal by the familiarity and attentiveness with which he described their individual characters. Charlotte was so pleased by this sleight of hand that she did not at first see how closely it was related to the effects of time; how it depended on the force of involuntary memory to release the deeper reality from the imprisonment of the years. The novel made it clear enough in the end, but Charlotte, still in her teens, had been too intoxicated by its sentences to take in its final significance. Monsieur Loiseau had not helped her; he had merely been delighted that such a French monument had so delighted his 'English' guest; Charlotte later suspected he might not actually have finished the book, but was merely proud of it as a French achievement and pleased by the coincidence of sharing a surname with one of the minor characters, a woman with a house beside the church in Combray with fuchsias in her garden.

At the Domaine Charlotte seemed to be coming as close as was possible to inhabiting that more profound reality, though it was possible only intermittently; for the rest, she was limited by the practical considerations of her life. She still did not quite believe that Gregory was dead. It seemed that he had not made contact with the garage at Clermont-Ferrand, but that proved very little. She had grown so used to his absence that that was now her way of knowing him, and marginal evidence that this absence might be final made surprisingly little difference. There were moments when she gave way to grief, and her vulnerability to such outbursts was kept at a certain pitch by the sheer anxiety of not knowing; at other times, she felt her emotions were simply not subtle enough to accommodate the perpetual uncertainty. Meanwhile there was always Mirabel, and the hope he represented.

She would carry on living, and eventually the pain would go, or at least she would reach a state of existence in which it was explained. While she waited for this enlightenment, she experienced none of the symptoms that had caused her mother to send her, in her teens, to the psychiatrist in Aberdeen; such depressions could not take root in the changed landscape of her mind. She had become galvanised, perhaps by grief, perhaps by some more intellectual process, in a way that left no room for the failure of energy that was the precondition of such despair.

In the Domaine she felt energetic, she felt precariously alive. She was in the right place, she was sure, and something was going to happen. Out there the foothills of the Massif Central were covered with summer darkness. In a lit window of a first floor Julien was telephoning quietly, smoking, drinking brandy from an antique glass. Somewhere Peter Gregory was hiding out, unhurt, and patiently planning his return. Downstairs, in the echoic rooms of this traditional manor house, Levade was doing whatever untraditional things he did at night. In Bordeaux the German soldiers stamped their feet.

I am almost happy, Charlotte thought, and it is a blasphemy to be happy in such grief. Something is going to happen.

★ ★ ★

Just before three o'clock, when Charlotte was lying many fathoms below thought, Peter Gregory was woken by a hoarsely whispering voice.

'Monsieur. Time to go. Come on.'

The couple stood in the doorway of his room. Béatrice held out a shopping bag in which she and Jacques had put a change of clothes, a dried sausage and a loaf of bread. The old man struggled with matches until eventually a flickering glow came up around him.

Gregory hated being woken in the night. It reminded him of days in Africa when the boy would rouse him before dawn because there was work to be done before it grew hot. The taste of aborted sleep also recalled days on the station when they would be scrambled to their planes just as the sun was rising.

He lowered his legs gently to the floor. He was fully dressed in clothes that Jacques had given him, the trousers ludicrously too short but lengthened by the addition of vaguely matching material at the bottom. He took his jacket from the chair and followed his hosts downstairs.

Outside, in the farmyard, a horse and cart were waiting. Jacques handed Gregory a walking stick and carried his bag to the cart. The moonlight was splashed over the mud and dung at their feet.

'Goodbye, Béatrice.' Gregory embraced the old woman and felt her hard little body sobbing in his arms.

The old man kissed him on both cheeks, his wiry bristles scorching through Gregory's shaved skin.

'I will come back,' said Gregory, also close to tears. 'I will come back.'

He climbed on to the cart, with Jacques pushing and helping him from behind. He settled his leg out straight on some old sacks while the driver shook the reins over the horse and moved off.

Gregory looked back at the grey buildings of the farm, three sides of a square in the darkness. He lifted his hand and waved to the old couple, minute figures, holding on to one another in the mud.

Part Three

Autumn – Winter, 1942/3

1

Robin Morris was late leaving his office for lunch. He was due to meet Dick Cannerley in the bar at a quarter to one, and it was already five past by the time he managed to find a taxi.

All morning he had been in an emergency meeting. The Minister and his civil servant arrived in a state of near-panic at half past eight, having received an intercept of a German communication presuming France was on the point of declaring war on Britain.

Taxis swooped towards the building like black ticking birds; the marbled floors rang to the sound of respectably hurrying footsteps; the oak doors of the committee room ground back and forth on their iron hinges. Morris and his senior officer, Sir Oliver Cresswell, presented the details of their own scrambled re-investigations with an air of ordered calm. Sir Oliver soothed the panting Minister and read each hastily ordered update brought into the meeting with no more than the detached interest he might give to an unfamiliar wine list.

'Our position,' he said, 'is that whatever Monsieur Laval may or may not wish to do, it is still Marshal Pétain who is the head of state, and if he compromises his neutrality, then his government is no longer credible.'

'Bloody nonsense!' said the Minister. 'It hasn't been credible since the start, and it's not Pétain who's in charge. It's Laval. The tail's wagging the dog, in case you didn't know. Don't forget that French forces have already fought with the Germans in Africa.'

'Not side by side, Minister,' said Sir Oliver. 'Against

281

a common enemy I concede, but not literally side by side.'

'Comes to the same thing.'

'It is admittedly a . . . political distinction.'

The Minister, rather admirably in Morris's view, did not rise to this provocation, but became more specific in what he required from Sir Oliver and his colleagues.

'I can assure you,' said Sir Oliver, 'that our chaps in the field have so far not missed a trick. Of course I do accept that the principal motive among the French people and their government is the avoidance of civil disorder, and I'm sure also that your own political analysis of Monsieur Laval's ambitions is a fair one. After all, if he believes that a German Europe — with France in the position, shall we say, of consort or dauphin — offers the only chance of a non-Bolshevist future, then it would make sense for him to offer armed assistance to his ally. The Germans are not, in our assessment, likely to accept his terms, however. Our understanding is that in return for French armed co-operation he has asked for a reinstatement of the 1914 frontiers with Germany.'

'I can make the judgements,' said the Minister. 'It's the information we're short of at the moment, particularly on the French side.'

Morris shifted on his unyielding mahogany chair and neatly shaded in his own name on the distribution list of the most recent report.

'I can assure you, Minister,' said Sir Oliver, 'that our endeavours are focused even more keenly on Vichy than on the Occupier. As far as the interpretation of events is concerned, there are well-established procedures, and I'm sure you would accept that a degree of processing of the raw material by ourselves is inevitable if we're not to swamp the ministry with detail.' He coughed and braced his shoulders. 'Now I wonder if we could look forward a little to how we might best co-operate in the coming months. Morris has prepared a short paper which he'd now like to read to you.'

Morris had received a telephone call from Sir Oliver at two o'clock that morning to tell him that he had better come up with something convincing. By six o'clock he had completed a paper he hoped was at least plausible. He had barely had time to bath and shave before putting on the new chalk-stripe suit he had had made by Cannerley's tailor. Its heavy jacket gave him an air of confident formality as he began with an assessment of the quality of information received, and went on to speculate on the procedures that might be necessary as the war developed.

'The German success in beating off the Canadian raid at Dieppe was greeted with enormous relief by the French populace. Our early reports last year on Marshal Pétain's preparations for defence against Allied invasion from the Bay of Biscay and from the Mediterranean were, as you know, subsequently borne out by military observation. Naturally, as the tide of war begins to run the Allied way, the fear of invasion from the Mediterranean may appear more acute both to the Occupier and the Occupied. Our reports at the moment, however, indicate no cause for concern.'

'Concern?' The Minister looked unbelieving.

'No concern that German unease might lead to any precipitate action inside France. Going into the Free Zone, for instance.'

The Minister grunted, 'Consort, dauphin — bloody concubine more like,' but said no more, which allowed Morris to give a detailed, practical analysis of future requirements in what, following departmental practice, he referred to as 'the field'.

As he slumped back against the seat of the taxi and watched the November leaves wheeling about the damp streets, Morris had the feeling of having escaped intact. The Minister's private secretary had fixed him

283

with a nakedly sceptical look throughout the reading of his paper, which had twice caused him to lose his place and stammer. For the rest, he felt he had earned Sir Oliver's *sotto* 'Well done, Morris', delivered in the lobby at the end of the meeting.

'I'd just about given you up,' said Cannerley, as Morris panted up the broad staircase, over the polished landing and into the bar. 'What'll it be? Sherry?'

'Thank you.' Morris found his hand was trembling a little as Cannerley gave him the fiddly little glass. 'Bloody chaos back at the factory.' He glanced round the bar whose walls were hung with oil portraits of distinguished, and some less distinguished, old members, before confiding in a lowered voice: 'They're convinced Laval's about to declare war on the Allies.'

Cannerley laughed. 'It would certainly be the logical outcome of his beliefs. Shall we go down? We're in the supper room — I hope you don't mind. It was either that or take pot luck at the long table, and the club bores are out in force. They appear to be indestructible. We need another Blitz, but rather better aimed this time.'

'How's Celia?' Morris asked as the waiter placed a carafe of the club claret between them on the table.

'Very well, thank you.'

'And the wedding plans?'

'God, Robin, you're worse than her mother. The wedding's postponed. I'm not sure I'm quite ready for marriage yet.'

'You mean you haven't finished playing the field?'

'That's a rather vulgar way of putting it, if I may say so,' said Cannerley. 'I do find that the hostilities have engendered a certain . . . *largesse* among one's female acquaintance. Don't you?'

Morris had not. He shrugged. 'The shadow of death, I presume. *Timor mortis conturbat me.*'

'Potted shrimps,' said Cannerley, to the waiter. 'Hell

of a price. I don't know where they get them from. But do have them, Robin, if you'd like to.' He pushed back a tumbling lick of fair hair from his forehead.

Morris's menu had no prices on it, and he felt inhibited.

'No, I'll have the . . . ' He scanned the menu for something modest. 'Sardine salad to start with. Do you remember that girl we met on the train from Edinburgh?'

'Och aye,' said Cannerley, 'the Scots lass. Thereby hangs a tale. Do you know what happened?' He leaned forward. 'You know we managed to recruit a G Section man over there? Fowler? He was supposed to get the girl to run a little errand, pass on a bit of misleading information. In return he was going to offer some sort of gen about the whereabouts of her boyfriend.'

Morris nodded.

'It's all gone rather haywire. Fowler had to get the hell out of the area. It was all getting a bit hot, apparently. He's only just managed to renew contact.'

'I thought she was only going to be there for a short time.'

'Apparently the bloody girl refuses to come home.'

'Why?' said Morris.

'God knows. It's all a typical G Section cock-up.'

'Does it matter, her still being there?'

'Not to us. In fact it's rather to our advantage because it gives Fowler a second bite of the cherry. But I imagine G Section are hopping about a bit.'

Morris laughed. 'Anyway, I'm seeing something of a friend of hers at the moment,' he said. 'A girl called Sally. They used to share a flat.'

'What's she like?' said Cannerley as the food arrived.

'She's rather nice. Delightful in fact. Trouble is, she's all moony about some naval commander.'

'God,' said Cannerley, 'I haven't had potted shrimps

since before the war. They used to do them at Goodwood.'

Since the hand of the clock had passed two by the time they finished eating, they were permitted to take a match from the box in the silver stand and light a cigar to go with the thin, sour coffee. Their conversation returned on a slow loop to where it had begun.

'I think it's very unlikely that Laval could pull off a declaration of war,' said Cannerley, 'although I'm quite certain he'd like to.'

'Why are you sure he couldn't do it?'

'Because he would try to link it with some sort of deal, and the Germans have never been interested in any sort of collaboration with Vichy.'

'They let them police the Occupied Zone.'

'It saves them the trouble. They allow Vichy to have the semblance of autonomy because it helps keep public order, but the Germans haven't seriously collaborated on a single issue. And even if they won the war they'd completely disregard all the sycophancy of Laval.'

'No place at the top table?'

Cannerley laughed. 'They'd be a hundred yards below the salt. Not even in the same trading zone.'

In a brief pause that followed, Morris said, 'I'm sorry about your father. I saw the obituary.'

Cannerley's face clouded. 'Yes, yes. Thank you. I sometimes feel . . . I don't know, it's more than just a death.'

'Are you all right? You look terrible.'

'Yes.' Cannerley laughed. 'Yes, I'm fine. Are you playing at the weekend?'

'Yes. Worplesdon. Foursomes. I'm rather looking forward to it.'

Later, they stood on the broad stone steps of the old, grey building and wrapped their coats about them as they peered this way and that in the dim afternoon, looking for the yellow lamp of a taxi.

Morris was thinking what London would be like under German occupation: sentries on guard outside the National Gallery, the Foreign Office requisitioned as the headquarters of some insane Nazi project, people scurrying through the streets to their shameful accommodations, a farcical shadow government, headed by Lord Halifax, sequestered in some genteel town — in Cheltenham, perhaps, or Leamington Spa. What providence of leadership, of geography, of political will, what desperate days of hungover young men staggering to their flimsy planes on all-grass airfields had so narrowly turned away the catastrophe? He shuddered as the November wind came gusting down the narrow street from St Martin's Lane.

★ ★ ★

In France Charlotte rose gently from the deepest levels of her sleep to find the reflected branches of the almost leafless chestnut tree undulating in watery shadow on the bare wall of her bedroom. Outside, the wind of autumn was hissing in the last dry leaves; the sound was not, despite anything the poet might have said, like sobbing violins, but like the muffled percussion of riveted cymbals.

Charlotte climbed out of bed, washed, dressed and went down the bare back stairs of the Domaine to the kitchen. The metal handles of the cupboard doors were cold to her touch; the large, flagged room held for the first time the prospect of winter. Charlotte was not displeased by it; after a Highland childhood she had never feared the rigours of the season, though she did wonder how a house the size of the Domaine was heated. She could light a fire in her bedroom in the evenings, and since Levade seldom emerged from his studio, a permanently stoked blaze in the large, marble-surrounded grate would do for him. The rest

287

of the unused rooms would have to be shut up and left to freeze.

That was her view, at any rate, and she would not be afraid to express it. Since arriving at the Domaine, she had learned that the quality Levade most seemed to value was frankness. His honesty about himself had prompted in her a reciprocal candour, and nothing would be gained by saying less than she meant. The only trick with Levade was to pick the right moment, not to trouble him when he was distracted by work.

When she heard his slippered footstep on the sprung floor of the dining room she made some tea and took it into him. His face was white, and there were grey smudges round the sockets of his eyes; his skin, she thought, was oddly expressive and changeable for someone of his age. His head hung still over the blue bowl of tea she placed in front of him, and she could sense the awful weight of sleeplessness suggested by his heavy movements. He would be better in an hour or so, when he had drunk more tea, smoked cigarettes and walked in the grounds of the house.

He lifted his head. 'I've been thinking, Madame Guilbert. I think perhaps we know each other well enough now, you and I, for you to come to my studio sometimes in the afternoon.'

Charlotte's reply was made incoherent by her surprise and by her uncertainty about what he wanted: she did not know whether Dominique Guilbert would thank him for the privilege, ask for more money or indignantly to refuse any such idea.

Levade smiled at her evident confusion. 'I just need a little help with tidying my papers to begin with. I suppose the room could do with cleaning as well. It must be two years since I let the last girl in there.'

'I see,' said Charlotte. 'That'll be fine.'

As she recovered her balance, Levade said, 'Of course there are other things you might help me with.'

Before Charlotte could discover what these might be, the telephone rang in the hall and Levade indicated by a nod of his head that she should answer it.

'Dominique!' It was Julien, in an excited state. 'They've done it. They've done it, they've broken through, they've overrun us, they've — '

'Julien, what are you — '

'Now it's all-out war. No more Pétain, no more deals, this is it. They're here in Lavaurette, they're everywhere.'

'Do you mean they've — '

'Yes, they poured through the line last night, whole divisions, they've taken over the entire country. They're heading down to the sea to protect the coast, but they're leaving their soldiers everywhere. We're going to have our own little German in charge. Come and see, Dominique. Come on.'

Charlotte ran back into the dining room to tell Levade, who shook his head and swore.

'I want to go to the village,' said Charlotte. 'Do you mind if I — '

'No, go on.'

In Lavaurette, everyone seemed to be on the street, murmuring in closed groups or looking in silent horror at the convoy of German motor vehicles that had pulled in along the side of the Avenue Gambetta. A small boy marched up and down in front of them with exaggerated goosesteps until rescued by his mother.

Charlotte found Julien surrounded by gesticulating people, who included two familiar to her from the Café du Centre — the quiet schoolmaster Claude Benech and Roudil, the veteran of Verdun who had placed his trust in the Marshal. For the first time since she had known him, Julien seemed to have lost control of himself; he was berating the other two men and pointing at the parked German lorries.

Charlotte knew with a panicky conviction that she

289

must stop him at once. She ran into the knot of people and grabbed his elbow; Julien glanced sideways at her, then carried on his tirade. He was shouting at Roudil, some insulting words about Pétain.

Charlotte took his arm again. 'Julien, you must come with me. You're needed at the Domaine. You must come now.' Julien looked at her once and pushed her hand away. Roudil's lined and weathered face had set horribly still; then his lower lip began to tremble, and large shameful tears rolled out from his closed eyes.

'As for you,' said Julien, turning to Benech. 'You — '

He got no further. Charlotte reached up to him and clamped her mouth over his. She wrapped her arms tight around him and squeezed as hard as she could. When she felt Julien's body slacken a little, she let go. With her lips still close to his, she said, 'You must come now. Your father needs you. Do you understand?'

Across Julien's gradually sobering face there ran successive expressions of surprise, alarm and furtive schoolboy pleasure. At least he understood, Charlotte thought, as he coughed, collected himself, and apologised briefly to Roudil, who was wiping his cheeks with a handkerchief. Julien and Charlotte walked up the hill, unspeaking, flinching beneath the curious eyes that followed them.

Two or three times Julien began to speak, then checked himself. 'I've been foolish, Dominique,' he finally brought himself to say. 'I must thank you for stopping me when you did.'

Up in the square, in front of the Hôtel de Ville, they sat on a bench and looked down. They could still see the German convoy, half a dozen troop-carrying lorries with canvas lashed over supporting hoops, an armoured car and a requisitioned black Citroën of the kind, Charlotte recalled, Monsieur Chollet had been working on in Clermont. German soldiers were sitting on the sandy roadside drinking from enamel cups while their junior officers went in search of provisions.

Charlotte watched Julien's face but did not dare to speak. He rested his chin in his hands, then shook his head.

'Perhaps this is a good thing, I don't know. Perhaps . . . ' He shrugged. 'At least it now means we're all in it together, there must now be a general, unified resistance . . . And yet, I just can't believe it — to see those men in uniform, those stupid farm boys and factory hands from Hanover or Bavaria or wherever it is they come from, here in Lavaurette . . . Somehow in Paris it seemed different. It was easier to think of it as diplomacy that had gone wrong and to see the German troops as just a new and rather impatient kind of police. You could see it all as just another political mistake — God knows, we'd got used to those. But here, they look so alien . . . ' He shook his head.

Charlotte felt very much for him in his confusion and in the frustrated sense he seemed to have that all of this could somehow have been avoided.

'We must be very careful, Octave,' she said.

'I know. And, by the way, you called me by a different name just now. When you kissed me.'

'I know. It would have been foolish to call you 'Octave' in front of people who know that's not your name.'

Julien looked at her, narrowing his eyes, not into their usual candid smile but into something more perplexed. 'You're a remarkable woman, aren't you, Madame Guilbert? Very decisive.'

'When I was sixteen I had a school report that said I was too passive.'

Julien let out a great snort of laughter. 'Passive! My God.'

'Anyway,' said Charlotte. 'Someone must take control in these circumstances.'

'I liked it when you kissed me.'

'It was nothing.'

'What do you mean?'

'It was political.'

Julien's full smile came out. 'I see. And it would take a comparable emergency for it to be repeated?'

'At least.'

There was a pause, and Julien looked down at the ground, sketching patterns in the dust with the rim of his shoe. He said, 'Do you remember when you first decided to stay, and you said you felt the real action had not begun?'

'Yes.'

'What do you feel now?'

'I feel this is it,' said Charlotte. 'But I don't feel downhearted. I think the enemy is now out in the open, and that's a good place for him to be — where you have him in full sight.'

Julien pulled a packet of cigarettes from his pocket and lit one. 'I know the Germans will try to squeeze us, they'll try to make us work for them in some way. And there'll be a war here in the south. Some people won't like that, they'll put the keeping of order above everything.'

'But you want to see fighting?'

'Of course I do. And you couldn't say we've been hasty. It's two and a half years since we were invaded.' He smiled. 'You look worried.'

'Yes,' said Charlotte. 'I was just thinking of all that quiet work you've done from your office — the times you've telephoned me at the Domaine or left a message with César's mother, all the calls from the wireless operator, the times you've spoken to the Communists — yes, don't look surprised, I know you've had no choice from time to time — and all this without once giving a glimmer of how you truly felt. I hate to think that all your work might be spoiled by one foolish outburst.'

'It's not true that I've given no indication of what I think. I was always honest about the failings of Vichy. Then, when I started this activity I thought it would look suspicious if I suddenly changed my tune. So it's become a double bluff.'

'But you've got to do something about this morning. That was too much.'

Julien laid his hand on hers. 'You're right. I shall go to the Café du Centre this evening and I shall confuse them. I'll say that on balance we have no choice but to co-operate with the Germans. I shall use the word 'realistic'.'

'Good.'

'Why don't you come too?' Julien looked into Charlotte's face.

'Servant girls don't go out to bars. And I'm a married woman.'

'I know, but after this morning everyone will think we're sleeping together anyway.'

'So are you saying we might as well?'

'No, I didn't say that, I — '

'Listen, Julien — I'm going to call you that this one time. You're a wonderful friend to me. I've never had a friend like this before. I can't tell you how much it's meant to me over these last few weeks. It's not just that we're co-operating professionally, as it were, we'd be friends anyway. Don't you feel that?' Charlotte's voice was eager and loaded.

'Yes.' Julien did not sound nearly as sure. 'Yes, of course, Dominique.'

Then why does he look so hurt? Charlotte thought, as she removed his hand from hers and gave it back to him. She said, 'I must go back to the Domaine. I have work to do. Will you telephone this evening and let me know if anything happens?'

Charlotte walked down to where she had left her bicycle, outside Madame Galliot's ironmongery, and on the way she went past the war memorial and its chiselled Marianne, with her seasick expression and her eyes dazzled by the list of names on which she stood. On the Avenue Gambetta the German lorries had started their engines and were beginning to move off in a loud, fuming line to the south.

★ ★ ★

Claude Benech was puzzled by developments. He had not expected to see German soldiers on the streets of Lavaurette. Their presence suggested either that the Occupier felt at liberty to override Marshal Pétain at any time it suited him or that there was a threat of Allied success to the south that made defence of the French ports imperative. He could believe neither of these possibilities. Of one thing he was quite sure, however: the German occupation of the whole country increased the chances of Communist disorder. There would be hotheads, like Julien Levade perhaps, and other more sinister Bolshevists, who would try to turn this new development to the advantage of their long-held wish to undermine the traditional France. Benech had thought a good deal about politics in the last year or so, and had grown quite confident of his analyses and predictions. If he was right, it would mean that a man such as himself, a patriot, would need to become firmer and more vigilant. Of course, that did not mean he had to be ponderous or crude: he would carry on as normal, and what could be more normal than a visit to the Café du Centre?

Irène Galliot greeted him with her minimal politeness as she swayed through the bar on her way to the dining room. Benech's eyes hung on the sight of her tightly-skirted rump as she smacked the swing doors open with her hip, bending a little forward to keep the four plates of food she carried away from her clean white blouse and, in doing so, inadvertently granting Benech a glimpse of her smooth cleavage, whose shadow was abbreviated by a prim yet suggestive line of white lace. Then she was gone, and Benech turned sadly back to the bar, where Gayral pushed over his drink.

The wireless was playing on a high shelf, a song of inappropriate frivolity about an absconding postman.

Benech inveigled himself into a conversation with a group of other men, who included Roudil and Julien Levade. Their talk was soft and depressed. Benech noticed how solicitious Julien was towards Roudil, bringing him coffee from the bar and inquiring about his building business.

The quiet mood of the room was violently interrupted by the sound of Marshal Pétain on the wireless, swiftly turned to maximum volume by Gayral.

The dozen people in the bar stopped what they were doing to listen to the old man's girlish voice with its dry, hesitant cough. Drinks were held half-way from the table. Irène Galliot froze in the doorway with a pile of empty plates. Roudil's ancient eyes looked up imploringly to the wireless as though he might actually see the face of the great soldier who had understood the plight of men such as himself in the furnace of Verdun, who had been their saviour then.

At the end of his hopeful, patriotic and unapologetic address, Pétain played the Marseillaise. The sound of the reluctant, rumbling march filled Benech with a cool certainty. Roudil, he noticed, covered his face with his hands. The emotions provoked by the music were evidently powerful: even Julien Levade appeared to be struggling to contain some turbulent inner conflict.

2

Once a week, after she had cleared breakfast and seen Levade safely into his studio, Charlotte took over the bathroom for the morning. The wood-burning stove that heated the water generally did so well enough for one deep bath, in which she washed her hair with a powerful concoction from the recesses of Madame Galliot's shop.

As she lay in the water, Charlotte tried to prepare herself for what Mirabel might say to her. Until the Germans arrived her existence, apart from visits to André and Jacob, had been free from risk. Presumably that would now change; she would have to see what Mirabel thought. He had cancelled their first meeting some weeks earlier, but, according to Julien, was more insistent than ever that they meet this time. Perhaps he would order her to return home, and she would plead with him that she could still be useful in France. Even if he insisted, it was still open to her to refuse: she could simply not turn up at the appointed time for the plane. It would mean that G Section would disown and dismiss her, but she had no long-term ambitions with them. It was not as if she would be in any more danger, because they could offer her no protection in France anyway. What they would not like about it was the thought of what she knew and that the longer she was there the more possible it was that she would be caught and interrogated. The German presence in the Free Zone made it more likely, but the truth was that she had little to tell. G Section's tactic of minimum information had worked well: she did not know Mirabel's assumed name, his real name or where to find him. She thought she could convince him that for the time being, at least, she was more of an asset than a risk. What excited her about the rendezvous was her hope, amounting almost to a belief that Mirabel, with his superior connections, would know where Gregory was hiding.

When she had roughly dried her hair, she set about re-dyeing the roots, where the natural colours were starting to show through. She wore gloves to protect her hands and worked the dye in with a paint brush borrowed from Levade's studio. She was two thirds of the way through Antoinette's bottle; as she upended it into her gloved palm, she thought of the steamy shop and wondered how Antoinette was managing up in the rainy mountains with Gilberte and her fortnightly visitor from Clermont-Ferrand.

Charlotte peered into the blue-framed mirror above the basin and saw the reflection of her anxious brown eyes. She smiled at herself, instinctively turning to a better angle beneath the harsh light.

There were days when she scarcely thought of Peter Gregory, days when she convinced herself that he did not exist and that her memory of him was false; yet she still believed that only she could give him back his life and that only he could plausibly join her future to her past. She had had time to inspect the feeling from every angle, to imagine, even wish for, its diminution, but while her mind offered many choices about emotions and their value — how much they should be honoured, how much resisted, how changeable they could be, how naturally mortal — her intellectual conviction remained stable. Now she was going to find him.

As she stood, naked from the waist up, inspecting herself in the mirror, Charlotte was stirred from her reverie by the sudden conviction that someone was watching her. Covering herself with a towel, she grabbed the door of the little bathroom and pulled it open. The corridor was empty.

That afternoon, her dulled hair wrapped beneath a scarf, she was sweeping the long corridor of the first floor when the door to Levade's studio swung open.

'Madame Guilbert? Would you care to come in for a moment?'

Charlotte followed him into the studio, broom in hand.

'What do you think of that?' said Levade, indicating the canvas on the easel. There was a picture of a woman in a green silk skirt whom Charlotte recognised as his model, Anne-Marie. He had caught her expression of slightly timid seriousness; he had made her look like an intellectual person, a teacher or philosopher, yet had depicted her bare-breasted in a green silk skirt and set her in an imagined room whose dimensions were surreal.

'It's wonderful,' said Charlotte. She did not think it wonderful, though she recognised it as the work of someone who was good at what he did.

'What do you like about it?' Levade stood with his arms crossed. He was for once wearing shoes, and had a jacket over his habitual untucked shirt.

'I just like the girl. Anne-Marie. I like the way you've painted her.'

'The likeness?' It was difficult to see how he managed to load the simple word with intense scorn.

'I'm afraid so. Look at her pale skin. And the way her eyes are almond-shaped yet not narrow, the centre so large and open. It's beautiful. I've never seen that in a woman before.'

Levade sighed. 'What about the skin?'

'It's lovely. The paleness. But not white or deathly — it still looks healthy.'

Levade gazed at the picture in silence. 'It's no good at all,' he said. He went over to a small circular table and lit a cigarette. 'As a matter of fact, I don't care. Anne-Marie is merely an exercise for me. There's something of her I'm trying to get right. Do you know what it is?'

Charlotte looked at the painting again. There was no doubt that the eye was drawn, willingly or otherwise, to Anne-Marie's breasts, whose exposure was the more obvious for the background against which the figure was set.

'It's her arms,' said Levade. 'The skin on her arms. That's why I asked her to be my model. She was working in a café not far from here, and I stopped there one day last year. It was summer and her arms were bare. She leaned across me to put down a plate and I was transfixed by the colour and texture of them.' He shook his head and flicked the ash of his cigarette on to the floor, then went and stood in front of a small table on which were some religious statues and a candle.

He gazed back at the painting with an expression of resigned distaste.

'The arms are very good,' said Charlotte. 'But perhaps one's eye is drawn away from them too much.'

'Does it worry you, the nudity? Even after so many statues and classical models? After Michelangelo and Ingres and — '

'I don't really think it's that kind of picture.'

'You think it's lascivious?'

'Not completely, because there are other things happening. But a little bit, yes.'

'Put that broom down.' Levade walked over to the window and gazed up at the thick woods that fringed the gardens to the north. His lined face looked older than his lean body in the mild, clear light of the afternoon.

'Sit down.' He thrust his arm towards the bed, and Charlotte perched herself, trying to look relaxed. Levade stayed standing by the window. She watched his half-turned face carefully: the thudding artery in the neck, the wizened Adam's apple dragging up between the flaps of skin on his throat as he spoke again.

'Have you heard any news of your husband?'

Charlotte felt repelled by Levade, but reluctant to admit that her repulsion was not absolute. 'No. Nothing.'

'Do you love him? Do you miss him?'

'No. There's another man I love.'

'What's his name?'

'Pierre.'

Levade turned into the room. 'Tell me about him.'

Charlotte hesitated for a second, but the temptation was too great. It occurred to her as she spoke how long she had carried the unshared weight of her feeling for Gregory; her waking and many of her sleeping hours had been filled with this sullen, secret ache. As she started to find words, the feelings formed themselves and rushed in through her abandoned discretion. She felt the emotions surge up and animate her movements; her hands were clawing at the air, rotating, and there was a flush rising in her neck, creeping over her jaw. In the most emotional moments of the story she still watched Levade's eyes, to see if he was listening, and she saw that his head did not move, that his eyes did not leave her, and she felt the radiance of his interest.

She was shocked when he said, 'I don't believe you.'

'What do you mean?'

'Oh, I believe the pain and the passion, but I don't believe this Pierre is a — what was it, airman from Rennes. I think he's English, as are you, Madame.'

Charlotte swallowed and looked down to her hands, now stilled and resting in her lap. 'Does it matter?' she said.

Levade pursed his lips and shook his head. 'Not in the least. The rest of the story is true, I imagine.'

'I came to France to find him. Everything I told you about how much I miss him, how I fear for his life — all the feelings of love I described, all those are true.'

'I don't think someone could invent those, Madame Guilbert. Shall I continue to call you that?'

Charlotte sighed. 'You may as well call me Dominique.'

'But why? Why another false name? It's no better than Madame Guilbert.'

'But even Julien only calls me Dominique.'

'It would be our secret, the sign of our confidence. If you wish.' He turned his back to her again and looked out of the window.

There was a long silence, which Charlotte was surprised to hear broken at last by the sound of her own voice. 'Charlotte.'

'Charlotte.'

She nodded. It was the first time she had heard her name for many weeks, and its intimacy was tender.

'And this Pierre,' said Levade, clearing papers from an armchair so he could sit in it. 'Did you make love many times? Did it surprise you?'

'Yes. I didn't realise it was like that. There didn't seem to be enough hours in the day. When I thought it was finished, even when he was saying goodbye it would begin again. He couldn't leave the flat, he would sink to his knees and start to pull at my clothes, and I was desperate, as though we hadn't been doing it all day, as though we'd never done it before. It was terrible. I didn't know if other people also . . . whether . . . '

Levade said nothing. Charlotte had a sudden fear that instead of sympathising with her anguish he was, in a voyeuristic way, enjoying the thought of her making love to Gregory.

She looked down at her lap, then up at him again. It was too late to withdraw her trust. 'I was frightened. I was really frightened. I wanted to devour him in some

way. Yet my feeling for him was so gentle. I so much
wanted to help him, to bring him back to health and
life, to undo all the harm that had been done to him.
What we did was awful, wonderful — I don't know
what you'd call it. But that wasn't why I came here
to find him. I came because I loved him, because the
feeling was . . . transcendent.'

'And he spoke to some weakness in you.'

'Of course he did. Why should I be ashamed of that?
Not every woman would have felt what I felt. I'm sure
it was my weaknesses and faults, my own wounds he
touched. That's why I so passionately loved him. That's
why I can't let go, because I believe there's no one else
who could do that.'

Levade breathed out a long, quiet sigh, which gave
no indication of what he thought. He watched Charlotte
as she struggled to control her agitation. She looked up,
red-eyed and resentful at his detachment.

'Don't you have anything to say?'

'Yes. Tell me how you thought it would end. What
did you imagine your lives would become? Did you
think you would stay together until one of you died?
That he would never be able to leave the house until
you had made love one more time? That your passion
would dwindle into some companionable friendship?'

'None of these things. It was enough to be with him,
to have his company. It was almost enough that he was
alive, even if I was not with him.'

'And you truly never thought about a future?'

'I never did. Though I admit that may have been
because I wouldn't let myself. A wise woman doesn't
indulge such fantasies about a fighter pilot in a war.'

'And you're a wise woman.'

She did not hear if there was a question in his
voice.

'I doubt it,' she said.

'Are you wise enough to know that the problems of

lovers seem to everyone else in the world, especially to their friends, like comic self-indulgence, like the antics of fretful children?'

'Yes, I suppose I do know that.' Charlotte's voice was grudging. 'But listen. If at the one moment in your life when the chance of something transcendental is offered to you, if you have this chance to move beyond the surface of things, to understand — and you say, No, maybe not, it's just a bore to my friends. What then? How do you explain the rest of your life to yourself? How do you pass the time until you die?' Charlotte was flushed and excited. 'Do you substitute for that an interest in what — eating? Do you spend the next sixty years trying to be fascinated by the act of breathing?'

Levade smiled as he stood up and crossed to the table where he had left his cigarettes. 'The lifelong love that young romantic Frenchwomen dream about — and perhaps most English girls as well, though maybe not you — that ideal they think so unattainable is in fact rather commonplace. I know hundreds of men and women who loved each other all their lives and died in that same condition. The feelings you describe are more unusual.'

'What do you mean?'

'The passion, that thing people call 'merely physical', is perhaps rarer than what they refer to as lasting love. Rarer, and therefore perhaps more valuable.'

'But it wasn't just that, it was more, it was — '

'Of course it was. That's the difficulty.'

Charlotte felt Levade was on her side, but still she resented it.

'I suppose you have a long experience of all these things,' she said.

'Long and sinful,' he said, pushing his hand through his hair. 'I came here to escape from it.'

He had moved across to the bed, where he sat down, at the other end from Charlotte. He turned to face her.

'I lived in Paris. Most of my life I lived there. I suppose we were all trying to forget what we had seen.'

'Seen where?'

'In the War.'

The features of her own father came up brightly in Charlotte's mind, and she turned her eyes away from Levade's old, knowing face. She did not want to hear him, and the word that had stopped her ears was 'War'.

There was something that revolted her. She would not confront it. She watched Levade's lips moving, heard his thin voice, weighted with grotesque experience and the awful compromises that he must have made, but she did not take in what he said. Words like Verdun, generation of my friends, slid off her mind like mercury running over polished glass. Only when Levade began to talk about his life in Paris, after the war, did the meaning of what he said begin to bite and register.

He appeared to be saying that he and his friends had indulged themselves because their faith in civilisation had been torn up and ploughed into the septic mud of the Western Front: they did what they liked because none of it amounted to anything. It seemed that what Levade was telling her, in his oblique way, was that he had become obsessed by women and been able to indulge himself without any practical or philosophical reserve.

'At the time of its peak it had become a compulsion. I remember in a butcher's queue in the rue des Acacias seeing a young woman standing behind me waiting to be served. She had a pinkness in the skin of her face I hadn't seen before. I couldn't drag my eyes from her. It was an area of such delicate colour that I had to have her, to touch her. I followed her home.'

'Did you sleep with her?'

'Yes. I can remember nothing else about her, whether

304

she was tall or short, fat or thin, only that pink skin.'

'Was it that easy to persuade her?'

'Yes. It always was. If you asked. If you could be bothered to try. It was these details of women that drew me to them. Sometimes it was a particular woman, sometimes I felt this passion for the entire sex. I would see a girl in a restaurant and the line of her thigh beneath her skirt would be enough. The fall of hair on a woman's forehead, the set of dark brown eyes.'

There was something almost chaste in the fervour with which Levade spoke; his gaze was fixed on the far wall, over Charlotte's shoulder.

'Did you fall in love with all these different women?'

He looked back to her face. 'That's not a phrase I ever used. What I felt was more pressing, more urgent than what I take that expression to mean.'

'But were none of these women different from the others? Didn't you form a lasting attachment to any of them?'

'The question of endurance wasn't important. What I had found was a kind of paradise, an attainable paradise. I had to see how it would end.'

'Did it make you happy?' Charlotte found that curiosity kept any edge of surprise or disapproval from her voice.

'Yes. For a while.' For the first time in their conversation Levade appeared to smile; at least his mouth expanded and rose at the corners before falling. He got off the bed and straightened his back a little stiffly.

'I understand your anguish, Madame. Everyone in your position thinks there is some uniquely unfair, tormenting aspect to her dilemma. For you it is the fact that in time of war so many men die. It seems selfish of you to worry about your Pierre — and you can't tell people about him. But, secretly, you believe that you love him more than any other woman loves

305

her missing lover. Don't you?'

'I wouldn't say that.'

'You're not allowed to say that, but that's what you think. If only this, if only that. If only the one you loved didn't live so far away. The married man who has fallen in love with a young girl can't tell his wife, his greatest confidante, and he can't tell his friends because they might disapprove. It's so unfair, he thinks. But every one of these situations has its own particular unfairness.'

'There's something else that troubles me,' said Charlotte. 'It's the shortness of the time we had together — only a few weeks. Can something valid have come from that?'

Levade shook his head. 'You worry that he won't want you if you meet again?'

'Some days I do. He had to learn French to come here. He had to go to lessons with some French woman in London, and he used to make me speak French to him, too, so he could practise.'

'You think he used you just to learn the language so he could go on this new assignment?'

'Sometimes I think that. He wanted this assignment because he wanted danger. I think he wanted to die.'

Levade was strolling round the studio. He picked up a book from the table and began to flick through the pages.

'We did discuss it once,' said Charlotte, 'the question of his learning French. But the terrible thing is I can't remember what he said. I've tried and tried but I just can't remember.'

'I think perhaps you should try not to think about that.'

Charlotte thought Levade's voice had lost its priestly tone and regained a note of sympathy. She looked up to where he had taken his position in front of the easel;

he had started to scrape a little area of paint with a palette knife.

Charlotte found herself once more gazing at Anne-Marie's breasts.

'Would you like to pose for me one day, do you think?'

Despite her misgivings, Charlotte was flattered. 'Do you mean like that?' She pointed to Anne-Marie.

'I don't know. I hadn't thought about it. Probably not.'

'Well, maybe. Let's see.'

She was relieved, but also a little affronted. What's wrong with my breasts? she found herself thinking. They could not be more beautiful than Anne-Marie's, it was true, but Gregory had always said that . . .

Levade suddenly turned and strode across the room to where a dozen paintings were leaning against the wall. He pulled one out and thrust it into Charlotte's hands. 'Look at that.'

★ ★ ★

Following directions from Julien, Charlotte met Mirabel in an old white stone farmhouse, an hour's bicycle ride from Lavaurette. At the end of the track that led to it was a roadside calvary turned green with moss and lichen; along the rutted way were the mashed leaves and rotting fruit of an overhanging horse chestnut.

The house was bare, with a vast white marble staircase rising from the hall to a straight single passageway above, off which opened half a dozen large rooms, each with bare boards and distempered plaster.

Mirabel showed Charlotte to the last room on the right, in which were two boat beds. As she walked in, her echoing footsteps told Charlotte that the floor was the ceiling of the room below.

In English, with a slight Midlands accent, Mirabel

said, 'Welcome, Danièle. It's nice to see a friendly face. Sit yourself down.'

Charlotte perched with her knees together on the edge of the bed. Mirabel walked round the room. He was a tall man with curly, light brown hair (almost a case for dyeing, Charlotte thought) and a worried expression. He was wearing corduroy trousers and a workman's blue canvas jacket. He had an enormously broad back, yet delicate fingers, she noticed, with which he made soft gestures as he spoke.

'Now I'm not sure exactly what your plans are, but I've been asked to pass on a request. I'm sorry I couldn't meet you before. I was unavoidably detained.' Mirabel coughed. 'To put it more bluntly, it was bloody dangerous. I had to get out.'

'If it's about going back, I — '

'Hang on. Listen to me.'

There was something masterful about him, but he seemed preoccupied — presumably with the cares of his position. He also seemed nervous.

'I think they're on to us again,' he said.

'Who? The Germans?'

'No. Some crazed French group.'

He looked out of the window for a moment, then seemed to collect himself.

'How good is your French?' he said.

'I can pass for French. For a while. Or on the telephone.'

'It'd be all right for a brief message then?'

'Certainly.'

Mirabel did not speak. He walked around a little more. Charlotte said conversationally, 'What about you?'

'What?'

'Your French.'

'I'm bilingual. Like most of us. My mother was French.'

308

Mirabel was standing by the window, looking over a fallen tree in the garden. Eventually he said, 'You're looking for someone, aren't you?'

'What do you mean?'

'Exactly that. You have another reason for being here.'

Charlotte was sufficiently alarmed to remember her training. Minimum information. 'No,' she said. 'I have no other purpose.' It occurred to her that she had no way of knowing if this Mirabel was who he said he was: it was Julien who had told her where to come, and although she was sure of Julien, it was possible that this man was not the real Mirabel. After all, if he was bilingual, why might he not be French, a Vichy policeman, with one English parent from whom he had learned the language, right down to the slight Midlands accent?

Mirabel looked at her with a weary and slightly superior smile on his face. 'All right. Read this.' He gave Charlotte a piece of paper on which was scribbled a single name and a street address; beneath them were a map reference, a date and a time.

Charlotte looked up. Mirabel said, 'Can you memorise that?'

'I already have.'

'The address is in Limoges. I want you to go there. Ask for the name. Then give him the other details. It's one of ours. It's details of a drop. You must say that you were sent by Frédéric. Got that? It's very important. Otherwise they won't believe you. Frédéric.'

'That's it?'

'That's all.'

'Well, that's easy enough.'

Mirabel looked at Charlotte suspiciously. 'Don't you want anything . . . I mean, can I help you at all?'

'No, it looks quite straightforward.'

Charlotte thought for a moment. 'I thought you were

going to order me home.'

'Why would I do that?'

'Because I didn't take my plane. I'm not supposed to be here any more.'

'I don't know anything about that. In any case, we need all the people we can get.'

'Will you tell them that? Tell the people in London that you need me?'

'I'll see. But in return I want you not to speak to anyone about what I've just asked you. Don't mention it to Octave.'

'Why not?'

'Just don't.' Mirabel's voice was loud in the bare room. He controlled himself. 'Then I might have news for you. About the person you're looking for. We should keep in touch.'

Charlotte breathed in deeply to still the hammering in her chest. She said quietly, 'I don't know how to reach you.'

'Don't worry about that,' said Mirabel. 'You deliver the message safe and sound and I'll be back in touch with you.'

Charlotte knew she should say nothing, but could not stop herself. In a quiet voice she said, 'Do you really know where he is?'

Mirabel looked her in the eye. 'Yes, love,' he said. 'I know where he is.'

3

'Good morning, Mademoiselle Bobotte. You're looking very well. Getting some early nights for a change, I dare say.' Julien Levade moved briskly across the hallway, inhaling the familiar smell of tobacco and wood polish which today had a new element, possibly of lavender, though less a woman's scent than the kind of vigorous alcohol a man might rub into his flayed pores after shaving.

'Coffee, Monsieur Levade?'

'Is that what you call it? If you insist.' Julien was safely round the bend in the stairs.

He sat at his desk and looked over the cobbled courtyard to the street door. Some fat Nazi squatted like a brooding toad in the best house in Lavaurette, requisitioned for the purpose; his country was in ruins, invaded from without, betrayed from within; his work was temporarily stalled for lack of funds; yet he felt an optimistic tremor as he looked across to where the low winter sun struck into the windows of the apartment building opposite.

He opened the half-dozen letters waiting on his desk, hung up his jacket behind the door and went over to his drawing board. He was satisfied that his conversion would work, though who would stay in this hotel, what nationality they would be and when it would open for business he had no idea. It was not like the numberless hôtels du Parc, du Lion d'Or or des Voyageurs, with their gold letters on black marble nameplates, their fusty dining rooms, swirling cress soup and long damp corridors of failed plumbing and doubtful assignations: it would be bold and simple; it would glory in the stripped-down elements of which it was made, and there would be no attempt to smother the stone flags with hectares of hatched parquet, to box in the beams and cover the ceiling with flowered paper. The walls would be whitewashed, the furniture plain, though he hoped the richness of the textiles and the efficiency of the heating system he had planned, the great boiler sunk into a former solitary cell below ground, would take away any lingering air of the penitential.

It would open, perhaps, in 1946. The mayor of Lavaurette would come, and there would be a party from Paris as well, the senior men in the parent company and their wives. On the first evening there would be speeches; the builders would be thanked and there would be a toast to the former abbot, driven up for the day from the old people's home. Julien would be in his dinner jacket, moving among the guests, modestly declining their congratulations; he would now be living back in Paris, with Weil, his old boss, reinstated at the head of the company. Weil's French citizenship, which had been revoked by Vichy, would naturally have been restored by the righteous and democratic government that followed.

Julien gazed at the floor plan of the bedrooms. Drawing was the part he liked best. The finished building was not worse, necessarily, than the plan, but it was always different; between the idea and the achieved reality the process of construction made a contribution of its own, so that what emerged invariably lacked the magnificent, beguiling, complex purity of the idea.

Poor Weil, Julien thought: how he had loved his work and his life in the city. He could picture him vividly, with his fair hair, and his quick eyes lighting up a fraction before his companion's at some irony, some gossip he had picked up at lunch in one of the restaurants he patronised on the Boulevard de Montparnasse. How proud he was — though silently: he would have thought it trite to say so — of being

French; how much he valued strolling through the sumptuous capital and its self-advertising landmarks of enlightenment — the Place de la Concorde, the Boulevard de la République. Now he was stripped of his job and his assets, forced to report daily to some surly prefect in the sixth arrondissement, and to wear on the lapel of his prized camel overcoat a cloth yellow star decorated with the word 'Jew'.

Julien was sure it would eventually be all right for men such as Weil. How could it not be? They must be patient; they must wait for the English and the Americans and for people such as himself who would clear a path for the friendly invaders.

There was a knock at the door, and Pauline Bobotte came in with the small white china cup of coffee.

She lingered by the desk. Julien looked up at her powdery pink face, framed by the chestnut-coloured hair she wore clipped close to her head in shiny waves. She ran a finger along the edge of Julien's desk.

'So, Monsieur Levade. The enemy is at the gate.'

'He's in the house, Mademoiselle Bobotte. He's been there for a long time, if only you had eyes to see.'

'Oh, I have eyes all right. I have eyes in the back of my head, my mother used to say.' She gave a small laugh. 'Nothing passes me by, I promise you.'

'I'm sure it doesn't, Mademoiselle Bobotte. You're a marvel. They say you can speak to three people at once on your telephone exchange.'

'People exaggerate.' Pauline Bobotte looked pleased. 'But they do tell me you've found a new lady love. Your father's servant-girl — if that's the right word.'

'Oh, do they? I wonder why they say that.' Julien had expected some comment and wanted to find out the current state of gossip.

'Apparently she kissed you, right out in front of a crowd, the day the Germans came.'

'The emotion of the moment, I imagine, Mademoiselle.

We were all a little distraught. I expect she wanted reassurance.'

'Reassurance! That's a funny word for it. They said you looked as pleased as anything.'

'Politeness, mere politeness, I assure you. One does one's best in these circumstances.'

'Anyway, I thought you had a fiancée in Paris, Monsieur Levade.'

'Oh, did you? I thought it was Lyon. You should really ask Pauline Benoit. She seems to know more about my personal life than I do.'

Pauline Bobotte pouted at the mention of the other Pauline. 'Anyway,' she said, 'you'd better be careful if you're going to carry on with a maid like that. People will talk.'

' 'People'?' said Julien. 'Well, you'd better go and stop these 'people', Mademoiselle Bobotte. Unless by doing so you think you might become one of them. Madame Guilbert is a married woman whose brave husband was taken prisoner in May 1940 and is being held by the enemy. She's utterly devoted to him. It would be not only immoral but quite unpatriotic of me to harbour any sort of amorous intention towards her. I see my role as protective.'

Pauline Bobotte grunted. 'She's pretty, though.'

'Is she? I suppose in a way she's elegant. For a servant-girl. I hadn't really noticed.'

'So why were you kissing her?'

'I didn't kiss her. She kissed me. I told you. She was overwrought.'

'But why should she — '

'Enough, Bobotte! Back to your switchboard, please. I have important work to do.' Julien handed her his empty cup, and Pauline Bobotte made her way unhappily to the door, where she paused as though to speak again but was forestalled by the sound of the telephone downstairs.

'Oh, Dominique,' said Julien out loud when she had gone. 'What am I going to do about you?'

He put his feet up on the desk and started to indulge a fantasy in which he contrived to invite Dominique to spend a night at the hotel with him before it opened. They would go to the largest room at the end of the western elevation, the one with the view down towards the river. The bed was unslept in, the sheets were of linen and new from their brown paper packing; the bath had never been filled. The bathroom itself was fragrant with the scent of gardenia, and the fixtures and taps were boldly modern, all chrome with porcelain insets. He would have ordered new clothes for her from Paris — a skirt, a suit perhaps, which he would help her on with. In the long intimacy of the night he would go beneath the layers of her acquired identities to find the English girl, and discover what it was that moved her, what it was that filled her eyes with that earnest and entrancing light.

★ ★ ★

At lunch-time Julien went to see the Duguay boys. Mlle Cariteau ushered him into the kitchen and poured him a glass of wine; her manner was as brisk and assured as usual, but her eyes were worried.

'I don't like to let the boys downstairs at all now,' she said. 'It's very hard on them being shut up on the second floor, but I just can't take the chance. I've asked Maman to spend more time with them while I'm at work so they don't get lonely.'

Julien found André and Jacob in a small bedroom at the back of the house. 'I've brought something for you,' he said. 'I got them in a second-hand shop in a town I went to the other day. I hope you like them.'

From his pocket he produced six lead soldiers whose bright Napoleonic uniforms were starting to flake away.

315

The boys grasped them eagerly. Julien fought a prim urge to tell them that they should say thank you. Then he saw the excitement in their eyes and remembered that they had probably not seen a toy since leaving their parents' house. Jacob had difficulty in making one of his soldiers stand up; it was a useless figure locked into some ceremonial salute and the base was warped. Jacob nevertheless chuckled with pleasure. André's response was more equivocal; he was annoyed that the sword had broken from one of his men and said he could not make much of an army with only three soldiers.

Julien remembered André's old lightness, the way he had skipped everywhere, and saw that he had lost it. He had become a sullen little boy; his clothes were getting too small for him and his hair hung down into his eyes. He seemed dissatisfied and to be looking for reasons to complain. Then, when Julien was at the door, on his way out, André suddenly began to leap up and down by his side, grabbing his arm, saying, 'Thank you, thank you,' and barking like a dog.

Back in the kitchen, Julien found Sylvie Cariteau preparing to return to the post-office.

'They seem all right, don't they?' he said.

'As well as they can be.'

'Listen, Sylvie, you do understand, don't you, how things have changed? When André and Jacob first came here, you could have given any number of excuses to the gendarmerie, who'd probably have connived with you anyway. Now it's different. They're taking Jews from everywhere, foreign, French, it doesn't matter. The Government is trying to bargain with the quotas, but they're co-operating. Now you're running a real risk. If they find André and Jacob they'll punish you too.'

'I know,' said Sylvie. 'But I can't turn them out now. It's Maman I worry about more. She doesn't really understand.'

'But is she safe? She won't tell?'

'No, I don't think so. I've tried to make it clear to her. And she's become fond of the boys. One thing I don't understand, Julien. Where do they take these people?'

'They go to Paris first, where they're put on trains.'

'Trains?'

'Yes. To Poland, I've been told.'

'And what happens there?'

'In theory they work. They put them in work camps.'

'In theory?'

'In fact . . . If they wanted them to work they would send them to Germany, not Poland. I don't know. There are rumours. These people are not like us.'

* * *

On his way back to his office, Julien came across Claude Benech on the Avenue Gambetta. He hesitated for a moment, then remembered the promise of duplicity he had made to Charlotte and held out his hand in greeting. Benech took it briefly and hurried on.

Benech would have rather not met Julien Levade at this moment; he was on his way to an assignation, and although it was perfectly proper, he didn't want to be questioned about his movements.

A couple of days earlier he had received a cyclostyled letter beginning 'Dear Patriot' beneath the double-headed axe of Vichy and the triple motto of Work, Family and Fatherland. It invited him to present himself at an address in a back street of Lavaurette where he could learn of an opportunity to serve his country. A minute or so before two o'clock Benech knocked at a thin blue door in a dark street optimistically called the rue des Rosiers. No

317

rose bush had forced its way up here for many years, Benech thought as he waited for an answer; it was an area of the village, between the garage and the factory, that he barely knew.

The door opened on to a gloomy hallway with a circular table at the foot of the stairs on which a black telephone was ringing. Whoever had opened the door was standing behind it in order to let Benech pass, and it was not until he was standing inside that he turned and saw a large man wearing a shiny, padded leather jacket with a cigarette in the corner of his mouth. The man led the way up the stairs, ignoring the raucous telephone. The room at the front of the house was bare except for a large deal table, spotted with white paint, and three hard chairs. The shutters were closed and the room was lit by an electric bulb that hung from the ceiling. In its light Benech could see the other man more clearly: he was in his middle thirties, with black curly hair, sideburns and thick eyebrows. He was solidly made but was starting to run to fat; his belly turned the buckle of his belt half way down towards the floor: he looked like someone who had been a footballer or boxer, and then let go.

'You can call me Clovis.' His tongue whistled on the final consonant; his accent was from the south-east. 'You're Monsieur Benech?'

Benech nodded. He felt a little unsure of this man. He had expected something more formal — flags, a uniform — and he was not certain that the Director of his school would approve of his being there. The telephone rang on doggedly downstairs.

Clovis lit another cigarette and pushed the packet across the table to Benech, who shook his head.

'I'm touring round the area to recruit for an organisation,' Clovis began. 'It's due to be launched officially in January, so there's no time to lose. This is a political party, but I'm not concerned with politics.

318

I'm looking for volunteers for the security force that will go with it. The aim of the force is to maintain order while political reform goes through.'

Benech licked his lips. 'I'm not sure. I don't want to belong to anything that's not part of the Marshal's vision of France.'

Clovis laughed, the deep, companionable sound Benech had often heard and envied among the men in the Café du Centre. 'There's no need to worry, Monsieur, this is a particular project of Monsieur Laval himself. He's to be the president of the organisation.'

Benech sat forward in his chair. 'Really?'

'Absolutely. The party will aim to unify all the different patriotic groups in the country. The security organisation will be open to all volunteers. It will have a youth section for boys and girls. But what I'm talking about are permanent staff, people we can rely on.'

Clovis was cleverer than he looked, Benech thought. Perhaps he could forgive the informality of his reception if this scheme had emanated from Vichy, from the brain of Monsieur Laval, and with the blessing therefore of the Marshal himself.

' . . . just a couple of questions about your beliefs. They're bound to ask you,' Clovis was saying. 'Who is the most serious enemy of the true France?'

'The Communists,' said Benech ' . . . and the English,' he added quickly, fearing that his first answer might not have been correct.

Clovis nodded and smiled. He pushed a piece of paper across the table. 'Read this. It's the oath of allegiance you'll be required to take.'

Benech read: 'I swear to fight against democracy, against Gaullist insurrection and against Jewish leprosy . . . ' It was phrased a little more strongly than he would have liked, but it was in essence the oath he had waited for all his life.

'It's fine.'

As Clovis raised his hand to his face to pull the cigarette from his lips, Benech noticed the numerous nicks and scars on his huge, thick fingers; there was something both soothing and stimulating about this man, he felt.

Clovis put his hand into a drawer above his thighs. Such was the size of his grasp that Benech did not see what he had taken out and laid on the table until he removed his hand with a flourish.

'Have you ever used one of these?'

Having been excused by reason of his asthma from military service, Benech had neither used, nor even previously seen from close quarters, a handgun. The packed, stubby handle and the long, gleaming barrel, sent a frisson through him; he felt something starting to be explained, some longheld injustice beginning at last to be put right.

'If you prove your worth, if you do what you're told, you'll get one of these,' said Clovis. 'You're lucky. Most of the volunteers are being told to stuff their holsters with paper. You'll get a uniform as well — khaki shirt, black tie and beret. You provide dark blue trousers and jacket. Do you want to hear more?'

The telephone in the hallway stopped ringing and it was suddenly quiet in the room. Benech felt Clovis's powerful, mocking eyes on him and knew that such an opportunity might never come to him again.

'Yes,' he said, 'yes, I do.'

★ ★ ★

All round the Domaine the darkness was cold and thick; through the night the wind had rushed and relented, softened and hurried on, hurling the rain against the bolted shutters. Levade shivered as he took a piece of paper from the desk in his studio and pulled the lit candle nearer to him. For someone concerned with making pictures he had ugly handwriting, distorted by the urgency with which he wrote.

21 November 1942. 04.45h. Man is alone in the world. A woman expects a baby, but that baby in particular, that character? No. She does not even know what sex it will be, would not recognise a photograph of it when grown. And in death there is eternal isolation. That will be my Hell. I am afraid of dying, but I know my fear is a sin.

By language men have made a show of congregation or society, because the individual is not born with language but learns to navigate with its means, which have been developed and bequeathed by dead men. This sense of being part of something greater is in fact an illusion. A man and woman may live together all their lives and still know little of the essence of the other. They rarely surprise each other, because what is essential to each is never communicated.

Like language, art struggles with what is common, to disturb the individual habit of perception and, by disturbing it, to enable men to see what has been lived and seen by others. By upsetting, therefore, it tries to soothe, because it hopes to free each person from the tyranny of solitude.

No child born knows the world he is entering, and at the moment of his birth he is a stranger to his parents. When he dies, many years later, there may be regrets among those left behind that they never knew him better, but he is forgotten almost as soon as he dies because there is no time for others to puzzle out his life. After a few years he will be referred to once or twice by a grandchild, then by no one at all. Unknown at the moment of birth, unknown after death. This weight of solitude! A being unknown.

And yet, if I believe in God, I am known. On

the tombs of the English soldiers, the ones too fragmented to have a name, I remember that they wrote 'Known unto God'. By this they meant that here was a man, who did once have arms and legs and a father and a mother, but they could not find all the parts of him — least of all his name.

God will know me, even as I cannot know myself. If He created me, then He has lived with me. He knows the nature of my temptations and the manner of my failing. So I am not alone. I have for my companion the creator of the world.

At the hour of my death I would wish to be 'known unto God'.

Charlotte had pushed the jagged grey pyramid of oyster shells to one side and was cutting into a plump Bresse chicken. She had ordered a whole one and was undaunted by its size, or by the steaming pot of fresh parsley sauce. From the mound of mashed potatoes on her plate a narrow trickle of butter ran into the margins of the oily vinaigrette that dressed the mountainous green salad. She tore off half a baguette, slit it lengthwise, plastered it with the ripe camembert the waiter had slipped on to her side plate, and made a bulging sandwich. As she sucked the fat meniscus from a balloon of burgundy, a remote jangling forced itself closer until the sound filled her head — and the dinner vanished.

She was, as usual, incredulous, and wished she had a watch against which to double-check the claim of the violent alarm clock. Seven o'clock? It was still dark; it couldn't be more than four or five. Reluctantly, she remembered that this was what she always thought, and that every morning the hands of the sullen Louis XVI clock in the dining room, mendaciously ticking in its absurd lacquered cabinet, pointed out her mistake.

The day proceeded as it had begun, cold and

dispiriting, until noon, when there was a call from Julien. The wireless operator had heard a coded message on the BBC and Mirabel had confirmed the codes: there was to be a drop on Thursday. Mirabel would not himself be there, and had entrusted Julien to pick up and store what was landed. They were expecting supplies, arms and explosives. It was to be the biggest drop of the war so far, and reflected London's expectation that, with the Germans in the former Free Zone, the action would become increasingly open. Julien sounded almost ecstatic with excitement, and Charlotte wondered what Pauline Bobotte would make of the news as she worked away with her busy plugs and headset. Julien thought it a good idea for Dominique to come into Lavaurette for dinner that evening to discuss 'tactics'. Charlotte knew the single tactical refinement to determine would be whether she or César rode the more decrepit bicycle, but was persuaded to accept, as Julien must have known she would be, by his use of the word 'dinner'.

Wearing both of Dominique's jumpers under her coat, her hair beneath a scarf, Charlotte set out on her bicycle, lowering her head against the flat drift of rain.

'Good evening, Madame. Monsieur Levade told me he was expecting you. A horrible night to be out, isn't it?'

'Yes,' said Charlotte, a little put out that she had got no further than two paces into the hall before Pauline Benoit's door opened. 'Though you look as though you're going out yourself.'

'Yes, indeed. I have no choice,' said Madame Benoit. 'Duty calls.'

Charlotte did not bother to think what she might mean; she was hungry, and the prospect of even Madame Gayral's cuisine in all its scorched uncertainty was enough to put other thoughts from her mind as she hurried up the stairs to Julien's apartment.

Julien sat her down in front of the fire and poured her a glass of wine. He seemed to find it hard to settle, but kept getting up and going off into a different room on some urgent but undisclosed business. Charlotte ascribed this nervousness to his worry about the imminent drop. He re-entered the room for perhaps the fourth or fifth time and filled her glass again. 'So, Dominique. You all set for Thursday?'

'Yes, Octave. Quite ready, thank you.'

'For God's sake call me Julien when we're alone. I can't bear this stupid Octave thing.'

'I apologise. I thought . . . All right. Julien.'

'Does my father know you're going?'

Charlotte crossed her legs and settled back a little further into the armchair. 'I imagine so. He's given me the whole day off. Your father seems to know a good deal about me.'

'Well, I can assure you it wasn't me who told him. I've been absolutely — '

'Relax, Julien. I wasn't accusing you. Your father seems interested in certain aspects of my life, though not what I might be doing tomorrow. For instance, he's guessed that I'm Scottish, or English as he calls it, but I don't think he has any curiosity about why I'm staying in Lavaurette. Or perhaps he was just too tactful to ask.'

'So what are these 'aspects'?' said Julien.

'Personal things. He knows my name, for instance.'

'Your real name?' A look of intense anxiety passed over Julien's face, which Charlotte presumed to spring from a worry about security.

'Yes.'

'And why did you tell him?'

'I was lonely.' She was glad Mr Jackson could not hear this abject excuse.

Julien nodded and made to speak, then stopped as

though on reflection he considered this a reasonable explanation. He sighed and stood up. Charlotte watched as he walked across the floor to the dresser to collect the wine bottle. In the tall, echoing room, with its austere furniture and pale colours, he looked for a moment vulnerable, a solitary man set against the background of his imagination.

'You drink too much,' said Charlotte, meaning to break his introspection.

'Probably.' He rolled his eyes as though she was always nagging him and smiled; it seemed to work.

'Have you booked a table?' said Charlotte.

'No. We're having dinner here. Hadn't you noticed the the smell?'

'I did notice something,' said Charlotte. 'I thought it kinder not to mention it.'

Julien drank more and more wine and Charlotte had to hold her hand over her own glass when he tried to refill it. He talked about the weather and how it could affect the operation; he muttered about Gastinel, whom he no longer bothered to refer to as 'Auguste', and cursed him for losing interest.

'Typical little shopkeeper just worried about filling his own till,' he said as he cleared the soup plates and brought in a china dish with slices of pink meat in gravy which he claimed were veal he had acquired from a friend of a friend. He had hardly begun to eat before he lit a cigarette.

'How do you manage to look so clean always?' he said abruptly.

'It's a wonder if I do. The stove that heats the wood takes about three days to warm up the tank. I only have one bath a week. Otherwise I wash in cold water.'

'You could use the public baths,' said Julien. 'That's what I do.'

'I didn't know there were any.'

'Behind the Place de l'Eglise. They're in an old school

building. They're very popular these days because fuel's so short.'

'I'll bear it in mind.'

'You don't look as though you need it. You look like the kind of woman who's always fresh and sweet-smelling, a little dab of scent behind the ears . . . Let me smell.'

He went over to where Charlotte sat and nuzzled his face into her neck, inhaling deeply. 'I knew it,' he said, 'delicious.'

Charlotte pushed him away. 'You're drunk, Julien.'

'Not really.' It was true; the dramatic amount of alcohol he swallowed seemed to have almost no effect on him except perhaps to make him slightly more affectionate: Charlotte sometimes wondered why he bothered.

Julien pulled up a loose chair next to Charlotte and reached out to her. He looked down at where his hands had imprisoned hers, then up into her face. His dark eyes were, Charlotte conceded, undeniably beautiful.

'We've been through some things, haven't we, Dominique? Whatever happens to us now, I think we'll remember.'

'Yes,' said Charlotte, 'though sometimes I feel guilty about having enjoyed it so much.'

'Exactly,' said Julien. 'As though we can't be taking it seriously. I think that's the point I'm trying to make. You think I'm your friend, and I am. You think that because we laugh together and work together then that limits the kind of friendship we can have. I don't think so. I don't think romance needs to be solemn. You can laugh with someone and still sleep with them.'

'Of course, but — '

'I want to sleep with you, Dominique.'

'Julien! I don't think you can just ask a woman straight out like that.'

'Why not?'

Charlotte did not know why not.

Julien said. 'Suppose there's a German ambush on Thursday night and we get killed by our fat German and his troops, mown down by machine guns. We would never know what it was like and, and . . .'

'It's a bit unlikely,' said Charlotte.

'Well, maybe . . . I hope so. But wouldn't you like to anyhow?'

'It's not a question of what I would like to do, it's a question of what is right.'

'But would you like to?'

'There would be worse things, I imagine.' She squeezed Julien's hands. 'I do like you, Julien, I promise you. I like you without reservation. But there's another man.'

'It's not quite without reservation, then.'

'Not quite.'

She leaned over and wrapped her arms round him. Julien laid his head on her shoulder, then raised his face to hers. Charlotte kissed him and, feeling his tongue slide between her lips, expected some violent retribution for her infidelity. Nothing in fact stopped her from kissing Julien and allowing him to run his hands over her; nothing except the fear that she was leading him on too far. She disengaged herself, reluctantly.

'I won't sleep with you, Julien. Now I don't know if you want to go on kissing me or whether that would make things worse.'

'I think perhaps it would make things worse.'

Julien stood up, ran his hand through his hair and, with an effort of self-discipline that seemed to weigh down his body, cleared the half-finished plates and took them out of the room.

★ ★ ★

327

Peter Gregory was standing in the Mayor's parlour. The Mayor was in his nightshirt, dishevelled and unwilling. Gregory was desperate.

'I need papers to get out of France.'

'How will you go?'

'Spain.'

'Do you have money?'

'Yes. I take trains. I can't walk very far.'

'But you'll have to walk across the Pyrenees.'

'Then my leg . . . better.'

The Mayor shook his head. 'It's a very long way. I've never been that far myself. I've never been further than Toulouse. You won't make it. Not with the way you speak French. And if I give you an identity card with the name of our commune on it, then it's not only you but we who'll end up in trouble.'

Once, Gregory had not much cared if he saw England again. Now it seemed to him to be the only thing he wanted; and, if he didn't make it, then to die in the attempt would be an almost equally gratifying outcome.

If only he had told Charlotte on the night he left. If only he had gone back, broken into the flat, woken her and told her how much he loved her. He twisted the ring on his finger, round and round. He would not move from the Mayor's house. There was no particular reason to trust the shaky line of sympathisers, beginning with the vet, that had brought him there, but he had no other grounds of hope.

'Monsieur, I would like to help, but I must put the well-being of the commune first.'

Gregory did not really understand. Although the Mayor was disparaging about Gregory's French, it did not occur to him to adjust his own speech in any way: he rattled away, gurgling, self-righteous, idiomatic.

The door opened and a woman came into the parlour: the Mayor's wife in a long nightdress, her hair beneath a cotton cap, her face dramatically white.

She looked at Gregory, crouched against the sofa, his leg at an angle obviously troubling him. In his midnight fatigue and in the enclosure of his pain he looked out to her and tried to summon up a remnant of flirtatious charm. God knows what I must look like, he thought, in Jacques's old clothes — how thin, how red-eyed. It's pathetic.

It was his only chance. He smiled at the woman and began his laborious, ungrammatical explanation once again. He adorned the story with smiles and shrugs which he hoped were winning. The woman left the room abruptly and Gregory stopped talking. His mouth now tasted of defeat and words could not form in it.

The Mayor looked at him, coughed and nodded. He, too, was silent. Gregory again cursed his inability to speak the language: if only he had talked more with Charlotte when she offered. The thought of her gave him a new resolve.

He calculated the practicalities. He would walk by night, steal food. They would give him a map. When he came to the Pyrenees he would trust to luck; if he could not find a guide he would follow the compass . . . It was not possible.

The woman returned with a tray on which was a bottle of spirit and three glasses. She poured one and handed it to Gregory. He thanked her warmly. As he raised the small glass to his lips, he thought of Leslie Brind taking down the glass yard from above the bar at the Rose and Crown. The fellowship of these men, foolish, drunk as they were, was not a reason to die but could be another reason to live. The liquor on his tongue freed the words and, thinking of these men, he began once more.

'You imbecile!' the woman screamed, and Gregory was stunned by her fury. Her face was so twisted by anger and indignation that it took him a moment to see that she was talking to her husband. 'Give this man a card! If you delay one moment longer I'll pack my bag and leave you.'

'But, my dear, I must think about the commune.'

'If you're not man enough to take responsibility for your actions in the town then God knows why you're Mayor. You're certainly not the man I married. Give me the cards.'

'There aren't any here. They're at the Mairie.'

'Then you will get one first thing in the morning.'

'But he'll need a photograph.' The Mayor's fleshy face was set about with anxiety.

Gregory had recognised the word 'photograph' and was rummaging in his pocket. 'Notes for pilots' by Wing Commander H.S. Verity DSO, DFC. He knew it by heart: 'You should carry a standard escape kit, some purses of French money, a gun or two, and thermos flask of hot coffee or what you will. Empty your pockets of anything of interest to the Hun, but carry with you some small photographs of yourself in civilian clothes. These may be attached to false identity papers. Change your linen before flying, as dirty shirts have a bad effect on wounds. The Lysander is a warm aeroplane, and I always wore a pair of shoes rather than flying boots. If you have to walk across the Pyrenees you might as well do it in comfort.'

Gregory handed the Mayor two photographs.

4

The painting that Levade had thrust at Charlotte was the only one he still owned from the best period of his work. He had kept it back when he sold the others, from some suspicion developing even at the time that the planets in his mind had moved into a favourable but temporary conjunction that would never come again.

Charlotte looked at it for several minutes; by the time she had finished she was less sure what it was she had seen than when she began. There was a square in a French town, painted in a clear and representational manner; the colouring was flat, the shadows thrown by the buildings were hard-edged: there was no deliquescence of form or colour as in an Impressionist painting; on the contrary, the technique was so realistic that it drew attention to itself. But against this assertiveness there was an element of mystery: the square was deserted, a clock on the church showed twenty to four, as though this blank hour of the afternoon were significant. Two figures in a side street faced in different directions, apparently trapped by some melancholy misunderstanding. The picture was suffused with a sadness that was both particular and irresistibly suggestive.

What gripped Charlotte was the sense of being strongly moved by a mysterious emotion, yet having the release of that feeling repeatedly closed off by the ambiguity of the image. In the days after she had seen it, Charlotte thought that perhaps what made it so affecting was that Levade had given the impression of seeing through the surface of the world into some deeper reality: he had unpicked one's natural assumptions of the way things looked and reassembled them in a different way; then, as one tried to adjust to this altered, truer state, the constituents of the picture once more unravelled. It was an entrancing feeling that Levade had evoked, but it was not reassuring; the powerful yearning, brought on by the immediate certainty that he had disclosed something profound, was frustrated by a metaphysical limitation. Perhaps there was an element of truth he had not been able to find. Perhaps he had reached a point beyond which it was not possible to go.

When she asked him why he no longer painted in this way, he sighed. 'It's simple,' he said. 'It's because I no longer dream. As a young man I painted in a very traditional way. Before the war I had a studio with some other people in the rue Carpeaux. We'd see what Picasso and the others were doing, and although I thought it was important I couldn't find my own version of it, my own language. I kept on painting in the style of artists I admired, Courbet, or Degas, then later like the early Matisse. When I returned to Paris after the war everything seemed to have changed. Suddenly I found I wanted to paint quite differently, and the subjects suggested to me the way they should be treated. They seemed to come to me more or less complete in dreams. At least, I didn't puzzle over how I should treat them, I just had to record them, as they were.'

Charlotte was sitting, once more at Levade's invitation, on the bed in his studio. 'And these dreams that came to you, were they of places you knew, or were they imagined?'

'Most of them are the places of my childhood. It was as though there were a landscape inside my head which I'd forgotten, and it was restored to me bit by bit each night. Perhaps it was the effect of the war in some way. I would wake up each morning and find that another small piece of myself had been rescued and returned to me, though of course, it now looked different. In the passage of time it had become more charged. My dreams seemed to capture the full meaning — something that had not been apparent at the time.'

'How long did this go on?' said Charlotte.

'For about five years. No more than that. All the good paintings I've done were in that small period. After that, something shifted, something changed. Although the process seemed to be spontaneous, I think there was also an element of will. I spent many hours at the easel — there was that sort of self-discipline — but apart from that I was unaware of any intellectual effort, although I suspect it was more than I realised at the time. When you're painting at that pitch of concentration, your mind is partly passive, you're in a state in which you surrender to the impulses you feel, but there's something active as well. You're making sure at the very least that the impulses stay in the right constellation. There's push and pull; even letting go is quite a conscious act. The fact that you're not aware of the active part doesn't make it any less demanding. Many painters become worn down by their efforts — Derain, for instance, in my view. Perhaps in the end that's what happened to me. I experienced it as a loss of these spontaneous dreams, but maybe I was really just exhausted.'

Levade coughed and gave one of his quickly vanishing smiles. 'So now I just put paint on canvas. The skin of a waitress's arm.'

'It must be frustrating.'

'Of course. I think about it all the time. Painting was my life and it failed me. I was bound to wonder why. And the solitude has given me time to puzzle over it.'

Charlotte pushed her shoes off and sat back against the bolster, drawing up her knees and wrapping her arms round them. Levade had spoken quite unguardedly, with a fluency that must have derived from having gone over the question so often in his mind.

'Have you talked to Julien about this?'

'Yes.' Levade sat on a little stool he kept in front of the easel. 'It was difficult at first because I hadn't seen him since I left his mother and I thought he might not want to know me. But he's a very forgiving man. He has a remarkable temperament. In the end I told him everything. When he first came to live in Lavaurette he used to come here for dinner every night. He cooked and then we'd talk for hours. Then I think he found a woman.'

'Who was that?' Charlotte's voice was even.

'He didn't tell me her name. Some woman in the village. He never stays with them long.'

'Like his father.'

'I think he has some difficulties. The difference is that he would like to be faithful, so he's always disappointed by himself.'

'But you didn't want to be?'

'Not until I married Julien's mother, then I did try.'

'And what was it about Julien's mother, out of all the other women?'

'It was a dream. I'd known her for five years. She worked in a baker's on the Boulevard de Rochechouart. I used to see her almost every day, and her brother knew a lot of people who were friends of mine. She was older than me, not very beautiful, a rather stout bourgeoise. Her father had a number of shops, they were quite well-to-do. Then one night I had an overwhelming dream of being in love with her. I awoke in the morning and found it was true. I was sick with the feeling. When I told you the other day that I didn't use the expression of being in love I should have excluded

334

this one instance. I took flowers to the shop, I followed her in the street. I was distraught, yet I had a sense of inner conviction that this was the woman I had to be with. The dream was not a vision or a fragment, it was the statement of a reality. I couldn't properly remember from that day on what I had felt before. I couldn't imagine what it had been like not being in love with her.'

'What went wrong?'

'I suppose it was the war. Julien was born in 1913 and the next year I was mobilised. I came home on leave from time to time, but it was difficult. The life I was living at the front was impossible to reconcile with what was asked of me at home. I knew it was changing me inside. I felt it was destroying me.'

Levade's voice was hard and emphatic. Charlotte felt he wanted to disclose more to her of what had happened to him.

'And yet,' he said, more ruminatively this time, 'it was the making in some way of my painting. I left Julien's mother in 1922 and it was then that my dreams began. But without the four years at the Front . . . I don't know.'

Charlotte looked out of the window and saw that it was dark. 'I should go and make dinner,' she said.

Levade did not answer; he seemed to be lost in recollection.

'Yes,' he said eventually. 'If you like. Perhaps you could bring something up here on a tray.'

After dinner Levade closed the shutters in his studio, handed Charlotte cigarettes, two glasses and a bottle of Armagnac.

'How did you find this house?' said Charlotte.

'A friend of Kahnweiler's. The picture dealer. It belonged to a family with several children but none of them wanted it or could afford it.'

Charlotte put some more wood on the fire, then sat

335

down in the room's only comfortable seat, a battered, rush-seated armchair. She thought for a moment of winter nights in the Highlands. Before it was somehow taken from her, there had in her childhood been a period of perfect contentment. She must have been very young indeed, yet the experience of it was still real in her mind: a sense of secure order in which the details of domestic life, the taste of redcurrants from the cage in the garden, the sound of a bicycle bell, the smell of paraffin with which her daily chore was to fill the heaters in the hall, the first frisson of hot water as she lowered herself into the bath in a cold but steam-filled room; and the lanes along which she walked — these had been of an enchantment that was complete, not tainted by comparison or loss.

And these remembered details would have amounted to nothing without love. For some short time at least, Charlotte recognised with a shock, there must have been harmony between herself and her parents. She had forgotten this brief childish paradise.

Levade took a glass and sat in the wicker chair by the window. He began to talk about his life in Paris. Then he told Charlotte about a house he had once lived in by the sea. It was summer time. Julien, aged about twelve, was packed off by his mother on the train from Paris to be met by Levade at the local station. The village had been inhabited by fishermen and their families for centuries and had yet to acquire a proper hotel. The house to which Levade took Julien was behind a small bay with pink cliffs topped by fir trees. There were upturned boats and lobster pots, tended by the fishermen whose boots left ugly imprints on the sand; no visitors from Paris had ever been before, and they were regarded by the people of the village with puzzled indifference.

Levade's whitewashed cottage had a terrace that overlooked the sea; inside, it was bare and simple, with two bedrooms and a small garden at the back. A girl from the village came in every day to clean and make lunch from whatever fish she had bought from her grandfather's early boat on the way. In the evening, Levade took Julien by the hand and led him across the sandy village square with a wind-battered larch, to the Pension that was housed in a squat brick building with bright blue shutters. Various friends from Paris were staying, also painters, some with small children in sailor clothes and sun-hats, some with their mistresses, and two men who dumbfounded the servant-girls by sharing a single-bedded room.

All day Levade worked out of doors, sitting on the top of the cliff with an easel or walking round the headland with a sketch book. Sometimes he would take a boat and row out of the bay, looking back at the tenacious grey village on the hillside, watching Julien's sunburnt face as his trailed fingers split the surface of the dark water. Occasionally there would be telephone messages from Paris, uncomprehendingly relayed by the woman on the switchboard; once a telegram boy arrived on the beach; but these urgent communications seemed no more than gestures from a forgotten world.

The reality was only in the swinging glass-panelled doors of the dining room at night, the snail's line of sand from the children's canvas shoes and the cream cheeses they ate with such glee for dessert, while their parents smoked cigars or persevered with the smaller limbs of lobsters; it was in the simple faces of the waitresses and the indulgent smile of the widow who owned the Pension.

As the summer wore on, the composition of the party changed and its numbers gradually diminished, but Levade felt there was no reason ever to go home. Each night he dreamed, sometimes useless stories, sometimes mere projections of the day that had gone, but also of buildings and cities, of landscapes given back to him from his past, now fully understood and released by the visit of his imagination. He painted with devotion, and the stretch of his mental energy did not deplete him but left his other senses stimulated and serene. He had formed an understanding with one of the girls in the Pension; he gave her books and presents; he talked to her, and in return she was a lover in whom the desire to please seemed limitless.

'I think of it often,' said Levade, who was now lying on the bed. 'Sometimes I can almost recapture it, but not quite. I can't find the exact reality of it.'

For all that she was interested by what Levade had said, Charlotte could not help a certain minister of the kirk reaction. Who had been looking after Julien when Levade was busy with his little girlfriend? What sort of durable Eden was it that saw children as little more than picturesque?

She said, 'Do you think all paradises are lost, that that's their nature?'

'I wouldn't say lost,' said Levade, 'but they must be in the past. What is present can't be imagined, and imagination is the only faculty we have for apprehending beauty.'

He stood up and walked over to the brass-topped table to refill his glass. 'Isn't that your problem, Mademoiselle? You have lost something, perhaps two things, two states of feeling. You don't wish to admit it, but perhaps there has been in one of them at least — your love affair — a diminution of your pain. If you admit that, then you're saying that the ecstasy was not as important as you thought, and since this was the feeling by which you organised your life, you can't afford to confess that.'

Charlotte said nothing. She did not know if Levade was right, but she felt a wish to hurt him, to expose his egocentricity in some damaging way. She said, 'I'm surprised you set such store by dreams. They seem an unlikely guide. I remember a colleague of my father's, a psychologist, describing dreams to me once as 'neural waste'.'

Levade laughed, a disconcerting sight that involved him throwing back his head so the sinews of his neck stood out. 'People always make fine phrases when they're frightened. I remember Proust, at his most desperate to break through the bonds of time, writing something like 'reality is the waste-product of experience'.'

Levade laughed so hard that he had to put down his glass.

'Did you like Proust?' said Charlotte.

'Yes, I thought it was a funny book. But I was young when I read it. I think there's a copy in the house somewhere.'

'Funny?' said Charlotte. 'I suppose it's funny,' she lied. She thought it was the most tragic book she had ever read. 'I think of it as sad as well. The loss of any hope of happiness through love, the disillusion . . . '

'Perhaps,' said Levade. 'Anyway, I don't arrange my life through dreams. I hope for them, I pray for them to help my painting. But I arrange my life through God.'

★ ★ ★

On Wednesday, the day before the parachute drop of arms and stores was due, Charlotte went into Lavaurette to buy food. Outside Madame Galliot's she remembered that they also needed candles and, as she leaned her bicycle against the shop, she saw the caped, official figure of Bernard attaching a piece of paper to the wall. Walking behind him to go into Madame Galliot's, Charlotte could not resist looking over his shoulder. The poster showed a man drowning, lifting up his hands for help; in the foreground

339

were shown the figures of de Gaulle and Churchill, with friendly arms round the shoulders of a sinister Jewish figure in a coat with an astrakhan collar. 'Remember Mers el Kebir! Remember Dunkirk!' read the black, smeared letters. 'DON'T LET'S THROW IT AWAY NOW!'

Bernard was staring at the poster in some puzzlement as he smoothed it down with his hands, though Charlotte thought it unlikely it could be the first he had heard of how the British fleet had sunk the French in the Algerian port of Mers el Kebir rather than let it fall into the hands of the Germans. When he saw her, Bernard shrugged. He uncurled another cartoon poster of a handsome Frenchman with chiselled cheekbones and improbably fair hair, lifting by the collar a wicked, unshaved Israelite with grotesque hooked nose and showing him the door of a building labelled 'France'.

At this moment a small, bald man with a raincoat and wire-rimmed glasses climbed out of a black car and came over to inspect Bernard's work. Charlotte had never seen him before in Lavaurette. He had a self-important air and wore polished shoes that seemed to come from a big city.

When he had inspected the poster, he turned to Bernard. 'Who's this?' he said, pointing at Charlotte.

'Madame Guilbert.'

Charlotte held out her hand, but the bald man kept his by his side. He looked her slowly up and down, walked round to look at her in profile, then marched off without speaking back to his car.

'Who was that extraordinary man?'

Bernard shrugged. 'He's called Pichon. The Government's sent him down from Paris. He's travelling round.'

'Is he a policeman or what?'

'He says he's from something called the Inquiry and

Control Section. Don't ask me what that is. Says he's helping the local mayors interpret all the new rules. In fact, he just sticks his nose in.'

Charlotte looked back at the posters. The odd thing about Lavaurette, she thought as she went past Bernard into Madame Galliot's shop, was that although on the surface it seemed a tranquil, inward-looking place with its municipal monuments, its empty shops and sleepy squares, it was in fact the site of continuous activity and secret meetings, of numbered postboxes, hidden boys, propaganda and smiling public deceit. Perhaps the Germans were right to leave a local commandant behind.

When she went back to her room in the Domaine she found that a piece of paper had been slid beneath the door. It was a note from Levade which he must have put there while she was out.

Wednesday. 05.15h.

On realising that his love for Gilberte has gone:

'Of the state of mind which, in that far-off year, had been tantamount to a long-drawn-out torture for me, nothing survived. For in this world of ours where everything withers, everything perishes, there is a thing that decays, that crumbles into dust even more completely, leaving behind still fewer traces of itself, than beauty: namely grief.'

Time Regained, page 9.

When Charlotte read it she thought that her teenage reading of Proust had left her with only clichés, and that she had not really understood the book at all. She resolved to think no more of it or of the unstable ecstasies it described.

★ ★ ★

At midnight Claude Benech felt for the first time the stout and pimply handle of a firearm against the soft skin of his palm. He laid it on a pile of school exercise books he was marking. What he had to do in order to acquire it had, in the end, been simple: a matter of intelligent observation and knowing whom to inform.

Benech felt his loyalty quicken and intensify in proportion to his new responsibilities. The gun on the table made him see the agony of his country in a clear light: it was time for action, it was time for the great majority of decent people like himself to fight for what they believed in. All his life he had patiently endured the triumphs of the undeserving, seen little men preferred to him, and he had stood quietly by because he believed in order. That was his passion, that was a proper and traditional belief; but order was not everlasting, it had no natural rights: from time to time true men must fight for it.

He lifted the gun again and weighed it in his hand. Its presence made him want to use it.

★ ★ ★

In the big house on the hill in Lavaurette Gerd Lindemann was reading orders delivered that afternoon by motorbike. The terse yet bureaucratic style of the papers was an affront to him. Until the winter of 1939 he had worked as a dramatic critic on a newspaper and had taken pride in the fact that his notices, while short and given little prominence by the editor, were always immaculately written: to be comprehensive in 350 words required a particular eloquence.

Lindemann's views on drama were more definite than his views on anything else. He had allowed himself to be left in this unimportant village, this under-sized town in the middle of nothing, through his inability to get himself posted anywhere more interesting. He

342

was not the gauleiter of Julien Levade's imagining, but a reluctant infantry officer promoted to middle rank by virtue of his education and the losses on the Eastern Front. And he was aware that many of the men under his command were not the swaggering, blue-eyed youths who so impressed the French by their arrogance and their self-discipline when they took control of the traumatised country in 1940. The half-dozen soldiers billeted in the attic of the house were surly, small and no longer young. None of them would have been in such an inconsequential place as Lavaurette were it not for the rail connections with the main lines that made the village both a useful junction and a possible target of resistance sabotage — not that there had been any notable activity in the area, Lindemann had been informed.

He went to the fireplace and rang the bell. He enjoyed this feudal procedure and relished the look of fear in the eyes of the little servant-girl who scuttled into the room a minute later. 'More coffee,' he said in his workable French. He had barely been able to finish the first pot of whatever it was she had brought, but something would have to keep him alert as he waded through the sheaf of orders. The military strategy was clear enough: get men in large numbers down to the southern coast to defend against Allied attacks from North Africa. This had meant over-running the Free Zone, but the tactic was to leave as few men as possible to administer it before the arrival of the SS, so the greatest number possible could remain in active units. It was important to encourage the French to do as much work as they could, and Lindemann's orders suggested ways of achieving this. Laval would launch his Milice in January, and in return for offering their help to the Occupier Laval would, as usual, ask for German collaboration in the matter of boundaries, prisoners of war, payments and so on. The request, as usual, would be declined.

Lindemann smiled. This Milice would consist presumably of various thugs and convicts given early parole, of young hooligans worried that they might otherwise be transported to Germany as part of Laval's eight-for-one exchange system for prisoners taken in the brief fight of May, 1940. Lindemann could not imagine that anyone else would want to join, but he might have to use these people, so he had better not prejudge them.

To have power over the lives of people was a seductive feeling to someone whose previous influence had been limited to suggesting whether his readers might or might not enjoy a new production of *Faust*. Lindemann was enough of a psychologist to relish assigning tasks to men under his command according to his own ideas of their abilities and limitations. It was irksome to him, however, that, in addition to his straightforward administrative role, he was now also required to participate in non-military projects.

The occupation of the Free Zone gave much easier access to the large number of Jewish refugees the French had obligingly detained in camps there, as well as to the French Jews who already lived there or had fled from the North. Lindemann was required by his orders to supervise the joining of two trains at Lavaurette and to supply a quota of Jews from the region of which he was nominally in charge. These people were to be transported to Paris and onwards to some unspecified destination in Poland. The official line was that they were going to be working in camps, just like the young gentile Frenchmen whom Laval was swapping for French prisoners of war.

However, it had occurred to Lindemann that if work was the purpose, they would hardly be transporting old people, pregnant women and large numbers of children, and he was rather surprised by the willing

344

acquiescence of the French government and police in the scheme. Perhaps the ever-optimistic Monsieur Laval was hoping for some concession on sovereignty in return for his help.

Lindemann found this part of his task slightly absurd. The girl came back with the coffee. Was *she* Jewish?

'Wait.' He looked at her. She was small, dark. She could be. But most of the French were like that — not as bad as the Poles, but not as fine as the Swedes or Danes. 'All right. You can go.'

How was he supposed to find all these people? What if they were only half-Jewish? Apparently Vichy had offered racial definitions which were even stricter than those issued by the Nazi Commission for Jewish Affairs in Paris. A man called Pichon, sent from Vichy on a tour of the region to help the local prefectures, had volunteered to help. Lindemann shook his head. He couldn't decide about this.

★ ★ ★

At the same time, Peter Gregory was standing in a doorway in a narrow street just behind the harbour at Marseille. Rain was dripping from the stone lintel above his head. A misunderstanding over trains had brought him into a city which a few weeks earlier might have offered him some hope of escape, but was now the centre of German military operations. He had his eye on a house diagonally across the street, but he could not move for the amount of activity all round.

His back and shoulders were aching from the three hours he had spent concealed beneath a train in the goods' yard, having observed that the Gestapo control at the station exit appeared to be questioning all travellers. The tenuous line of sympathisers that had kept him going from the site of his crash to the Mayor's house and on for four more days towards the Pyrenees

345

had been broken by his mistake with the train.

Having managed to escape from the goods' yard over a brick wall, Gregory walked for a mile until he found himself in an apparently unpopulated area. He spotted a café through whose windows he could see only empty tables and went in; a barman was moving a greasy cloth back and forth over the counter. Gregory stuck a cigarette in the corner of his mouth to muffle his voice. 'Telephone,' he said in an abrupt way he hoped would discourage conversation, and the man jerked his head towards the back of the room.

In a dark alcove next to a narrow door marked 'WC' he dialled a number in Clermont-Ferrand. He had never been happy with the vet's diagnosis of his 'fractured' leg, and the exertions of the last four days, culminating in the walk from the station, had produced an excruciating friction in the shin, as though parts of the bone were rubbing together. He bit his lower lip as he heard the telephone let out its desperate, single peal in the distant mountains of the Massif Central.

The voice of a garage owner, wakened from a wine-heavy sleep, came on the line. Gregory went through the passwords he had been taught in London and hoped his accent would be comprehensible to 'Hercule'. In the long and painful exchange that followed, Gregory found it almost impossible to understand what Monsieur Chollet was saying. Eventually, he extracted from him an address in Marseille which he repeated and checked as many times as he dared until he heard Chollet's patience become exhausted.

'Thank you, Monsieur,' Gregory said. 'Goodbye.'

'There was a woman looking for you. In the summer.'

'What?'

'An English woman.'

'Did she leave a message?'

'No. Goodbye.'

Gregory put down the receiver. An English woman. How Charlotte would hate being called that. He leaned for a moment on the top of the telephone, and tears — presumably from the pain in his leg — blurred his vision.

Now at midnight, one hour later, he was waiting in the doorway. He would get into this house. The English woman. He smiled. Whatever it took, he was going to get in.

★ ★ ★

It was midnight when André Duguay sat up in bed and called out his mother's name. There was nothing soft or tender about the call; it was a sound of primitive panic, the expression of a fear that had been rising and working slowly in his mind for several weeks and had finally found utterance in a response to the pictures shown to him in his dream.

Madame Duguay's face was not clear, but then it was not seen objectively in André's mind even when he was awake. Yet in the dream he was with her, and he saw those dark features, the face bent over his cradle, whose outline he had over the years uncritically absorbed, so that it had become the face of love.

He was with her, he saw her, and she was in darkness among crowds of people wailing.

Down the corridor came the running footsteps of Mlle Cariteau. She had had time to throw a flannel dressing gown over her nightdress, and she stumbled into the boys' room, not wishing to turn on the light in case it woke whichever one had not called out. She could not tell from the cry alone which it was, and at first went to Jacob; then she heard a voice from André's bed and went to him.

Sylvie Cariteau wrapped the boy in her arms and stroked his hair. Childless, she felt the torrent of

347

maternal tenderness go out of her to the weeping child, a force that was angry in its desire to protect him.

On the walls of the bare upstairs room there were daguerreotypes of Sylvie's respectable grandparents, uneasy in their Sunday clothes; there were two plaster crucifixes.

For half an hour the granddaughter with no husband rocked the unprotected little boy against her bosom, back and forth, back and forth in the awful night.

★ ★ ★

Levade had lit a candle at the writing table in his bedroom. An hour earlier he had said goodbye to Julien and his mind was still full of the boy. He wrote:

Midnight.
I thank God for Julien. The joy I have in him is simple. Merely to be near his life brings me delight. This makes me think of dying, because I feel my spirit is one with his and that only by death will our separation be dissolved. I believe we will be in paradise together, and I believe we will become one, as God, through the Trinity, is indivisible from His own Son.

Of course I believe this. I believe it since Christ showed himself to me that night on Dead Man's Hill at Verdun, without arms and legs, nailed to a tree trunk. I didn't understand at the time, but later He came to me again, the same body, this time on a cross. It was the night my cousin appeared to me in a vision; his face was illuminated, though we did not know until the morning that he had died. I believe, because God showed me in a dream my dearest mother as a child, her happiness secured, and I was able as a grown man to care for her, as, when death at last folds time away, I shall again.

And hell will be the absence of God, the complete loss of Him. I have lived in this place and I have felt its void. I lived this time without God because I was not worthy of Him. The chances that I was given I ignored or spurned because I was sunk so deep in sensual things, ambitions, self-deceit. Every day I must affirm my faith. Every day I must be reconverted.

When I write at times like this, the voice I hear does not sound like my own. But I hope this voice of devotion is the most true of all the different voices I have. My friend Madame Guilbert (she is my friend; I do admire her) has made me think about this. Yet I hope there is some core of goodness in me, and of faith. After all, what else is it that will die?

And when I go, will it be in a hospital for the old, or here in my dreamless bed? When it comes, the doctor will prolong my breathing for a few more useless hours, the priest will lean over me to hear my last and most sincere confession. Some friends will come and be polite. Some will cry at the recollection of their own lost youth — experiences they must now concede are for ever gone, beyond the redeeming power of the imagination, in the abyss of time closed. And my sinful life will offer them no fine or comforting example.

Somehow they will stick my gaping jaws together, weigh down my staring eyes. And my head, which has teemed with thoughts for so long, will hold not even the flicker of an idea. My once hot, mobile hands will not be capable even of picking up a paintbrush. Someone will lift up my arm on the bed and it will fall back by my side. They will bundle up the rotting meat and put it in a box. The millions of people who have lived without knowledge of my small life will be ignorant still; the handful who knew me will forget.

But I have faith in God. At moments I have seen — with His blessing and through the light of art — into a world that transcends this one but lives beside it, like a lost city visible through the now-impenetrable, now-translucent waves.

These things I have believed in, and I believe also in the love of my son. Death does not separate us from those we love. It is life that keeps us frustratingly apart. I trust in God that on the Day of Judgement He will reunite me with those I have loved, and that our spirits will at last become truly one.

5

It was the day of the drop; but before the evening came, Charlotte had an errand to run in Limoges. She dressed quickly and went down to the scullery, where she found some bread and a tin of what was referred to by the ration ticket as fruit condiment. She swallowed it with a glass of water, tied her headscarf, checked that she had Dominique's papers in her handbag and went outside to get her bicycle. As she pedalled beneath the arch of the pigeonnier she turned back to look at the front of the house, and saw the sun glistening on the tightly closed shutters of Levade's studio. The bicycle juddered over an unseen pothole and water splashed up over Dominique's admirably hard-wearing shoes. All down the avenue of flaking plane trees the birds were singing.

There were only two other passengers waiting for the early train, both elderly women with empty baskets on their arms. Charlotte smiled at them and mouthed a polite greeting, while making it clear she had no wish to talk.

The second-class carriage of the train had seats to spare, and as they nosed into the open landscape, leaving the town of Lavaurette to foment its closed and unsuspected conflicts, she saw the country of her heart reveal itself once more in all its old beguiling colours.

Tonight, unless there was some drastic change in the weather, the drop would go ahead, and in Charlotte's mind it had become an important occasion. She would need warm clothes, and she would wear beneath them whatever she managed to buy in Limoges; she would have a bath, and since the water at the Domaine would

351

not be hot, that would mean braving the public baths at the women's allotted time of six o'clock. There would be dinner with Julien and perhaps with César and some of the other men; then there would be the big plane from home hurling the contents of its hold out into the beleaguered darkness.

The flashing pictures revealed by the train's windows were like the country Charlotte remembered, with its effortless harmony of church and meadow, grey villages and their rooted inhabitants; but the streets of Limoges showed the strains of the present. There was a shoddiness in the way people were dressed and an unhealthy calm caused by the lack of motor vehicles. It did not lower Charlotte's spirits as she walked up past the Jardin d'Orsay, where the flowerbeds were still well tended, though it was only as she came closer that she saw that they had been planted with vegetables.

In her mind she repeated to herself the details of the message Mirabel had given her. Her destination was in the Place des Jacobins; the person she needed was called Georges. She felt no fear as she walked through the streets of the city, though she did not congratulate herself for it. You were frightened or you weren't: it was not something in your control.

She did glance briefly round her, however, as she rang the doorbell. There was no reason for alarm: Limoges was sunk in provincial peace. The door opened and a concierge looked out.

'Good morning, Madame. I'm looking for Georges.'

'Who shall I say is calling?'

'A friend of Frédéric.'

The woman disappeared, leaving the door open. A few moments later, a portly, unshaven man in a cardigan came to the entrance.

'Are you Georges?'

'Yes.' He nodded, dislodging some ash from the end of the cigarette stuck in the corner of his mouth.

'I have a message from Frédéric.' She gave him the time, the date and the map reference.

To her surprise, he took a pencil from the pocket of his cardigan and wrote down the figures on his cigarette packet. Clearly he had not had the benefits of G Section's mnemonic training.

Georges smiled. 'Would you like to come in for a glass of wine?'

'No, thank you,' said Charlotte.

He shrugged; they shook hands and she walked swiftly away. The reward that Mirabel had promised her was so great that she did not wish to jeopardise it by staying.

In any case, there was something more pressing than wine. There was a shop just off the Boulevard de la Cité, where — she had been told by Pauline Benoit — it was possible to buy clothes, provided you were not fussy about the material. The directions Charlotte had received were precise, and the shop itself was unmissable. Its glossy black-painted front contained a window display that would not have disgraced the rue du Faubourg St Honoré ten years earlier. The window on one side contained mannequins in dresses and suits, their plastic wrists cocked and their slender feet dipped into crocodile shoes: one held a long lapis lazuli cigarette holder to her lips, another appeared to be wearing a mink stole. The other window revealed an encyclopaedic array of underwear. Charlotte looked in amazement at the brassières, slips, foundation garments, drawers, roll-ons, petticoats, corsets and other devices of whalebone and pink flannel.

As she stood staring, the door opened and a man in shirtsleeves with a tape measure round his neck came on to the step.

'Do come in, Madame.'

Charlotte followed, with misgivings. This array could not be legal.

'All these things,' she said, pointing to the window, 'do you have — '

'Alas not, Madame. Do take a seat.' The shopkeeper pulled a high stool up to the counter. 'Those are remnants from the days before the war. We keep them to remind us of what life was like.' He was about sixty, with a round face and a small moustache; he was respectable but with a humorous eye, and Charlotte found that she could not distrust him.

He smiled. 'We have a little stock, of course. Is there something in particular Madame was looking for?'

Underpants that would not take two days to dry; shoes that did not make her feet look deformed; something pretty to wear in the evening . . . 'Perhaps a blouse?' she said cautiously.

From beneath the counter the proprietor pulled out a long drawer. It contained four white or off-white blouses made from some synthetic material.

'Hmm . . . I'm looking for something a little more colourful. If you haven't any blouses, maybe something knitted.'

'Ah-ha, a little knit, yes.' The man took a step-ladder and walked down the bare boards of the shop to the back.

While he pulled out various boxes from the top shelf, inspected and replaced them with a mutter, Charlotte thought of the wardrobe full of clothes she had in Scotland: the plum-coloured cashmere pullover, the lilac cardigan, the silk and cotton shirts, the kilts, the pleated skirts, the sleeveless summer dresses so seldom worn north of Berwick, the piles of cotton and silk underclothes.

The shopkeeper returned with half a dozen woollen items and laid them on the counter. To Charlotte's eye, most of them appeared to have been knitted by his mother. He read her disappointment and said,

'One minute, Madame. There's something I'd like to show you.'

From the back of the shop he produced a burgundy-coloured dress, with a discreet pattern of golden curlicues, made in light wool, like a Limousin version of paisley. 'I think it's exactly your size,' he said encouragingly. 'If you'd like to try it on.'

In the changing room Charlotte slid off Dominique's skirt and jumper. She looked at her reflection and smiled as she pulled on the dress. It was cut high at the neck but rather tight over the bust; she pulled it from the waist to loosen it, and smoothed it over her hips. The hem swung loose below her knees. With Dominique's porridgey stockings it did not exactly look elegant, but it was well made and, while middle-aged in style, it was at least slightly feminine.

Charlotte walked into the shop and turned round a couple of times in front of the mirror.

The shopkeeper told her it fitted perfectly. 'Very, very pretty, Madame.'

'How much is it?'

'Aah.' He held up both hands and then leaned forwards to put his mouth against Charlotte's ear. 'You are from the country, I think, Madame?'

'Yes.'

'Shall we say . . . could you manage . . . ' His voice dropped to a whisper, ' . . . a leg of ham?'

'I beg your pardon,' said Charlotte through her laughter.

'A shoulder then.'

'Monsieur, I'm sorry, I think there's some misunderstanding. I can give you cash.'

The shopkeeper's mouth turned down sadly. 'I have cash, Madame. That's not a problem. The trouble is, I have nothing to spend it on.'

Charlotte smiled. 'What about the clothes in the

window? Are they for sale? How much for the dress? A whole pig?'

'At least. Made into ham, into chops and black puddings. One could begin with the belly roasted in sea-salt, or the liver fried with onions in butter and olive oil.'

Charlotte eventually persuaded him to accept some of her G Section bank notes in return for two pairs of silk drawers and the woollen dress. He made them all into a parcel and tied it with string, carefully knotting and snipping, as though he knew it might be all the work he had that day.

The winter sun was still bright when Charlotte stepped out of the shop and began walking. She had plenty of time before taking the two o'clock train and intended to look at the cathedral, but was sidetracked by the noise of a crowd. She followed the sound into a square she recognised as the one obliquely visible from her bedroom when she had spent that first night in Limoges. A man with a megaphone was standing on the steps of a monument and addressing about three hundred people, many of whom carried placards and flags.

Charlotte moved to the edge of the crowd, from which she sensed a surprising degree of animation.

The word 'assassins' was used frequently by the speaker and was angrily echoed by the crowd. It took Charlotte some time before she understood that the object of this term and the focus of the crowd's hatred were the men of the RAF. She was startled at the passion they evoked. Their bombing raids over France had killed hundreds of civilians, according to the speaker, and all of the deaths were quite unnecessary. 'They say they're destroying German installations and French factories that supply the German war effort, but that's a lie. The English have always been our enemies and the Monster Churchill is prolonging the war for his own selfish ends! This is war for Wall Street, war for the City of London, war for the Israelites!'

The name of Churchill was greeted by a wide range of expletives from the throaty crowd, the most common of which was 'Jew'. A couple of drums started up a regular beat, though the people could not decide whether the chant should be 'RAF-Assassins' or 'Churchill, de Gaulle — Jew!': the first had a good hammering rhythm, but the latter had a catchy, iambic quality. Charlotte looked at some of the banners and placards being waved and saw the usual demonic faces of ringleted, black-coated figures, depicted in the act of thieving, hoarding and plotting in connivance with the British, Russians and Americans. One had a photograph of a Lancaster bomber imaginatively decked out with stars of David.

Poor Gregory, Charlotte thought as she moved quietly away from the square. She glanced back once over her shoulder at the crowd, whose breath was making angry statues in the freezing air.

By five o'clock she was back in Lavaurette. Pauline Bobotte told her that Monsieur Levade was busy, so she left some packages of food she had brought for dinner at the desk and made her way slowly towards the public baths. The thought of the drop that evening had chased away the bitterness she felt at watching the demonstration: the people who would hold the torches in the field did not see things in that way; nor did Antoinette, patiently tapping out her messages in the drizzly hills of Ussel.

★ ★ ★

The public baths had been installed eight years earlier by a socialist mayor anxious that Lavaurette should move with the times. They had become popular during the fuel shortages, though even now they were disdained by the town's élite who preferred to wash in cold water or not at all than to mingle with the shopkeepers and the proletariat.

In the tiled vestibule Charlotte was given a ticket and a towel by an old woman stationed in a glass-fronted box. On the opposite wall was a giant framed photograph of Marshal Pétain, looking down indulgently on his clean people; beneath it, to the words Work, Family, Fatherland, a local signwriter had neatly added: Hygiene.

Although it was only a few minutes after six, the baths were already almost full. A long, concrete-floored space had eight tubs on either side, and was divided down the middle by wooden benches with attached rails at head height on which were hooks for clothes and towels. Charlotte could taste on her tongue the steam that rose up against the cold air and made it difficult to see if there was room for her. She walked along the duckboards until she came to a free place, where she put her parcel on the bench and began to undress.

As she quickly slipped Dominique's brassière over her shoulders and ran it down her arms, she found herself addressed by a naked Mlle Cariteau, who was about to climb into the bath next to her. Charlotte was unsure of the etiquette and found herself blushing, unseen, in the steam. Sylvie Cariteau was making conversation in the positive and factual manner she favoured in the post office and Charlotte did her best to respond in the same style.

Sylvie Cariteau turned away and walked round her bath to feel the temperature of the water. Charlotte watched the departure of her strong back and solid haunches with relief as she quickly finished undressing and climbed into the high-sided bath. On her other side was Madame Galliot from the ironmongery, though without her glasses and with her hair let down her back it was a moment before Charlotte recognised her.

Naked, she seemed younger and less formidable. She walked up beside Charlotte's bath and leaned over to take one of the bars of soap that were perched on the taps. As she did so, Charlotte's eye took in Madame Galliot's torso and the huge lower expanse of black hair which looked for a moment like the giant sporran of some fabulously virile clan. Charlotte lowered her head and splashed water into her face.

Above the thunder of water on porcelain and the swishing waves of women mixing hot and cold inside their tubs, there were shouted conversations and splashing. Charlotte could make out Pauline Bobotte's plump, shiny body with its pointed breasts and roll of fat around the middle that no privations appeared to have threatened. As she vigorously dried herself, the flesh of her buttocks wobbled like that of a woman in a Rubens painting, and Charlotte wondered if this was what men liked. Would Gregory like it? He would certainly enjoy being here, she thought, though he would have noted sadly the absence of Madame Galliot's daughter. Perhaps Irène was too proud to take her clothes off in front of other people.

Cakes of soap, so severely rationed outside, were in abundance here; they smelt of something harsh and chemical, but there were plenty of the palm-sized pink bricks. Charlotte washed with luxurious pleasure in the deep water, replenished from the unlimited supply, and when there was no reason to prolong her immersion, she reluctantly stood up and turned towards the central bench.

She had lost weight in the months she had been in France, though to her irritation it had gone from her hands, her feet, her cheeks, places from which she had no need to lose it. She was aware that above each hip-bone there was still a little surplus flesh and that a slight roundness persisted in her belly, even though the ribs above were protuberant. As she stood by the bench and raised her leg to dry her thighs and her knees with their fine bones, Charlotte found that she was staring at Pauline Benoit, naked except for her cherry lipstick and a ribbon in her hair, or rather that Pauline was staring at her, and in particular at her groin. Charlotte followed the other woman's eyes to the thin, inverted plume of golden hair that her raised leg only half concealed; then she looked back at Pauline, saw her eyes now on her face and on the dark, cropped coiffure. She understood what had intrigued Pauline. After almost five months in France, it was the first evidence of a mistake by G Section.

When she had put on the new dress, she took the rest of her clothes out to the washroom that adjoined the baths, where she towelled her hair vigorously and tried to arrange it in the mirror. Sylvie Cariteau combed her black bob and smiled her candid smile at Charlotte.

'Will you come and have a glass at my house after dinner with Monsieur Levade?'

'Thank you.'

'To wish you good luck.'

In the vestibule, Charlotte wrapped her coat about her, put on her scarf and handed in the sopping towel. It was not far to Julien's apartment, and for the first time ever, unless Pauline Benoit was going to run naked across the Place de l'Eglise, she would reach the staircase unchallenged.

'My God, Danièle, you look wonderful,' said Julien when Charlotte stepped into his apartment. 'You remember César, don't you?'

The head boy of the lycée stood up and held out his big hand to be shaken, apparently not daring to offer his cheek; Charlotte kissed him anyway and accepted the glass Julien held out to her.

'We're expecting a couple more for dinner,' said Julien. 'Lepidus is bringing some pâté and Antony is supposed to have a pear tart. Don't ask how they manage it.'

'What am I drinking?' said Charlotte.

'It's an alcohol made from apples, a sort of local calvados. Madame Benoit gave it to me. It's a little rough, I'm afraid, but I haven't been able to get much wine. I like your dress. Was that from the shop Pauline told you about?'

'Yes. It makes me look a bit like my mother, but it was the best they could do. Is everything all right for tonight?'

'Yes, there was confirmation on the BBC. It's not till midnight, but I want us to be there by half past ten. We'll meet the others there. We've got a new man in to replace Auguste.'

'Good,' said Charlotte. 'Don't tell me his name. Caligula?'

'This is a serious business, Madame. As a matter of fact it's Tiberius.'

'I knew it was only a matter of time before you reached the perverts.'

'That's enough. César, amuse Danièle, please, while I finish making dinner. I have a little surprise for you.'

The prospect of action seemed to have restored Julien's old humour and Charlotte heard him singing as he clattered about in the kitchen. Antony and Lepidus arrived together, bringing their promised contributions, which they laid on the table before helping themselves eagerly to Madame Benoit's apple spirit. Antony was a plump man with thick-rimmed glasses whom Charlotte recognised, though she did not say so, as the local optician. Lepidus, the third member of the peculiar triumvirate, was well into his seventies, red-faced, and with a hand that shook so badly that he had to steady it with the other when he clasped his brimming glass. A minute or so later his eyes were still watering, but his hand was calm.

Julien's surprise turned out to be a brace of rabbits he had shot in the grounds of the Domaine that morning. He had prepared them in a sauce whose main ingredient was mustard, referred to on its packet by the new régime as 'condiment'. He had put some of the rice with the offal to make a stuffing and served some macaroni on the side in place of potatoes, or 'feculents' as the ration-masters called them. There was also a small heap of something orange which even in their extreme hunger Julien's guests treated cautiously.

'They call it 'rutabaga',' Julien explained to Antony, who had lifted a forkful up to his spectacles for closer examination. 'I think it's something they normally give to cattle. The commissars of Vichy have strongly recommended it to their loyal, hungry people.'

'Hmm,' said Antony, inspecting the blob on the end of his fork. 'I don't suppose it features very often on the menus at the Hôtel du Parc.'

'I dare say not,' said Julien.

Even César, with the appetite of three men, managed only a little of the curious vegetable. Charlotte, who recognised it as swede, wanted to tell them that where she came from it was considered a delicacy when accompanying the haggis; but as Danièle she could only shrug and share their puzzled revulsion. Julien poured wine into glasses that were always empty and pushed affirmatively towards his bottle. Watching Lepidus's lip hook avidly over the rim of his glass and suck, Charlotte wondered to what extent political idealism was his motive in risking his life on a freezing winter's night.

Reaching the agreed drop zone was no longer the simple matter it had been before the advent of the Germans. They left the house separately, at a quarter to ten in order to beat the curfew, and were instructed by Julien to make their own way to the farm, without lights on their bicycles. 'You can come with me, Danièle,' he said. 'We'll bring up the rear.'

As Charlotte free-wheeled down the rue de l'Eglise, the wind whistling through the insubstantial fabric of Dominique's overcoat, she was aware both of how much she had drunk and of the fact that, whatever the amount, it was less than half that consumed by any of the others. She followed Julien to Madame Cariteau's house on the main road.

'We've got half an hour,' said Julien, rapping on the glass of the back door.

Sylvie Cariteau, her hair shiny from the effects of the pink carbolic soap, let them into the kitchen where she had set out six glasses on the cleared and scrubbed table. In answer to her daughter's call, Madame Cariteau appeared at the door to the main part of the house with André and Jacob.

'I don't know what all this is about,' the old woman muttered, 'and I don't think I want to know, I'm a loyal citizen. Sylvie doesn't tell me anything.'

'We should have a song. A song from each of us,' said Sylvie Cariteau, and sat down at the piano. 'Who'll go first?'

'Madame, Madame, you go,' said André, looking up at Charlotte.

'I think you have an admirer,' said Mlle Cariteau.

The only song Charlotte could think of was 'Alouette', which she sang, with some help with the words from Sylvie and André. Julien drained another glass before starting up an old folk song about a man who was jealous of his wife but was cuckolded all the same. Madame Cariteau's clucking disapproval was drowned by a chorus full of 'la-la-las' with which the boys were able to join in.

Madame Cariteau walked over to the piano and folded her arms across her chest. She launched herself precipitately into something that her daughter was not expecting, and there were some family words before they agreed to start again.

Madame Cariteau's voice, once it had found the right key, turned out to be surprisingly clear and firm; no trace of self-consciousness blurred the high notes of the traditional song she had chosen. Looking at the old woman's stout, worn body, Charlotte was amazed by the youthful purity that had been preserved intact within it; it was like watching a clear stream erupt from dark, decaying undergrowth. The chorus went: 'But then I was young and the leaves were green/Now the corn is cut and the little boat sailed away.' It was a song of the most self-admiring sentimentality about the different ages of a man's life. One of the verses began: 'One day the young men came back from the war, the corn was high and our sweethearts were waiting . . . ', and there was a silence in the Cariteaus' kitchen as though the music had exceeded the sum of its modest parts. Charlotte could not help thinking of Madame Cariteau's husband and of all the men who did not come back for Sylvie. She found tears filling her eyes and was appalled both by the feeling and by her lack of musical taste.

Julien called out a virile 'bravo' to break the mood and brought Jacob forward to the piano. He sang a tune he had learned at school, though his shyness made it difficult to understand. It was something about 'To the right, to the left, please take my hand, and come and dance, and . . . ', but after two or three attempts the words seemed to peter out at this point.

Sylvie Cariteau sang a canon by Bach, her voice oddly coarser than her old mother's. Finally, André sang all the many verses of the story of a little ship that had never sailed and set off on a long voyage. The chorus involved Julien conducting with the empty wine bottle: 'Sailors sail upon the waves!' It went down so well with the boys that they had to go through it again.

On the final note, Julien embraced both women warmly, kissed the boys, took Charlotte by the elbow and out into the night. They were ten minutes up the road before Charlotte had caught her breath.

In the farmhouse they met the other members of the group, standing round beneath the lanterns hung from the beam of the kitchen, smacking their upper arms with their gloved hands, drinking from coffee cups and enamel mugs they filled from an unlabelled bottle on the table. Charlotte watched in disbelief as César, Lepidus and Antony helped themselves again. One of the other men produced a dry sausage, which he cut into lengths and handed round. A youngish man with curly hair and a beard took a pistol from his jacket, emptied the bullets into his hand, twirled round the empty chamber, held it up to the lantern, checked the sights and carefully reloaded it. Most of the others had firearms of some kind. Charlotte knotted her headscarf more tightly under her chin and smiled at César as she declined his offer of a sunflower-leaf cigarette. The men muttered and growled at each other as they shrugged, lit cigarettes and occasionally punched one another on the shoulder.

On the bare table Julien placed two cups to show the location of the farm building and of a barn the other side of the drop zone. Then he drew tracks in the wood with this finger to show the plane's path and the line that the men's torches must make. It was a large bomber, he didn't know what make, but it would be heaving out sixteen containers into the void. It was dangerous to be underneath because of the weight of what was coming down, so no one was to move a pace from his designated spot.

'Listen,' said one of the men, slightly less agricultural-looking than the others, 'my brother-in-law was in the air force and I know a thing or two about flying. The chances of a bomber finding that little clearing and being able to drop on the lights you've described — it's hopeless.'

Julien smiled tolerantly. 'They've done it before.'

'Just on co-ordinates and a couple of torches, you don't think — '

'If you don't want to take part, you can leave now. Go on.'

The man shrugged and puffed for a moment, but stood his ground. 'It's all right. I'll stay.'

'Good.' Julien turned to a small man who looked from his torn clothes and bedraggled appearance as though he had spent several nights in the woods. He had an unwashed smell that reminded Charlotte of a beggar who had once lurched at her from a doorway in Glasgow, but Julien seemed to defer to his knowledge of the terrain, and particularly of a wood they needed to cross. He told them he had heard the second BBC bulletin and that the drop had been confirmed; they would meet four more volunteers at an agreed clearing in the woods.

Julien looked at his watch. 'Is everybody ready? From the time we make contact with the other four until the drop is completed and everything has been cleared away there must be no talking. Do you understand?'

The men shifted their weight and stamped their feet on the cold stone floor. Charlotte thought they looked like ghillies preparing for a rough shoot on the estate of some minor aristocrat fallen on hard times. She saw two of them fill flasks from the bottle on the table and slip them into their pockets.

As they left the building and clattered over the moonlit farmyard, Charlotte felt the sweet illicit thrill she remembered from her childhood when, on the endless summer nights beneath the northern skies, she and Roderick would climb out of their bedroom windows, go down a ladder they had left beside the house and make for the fields. The aching cut of the

December wind brought her back to the present, but the moonlight was as white and as evenly spread as on a Highland night in August. ' 'Charlotte' . . . admirable,' she thought.

They walked in single file, obediently silent, down a narrow path beside a field in which half a dozen cows stood like iron statues. The tramp-like man in front, who, Julien whispered to Charlotte, was a poacher, then made them drop down into a ditch and up the other side into a dense wood. Hearing the noise of breaking twigs and shuffled leaves, Charlotte shivered at how easy it would be for a German patrol to run a machine gun swiftly down their line. After about twenty minutes they emerged on to the rim of a large clearing, which Charlotte could make out was edged on all four sides by woods.

Charlotte jumped at the sound of a creature coming through the thick undergrowth at her shoulder. She had no gun and found she had let out a small cry as she grabbed Julien's arm. The creature was followed by three others. They whispered greetings to Julien who motioned them to go forward into the field.

In the twenty minutes before the plane was due, Julien placed the men with torches at intervals of a hundred yards and told the others that each of them must count the number of parachutes with the utmost care. He took Charlotte by the wrist and positioned her on the edge of the field. 'Watch carefully, Danièle. And count. One parachute missed means we can never use this place again. And they'll be on to us.'

Charlotte watched the sky, picking out the tilted saucepan of the Great Bear, from which northerly direction the plane would presumably arrive. The thought of the English plane with men from London, Lincolnshire, perhaps from Aberdeen, that had ploughed through the night and would by dawn have taken its men home to tea and English newspapers made her feel, for the first time since she had been in France, a lurching homesickness.

Above their heads was a narrow crescent moon in a sky almost yellow with the light of sludgy galaxies. The curved shape reminded her of some lines by Victor Hugo that she could never, irritatingly, quite remember, about a careless god who had been reaping in the sky, then stopped and 'left his sickle in this golden field of stars'.

They stood in their places, listening to the darkness. The huge country lay peacefully all about them, indifferent to the whereabouts of some tiny plane. How futile it seemed, Charlotte thought: the villages in the Cévennes would still cling to their rocky defiles, the Loire would still broadly flow; the vastness of the silent, undisturbed country made their sincerest efforts look quite useless.

She strained against the silence of the night. There was the sound of some night-bird, fussing over the limits of its territory, a sudden rattle in the undergrowth of the woods, perhaps a rabbit or a grounded pheasant, then the icy stillness once more all round. Then there came a sound like breath, like a soft grunt caught and stifled on the beat of a pulse. She reached out and touched Julien's hand. She pointed upwards. 'Yes?'

Julien put his finger to his lips and listened. The noise grew louder, becoming a whirring growl. 'Yes.' Julien ran out into the field and shouted to the men in the line.

The sound was now continuous, and above the deeply pulsing engine there was a whining note as though it was straining to slow down.

At last the plane came into sight. A black square against the white moonlit clouds, it grew swiftly in size as it began to descend on them. With no lights, it was like a thunderous animal coming down closer and closer, until it filled the sky to one side of the torches only a few feet above their heads and made the ground tremble with the huge sonorous notes of its exhaust. Charlotte saw four vast engines, then the belly of the plane, then square rudders on the tail as it passed over them and began to climb. It dropped nothing, but started to rise and bank slowly to its right.

'What's wrong?' called Charlotte to the figure nearest to her. 'Wasn't it ours?'

'Yes.' It was the man with the brother-in-law in the air force. 'It was a Halifax. It'll come back.' His tone was grudging.

The sound of engines was almost lost as the heavy plane made its long, heavy turn, then, at the point of vanishing, it began a slow crescendo. Once more the black, ragged square approached beneath the lights of the Bear and this time it came in almost flat on the line of the waiting torches. The noise of the propellers seemed to echo and ring off the frozen sky, and as the plane levelled out above them the moon struck a tingling reflection in the perspex canopy.

At the moment the four engines seemed on the point of stalling, the belly of the aircraft broke open and heavy dark blossoms filled the sky behind it like a handful of black confetti. They swung on swift, narrow arcs and landed with a tinny sound on the hard earth. Before the plane was out of sight, the field was full of people running to the collapsed parachutes and wrenching them free of their metal cargo. In the excitement Charlotte had forgotten to count.

Julien was running round trying to find out how many parachutes had come down. Charlotte hurried over to the nearest one, where she found the poacher opening the cylinder down one side. There were three further canisters inside with two wire handles for carrying. He pulled one out, handed it to Charlotte, and pointed her to the corner of the field while he folded the parachute into the empty outer container.

The squat little tube was extraordinarily heavy, and the wire handles cut deeply into Charlotte's hands. She noticed that most of the men had somehow hoisted the tubes on to their shoulders. She took off her headscarf and wrapped it round her palms to protect them as she lugged the cylinder across the field.

There was a growing pile inside a small clearing at the edge of the wood where Julien was discouraging the men from opening the containers until everything had been brought in from the drop zone. The rule of silence had been completely forgotten in the exhilaration of the moment as they smoked and laughed and congratulated themselves on the successful drop.

As Charlotte went back into the field to retrieve another of the heavy packages she heard the sound of the plane again. It came down on a different angle this time, not directly overhead, but on a slow, wide turn from east to west. As it dipped in above the clearing it seemed dangerously low, and the sound of its groaning engines made Charlotte think for a moment that it was going to stall and bury itself in the ground. A torch to her left was flashing a morse signal to the roaring, juddering plane, and as her eyes ran up along its beam, Charlotte, alone in the field, her hair whipped against her face, looked up and saw for a second in the black open cave of the bomb bay a kneeling English airman looking down on her.

His silhouette was caught for a moment, lit from behind by a light in the fuselage. Then the plane was climbing as swiftly as its bulk would permit, the engine noise rising in pitch as it completed its turn and pointed north for home.

★ ★ ★

'They like to have a look at their clients sometimes. It's their way of saying hello.' It was Julien. 'Come

370

on. Let's see what they've brought us.'

Charlotte followed him back to the wood. She was shaking.

In the clearing the men were transferring the contents of the metal containers into sacks. There were Bren guns, pistols, ammunition and hand grenades; there was also plastic explosive, which the men inspected doubtfully, and a huge number of cheap-looking Sten guns with magazines and loaders.

César let out a cry of delight as his canister disgorged bars of chocolate, butter, tins of food and prime Virginia cigarettes, a packet of which he opened at once and handed round.

'You've got to stop them taking the parachutes,' said Julien. 'They'll try and make them into clothes and anyone can see from the stitching where they've come from.'

Eventually they finished burying the stores and covered the place with leaves and loose branches.

'The horse and cart'll be here tomorrow night,' Julien said, 'but it's too dangerous to take it all back to Lavaurette with the Germans there. We'll have to keep it at the farm. Is that all right?'

The farmer he had turned to shrugged as he pulled deeply on his English cigarette. 'We had a visit from the police two weeks ago when we had two calves and a pregnant sow in the cellar. They didn't see a thing.'

'Come on, then.' The men began to file back through the wood, with the poacher leading, then out on to the narrow track. Many of them stumbled and swore as they went. One of the men passed Charlotte a flask. Although she had already drunk more than ever before in her life she felt the bonds of comradeship required her to accept. Here was service at last in the ill-defined but urgent moral cause that had first sent her south to London; here was the reason she had decided to stay in France. She was not going to appear half-hearted at this late stage.

'Are you all right?' Julien asked her at the farm, as the men mounted their bicycles and rode off shakily towards their homes.

'I think so.' It was hard to say precisely. She had been frightened by the dangerous proximity of the plane and by the noise it made, then felt tricked and wounded by the vision of the single airman looking down on her. She also felt a powerful bond with these absurd drunken men stumbling about in the darkness, a sense of gratitude to them for having understood what needed to be done. She was one of them, and wanted to be closer.

Her skin felt swollen with this odd mixture of emotion as she followed Julien back into Lavaurette, her bicycle wobbling dangerously as they turned the sharp corner out of the Place de l'Eglise.

'Will you be all right to get home?' said Julien, leaning his machine against the wall.

Charlotte nodded.

Julien put his face close to hers; he seemed to be inspecting her in the darkness. She closed her eyes for a moment. She was aware of how strange and sleepy she must appear; it was as though she were anaesthetised by drink, yet beneath the painless surface she was turbulently conscious.

'Do you want to come in? We could have a nightcap. Or you can sleep here if you're too tired to go back to the Domaine. I don't mind the sofa.'

Charlotte nodded and Julien took her arm as they made their way across the hall and up the stairs. He turned on a lamp in the sitting room and handed her a glass. She put it down on the table and opened her arms. Julien embraced her and she rested her head against his shoulder.

'It's all right, Dominique, it's all right.' He kissed her hair.

She pulled her head back and smiled at him. 'I'm so tired,' she said.

'Of course you are. It's late. It's almost dawn. And tonight was . . . different.'

'Yes.' Charlotte wanted to explain her conflicting passions to Julien, how strong they were, how important, but she was too tired to find the words, and too drunk.

'Kiss me,' she said.

She had no wish to leave Julien's apartment; she had been so long alone, so long thrown back on the resources of her own mind and feelings that she wanted to take strength and comfort from someone else.

'I'd like to stay with you,' she said.

Julien appeared once more to be earnestly, almost clinically examining her face. 'Are you sure? You won't regret it?'

Charlotte smiled. She would not regret anything that brought her closer to the companionship of the men with whom she had spent the evening. They had understood their past and they had made some effort to keep a thread intact, a link that would enable their country to survive because the connection to better days, before the Fall, though tenuous, would be unbroken.

'And Monsieur Guilbert?' said Julien. 'What would he say?'

'I don't care.' She opened her hands in shrugging dismissal. 'You can kiss me again, Monsieur Levade, if you like.' She saw in Julien's eyes the look of furtive schoolboy pleasure she had seen when she first kissed him in Lavaurette, as though he could not quite believe his luck. It made her start to laugh, so she had to pull her mouth away from his.

'Your face,' she said.

'What's wrong with it?'

Charlotte looked at its expression, now agitated and serious. 'Nothing,' she said, 'it's a beautiful face.'

'Madame Guilbert, you're a very teasing, wicked woman.'

'Shall we go into the bedroom?'

Charlotte sat on the end of Julien's bed; she remembered how she had slept in it the first day she had arrived in Lavaurette with her detective story, her identity fiercely subdued in that of Dominique. Now it would be wonderful to do something spontaneously affectionate, free from the weight of anguish and uncertainty.

'My husband has a mistress, anyway,' she said, as she pushed off the ugly shoes. 'It serves him right.' She reached up and undid the buttons on the back of her dress; she stood to let it fall to the floor. She was not quite too drunk to calculate that, unless the cycle of her body had played an unprecedented trick, there was no danger of her becoming pregnant.

'Oh, Dominique,' said Julien, running his hands down the small of her bare back, then slipping a finger inside the waistband of her new silk underwear. 'I've always wanted to make love to a stranger, someone whose name I don't even know.'

Charlotte felt him slide away her remaining clothes and tightly shut her eyes, some modest hope persisting that she might thus herself become invisible. Julien pushed her gently back on to the bed and she felt the mattress shake as he tore at his own clothes.

'Quickly,' she said, aware that her churning emotions might move into a new pattern that would make her want to stop, or that the serene sense of not caring might desert her.

She felt Julien's lips kissing the skin of her inner thigh and for a moment thought of what he might be seeing, and wondered whether it was yet light enough in the seepage of the grey winter dawn through the shutters for him, like Pauline Benoit, to be puzzled. She lifted him by the shoulders and felt his body loom over hers as he kissed her mouth.

Between her legs she felt the touch of his hand while he whispered in her ear. 'Madame Guilbert, you are a remarkable woman. If you were not married I might think myself in love with you.'

'Please, Octave. Please.'

Charlotte heard her own voice as she begged him to begin, but he kept her waiting, whispering, 'Dominique, you're so beautiful,' while his hand caressed her until she could take no more but reached out and pulled him into her.

She felt Julien clench his body in desperate self-control. He moved slowly back and forth for a few minutes, then briefly stopped.

'Dominique,' he breathed, 'this is so wonderful I feel I might disintegrate, I might break into a million fragments.'

She pushed against him, reclaimed him, and he began to move more vigorously, then sigh with sad rapture as though he recognised his time was limited. Though she sensed how he tried to hold himself back, Charlotte felt buffeted by the urgency of his desire, too much so to venture off into her own imagining, and so she merely went with him, in a willing indulgence.

At the last moment she did feel a rise of feeling in herself as he groaned out her presumed name for the final time; but what name she called out in return she could not have said, as her mind was full of the picture of Julien being annihilated, as he slumped down gasping on top of her, breaking into tiny dying fragments.

6

For more than twenty-four hours Peter Gregory had waited and watched. He left the busy port area during the day and looked for somewhere to sleep where he would not draw attention to himself. Although he had cash in his pocket, he was wary of trying to buy food without tickets. In order to look less suspicious, he also needed to shave, but having previously borrowed equipment from Jacques (it was seldom used by the old man himself), he was not sure whether razors and blades were also rationed.

By midday the pain in his leg was so severe that he decided to risk a hotel he had seen a short walk back from the waterfront. Despite the harsh light overhead, the lino-covered vestibule had a dim, crepuscular feeling, unmitigated by the sweet smell of some recent disinfectant. Behind the high front desk sat a woman in her sixties with greying hair piled up in a bun and thick glasses that rendered her suspicious eyes unnaturally large.

Gregory stuck an unlit cigarette in the corner of his mouth to make his speech less distinct. 'Room?' he barked, laying down his identity card on the counter. In the course of the afternoon he had rubbed it on the ground and scuffed the edges to make it look less new.

The woman turned to a board behind her and took a key from its hook. She said something Gregory did not understand, in answer to which he smiled as charmingly as he could manage and yawned melodramatically.

She spoke again and he thought he made out the word for money. He rapidly calculated that even if he was mistaken she was unlikely to be displeased by being offered cash at this stage, and put his hand to his pocket; perhaps it was not the sort of hotel where people actually spent the night. The exchange of money lightened the atmosphere, and it occurred to Gregory that the woman was as frightened as he was. They had told him in London that there were no fewer than fifteen police and security organisations working in France and doubtless the landlady like everyone else had something she did not wish them to find out.

He climbed the stairs and went along the passage to room number 14. The grimy little window overlooked an interior courtyard in which the cooker outlet from the kitchen emitted a grey, unwholesome vapour. Gregory lay down on the bed and, despite his best intentions of only resting, fell asleep.

It was dark when he awoke. He made his way back to the street by the harbour. There was still the same bustle of German troops unloading stores, standing behind lorries, smoking; there were still French police strutting about in pairs.

It was past midnight when he decided he could wait no longer; if he did not move soon he would faint with hunger and fatigue. When the door of the house he was watching opened at last, he went across the street and stopped the middle-aged man who was leaving.

'Pascale?'

'First floor.' The man jerked his head backwards and hurried off.

Gregory went up the bare stairs and knocked at a green-painted door on the landing.

It opened a few inches and he found himself looking at a woman with stern, grey eyes.

'What do you want?'

'Pascale. I . . . ' Gregory's French deserted him. He closed his eyes and felt the floor begin to buckle underneath him. 'I'm English,' he said in his own language. 'For God's sake help me.'

The door opened and he stepped inside.

'Take it easy,' said the woman, also in English.

'My God, you're American.'

He fell forward against her, and she dragged his bony weight across the room to a divan by the window.

* * *

Charlotte became particular in her work at the Domaine, as though it were something that interested her. She forced herself to take pride in the cleanliness of the floors and furniture and to make dinner, even if it was barely edible, at least a punctuation of Levade's undifferentiated hours.

She began to think more and more about home. The sight of the black-bellied Halifax above her, the curious pilot making one more sweep above the benighted land before heading north for England, had made her think of those laconic men, their flying suits, their beer, their shoulder-shrugging that concealed an inglorious belief in what they did. She thought more and more of her parents and of her brother; if he was now abroad, as he had so long hoped, they would be worried for his safety. Roderick had a way of being at the centre of improbable storms; he was always on the train that broke down, invariably in the foyer of the cinema that caught fire.

The combination of fatigue, exhilaration and the after-effects of drink made her able to postpone thinking about her night with Julien. Then, as her mind became rested and clear, she found her first response was a self-righteous sense of loyalty to herself. Why not?, she caught herself saying to her reflection when she combed her hair in the morning: it's my life, I'm responsible to no one but myself. She rather admired her own daring, and felt protective of the vulnerable being that was still there in the centre of her — child, woman, it made no difference — and to whom she owed her greatest allegiance. I will stick by my own decisions, she valiantly thought, as she laboured in the icy rooms of the Domaine.

Yet her bravado was slowly deflated by feelings of shame and insecurity. She loved the idea of Dominique, had used her without compunction for her own advantage, and regretted having descended to invoking her as an alibi for her own idle lust, betrayal or selfish need for reassurance. Dominique represented to her the plight of a typical woman expelled from some domestic paradise by forces outside herself, and Charlotte was deeply sympathetic; for a few days her misuse of Dominique weighed more heavily with her than her infidelity to Peter Gregory. He had been for so long absent, for so long kept alive not by any realistic belief but more by her neurotic need for him, that to believe she had been unfaithful required a sophistication of feeling that was beyond her.

Slowly, however, guilt cleared its ingenious paths, and Charlotte began to suffer fears that only her fidelity had kept him living — a superstitious dread that he would now give up or die. She felt she had compromised the only thing in her life that had had the redeeming power of goodness and purity; it made no difference that it was just one night, with a man of whom she was profoundly fond. Fidelity was a matter of absolutes, not degree; it would have been no worse if she had slept with every man at the farm that night. Her long patience was about to be rewarded by word from Mirabel, and, at the crucial moment, she had failed.

From day to day her most pressing problem was with Julien. She felt embarrassed by the difference she presumed in their feelings; she thought he was in love with her and that she was bound to disappoint him. Her only hope was that men, perhaps, were different in such matters and that his obvious desires for her were not necessarily eloquent of any deep feeling. Meanwhile she discovered some reflex in herself — so contradictory of her conscious feelings that she could only imagine it as a primal instinct — which craved reassurance that he did actually care for her, and that their night together would not be a single, unrepeated act. She wanted to go back to him.

Charlotte despaired at the confusion of her feelings, but managed to decide one thing clearly at least: that she would as far as possible avoid seeing Julien until her thoughts were clearer.

One morning she was washing in the icy water of the bathroom basin, splashing it all over and scrubbing with soap to store up cleanliness so she could postpone a return to the public baths. Again, she had the strange sensation that someone was watching her, but this time she did not have time to cover herself and investigate because the door was opened from outside.

'Ah, Madame Guilbert. Excuse me. I need to go out and I wanted you to know that I am expecting a delivery this afternoon. Some paints.' Levade shrugged. 'Pointless, I expect. I'll just smear them on the canvas. But you never know.'

Charlotte, dripping, cold, and hastily arranging a towel about her, felt embarrassment for them both. Levade simply stared at her with level eyes. She began to protest at his intrusion, but it seemed quite pointless.

'All right,' she said. 'I'll listen for the door.'

'Thank you. I'll be back by two.'

He walked away down the corridor, and Charlotte quickly dried herself. Did he really see only through the eyes of art? Was his gaze so pure that he saw only the shapes of Renoir or Modigliani? She was slightly nettled by his indifference. At least now perhaps he'll consider

380

my breasts as fine as Anne-Marie's, she thought, as she pulled on her clothes.

Downstairs there was a letter for Madame Guilbert. On a single sheet inside were the words: 'Meet me Wednesday, 16 hours. Same place. Mirabel.'

Charlotte crumpled the paper joyously in her fist. She loved Mirabel; she loved the way he kept his word; she loved the care he had taken to make his handwriting look so French.

★ ★ ★

'I think I'm dreaming for two,' Charlotte told Levade that afternoon when he had invited her into his studio to examine his new paints. 'Something has caused a great storm of dreams in me. They're not pictures, though, they're more like actions.'

Levade seemed uninterested. Other people's dreams, Charlotte remembered her father telling her as a teenager, are the most tedious conversational topic on earth. You can fabricate an interest in gossip on the grounds that it at least springs from an actual experience, however trite; dreams lack even this weak claim on our attention. Dr Gray had resented the importance ascribed to dreams by most practitioners of his science and had himself tried to hurry his patients through their recitations.

Levade was looking at the painting of Anne-Marie. 'She's a charming woman, isn't she?' he said. 'There's something powerfully feminine about her. But the painting tells us nothing. It might just as well be a photograph.'

'What about the skin on her arms?' said Charlotte, though she still found it was not to Anne-Marie's arms that her eyes were drawn.

'Just paint.'

The dream Charlotte wanted to tell him about

was one from the night before, in which she had re-experienced the moment in her childhood when her father had betrayed her. To overcome Levade's resistance to the topic of dreams, she had to cast it as truth, as something that had happened, as in fact — so far as she could tell — it had.

She climbed off the bed where she had been sitting and walked across the bare boards until she stood between Levade and the light from the window, so she could be sure of his attention. Her tongue seemed stuck for a moment to her teeth; she licked her lips and looked over at him.

'When I was a child of about seven my father did something to me that has troubled me ever since. He caused me pain in what seemed like an innocent embrace. I opened my arms to him as a child would, and when he let me go something terrible had happened. Everything was changed.'

Levade's hand was motionless, the paintbrush poised a small distance from the canvas.

'He assaulted you?' Levade's eyes were fixed on Charlotte's face.

'He hurt me.'

She told him how she had come upon her father weeping, and how, when she had tried to comfort him something had taken place. He had pushed her away, he had slapped her . . . but the pain felt worse than this, like a violation, like an end of innocence.

'Did he really hit you? Or was it more like . . . '

'It sounds extraordinary,' said Charlotte, 'but I don't know. There was physical pain, but I couldn't say in what part of my body. The damage he did me was so personal and wounding that I've often thought it must have been sexual. Yet the truth is that I can't remember. My mind didn't understand at that age, and I just shut it away. I was left with a fear that it might happen again. It was the most real, most powerful thing that's ever happened to me, yet I can't remember exactly what it was.'

'It's not strange,' said Levade. 'I understand.'

'You do?' Charlotte looked at him in disbelief. For almost twenty years this half-assimilated thing had lain in her mind unconfessed, a trouble to her thinking, feeling life, and she had never thought that anyone could comprehend.

Levade breathed in; his face became radiant with interest and his body seemed to slough off its habitual air of defeat. 'What would a child's mind do with such an experience? It could only push it to one side and try to bury it. It's possible that you may never know what happened; it may be beyond the reach of memory. And perhaps that's not a terrible thing. Human beings can live with mystery, with unresolved conflicts.'

Charlotte thought of the painting he had shown her. 'Yes, but the trouble is that it affected my life. My childhood until then had been wonderful. There seemed to be no flaw in it. Although my father was not a demonstrative man, I felt surrounded by love, I was insulated from the world. Every taste and every sensation came to me with this innocence, with this guarantee of love and safety. Then, from that moment, all that certainty, all that bliss was gone.'

'How did it show itself? Did it make you unstable?'

'Later, in my teens, I was ill, I was treated by various doctors. They called it 'depression', but I don't think they knew what it was. Perhaps it wasn't related to the incident.'

'What did the doctors say?'

'I only told one of them. It was in Aberdeen. He didn't believe me. He got up out of his chair. He was angry.'

'And what did you do?'

'I felt trapped. I had to break out of it. I . . . ' Charlotte was finding it difficult to breathe.

'What did he say?'

Charlotte began to sob, long, scorching breaths from deep in her abdomen. 'He said I was . . . a liar . . . an evil girl. He . . . '

Levade put his arm round her shoulder, and Charlotte thought how strange it was that something that had been so long suppressed should emerge in the embrace of a person she had until then so distrusted.

Levade made her sit on the bed while he went downstairs and prepared some tea, which he told her would be soothing for an 'English' woman. He returned with a small pot of black herbal tea and pressed a cigarette on her as well.

'There you are, Charlotte,' he said, and it occurred to her that although he made an issue of discovering it, he had never until that moment used her name.

Levade began to cough, a horrible, deep retching sound that left him panting and momentarily incapable of speech.

'Are you all right? That sounds terrible.'

'This house is cold at night. That's all.' He waved away her concern.

'How old was your father when these things happened?'

Charlotte sucked at the bitter tea. 'I was born in 1917 and I was about six, so if he was born in 1887 — '

'So he'd been in the war?'

'Oh, yes. All the way through. I think he must have been very lucky. He once told me almost all the officers were killed.'

'Did he tell you much about the war?'

Charlotte struggled to overcome her habitual repulsion at the thought of conflict, and her father in it.

'Not a great deal. He took us to see the graveyards when we were children. He told us it must never happen again. I think my brother and I found it hard to take in. I don't think children can understand things on that

384

scale. Then, as we grew older, he spoke of it less and less. He became more withdrawn in every way, not just about his own past experiences.'

'Did he ever tell you stories about it?'

'Not that I recall. We had a general impression of waste and death. Though I do remember one odd thing he mentioned. I remember it because it was so incongruous. It came out of the blue. I suppose I was about ten and it was one of those rare days when we did things together like a real family. We went to a loch and rowed on the water. Then we had a picnic lunch . . . '

★ ★ ★

. . . Gray was lighting a pipe to keep the midges off. He held the box of matches over the bowl to help it draw, then puffed a blue cloud into the thin and silent air. His wife laid out a tartan rug on the heather and took a thermos from a wicker basket.

'Would you like a cup of tea, William?'

'What? No. I'll have a dram. Did you put some in?'

Amelia Gray handed him the whisky flask in silence, and he filled the little silver lid, then raised it to his lips. The familiar spirit spread its slow comfort through his body as he propped himself against a rock and looked down towards the glistening water where his children played.

'Would you look at that lassie, Amelia? Look at the way she runs. She's like a boy.'

'She's lovely,' said his wife. 'We're so lucky, aren't we?'

Gray raised an eyebrow and looked over at her, his head nodding in the interested but sceptical manner he had developed in the lecture-room. There was the golden-legged girl chasing her brother up the margin of the loch; he heard her shrill, protesting voice and saw the tireless movements of her twisting body, as slim and muscular as an eel. So what was that storming sadness in her brown eyes when he spoke to her alone?

There was his boy, raw-boned, his voice already cracking with unexpected bass notes, a brave and vigorous child he had welcomed with all his proud young father's heart into a world that was still then, at that innocent time, with whatever fitful setbacks, becoming slowly and demonstrably more civilised, more habitable for his children and their future sons and daughters.

On this summer morning in the Highlands, the last coldness of the air just burned off by the sun, he could almost believe that nothing had been lost, that the powerful harmony of the rocks and water, the sound of generations and their laughter, were rolling on to some natural and joyous end. But everything had changed.

Sometimes at night he woke to find himself screaming, drenched with sweat. Usually, he was at the head of the communication trench, looking into the eyes of his disbelieving platoon commanders as he told them the attack would be in daylight. *In daylight?* He saw their stricken faces. Something they had concealed from one another, even from themselves, assumed at that moment the contours of a clear, impending truth. Twelve hours later, the size of it had become apparent; but even as he went among the emergency dressing-stations, encouraging the shattered men with his acquired brusqueness, Gray knew that it would take years to understand what they had seen that July morning.

He began to curse his survival. He was viewed by his men with incredulity: he not only had the will to survive, he even seemed to care who won. His unyielding efficiency, his brightness of manner and intellectual curiosity made the men fear him, as though his reserves were more than human. But the weight he carried was concealed from them; it was the burden of continuation. He watched the companies in his battalion renewed from top to bottom as the years wore on, their officers the first to go, but only he seemed unable to attract the fatal release. He knew that each day he nerved himself to carry on was a depletion of the life he might hope to lead when the war was over.

One of his platoon commanders, an inward, difficult man called Wraysford, had seen at one moment what it was costing him. He had looked into Gray's eyes and described the perfect blankness he had seen there, though Gray was doubtful whether he had diagnosed its cause. He had tried once to confide in this man, but when he reached out to him, he saw that his soul was too far shrunken down inside him to be capable of responding.

Charlotte and Roderick ate sandwiches on the rug and played with the small white dog who sniffed about the plate of hard-boiled eggs. When Gray looked at his daughter's wide brown eyes and the fine white down on her bare arms he felt indescribably old and tarnished. Yet he loved the girl, still, in his shocked and weary heart, he loved her, and he wished until the wish became an agony that he might have passed on to her a world that would have been worthy of her childish glee.

Roderick had just outgrown the high point of his boy's inquisitiveness, but there were still occasions when he turned to his father for information. Now he asked about soldiers and dungeons and why kings and barons didn't simply kill the prisoners they took.

Inspired by the beauty of the open landscape, the sound of birdsong from the bright sky, Gray for once did not tersely deflect the question but answered as the father of a boy and girl should, with friendly interest and detail.

The trouble with Roderick's questioning was that he was never satisfied; his endless cross-examination always drove Gray to some slight excess to make him stop.

'Of course they did, Roderick. Of course they sometimes did bad things, especially in the Middle Ages. Even in the war I fought in, it was not unheard of. Some people in my division — not in my battalion, I hasten to add — once had some German prisoners. It was not long after the Somme, that big battle I told you about once, when they'd seen almost all their friends killed one summer day. Then there'd been a long bombardment, day after day the shells falling, and some of the men were almost out of their mind with it. They went on a raid one night, crawling across no-man's-land on their bellies, and brought back twelve Boches. They took them down the line to the rear area, and the officer in charge told them they had to march them five miles, most of it uphill, in the pouring rain, to some depot where the prisoners would be guarded. These men were desperate, they were exhausted. At times like that you're not quite human. They had gone about half a mile, when they went into a little wood to rest. They went no further. They asked the officer to stand aside, to take himself off a hundred yards or so, then they shot all twelve where they stood. They told the officer the Germans had escaped. He knew quite well what had happened. They left the bodies there to — '

'That's enough, dear. Roderick understands, don't you?' Amelia Gray took a big tin from the picnic hamper. 'It's such a lovely day, we don't want to spoil it, do we? Charlotte, would you like a piece of fruit cake?'

Charlotte was sitting on the rug with her chin on her

drawn-up knees, and her arms wrapped round her bare legs. 'Thank you,' she said, her eyes averted from her father . . .

★ ★ ★

' . . . all that I remember,' she said to Levade, as she came to the end of her version of the story. 'Otherwise he never talked in detail.'

Levade stood, tapping his front teeth with the wooden tip of his paintbrush. 'I suppose such things did happen,' he said. 'Everyone who went through those years could tell you some horror.'

'And you?'

'I put it from my mind. I could never explain it to people who hadn't experienced it. The choice was either to think about it all the time or not at all. Then other things eventually came to distract me. Women, painting, the pointless joy of being alive.'

Charlotte looked at Levade's impassive, lined face and thought how little she had understood him. 'You fought all the way through, like my father?'

'Yes. I volunteered because I wanted to fight. I had inherited my father's love of this country. I was at Verdun. So were most of us. I was a Jew, but that was all right in those days. We were considered fit to fight and die with the rest. I was a bad soldier. They made me into a soup-man eventually. They were the most expendable. They tied a dozen flasks of wine to my belt and wound me round with loaves of bread which they'd knotted together with string. You could hardly stand up under the weight. Then at night they'd push you out, and you had to run or crawl through the fields and mud from one trench to another. To reach the hill they called the Dead Man, you'd be on your belly for an hour, and when you got there the men would spit and curse at you because the bread was caked in filth and half the wine had leaked away. The Germans knew the routes we took and used to shell them. They only used old men or weak people like me to be soup-men. You didn't last long. I remember lying in the slime one night, it was in my eyes, my ears, and I looked up and saw the torso of a man pinned against a tree by a splinter of metal. It had no head, no legs, no arms. There was a drip of offal from the waist. Many years later that image came back to me. In a vision of Christ.'

'How did you manage not to be killed?' said Charlotte.

'I was lucky. I was wounded. I was out for three months. When I rejoined my unit Pétain was in charge. He cared for the lives of his men. We still died in thousands, but he didn't waste our lives. He understood that Verdun was where the honour of France would be held and won, but he knew the price we had to pay. To have a man like that at such a time — someone who understands that all the history of his country hangs on what he does, and has the bravery to do it . . . Yet he cared for us too, like a father, he worried for our lives. My God, we loved him then.'

Charlotte saw the rims of Levade's eyes redden, but there seemed to be no tears. 'A group of four of us came on a dead horse one night. It was difficult to avoid them. It stank as though it had been there for weeks. My friend cut a piece from its flank and began to eat it. We chose the most putrid parts to make us ill. Two of them got taken into rest, one of them died. But I couldn't keep it down. I kept vomiting it up. There seemed to be no escape.'

'But you survived?'

'Somehow. I was taken off the soup run and went back to join the others.' Levade unbuttoned his shirt and pulled it to one side. 'This is the first wound I had.' A long red scar ran round from the top of his shoulder to his armpit, its edges raised into a purplish ridge. Charlotte could see the rough stitching that held the two welts together, presumably accomplished by the lamplight of some field dressing-station. 'It looks worse than it was. It wasn't really bad enough, that was the trouble. I would sooner have lost a leg.'

Charlotte said, 'And what do you think about the Germans now? Do you hate them?'

Levade smiled. 'I hardly think about them. When I do, I pray for them. I pray for God's forgiveness for what they have done. And what they are doing now.'

★ ★ ★

Charlotte still had not spoken to Julien by the time she set off on her bicycle for her rendezvous with Mirabel.

It was an icy December day and she pedalled fast to keep herself warm. In all the time she had been in France she had never had cause to doubt the justice of her decision to stay. It must be rare, she thought, that all one's duties and impulses pointed in the same direction. She had been useful to Julien and Mirabel: she had, as far as it was possible with so little active resistance yet taking place, done her job. She had frequently visited André and Jacob and brought them comfort. More than this, she felt that the time she had passed in Lavaurette and the conversations she had had with Levade had helped her in a personal way. Living in the Domaine, under a different identity, had soothed and educated her.

Yet however much her staying in France had satisfied her various desires, the most important matter of all, the whereabouts of Gregory, had been set to one side. She remembered her last night of training in England when she had pulled back the curtain to see the misty moon outside, 'Charlotte' unclear. She had vowed to

Gregory that she would find him, and now at last she was on her way.

The narrow road wound between bare fields, then through a hamlet where a farm straddled it: the house on one side, the barns and outbuildings on the other. Geese spat at her bicycle as she pedalled through, and scrawny chickens flapped angrily from the rolling tyres.

After one more dip, the road swung sharply to the right, over a crumbling concrete bridge with rusted iron rails, and climbed for the last time. On the brow of the hill was the moss-covered calvary and the rutted path to the white stone house. Two thin lions sat on top of the gateposts, grimacing over the cold countryside. The stone chippings of the driveway clotted the wheels, and Charlotte dismounted, propping the bicycle against a low wall that enclosed a terrace.

A momentary thrill of self-consciousness went through her as she stood at the front door. She saw herself and her desperate errand as through the eyes of an incredulous stranger. Then it was gone, because the urgency of what she did was too great, as she turned the large handle and pushed open one half of the heavy double door.

The great staircase rose in front of her, its broad white steps illuminated by candles gripped in iron holders on the walls. Charlotte went slowly up, feeling the lovely surface of the stone, polished by the passage of centuries, beneath her feet. She walked down the straight, broad passageway ahead, her shoes now cradled and sprung by polished oak. From the last bedroom on the right, the one where they had met before, she could see a light flickering through the open doorway, over the pinkish markings in the white distemper of the walls.

She should have breathed in deeply at the threshold, she thought; she should have sent a small prayer arrowing to heaven; but she wanted too much to hear what was waiting for her: she wanted the words that would bring him back to life.

She knocked and entered the shadowy room. The two boat beds were on the right; on the left sat Mirabel with his back to her, looking through the window over the fallen tree in the garden below. Hearing her knock, he turned slowly round in his seat, and when his face came into the light of the candle, Charlotte saw that it was not Mirabel at all, but Claude Benech.

'Thank you for coming,' he said. 'I knew you would.'

Charlotte was too shocked too speak.

Benech was smiling. 'You were expecting Monsieur 'Mirabel', I believe.'

Charlotte said nothing, not because her training required it and not from any sense of self-preservation, but because the absence of Mirabel meant she had lost Gregory.

Benech coughed. 'He asked me to apologise. He's been detained.'

Charlotte remembered how nervous Mirabel had been the first time. There seemed no point in denying that she knew him. 'Where is he?'

'With the proper authorities. He is an enemy and will be treated as such.'

'And you. Why you?'

'Do you remember, we met in Lavaurette one day?'

Charlotte nodded. 'I've seen you.'

'I have taken an interest in your life, Madame. I saw you kiss Monsieur Levade the day the Germans came. I was intrigued by you. I belong to a patriotic organisation. For some time this Monsieur 'Mirabel' has been watched. Then there came a time to act. I was able to help.' Benech put his hand inside the pocket of his coat. 'And this was my reward.'

In the candlelight Charlotte could see the gleam of

gunmetal in Benech's pale palm. She wondered if he was deranged. The orderly, articulate way in which he spoke was perhaps too controlled. She must not provoke him.

'And you're here for them?' she said. 'For your organisation?'

'Oh no. This is a private matter.'

Charlotte thought of Mirabel's 'French' handwriting in the note. She should have suspected. The contact should have been made through Julien, but she had been too excited to think.

'I don't know what your plans are, Madame,' said Benech, 'but clearly you might feel it worthwhile to make them fit in with mine. The authorities in time of war are efficient and direct. We are fighting for the heart and soul of our country. I'm sure you understand.'

Charlotte inclined her head slightly.

'They have dealt with your friend. They would be interested in you, too. And perhaps in others that you know.' Benech smiled again. 'Do speak to me, Madame. You're making me feel uneasy and I'm trying to be helpful.'

Charlotte swallowed. 'What do you want me to do?'

'I want you,' said Benech, 'to be my friend.'

'I don't understand.'

'I want you to come and see me at my apartment. There you will tell me things I ask. We will develop a relationship of trust. And our friendship will of course take other paths.'

'What paths?'

'The natural paths between men and women.'

'Why should I do this?'

'I don't think you really need to ask that,' said Benech, standing up and putting the gun back in his pocket. He walked over to Charlotte and grabbed her jaw in his right hand, twisting her face from side to side.

'Monsieur Mirabel is dead. Before he died, he talked a great deal. Don't play with me, Madame, don't play.'

There was no strain in Benech's voice, Charlotte thought. In his work he was used to issuing threats and orders and to having them obeyed.

'All right,' she said. 'I'll come to you tomorrow evening.'

'Good.'

Benech, still holding her face, pressed his mouth over hers.

'Tomorrow,' said Charlotte, pushing him away. She managed a halfsmile. 'I must go now.'

Benech held her by the arm. 'Don't try to leave the town,' he said. 'I will track you down and find you.'

She nodded.

'And if you tell one word of what's just passed between us . . . ' Through the fabric of his coat he pushed the gun against her hip-bone.

He had released her arm. Charlotte moved quickly to the door. 'Tomorrow,' she said, and ran down the wooden landing to the stairs.

As she grabbed the bicycle from outside and rode off through the gates, she heard Benech call out after her. He had changed his mind; perhaps he couldn't wait until tomorrow. But Charlotte did not hesitate as she plunged into the darkness.

★ ★ ★

She arrived at Julien's apartment in Lavaurette, ran upstairs and hammered on the door.

'Julien, thank God you're here.' She was so out of breath she could hardly speak.

Julien's momentary expression of delight at seeing

395

her was replaced by anxiety and anger as Charlotte told him what had happened. She omitted all mention of Peter Gregory, giving the impression that her second rendezvous had been merely at Mirabel's supposed instigation.

When she had finished, Julien said, 'You must leave. That's the first thing we must do. Get you out.'

'What about you?'

'I'll be all right. I've done nothing wrong, nothing they know about anyway. But listen, Dominique, I had some other news today. Something else that worries me. You know Gastinel, the butcher?'

'Auguste?'

'Yes. You know he left us to join a fledgling Gaullist network in Limoges. Well, I gathered from Pauline Benoit, who's a friend of his and a bit of a Gaullist herself, I suspect, that they'd been set up. They went to some agreed place for a drop and the plane didn't come. In fact, the only other people there were the local gendarmerie, who wanted to know what on earth they were all doing. They spent the night in prison. They're certain they were betrayed by someone.'

It was the word Limoges that filled Charlotte with a sense of lurching emptiness. 'Do you know exactly where this drop was?' she said.

'Pretty well. Why?'

'Have you got any maps?'

'Yes, over on the shelf.'

From among the dusty atlases and tourist guides, Julien eventually produced a detailed map of the area. Charlotte spread it out on the floor beneath the light. She could still remember the references Mirabel had given her. She peered at the small figures at the side of the map for a moment, than ran her finger slowly across the paper.

'There,' she said, her face turned anxiously up to Julien's. 'Was it there?'

'Pauline said something about a stream and a church. Yes. Look, there they are.'

Charlotte could not bring herself to speak for a moment. At last she said, 'Oh, Julien. Something terrible has happened. It was me. Mirabel asked me to take a message to someone in Limoges. I must have got it wrong, the wrong co-ordinates. But if it was one of our people, why were the Gaullists there? I don't understand. My memory is . . . well, almost infallible. I must have given it to the wrong person.'

'Why didn't you tell me what you were doing?'

'Mirabel told me not to tell you. Minimum information. Anyway, it didn't seem important.'

'He told you not to tell me?'

'Yes, he said, Whatever you do, don't tell Octave.'

Julien shook his head. 'Oh, God. They've used you, haven't they?'

'I don't understand. Surely Mirabel is — '

'Mirabel's like everyone else. He's under orders from the politicians. And the English are no better than the French.'

'You mean he deliberately misled me?'

'Whoever you gave the message to wasn't one of ours. It was a Gaullist. I don't quite know why the English would want to mess it up for them. But the reason doesn't really matter. What did he promise you in return?'

'I . . . Nothing. Nothing, really.'

'Nothing 'really'?'

'Well, he intimated that he might be able to help me find someone. If I did what he asked, if we kept in touch. It was rather vague.'

'The airman?'

'How did you know?'

'My father told me.'

Charlotte nodded without speaking.

'You really thought he might know where this man was?'

'I suppose I did hope. I mean, he knows people, he's in touch with them. And . . . And . . . ' It all sounded too foolish.

'Oh, Dominique, you poor girl.' Julien opened his arms and hugged her tightly to him. 'You poor, poor girl.'

Charlotte was reluctant to disengage from the safety of Julien's arms. 'And what should I do now?' she said.

'You must go home at once. I can get a wireless message to London. You must get out as soon as you can.'

'But, Julien, I've only just begun.'

'If you stay, they'll get you. The Gaullists will tell the police even if Benech doesn't. The fact that you're from England makes it worse. Perfidious Albion.'

'But we're all on the same side.'

'Not now you've betrayed them.'

'Oh God, Julien. What about Peter? He can't manage without me. He'll never get back now. It's only my being here in France that's kept him alive.'

Julien looked crushed by what she said, as though he had not really believed until then in the depth of her feeling for another man. He took her hand and said gently: 'If you love him, leave tomorrow. If you stay, they will kill you. Men like Benech are worse than the Germans. If you love him, for God's sake go.'

7

Dinner at the Domaine was late that night, and Julien asked Charlotte to eat with him and his father. It was the first time she had seen them together for any length of time, and she kept imagining the ten-year-old boy returning home from school to find his tearful mother telling him that his father had deserted them. What would the distraught Madame Levade have thought if she had been told then that, twenty years later, the two of them would be sitting with a Scottish woman in the vast panelled dining room of a draughty manor, miles from Paris, the Germans in possession of their country?

'How long have you been coughing like that?' said Julien, laying his hand on his father's arm.

'A couple of weeks. It's nothing. The house is draughty, that's all.'

Julien raised his eyebrows. His attitude to his father was of slightly teasing reverence. Levade was not old enough to need concern or looking after, but Charlotte sensed that Julien was in some way preparing for the day when he would be. In Levade's manner towards his son there was that moving indulgence Charlotte had so missed in her own parents: he disagreed with him, shrugged off Julien's humorous remarks, but looked at him throughout with a passive and slightly incredulous pride.

In a few days' time, Charlotte thought, she would be back in London, and then she would really have no excuse for not making the long journey north to Scotland. For all the danger of her position, she found the thought of leaving unbearable.

The food she had prepared was quickly finished.

Levade asked her to bring more wine and anything else she could find to eat in the kitchen. There was a tin of sardines, some macaroni, a couple of handfuls of which she set to boil on the range, three apples and a bowl of walnuts from the garden. With these and the wine she returned eventually to the dining room, where dinner started up again.

Charlotte had recovered her composure. As she sat with the two men, prising open a nut with an old oyster-knife, she was calm enough to know that this would be her last night at the Domaine, and she was saddened by the thought.

It was almost midnight when there came a thunderous hammering on the double doors of the house.

'My God,' said Levade, pulling a watch from his pocket.

'Wait here.' Julien had already pushed his chair back. There was something anxious in his voice that made Charlotte feel nauseously sober.

There were voices from the hallway, then the sound of numerous pairs of feet coming towards them. Julien was followed into the dining room by two men, one of whom was a uniformed German officer. 'I am Oberleutenant Lindemann,' he said. 'Are you Monsieur Levade?'

'Yes.'

Lindemann nodded to a small man standing next to him. He was wearing a fawn raincoat over a stiff collar and dark blue tie; he was of middle age, almost bald, with a little shiny dark hair above the ears, and a round, soft face, in which was set a pair of wire-rimmed glasses. Charlotte recognised him as the man who had been watching while Bernard put up the posters outside Madame Galliot's.

He came towards Levade and held out his hand. 'My name is Paul Pichon. I work for the Inquiry and Control Section.'

Levade gave a thin smile. 'That's a distinguished-sounding organisation.' He declined the offered hand.

Monsieur Pichon said, 'We have taken over some functions of the Police for Jewish Affairs, which, as you probably know, has been disbanded in all but name.'

Levade raised his eyebrows in a gesture of ignorant indifference.

Lindemann coughed. 'We must go into a different room. There are some questions to be answered.' His voice, despite its clumsy accent, was curiously diffident, as if he was not sure who was in charge.

'We'll go into the drawing room,' said Levade. 'Is it open?'

'Yes,' said Charlotte. 'I'll go and turn on the lights and make a fire.'

Charlotte's heart was big inside her ribcage as she went down the corridor. The lights came on dimly in their gilded wall mountings. She went to the long desk at the far end of the room and turned on the lamp. The room had its usual smell of fine, old dust. Behind her she heard the tramp of footsteps on the uncovered parquet. Why were there so many people there? There must be at least four others on their way from the hall that she had not yet seen.

Levade came into the room and gestured towards the fussily upholstered nineteenth-century furniture, but Lindemann made for the far end of the room. Charlotte busied herself with the fire, which had not been lit during the winter, and when she looked up she found the men had arranged themselves at the long desk. In the middle of one side sat Lindemann, with Pichon on his left; on his right was a German corporal, a small, sour-faced man with grey hair; on Pichon's left was a man with a mealy skin, a moustache and a nervous smile. It was Claude Benech, and Charlotte found that his smile was directed at her.

By the door into the library Lindemann stationed

a single German private, while Pichon indicated to the gendarme, Bernard, that he should remain by the principal door leading back into the house. Bernard gave Charlotte a self-conscious grimace as he took up his post. Julien sat on the edge of an armchair towards the centre of the room, while Lindemann told Levade to take a seat on the other side of the desk, so that he faced, from left to right, the corporal, Lindemann, Pichon and Benech.

Charlotte was still kneeling by the fire, unable to move, when Lindemann spoke. 'I am for the moment the commanding officer in Lavaurette. I shall leave soon when . . . others arrive from Paris.'

'You mean the SS?' said Julien.

'I believe so. I have orders from our Military Command in Paris. I don't need to tell you the details. The administration of law during the Occupation has been carried out by the French police. You know that.'

'Why don't you tell us what you're doing here?' said Julien.

Lindemann opened his left hand to Pichon, who cleared his throat. Lindemann seemed relieved to stop talking; and where his voice had carried a degree of uncertainty, Pichon seemed calm and authoritative. 'Certainly,' he said. 'There appears to have been some procedural irregularities with your papers, Monsieur Levade. In June last year, as you are no doubt aware, there was a detailed census carried out by the Government of all Jews in the Free Zone. I have here the lists for this commune and your name does not appear on it. Do you have a certificate of non-belonging to the Jewish race?'

Levade spread his hands in a small, contemptuous gesture of dismissal. 'A certificate of what?'

'Such papers were freely available from the Commissariat General for Jewish Questions.'

'I don't know anything about these German bodies.'

'It's not a German body, it's a Government department, Monsieur Levade, responsible for the various Jewish statutes. Surely even you have heard of those?'

'Confiscation of property, you mean, wearing the yellow star, persecution of — '

'The policy is called 'Aryanisation',' said Pichon. He paused for a moment and Charlotte saw him peer closely across the table into Levade's face. 'I think you would do well to adopt a less remote attitude, Monsieur. Ignorance, even credible ignorance, has never been a defence before the law. In difficult times citizens more than ever owe a duty of conformity and awareness. Full citizenship carries obligations. That, Monsieur, is the nub of the whole Jewish question.'

Levade said nothing, but glanced across at Julien, who seemed to be holding himself back with difficulty, convulsively clenching and unclenching his fists.

'Let me explain a little further,' said Pichon. 'I have no wish to surprise or intimidate you. I want you to understand the full authority of these proceedings.'

Charlotte stood up from the gently smoking fire; Pichon's voice carried no obvious emotion, but it made her feel sick with foreboding. Her initial relief that no attention was being paid to her was replaced by a fear that some worse fate was being prepared for Levade.

'Authority?' said Julien. 'Authority? What on earth authority can you have, some fabricated organisation who — '

'We have the authority of the French government, Monsieur. The law of 2 June 1941 gives the right of internment to the local prefecture of any Jew, foreign or French. Juridically,' said Pichon, removing his glasses as though to savour the word better, 'the distinction between native Jews and refugees collapsed with that statute.'

'But in the Free Zone,' said Julien, 'you can't — '

'There is no longer a Free Zone,' said Pichon. 'Surely even here in Lavaurette you have noticed that. Please let me continue. Since the events of 1940 the government, as you know, has endeavoured to maintain the sovereignty of France by vigorous independent action. The principal aim has been to collaborate with the Occupier in order to safeguard more completely that independence and, in the fullness of time, to extend its limits. All this has been successfully achieved by the Government, acting in the interests of its citizens, though the full rewards for such negotiation will not be apparent until the Allies are defeated. However, the course of events in the summer has imposed a degree of urgency. In June, there was a visit to Paris from Herr Eichmann, in which he proposed that a total of one hundred thousand Jews be deported from France, half of them to come from the Free Zone. In case you are still wondering about what we call the authority for such measures, you might like to know that the inclusion of Jews from the Free Zone was the suggestion of the Head of Police, Monsieur Bousquet.'

'I don't believe you,' said Julien.

Pichon shrugged. 'Monsieur Bousquet's deputy, Monsieur Leguay, was informed by Herr Rothke of the German Military Command in July that French nationals of Israelite stock would be included in the deportations and that Monsieur Laval had not demurred. There have been some minor administrative difficulties in dealing with families, as you can imagine. Children have been left behind and this has caused some confusion. However, Herr Dannecker, who as most people know — though perhaps not you, Monsieur — is head of the German Section for Jewish Affairs in Paris, reported to Berlin on 6 July that Monsieur Laval himself had suggested that, in the case of families being deported from the Free Zone, the children under sixteen could also be taken.'

Pichon looked round the silent room and smiled. 'I have a confession to make. I am a lawyer. And the neatness of the arrangement pleases me, I am bound to admit. One has so many difficulties with the question of the sphere of jurisdiction that it is a pleasure to come across a case in which everything has been done in such an orderly and co-operative way.'

Julien spoke in a voice that seemed blanched and weak compared to its truculent tone of a few minutes earlier. 'Laval volunteered the children?'

'Yes,' said Pichon. 'I have a copy of Herr Dannecker's report to Berlin.' He began to search among the papers on the table in front of him. 'It intrigued me, and I had a clerk write out the actual text. Here, if you'd like to . . . '

Julien shook his head.

No one spoke. Benech fiddled with some papers he had placed on the table in front of him; he seemed to be finding it difficult to suppress a smile of some kind. The corporal on Lindemann's right stared straight ahead of him.

Eventually, Julien said, 'Why all this talk about deportation anyway?'

Lindemann turned to Pichon. 'Please continue.' He seemed to be the only person with any sense of urgency.

Pichon cleared his throat. 'One of the inevitable results of such a formal system of co-operation is that it does generate a large amount of paperwork. Many local mayors have not been able to deal with all the directives they have received from the departmental offices in Vichy, which is why various people such as myself have been dispatched to help them. The mayor of Lavaurette, for instance, an estimable man no doubt, has been grateful for our assistance. I understand that

405

by profession he is a smallholder.'

'He grows melons,' said Bernard from the doorway.

'Thank you, Monsieur,' said Pichon. 'Now, Monsieur Levade, we come to your case.' Pichon pulled out a single sheet of paper from the pile in front of him, smoothed it down, then held it a little away from him so that it came into the long-sighted focus of his sparkling glasses. 'Absence from the census we have dealt with. Now I must ask you to show me your documentation, please.'

'My what?'

'Identity card, work permit and ration card. Please don't tell me you don't posses any. Every French citizen has been issued with them. How else have you bought food?'

'I really don't know. It's possible that there's something in a drawer.'

'Go and look.' Pichon's voice became sharper as he flicked a dismissive hand at Bernard to indicate that he should go with Levade.

Charlotte watched as Levade stood up and crossed the room.

'Her.' Lindemann nodded in Charlotte's direction. 'She shouldn't be here. Nor should he, the son,' he said, looking at Julien.

'Oh, I rather think he should,' said Pichon smoothly. 'I think the presence of Monsieur Levade junior is entirely . . . germane. As for the maidservant, I have no objections. I think it is a good idea that the lower orders should see the proper working of the legal process.'

'So do I,' said Benech, fixing Charlotte with a slow, conniving smile.

Levade returned to the room with an envelope which he dropped on to the table in front of Pichon. 'I don't know if this is what you mean,' he said. 'It's all I could find.'

He began to cough violently and turned his head

away from the men at the table.

Pichon pulled out the contents of the envelope and inspected them. 'Indeed,' he said. 'As I thought. Why are they not properly stamped?'

'I don't know what you mean.'

Pichon said, 'I think you do, Monsieur Levade. On 11 December the Government ordered that all relevant identification cards be stamped with the word 'Jew'. Everyone knows that. There are notices in town, there were broadcasts. It's the law.'

Levade shrugged. 'I don't know anything about these German things, these — '

'It is not German,' Pichon said, standing up and spitting out the negative across the table at Levade. 'It is a law passed by the French government which, if you had any idea of citizenship, you would have obeyed.'

Lindemann cleared his throat. 'Are there other things? It's late.'

Pichon sat down again. Levade shook his head slowly from side to side. Charlotte, who could only see him from behind, thought from the gurgling noise she heard that he was crying. As she went over to comfort him she recognised that the sound was of soft laughter.

'Sit down, Mademoiselle,' said Pichon. 'The list of charges here is enough for me to recommend any disposal. It is only a question of what route we choose.'

Julien walked over to the table. Charlotte could tell that he had made an effort to restrain himself and was going to speak carefully. 'There seems to be one thing missing from your case, Monsieur, and that is any proof that my father is Jewish. I think you will find if you take a look round the house that the evidence is that he is in fact a devout Catholic.'

'Ah, indeed. The question of definition. The precedents are very interesting, and the law is developing all the time, though its basis remains perfectly clear. It is a matter of ancestry.'

'My father is a second generation Frenchman,' said Julien. 'He is also a war veteran.'

'How admirable. When Monsieur Vallat was head of the Commissariat General for Jewish Questions he was inclined to look tolerantly on such cases; his successor, Monsieur Darquier de Pellepoix, rather less so. Under the first Jewish statute a Jew was defined as someone with three Jewish grandparents. Monsieur Vallat was prepared to allow religion to play a part, so in his second statute someone confessing to a recognised non-Jewish religion might be deemed to have ceased being Jewish, provided he had only two Jewish grandparents. Those with three remained Jewish whatever religion they claimed. In Monsieur Vallat's view Baptism was not conclusive, because Jewish tradition is passed down racially. Heredity is stronger than holy water. He began to talk of families in which the hereditary atmosphere was 'predominantly Jewish'. It is fair to conclude that Monsieur Vallat had become somewhat confused by the time he left office, though the provisions of his statute remain useful. Let us look at your family, Monsieur Levade.'

Charlotte glanced expectantly at Levade. At last he was being given a chance to speak for himself, and surely he would now understand the horror of his situation. Surely he would now shake off the amused torpor in which he seemed sunk. He looked feverish and unwell.

'Come now, Monsieur Levade, would you not like to tell us a little about your ancestors, your very French ancestors?'

There was a silence in which Charlotte could hear the clock above her head. Levade began to cough again. Eventually, he spoke. 'My father was a schoolmaster in a small town near Paris. He was the most patriotic person I've ever known. He used to quote that little saying, 'As happy as God in France'. He was perhaps a rather innocent man, now I come to think of it, but he was very contented. He had very little religious belief. I suppose he must have been nominally Jewish at least, because his mother was, but he seemed to lack any spiritual life. I never saw him go to a synagogue or to a church. His joy came from his family and from his country. He was always involved with Saints' Days and public meetings and celebrations. He was very conservative about the old ways.' Levade smiled. 'Like a lot of fairly recent arrivals.'

'Would you care to be a little more specific about your origins?' Pichon's voice had taken on a light, ironic edge.

'I think not, Monsieur. I have told you all I want to.'

'I'm not sure such reticence is a very good idea for someone in your position, Monsieur Levade. Perhaps your son would care to be a little more forthcoming.' Pichon looked over the top of his spectacles towards Julien, who had resumed his seat on the edge of an armchair.

Julien shook his head. 'Not if my father doesn't want to.'

'Very well,' said Pichon, 'let us continue with the question of definition.'

Charlotte noticed how much Pichon was enjoying himself. There was a forensic construction to his sentences which obviously gave him pleasure.

He picked up some more papers from the table in front of him. 'Now then, Monsieur Vallat was replaced at the GCJQ in the summer. It is hardly for me to comment, but it seems he had become somewhat competitive with the Occupier. Apparently he told one of Herr Dannecker's SS officers that he had been an anti-semite far longer than the German gentleman. This was perhaps the last straw for Herr Dannecker.'

Pichon gave a little laugh in which Benech briefly joined. Lindemann looked at his watch as Pichon set off again on an exposition of the French government's policy, which he explained had first been set in place in response to the refugee crisis of a few years earlier, when Jews began arriving in France from Eastern Europe. Occupation by the Germans forced certain changes in policy, and men such as Vallat objected to having their own solution to the Jewish problem influenced by outside agencies who were less strict in their definitions but probably more crude in their aims.

Eventually, Lindemann interrupted him. 'It's after one o'clock,' he said. 'I want to finish tonight. Please talk to Monsieur Levade.' Lindemann's voice for the first time sounded decisive.

'Very well,' said Pichon, 'but I insist that this is done correctly. The difficulty of course is in establishing the religion of the grandparents. However, in recent cases of foreign Jews, the courts have been persuaded to accept a presumption of Jewishness where non-Jewishness cannot be proved by baptismal certificate or similar. This is likely to set a precedent in the case of French Jews as well. The degree of assimilation of a Jew is not necessarily relevant. Monsieur Vallat in theory was prepared to tolerate certain Jews who had been subsumed into French culture — though not all, it must be said. The Prime Minister Monsieur Blum epitomised all that he disliked. Monsieur Vallat was again a little inconsistent on this point. Not so Monsieur Darquier de Pellepoix, who shares the Occupier's view that the Jewish influence is a racial not a cultural one, and that the most assimilated Jew is therefore the most dangerous. This has made for a greater congruence of outlook with the Occupier, and a greater efficiency. Our department has in fact been sent a copy of a telegram of congratulation received by Monsieur Bousquet, the police chief, from his opposite number in the SS, General Oberg.'

All the time Pichon was speaking, Charlotte was watching Levade's back and thinking of the painting of the deserted square, with the clock at twenty to four and the two figures with their sense of imminent separation. Her feeling for Levade had utterly changed; all trace of censure had now gone from it. It was partly that, since sleeping with Julien, she no longer felt in a position to disapprove of his amorous past, but more that she no longer feared him. Instead, she saw that the events of his life had not been easy, the crawling through the mud with loaves and wine roped round him, the interior battle with his art and his patient knocking at the door of his unconscious. Approval of him, or its absence, now seemed like a trivial issue; when she looked at his bowed head, she felt a horrified compassion.

Pichon's skin gleamed softly in the light from the shaded lamp on the table in front of him. Charlotte thought it was the face of a man who had always been right, who as a schoolboy had had all the answers and was puzzled that his demonstrable success brought him fewer friends than he might logically have expected. The adult world to him, however, had not been disappointing; there were systems he could operate and areas of work in which his precision was valued. Behind him, painted in the plaster just above the wainscotting, were various heraldic shields, extravagant family claims and noble mottoes, bleached over by a later decoration and now showing through only as little patches of distempered colour; and over them was an oil painting, clotted with dark grease and smoke, of a traditional château in the Limousin.

Pichon replaced his glasses which he had been polishing with a white handkerchief. His little face

411

looked soft and vulnerable for a moment, as he blinked his eyes rapidly like a new-born creature. 'Monsieur Levade, there are a number of courses open to me. Which one I choose depends on the degree of your co-operation. I am entitled to order your arrest and trial in the usual way, but I am also empowered to order your detention in one of a number of camps, and can further recommend whether you should be removed from there to Paris.'

'And what happens in Paris?' said Julien.

'Railways, Monsieur Levade. Trains.'

'If you're threatening us, Monsieur,' said Julien, 'it would be better if you spelt it out.'

'The law carries no threats, Monsieur Levade, only procedures. Now,' said Pichon, turning to Levade, 'will you help me?'

Levade sighed heavily. 'I'm a painter. That's all I have to say.' He lifted his hand to his mouth as he began to cough again.

Charlotte was watching Julien, who seemed to be trying to catch his father's eye. Levade, however, stared either down towards his feet or straight at his accuser.

'I'm going outside for a minute,' said Julien. 'I'm going to find a cigarette.'

Pichon gestured to Bernard to go with him, and Benech rose clumsily from the table. 'I'll go too,' he said. He walked quickly across the room, and Charlotte heard his footsteps in the corridor as he hurried to catch up with the others.

Lindemann spoke rapidly to his corporal; Charlotte did not understand what he said, but his attitude expressed impatience. The gilded clock on the mantelpiece showed it was nearly half past one.

When Julien returned, his face had gone a peculiar grey colour; his eyes seemed focused on some invisibly far horizon. 'Are you all right?' said Charlotte as he

412

went past her place at the fireside, but he appeared not to notice her. It was clear to Charlotte, from her knowledge of Julien, that something dramatic had taken place outside the room.

'I want to explain something to my father in private,' he said.

'No,' Benech said.

Benech whispered in Pichon's ear, and Pichon said something inaudible to Lindemann, who gestured to the German private by the door into the library.

Lindemann gave an order; the private crossed the room and pushed Julien back into his chair with the butt of his rifle.

Julien's voice was shaking when he managed to speak. He said to Lindemann, 'You're going to lose this war. You know that, don't you?'

The private raised his rifle, but Lindemann motioned him back to the doorway. He seemed amused. 'Not in France, I think,' said Lindemann. 'Not here.'

'Yes,' said Julien. 'Even here eventually.'

'I think not,' said Pichon. 'People prefer order to resistance, as we have seen. Acts of sabotage merely lead to reprisals by the Occupier: ten hostages shot for every German killed. Any organised resistance would also open the gates to the Communists. It would mean the Americans and English would have to invade, which no true Frenchman wants. The upheaval would be terrible, especially at a time when the Marshal has just managed to set France back on a stable course.'

'You're wrong,' said Julien. 'Resistance will come in the end. It will come when people see that they've been misled. Your problem, Monsieur, the problem of the government you support is this — that you took a gamble. You decided to act in a way that you considered practical. All considerations of honour or morality were put to one side because they looked subsidiary in the light of events — the overwhelming probability that Germany would win the war. And that, Monsieur, is the danger of that kind of politics. If its practical assumptions prove to be false, you have nothing left to fall back on, because you have already sacrificed morality. You were not just immoral, Monsieur, you committed the unforgivable crime of practical politics — you got it wrong.' Julien's voice caught on the contempt with which he spoke the final word and for a few moments his breath would not come.

Pichon laughed. 'Every plan has occasional setbacks, but there is no doubt that we will play an important part in the new European alliance.'

'You will lose in Russia and you will lose to the Americans and the English in Europe.'

Lindemann said, 'And France? Who will rescue France?'

'It doesn't really matter.' said Julien. 'Provided there is still something that has not been corrupted, provided there is something worth rescuing.'

Lindemann said, 'We must finish. Monsieur Pichon — '

'Tell me one thing,' said Julien. 'If the people you deport are going to work for Germany, why do you take them to Poland?'

'I don't know,' said Lindemann. 'That's enough.'

'And if they are going to work, why do you take children and women?'

'That's enough,' said Lindemann.

'There were two people in Lavaurette who were dragged off in the summer,' said Julien. 'What did you do with them? They were French, too.'

'I believe not,' said Pichon, going through his pile of papers. 'Are you referring to Monsieur and Madame Duguay? They had come from Alsace-Lorraine, like many Jews down here. She was of Belgian origin. There were fewer Jews in the camps than the Government had thought, but Monsieur Laval insisted on honouring his pledge on numbers to the Germans. These people were classed as refugees. You can see here. Look.'

'But they were French, they — '

'That is enough,' said Lindemann, suddenly standing up. 'Is this man a Jew or not?'

There was a heavy pause before Julien eventually pulled himself to his feet. He was staring at Benech, Charlotte noticed, with a violent hatred. Something had passed between them.

'Yes,' Julien said at last. 'My father is a Jew. Three of his grandparents were Jewish. It's in his blood, in his mind, in his culture, in the essence of who he is. It's in mine, too.'

Levade's hand was inside his shirt. He had been gently rubbing the skin below his collarbone, and Charlotte pictured his fingertips going over the risen seams of his wound. When Julien spoke, his hand stopped moving.

He turned sideways in his chair to look at his son, but, having spoken, Julien turned his head away and looked down at the floor.

Charlotte held her hand across her mouth.

It was Claude Benech who eventually dared to break the silence. 'So that makes two for the quota.'

Pichon lifted his head from his papers and looked at Julien. 'I understand that your mother was French, a good Catholic.'

Julien kept his head averted. 'I'm a Jew,' he said.

'I suggest this is something we might resolve at a later date,' said Pichon.

'Take the old one,' said Lindemann. 'The train leaves at two o'clock tomorrow.'

Pichon gestured to Bernard. 'Take him to the police station and keep him in the cell.'

Charlotte stood up. 'Let me put some things in a case for him.'

Lindemann nodded. 'Quickly.'

Charlotte ran upstairs to Levade's bedroom, where she found an old suitcase. With shaking hands she threw in shirts, underwear, a thick tweed jacket she found in the wardrobe, washing things, the books on the table and, from by his bed, the pad of paper and the pen. She ran to the studio, where she took a Bible, a missal, a crucifix, a sketch pad and pencils. Then she rummaged through the canvases stacked in the corner until she found the one he had shown her. It would not fit in the case, and she could not prise out the nails by which it was attached to the back of the stretcher. She began to pull at it in a frenzy; then she heard footsteps and voices calling her from the stairs. She ripped the canvas clear of the stretcher, tearing it along the edges, rolled it up and stuffed it down inside the suitcase.

She arrived breathless in the hall to find Bernard with his arm linked awkwardly through Levade's. She put the case down on the floor and threw her arms round Levade's neck, holding him close to her. She felt his touch on her back, his hand gently patting her shoulder blades, as though it was she who needed consolation.

She pulled back and he looked into her face. 'Don't worry,' he said. 'I have faith in God. I'm not afraid. See that Julien's all right.' His voice was calm.

Charlotte went back reluctantly down the passage to the drawing room.

Pichon was speaking. 'I really think it would be better to have the proper documentation. By tomorrow lunch time, I'm sure we could — '

'Do you want me to stay or go?' said Julien. All three men were now standing in front of the fire.

He looked towards Lindemann, who was clearly undecided. 'I . . . I don't know. I have to fill a quota. I wish I could leave it. Very soon all the prefectures will have officers of the SS and they can decide . . . I . . . '

He seemed at last to remember that he was no longer a drama critic but a soldier. He stood up a little straighter and spoke briskly to the German private. Then he translated, 'I told him to stay and watch tonight. We come tomorrow.'

Benech's nervous smile became a grin of wide relief; Pichon began methodically and contentedly to clear his documents with the air of a man who has completed a demanding task, the onerous nature of which has gone unappreciated by his colleagues.

He looked at his watch and lit a cigarette that smelled powerfully of real tobacco; then he turned to Charlotte with a smile. 'There, young woman, you have seen an example of correct procedure. Remember it. Our domestic problem solved by legal co-operation, and at no cost to ourselves.'

Lindemann began to laugh. It was the first natural emotion he had shown, and it made a curious sound in the echoing room, surrounded by the silence of the winter night.

'No cost? I'm afraid not. The cost of the deportations is paid by the French government. It is seven thousand Reichsmarks for each Jew, and food for two weeks at their destination.'

Pichon began to stammer. 'Surely, the Occupier would not — '

'Look in your papers,' Lindemann said, still snorting. 'You'll find it somewhere.'

Pichon set his lips together tightly, as he followed Lindemann and Benech from the drawing room. Benech turned on the threshold and looked at Charlotte. 'See you tomorrow,' he said quietly.

When the sound of their footsteps had died away, Charlotte went over to Julien. He could not look at her.

She put her hand on his arm. 'Are you going to say goodbye?' she said.

Julien shook his head and bit his lip while tears flowed from his eyes. 'Give him my love.'

Charlotte returned to the hall and embraced Levade for the final time. She whispered Julien's message.

Levade said nothing, but the serenity of his expression was undisturbed. Bernard went to the door, then glanced down at his gendarme's uniform as though unsure of some order of precedence and etiquette. He stood back for the others to leave, then, when they had gone down into the cold darkness, he took Levade once more by the arm and ushered him out through the double doors of the Domaine.

★ ★ ★

Charlotte stood alone in the empty hall. She remembered the first day she had come to be interviewed, how she had looked up to where the staircase doubled back to a remote ceiling and seen Levade's bare feet quietly descending. Around her now the white stone and faded pink plasterwork had a cold, deserted feeling, as though they had never truly enclosed human activity and the paintings of family forebears on the walls belonged to a line long defunct.

She shivered in the night air that had come in through the open front doors; then, wrapping her arms around her, she went slowly and reluctantly down the corridor towards the drawing room.

The fire had gone out and the room was cold; the chairs at the long desk were left untidily at the angles to which the men had pushed them in their hurry to leave. A piece of paper from Pichon's pile had fluttered clear of his precise tidying and lay alone on the floor beneath the chair in which Benech had been sitting. Julien was in the armchair, his elbows on his knees, holding his head in his hands.

Charlotte felt wary; she did not know how to

approach him, so stayed a little distance away, her back to the extinguished fire.

Julien said nothing. He did not move. To Charlotte it looked as though his body were immobilised by the weight of some crushing force. Eventually, she went to a small table by his chair and lifted his packet of cigarettes; she moved it in an interrogative gesture towards him, asking his permission, and he waved his hand.

She had no matches. She looked round the room and only at that moment became aware of the German soldier, who was standing where he had been left, in the doorway through to the library.

Charlotte went towards him. He seemed quite old to be a private soldier; his demeanour held nothing of the youthful pride and snap she had heard French people admire in the young men who had first taken Paris and Bordeaux. She put the unlit cigarette in her mouth as she approached, and he produced some matches from the breast pocket of his tunic.

Charlotte smiled and thanked him in one of the few German words she knew. The man nodded uneasily and shifted his weight.

She felt strong enough to go and sit on the arm of Julien's chair. She put her hand tentatively on his wrist. 'What happened?'

Julien put down his hands and turned his face up towards Charlotte. His complexion had the same grey colour she had noticed when he had returned to the room after briefly going out, and his eyes still seemed to be gazing beyond the walls. He coughed, and with an obvious effort brought his eyes to focus on her face.

'Benech. That man.' He waved his hand in the direction of the chair Benech had occupied. 'When I went out to find cigarettes I was really going to make a telephone call, but I couldn't because of the

419

gendarme coming with me. And then this . . . this creature, Benech.'

Julien's voice was toneless and flat, but at the second mention of Benech's name a trace of colour returned to his face. 'I went to the desk, I fumbled about in a drawer pretending to look for cigarettes. Benech came hurrying up behind me and pulled me over into a corner so Bernard wouldn't hear. He put his lips against my ear and said, 'If you don't tell the truth, we'll have to look elsewhere.' '

'What did he mean?'

Julien sighed and shook his head. 'He stood away from me a little and smiled. It was a big, broad smile. He said, 'I'm a schoolmaster. It's my business to know the whereabouts of children.' '

'My God.'

'I said, 'What do you mean?' He still had this big smile, as though he had done something clever and was taking me into his confidence. He thought for a moment and said 'Mmm'. He was trying to find a subtle way of saying something. Then he said, 'Let's just say I always know where to look if I need a telegram sending after hours.' '

'Oh my God, those poor boys.'

Julien nodded. 'I said, 'I don't know what you mean.' I had to say that. He just kept on smiling. Then he said something like, 'The numbers in the camps are disappointing, so the police have been scouring the fields and villages. Lavaurette's a small place and two people's enough for the quota.' Then he said, 'For the time being.' '

Julien breathed deeply and struggled to take control of himself. He said softly, 'We'd better go and talk about this.'

He stood up and turned to the German soldier, 'We're going to sleep now. Bed.' He made a gesture of sleep with folded hands.

The German nodded and pointed at each of them in turn. He raised one finger, then two, then made a circle with his arms.

'Yes, together,' said Julien, putting his arm round Charlotte.

The soldier looked relieved at the prospect of guarding one room only.

'Come,' said Julien, beckoning with his hand. 'I'll show you.'

They went up the stairs and along the musty passageway, past Levade's studio, with the German's footsteps ringing out behind them.

Julien stopped outside one of the many vacant bedrooms and twisted the handle in the door. The room was large but bare, with pale grey panelling and one solid wardrobe with dark iron hinges. The German went over to the windows and looked out; he opened the catch, pushed apart the two heavy sections of framed glass and ran his hand along the sills outside as though looking for a ladder or perhaps a concealed machine gun.

He nodded affirmatively, went over to a chair in the corner and sat down.

'No,' said Julien. 'You. Outside.' He pointed.

The man shook his head and lifted his rifle a few degrees.

Julien said, 'Man. Woman. Last night together.'

The soldier looked blank. 'Can you speak German, Dominique?'

'No.' She looked at the German. 'Italiano?'

He shook his head, distrustfully.

'I don't want to speak in English, it might make him suspicious,' she whispered in Julien's ear. 'But I could tell you the English words and you could ask. Say, 'Do you speak English?' '

Julien repeated the words slowly and some small light of comprehension came into the German's eyes.

Charlotte whispered, 'Say, 'Man, woman.' Point to the bed.'

Julien said the words and raised an eyebrow expressively as he pointed.

The German angrily shook his head.

'Please, please,' said Charlotte, again in German, holding her hands together and giving the man her most supplicant, flirtatious smile.

He was unimpressed.

'It doesn't really matter,' said Julien. 'We'll just have to talk in front of him. He doesn't understand anyway.'

For a long time Julien sat staring at the bed, running his finger over the faded pattern on the cover; then he lifted his head and looked into Charlotte's expectant eyes. 'I think my father will be pleased to die. I think he has no fear of it.'

Julien's voice sounded unsure.

'You made the right choice,' said Charlotte.

'He's unhappy. He hates what he calls his sensual urges. He's lost the ability to paint good pictures. His faith will make it easier for him.'

Charlotte stroked his hand. 'I'm sure you did the right thing, I'm sure you did. It must have been awful for you, but — '

'I felt like Judas. I'm glad I couldn't see the expression in his eyes.'

'I think he understood,' Charlotte said. 'When I said goodbye and gave him your love I really think he understood.'

She did not believe what she was saying, and she could not bear the thought that Levade might be taken to his death believing that his son had betrayed him. She said, 'He must have guessed that you had a motive. He knew how much you loved him.'

'Did you tell him anything?'

'I didn't know what to say. Why didn't you call out to him and explain?'

'Then the Germans would have known about the boys.'

'Don't you think they know anyway?'

'No. I'm sure it's just Benech. He wants his own power. For the time being. I don't think the German officer was really interested, I think he just wants to get back to his unit. He's only here because of the railway junction. I don't think he's even interested in me. Otherwise he wouldn't have left me behind with this old fool.' He did not look at the guard.

'I thought he was just waiting for the documents.'

'He could have taken me if he wanted. I said I was a Jew. He could have told the police to take me in for not having my card stamped with the word Jew.'

Charlotte looked down and found she was still holding Julien's hand. 'And what are you going to do?'

'Insist they take me. Otherwise Benech will tell them about André and Jacob.'

'They wouldn't really,' said Charlotte. 'They couldn't. Not in cold blood. Two little boys. They — '

'We've gone past that point,' said Julien. 'They'll do anything. This is going to get worse. I have a dreadful feeling that it's all just beginning. Everything till now has been manoeuvring. Now all hell's going to break open.'

Charlotte was thinking of Levade, alone in the police cell. He had lost hope in his country and in his art; despite what she had told Julien, she thought Levade also believed that Julien had betrayed him. What else could he have thought? His attitude at the end when he embraced Charlotte in the hall was not of understanding, but of resignation: all this, his fatalistic expression seemed to say, and my son, too . . . But somehow she would get word to him; no one could be left alone in such ruins.

'Listen, Julien,' she said. 'I'll go and warn Sylvie Cariteau to get the boys moved somewhere safe, and you see if you can escape.'

'How?'

'You said he was just an old fool. You can think of something. Perhaps he'll fall asleep.'

Julien thought for a long time. 'I don't want to risk it. I couldn't bear the thought of them taking André and Jacob.'

Charlotte said, 'I think you're wrong. You're important, Julien. You could carry on your work. If it's going to get worse, as you say, then you must be here to fight. I can get the boys out of Sylvie's house.'

Julien shook his head. 'It's too dangerous. I'm not going to be responsible for the death of the children. I'd rather die myself. This is exactly the problem I was talking about downstairs. Suppose I escaped, suppose they took the boys and then they caught me, too? If you don't base your actions on what is right, then you have nothing left to fall back on if the practicalities fail.'

'I love those boys, Julien. I'll do anything to help them. But for you to give yourself up is a futile gesture. A fine one, perhaps, but quite futile. If you stay free you can save the lives of many more people.'

'I must kill Benech.'

'What?'

'That's the only solution. He's the only one who knows. It's the one thing that would help and also somehow be right.'

Charlotte thought for a moment. 'All right.' If it meant Julien would try to escape then she was in favour of anything. 'And then what?'

'Then I'll have to leave Lavaurette. I'll go and join a network somewhere. Pretty soon there'll be proper groups of fighters, I'm sure.'

'Good,' said Charlotte. 'Good, that's right. And I'll make sure the boys are moved anyway, just to be on the safe side, just in case Benech has told Pichon.' She paused. 'And you're not worried about killing a man?'

Julien shook his head. 'Not any more. Not that man. It's a war now. If you fight in a war you take the risk of being killed.'

There was a pause as they both inspected the new plan, neither of them quite able to believe that they had come to an agreement.

Julien said, 'The important thing is to move the boys quickly, so if anything goes wrong they're already out of Sylvie's house. So you must get there now. I'll deal with Benech later in the day. Then you must go to the monastery. You know where it is, the one I'm working on?'

Charlotte nodded. She felt a small metal object being pressed into her hand.

'That's a spare key to the temporary fence, on the building site,' said Julien. 'Then in the morning, go straight away to the wireless operator.' He put his lips to her ear and whispered a name and address. 'The operator will find a safe house for you till the plane comes. But you mustn't stay a second in Lavaurette. Do you understand? For God's sake go now.' He was squeezing her hand.

'Yes, I promise. But in return I want you to keep in touch with Sylvie. See if there are messages from me. Do you promise?'

'The post office is under German control now. Since they came into the Free Zone.'

'Sylvie will find a way. Promise me you'll be in touch with her.'

In Charlotte's mind there was already the outline of a plan for not going home. She had not finished yet.

Julien looked at her quizzically. 'All right,' he said.

'But don't do anything stupid. Don't try and find him, will you? Just go home.'

'You're hurting my hand,' said Charlotte. 'Now how do I get out of here?'

Julien shrugged. 'Ask to go to the bathroom. Say it's urgent.'

Charlotte smiled. 'I don't know the German for bathroom. I'm not going to mime it.'

'If I ask he'll tell me to do it out of the window. It has to be you.'

'He'll tell me to do it in the washstand. Don't look now, but there's even a chamber pot underneath.'

'I have an idea,' said Julien. 'Do you remember what I said about man, woman, last night together?'

'Yes.'

'That's what we must do.'

'In front of this man?'

'He'll have to stop it in some way.'

'But . . . Julien. Then, then . . . ' The objection that came to Charlotte's lips surprised her. 'Then I must say goodbye now. Before we . . . begin.'

Julien nodded. Whenever he had talked to Charlotte about love or about his desire for her, he had always been smiling, and now his face was grave. It seemed quite wrong to her, to begin in this way, without his laughter or cajoling.

'I don't want to say goodbye.'

'Nor do I, Dominique. We've been friends, haven't we?'

'We've been friends.' She nodded, biting her lip.

'It's a good thing to be. But I'm not your lover.'

'No.'

'I know about him. You must wait for him.'

'I will wait for him.' It was clear. There was no doubt in her mind. 'But you, Julien, I've never had a friend like this. I don't want to say goodbye to you now.'

She was gripping his hand very hard on the bed.

426

'Don't look at me with those eyes, Dominique.'

'I'm frightened, Julien.'

'You'll be all right. As long as you don't delay. If something goes wrong, get in touch with Sylvie Cariteau.'

'I'm not frightened for me. It's for you.'

She pictured Julien slipping off in the night to kill Benech, then vanishing somewhere into the hills. There were not yet enough people for him to join, no proper network; he would be tracked down and shot. She could not bear to think of him hunted and afraid because it was not in his nature to be like that; she wanted him to be in his office, bantering with one of his Paulines, pouring out wine while he spoke into the telephone.

'I'll be all right.' His solemn face at last broke open in a narrow smile. He leaned forward to kiss Charlotte on the lips.

She had seldom felt less lustful, but in the interests of André and Jacob she forced herself to dissimulate a passionate response. She stroked Julien's hair, she murmured as he kissed her cheek.

She lay back on the bed and circled Julien's neck with her arms. She felt his hand run up her leg and begin to lift her dress. There was still no sound from the German.

Julien was whispering, 'I don't know what more I can do. He doesn't seem to have noticed.'

'Just hold me,' she whispered back hotly in his ear.

'It's not enough. Make more noise.'

Charlotte closed her eyes and felt the bed rock in the way she remembered from the night in Julien's apartment. She tried to sigh passionately, but her breath caught in her throat. His hands again lifted the skirt of her dress and began to pull at her underclothes. She could not go on with this much longer. Of all her mixed feelings, the one that was rising to the surface was the shame of being watched.

427

She felt Julien lower himself on top of her, then she heard at last a sound she would never have thought welcome, a coarsely uttered German order. Julien made no movement, but continued to manoeuvre himself on top of her. Charlotte, still with her eyes closed, heard the German voice a second time, nearer, and felt Julien's body being pushed sideways.

Julien rolled to the side of the bed and pulled Charlotte up with him. As she desperately pushed down her dress, he persisted in his passionate embraces, pulling at the buttons on her back, lowering his head to her breast, compelling the German to force Charlotte away. He pushed her strongly back against the door and shouted at Julien who was half undressed.

'Run!' screamed Julien, but Charlotte stood for a moment, her hair disarrayed, her clothes rucked and caught, unable quite to let go.

As the German turned to look at her, Julien threw his arms round the man's neck and wrestled him towards the window. 'Go!' he screamed over his shoulder, and Charlotte turned, twisted the handle of the door and plunged out into the cold, dark corridor.

She ran past Levade's studio to the top of the stairs, caught the banister and, half-tripping, slithered down the wooden steps. In the hallway she thought of going for her coat, but the frantic urgency of Julien's voice was still in her ear.

She heaved open the double doors of the Domaine and went down into the winter's night. She ran to the barn where her bicycle was kept. Thinking it better to be in darkness, she did not attach the dynamo, but pedalled off beneath the arch of the pigeonnier, then, panting, swung the bike into the long drive, where she lowered her head against the freezing drizzle of the night and strained her eyes to see the potholes and the grassy verge beneath the rows of darkened plane trees.

8

Peter Gregory was in a deplorable state by the time Pascale had undressed him and put him to bed in her apartment above the harbour in Marseille. He had a high temperature as a result of the infection in his leg and he was exhausted by exertion and from lack of food. Pascale called a doctor, who drained the wound and said there was nothing more he could do; the activities of the previous days had made things worse and he could only recommend rest.

At the height of his fever Gregory called out, and Pascale came to him.

She sat by the bed and held his hand. 'Hold on to me,' he breathily begged her.

When the delirium took him from her again, she ran from the room and soaked cloths to press on his forehead. At last, his face scarlet and dripping, his hair plastered to his head, he subsided into sleep.

Pascale, under her real name of Nancy Brogan, had been married to a French industrialist, for whom she had forsaken her Pennsylvania home and her job with a news magazine to move into a house in Lyon. He had died of a heart attack, leaving Nancy a widow at the age of thirty-nine, three years before. She shuttled back and forth between her friends, most of whom were in New York, and her new home in Lyon. Her old college classmates told her she was crazy not to come back; one of them even secured her an offer of a job with a publisher. Yet she felt drawn back to her husband's country, and when a visiting Englishman tentatively suggested she might be of help to him, the decision to stay was easy.

She liked washing and tending her passive patient.

It brought back some childish satisfaction, a feeling of control. She felt that her own life was at a critical stage, and that caring for this man might help. She felt no older in herself than she had done on the day of her graduation from Vassar; she had discovered that ageing and what they called 'maturity' were myths, that all the years did was disqualify you from various pleasures, one by one.

As Gregory grew better, he began to talk to her about his life. Unable to look after himself, he depended on Nancy, and from such dependence a sense of trust grew naturally. Physically, he prospered. She gathered from his stories how active he had been in planes, in playing golf and other games; she saw an underlying health begin to reassert itself as the infection retreated from his leg and he felt the benefits of her care. Yet she sensed exhaustion in him too: a spiritual fatigue that was unrelated to anything the doctor diagnosed.

He told Nancy about a woman he loved. He told her he felt unworthy of her, so much so that he wouldn't even say her name. He was not sure that she would want to see him if he managed to get back. He had not appreciated her at first, had not seen how much he loved her until it was too late, and now he cursed himself for his stupidity.

For all his passion when he spoke of this absent person, Nancy found that she straightened her wavy brown hair before she went into his room; she wore a little red lipstick. After all, she was young.

She tried to make a place for him outside the cares of war and the fatal ties of human obligation. She brought him food she conjured with American dollars from the blackest market of the port; she brought him half bottles of Burgundy she had had dispatched from the replete cellars of her husband's old house; she brought luxury to her unreal world.

For his part, Gregory liked to pass the time by

thinking about Charlotte. It comforted him to imagine that while he had fought his way through injury and fever to this temporary haven and that while he braced himself for the danger of his return, she would be quietly going about her routine in London.

He saw her in the narrow room at the end of the corridor, hurriedly dressing in the morning after one of her motionless sleeps. He could not quite remember what the FANY uniform was like, but he was sure that Charlotte would not care for it. She would for some time have been safely back from whatever errand she had been assigned in France, unless, of course, her Lysander pilot had also crashed and therefore failed to pick her up. It seemed unlikely.

She would take a taxi (she would be too late for the bus) to some office, where she would pass a long day which to him would have been intolerably tedious but which to her would seem useful. Then in the evening she would busy herself in the flat, making dinner, listening to the problems of her ridiculous flat-mates. He imagined her curled up in bed, reading into the small hours, and the picture brought him a profound sense of peace.

★ ★ ★

Levade sat on the train to the concentration camp writing letters to his friends.

Dear Anne-Marie,

I'm afraid our sessions have come to an end. Please take the painting if you want it. It's no good, but you might like a souvenir of those long afternoons that you so bravely bore. Never lose the grace you have, however the years deprive you of your swift movements. Your arms, I remember so well from that lunch on the terrace of the restaurant, were so beautiful that they obsessed me. But I am a feeble painter who has not for many years been able to go behind these surfaces to what lies beyond. Forget me now, but I will remember you in my prayers.

He was in a third-class compartment guarded by gendarmes in the corridor. They were unhappy in their work and averted their eyes from Levade and his five fellow-prisoners. Instead, as the train rattled north, they leaned against the window and carefully watched the weak afternoon sun decline on the foothills of the Limousin.

Levade sealed the letter to Anne-Marie and began another.

Dear Julien,

I'm sorry we didn't have time to say goodbye. There are many things I would like to have told you. I feel ashamed to have been absent for so much of your life, not having been there to help you. It is a passionate regret to me. The love of a man for his son is a terrible and wonderful thing, one of the greatest that God has given to us. It is comparable to the love of God for man. Think of Abraham, prepared to kill his long-awaited son Isaac, to plunge his knife into the living boy. God chose that test because it was the hardest. And to save the world he gave his own Son. In what a father feels for his son there is much stern hope, but so much tenderness that I cannot describe it to you now. If you have sons of your own you must hold them when they're young. But you will never keep them in that embrace. They are separate from you, however much you love them, and all you have done, in a moment's passion, is create the circumstances for their existence.

As for the manner of my leaving . . .

Here, Levade put down the pen because he hadn't the heart to examine what had happened, or to think what Julien's motives might have been. He had thought himself into an elevated state of mind in which he was able to accept that what had taken place was in some way ineluctable. The truth had been told: he was a Jew; and he was prepared to live in the consequences of that truth with a providential hope. He became momentarily aware of a selfish desire: he wanted to die; but he was able to deny this wish, or at least subsume it into a more general sense of tranquillity in which his own desires had no active part. Not my will, he repeated to himself, but Thy will be done.

He would return to the question of Julien. Meanwhile he began another letter, to Charlotte.

Dear Madame,

I am addressing this to you at the Domaine, though I don't know whether you will still be there. I shall give it to the young gendarme in the corridor who manically avoids my eye. Perhaps it will make him feel better.

Is it too late to thank you for your company in my house? I was a bad friend and landlord to you, but to have you there was a comfort to me in many long days and nights. I wish very much that you did not so much love another man, as I believe you could have loved my son. One wishes for things to be content and permanent in a way that one has failed to achieve oneself. But you are a fine person, Madame, you have such courage in your heart, and if not with Julien, then so be it, with someone else.

Did I tease you too much? I wanted to make you strong. The happiness of young people becomes almost the only source of delight to someone of my age. I remember when you told me about your father, and I was pleased that you confided in me. I told you that we can live with mystery, with unresolved conflicts. Now I'm not sure if that's true. In art, perhaps, these things are good. In your life I think you should try to remember, though whether you can do this by an act of will, I doubt. Memory works at its best unasked.

I wish you very well. For the sake of those who are old and those about to die you must make something glorious of your life. That would mean something to those less free to choose.

When he had signed the letter, placed it an envelope and addressed it, Levade returned to the piece of paper on which he was writing to Julien.

For a long time he stared at the abbreviated paragraph, but still he remained unwilling to break the tranquillity of his mental state. So lost was he in thought that he did not notice the train slowing down as it neared its destination.

Eventually, he continued:

There was an English mystic who came back from her most joyful communion with God saying, 'All will be well; all manner of things will be well.'

So, Julien, I believe . . .

But, at this moment, the train stopped at the station with a heavy jolt, and the gendarmes pulled back the doors of Levade's compartment. He had barely the time to write, 'I love you' at the bottom of the letter, to seal and hastily address it before he and his fellow-passengers were hurried down on to the platform.

The station was at a town in the flat pastures of the Bourbonnais. The travellers on the platform looked with sheepish interest at the small group of men and women under guard. A senior gendarme took the papers offered to him by a young man who had been guarding them on the train. He told them to arrange themselves in a line and follow him.

Levade picked up the suitcase Charlotte had packed and felt inside the pocket of his jacket for the three letters. As he passed the youngest of the gendarmes, he held them out to him. 'Would you post these for me? They're just letters to my son and a couple of friends.'

The young man looked down at his feet, then glanced to see if anyone had seen. He stuffed the letters into his pocket and grunted.

The senior gendarme led his half-dozen charges down the platform, over a metal passenger bridge and down to a goods' siding where half a dozen wagons had been coupled.

The men and women waited, looking round for their train and wondering whether the officer had made a mistake.

Then the gendarme went to the side of one of the wagons, unbolted it and pulled it open. It was full of people standing. The gendarme motioned towards the wagon with his hand.

Levade recognised this kind of wooden truck. When he had been released from duties as soup-man at Verdun he had spent a pleasantly undangerous period working in stores at the railhead. Such transport had arrived almost daily, bearing horses.

Perhaps this wagon had once carried the very horse he had tried to eat.

Part Four

1943

1

André Duguay ran down the stairs when he heard Mlle Cariteau's urgent call. It was six in the morning. In the kitchen was the nice young woman who sometimes came to visit them and read stories. André smiled briefly at her, then turned his eyes to the floor. Mlle Cariteau attacked his face with a cloth from the sink while he grimaced and tried to wrench his head away.

'We're going to say goodbye,' said Mlle Cariteau. 'For a few days you're going to another house, just for a holiday.'

'It'll be nice,' said Charlotte. 'You're going to be on a farm with animals, you and Jacob. Would you like that?'

'No,' said André. 'I don't want to.'

The two women set about trying to persuade him, by painting pictures of outdoor life with dogs and chickens and games in old barns. André felt suspicious of both.

'I don't want to leave, I like it here.'

'And Jacob's coming too,' said Charlotte. 'You'll have wonderful games together. Then you can come back later and visit.'

André, who had seemed to be on the point of acquiescing, suddenly shook his head. 'I want my mother. I want to know where she is.'

Charlotte said gently, 'André, there really isn't any choice. Soon this war will be over. Things are beginning to happen. And soon, when it's finished, you will see your parents again. I'm sure you will. But just for the time being it would be better if you do what we ask. Trust me.'

André was beyond the reach of reason; he felt he had been trusting enough already, and still his parents were not there. His small, muscular body set itself in resistance to all these adult plans; he grasped the edge of the chair next to him and began to wail his defiance.

Mlle Cariteau said, 'I'll go and get the little one.'

In the middle of the previous night, André had heard a hammering on the kitchen door, then the sound of voices. He crept to the top of the stairs and through the banisters was able to see Madame and Mlle Cariteau talking urgently to the young woman, Madame Guilbert. As a result of their conversation, he and Jacob had been pushed up into the attic for the night and told to sleep on a pile of old blankets. They clung to one another for warmth in an unaccustomed embrace.

Sylvie Cariteau returned to the kitchen with a suspicious Jacob and the suitcase the boys had once used for tobogganing downstairs. It now held a few clothes Sylvie had managed to extract one evening from the Duguays' house, the tin soldiers that Julien had brought, the book about the crocodile who lost her egg, an old adjustable spanner of which André had become fond and one or two other small objects of mysterious but intense private significance.

'Listen,' she said, 'a friend is coming to pick you up later in the morning and take you to the farm. I just want you to say goodbye to Madame Guilbert now.'

Madame Cariteau appeared in the kitchen and, seeing that André was upset, clasped him against her bosom, where he breathed in the old sour smell of her and felt the heat of her embrace, which once had reassured him, being soft and vaguely female, but now seemed only to emphasise the extent to which she was not his mother.

★ ★ ★

440

The night before, Charlotte had arrived, dripping wet, from the Domaine and woken the Cariteaus with her knocking. After she had explained the situation to Sylvie and they had moved the boys to the attic, they sat at the kitchen table and tried to decide what to do with them.

'I think our best chance is Pauline Benoit,' said Sylvie.

Charlotte remembered what Julien had said. 'Isn't she a Gaullist?'

'Does that matter?'

'Maybe not.' Charlotte wanted to say as little as possible.

'She's a kind woman. She'd certainly want to help two children.'

When Charlotte left Sylvie Cariteau and bicycled off, as instructed by Julien, to the monastery, Sylvie went quietly through the dark streets to rouse Pauline Benoit. Initially resentful at being woken, Pauline was intrigued by the plight of the boys and and amazed at how successfully Sylvie Cariteau had concealed them.

'I can't have them here,' she said. 'Obviously. Especially now with Monsieur Levade in difficulty. This is the first place they'd look. We want to get them out of the village. There is one person I can think of. I don't know her very well, but . . . '

'Who is it?'

They were sitting by candlelight in Pauline's small front room. 'Wait a minute. Let me think.'

Eventually she said, 'Yes, I think it'll work. She's called Anne-Marie. She sits as a model for old Monsieur Levade. Her father has a farm about twenty minutes from here. He knows how to keep his mouth shut. God knows, he's got enough to be discreet about.'

'Are you sure they'll co-operate?' said Sylvie Cariteau.

'I'm pretty sure. We can always offer to pay them. And the boys will be much better off on a farm. They might even get some eggs. I'll take Gastinel's van and go and see them. I'll be back by dawn.'

* * *

Julien Levade was not a particularly strong man, but he was younger and bigger than the German soldier guarding him, and in the struggle that followed Charlotte's departure he had more reason to fight. With his arm round the German's throat he said, 'Put down your gun and I won't hurt you.'

His words meant nothing to the other man, who continued to wriggle in Julien's embrace and to thrash out with his elbows. It was so long since he had fought as a boy, playground disputes with trembling lips where the loser was the child who cried, that Julien could barely remember how to go about it. There was a repellent intimacy about the other's man hair against the skin of his face.

Julien held a forearm across the German's throat and locked one hand with the other to increase the grip; in this way, he was able to pull him slowly backwards to the floor, while he retreated step by step to make room. As the German finally lost balance, Julien was obliged to let go, at which moment he kicked out at the rifle the other man still clutched in his right hand. He watched it slide a few feet over the bare floorboards. He drove his heel as hard as he could into the German's ribs and, while the man gasped, he was able to dive across and grab the gun himself, then scuttle over the floor on all fours and turn round, kneeling to face his enemy with the rifle in his hand.

The German levered himself into a sitting position, in which all soldierly pretence fell away. Panting and snorting from his exertion, he placed his hands together and prayed Julien not to shoot.

Julien stood up slowly and walked back towards the door. Now that he had gained control, he still faced the awkward question of what to do with the man. He could tie him up, but with what? He could shoot him, but really he wished him no harm. As his tearful imprecations made clear, he was just a pathetic creature, caught in a job he did not want, anxious to return to the children he had left behind and whose photographs he was now, to Julien's embarrassment, fumbling to produce from a wallet.

Perhaps he should just shoot him in the leg, to disable him. Really, these were considerations of war of which his own activities had as yet given him no experience. But there was no use being squeamish, he thought. 'Take your clothes off,' he said.

The German looked at him, head on one side, striving to understand. His thinning hair had been tousled by the struggle, and a single long strand hung down over his ear; his face was flushed and looked exhausted in the shadows and pouches of his incipient middle age. Julien mimed what he meant and the German, in ecstatic relief at having understood his captor's wish, did his best to please him.

'More.' Julien gestured with his rifle. The pile of clothes mounted by his ankles, and when he was naked Julien pointed to the door.

Shivering, and no longer pleased, the German soldier walked across the room, his eye on the barrel of the gun as Julien retreated to one side to let him pass.

Down the corridor of the first floor they went, past the door of Levade's studio, the man's white buttocks a dim beacon in the darkness. At the top of the stairs Julien stuck the tip of the rifle into his back to remind him that he was serious and kept it there as they groped their slow way down.

In the hall, Julien turned on a light and, keeping

the gun steady on its target, backed over to the desk from which Levade had earlier taken his identity papers. Among the letters and documents was a bunch of keys which he took over to the door beneath the stairs that led to the Domaine's enormous cellar. When he had found the right key, he indicated with his head that the German should go through the door.

'It's all right. In the morning your friends'll come. They'll hear you. Go on. Go on.' He raised the rifle and fired a shot into the ceiling.

Each angle of his body protesting reluctance, the man moved slowly over the floor of the hall to the open door, one hand raised to protect himself, the other placed across his genitals, in self-defence or in some reflexive modesty beneath the light snow-shower of fallen plaster.

Julien smiled. 'You'll be all right. I'll leave the key here on the table. Go on.'

At the last moment, faced with the icy darkness, the German suddenly protested and turned to fight again, but Julien kicked him through and closed the door against his struggle.

He returned to the bedroom and went through the man's clothes to see if there was a handgun or anything else that might be useful to him in the days ahead. There was nothing but a few extra rounds for the rifle, which he slipped into his jacket pocket.

He let himself out of the Domaine and took a bicycle from the barn. He could still be clear of Lavaurette by dawn.

★ ★ ★

Charlotte was unable to sleep in the monastery. She paced up and down in a book-lined room that looked like an office, and, shortly before dawn, returned to the Cariteaus' house.

444

She leaned her bicycle against the wall by the back door and remembered all the times she had done this on her visits to the boys; she thought of the night of the drop and of the excitement she had felt as they pedalled away into the night.

She knocked quietly at the door and Sylvie Cariteau let her in. She looked anxious. 'Madame, it's dangerous for you to be here.'

'I wanted to know about the boys. Are they all right?'

'Yes. Pauline's just been here. They're going to live with Anne-Marie.'

'She didn't mind?'

'No.' Sylvie Cariteau shook her head. 'I don't know if she really understood the danger. But she's a kind girl, Anne-Marie.'

Charlotte looked about the kitchen, with its huge, blackened range, its pitted oak table and traces of the Cariteaus' frugal meals.

Now that the time had come, she could not bring herself to leave. In this raw, square room something valuable had taken place. With Sylvie and her mother she had formed an understanding that went far beyond their differences. Something elemental and loving in her had found an answering spirit in these two French women, and parting from them now, before they knew how it would end, would be like leaving behind some vulnerable element of herself.

She felt Sylvie Cariteau's eyes on her. 'You must go, Madame. It's almost light.'

Charlotte went to the door, then hesitated. She turned and saw that Sylvie's eyes were full of tears.

'Oh, Sylvie,' she said, going back and throwing her arms round her.

They clung to each other for a few moments. Charlotte struggled to find words, but then gave up. She knew that they were thinking the same things.

'I will come back,' she said.

'Do you promise?' Sylvie Cariteau was smiling now, wiping the tears from her cheeks with the backs of her large, red hands.

'I promise.' Charlotte kissed her on the cheek and ran from the house.

Then, in the early morning light, she pedalled hard out of Lavaurette, Julien's fearful warning still loud in her ears. She reckoned it would take her a day to reach the small town where the wireless operator lived and she knew she should not delay. The further she went, however, the more tormented she felt by the thought of Levade being held in some detention camp and Julien, exiled in the chilly countryside, unable to reach him to explain what he had done. Her business was not finished, and, until it was, she could not go home.

Late in the morning she stopped to rest at the edge of a field. There was a small stone-built hut, presumably a store or shelter of some kind, but now dilapidated. She pushed the bicycle inside and lay down to rest, but it was very cold. She thought longingly of Dominique's woollen vests.

Somehow she dozed in the sunless afternoon, and when she awoke, stiff and hungry, she knew that she had to return to Lavaurette. She would give it a day for the alarm to subside, then go back to the Domaine. The reason she gave herself was that she needed her identity card and some money, which were still in her bedroom. She did not listen to an inner voice that told her the wireless operator could in due course supply her with both.

She bicycled into the nearest village, but the food shops were closed and there was no café. At least there were still some tins in the store cupboards of the Domaine, she told herself, as she went back to her stone shelter.

She passed a long night without sleeping. She spent

the first part of the next day walking up and down to keep warm, then began to bicycle slowly back. She timed her return to Lavaurette for eight o'clock in the evening, well after dark, but before the curfew. She went on a long circuitous route that avoided the village and brought her through the woods at the side of the house.

She found the front door of the Domaine ajar, as though someone had left in a hurry. There were no lights burning. She paused in the hall and looked round: something was not right; she noticed that the door to the cellar was open and that the bunch of keys was in the lock. She took a torch from the desk and went down the steps into the cold gloom. The beam of light travelled over the dusty wine bins, some of which had empty bottles spanned by cobwebs in whose sticky grip were long-dead flies and globs of thicker dust.

Charlotte walked carefully over the uneven floor of beaten earth, hosing the walls with her torchlight. It was intensely silent, aromatic with the passage of damp centuries.

There was no one there. She climbed back to the hall behind her, replacing the keys in the desk, in their proper place, some housekeeperly instinct prompting her. Still using only the torch, she went into the kitchen, where she opened a tin of ham that she had been saving for some special occasion. She sliced it hurriedly and consumed it all, with a crust of bread, some walnuts and a glass of stale wine from an open bottle on the sideboard.

Then she crept for the last time over the sprung floor of the dining room and went to the top of the house, where she once more packed the possessions of Dominique Guilbert in their tattered leather case and cast a farewell look at the little bedroom in which such extraordinary days of her life had passed: the toile with its figures of eighteenth century gaiety, faded and worn;

the servant's bed, the threadbare rug and the view down towards the lake.

She walked along the corridor of the first floor. In the room where she and Julien had been held, she straightened the bedclothes, still rumpled by their simulated passion. She noticed that a chair had been turned over, presumably in the struggle that followed her leaving. She had no doubt that Julien would have prevailed: in the last picture she had of him, he already had the German by the neck.

The door to Levade's studio was open. Inside, the chaos of his work was undisturbed, except where she had wrenched the painting from its stretcher; some shreds of canvas, mostly white but some that he had painted on, still clung to the nails in the beam of her torchlight. She smiled at the portrait of Anne-Marie in her green skirt. Her unreadable, almond-shaped eyes smiled back, unembarrassed by the strangeness of her situation. All around was the evidence of Levade's furious and fruitless effort: the stacked canvases, the open books, the palettes, tubes and exhausted brushes; and none of it, according to him, of any use at all.

She went, tidying and straightening, through all the other rooms of the Domaine. It had been many years since a family, rooted in the events of the day, had lived there. Levade was an outsider, presiding over something that was already moribund; and she, the last inhabitant, was an impostor, a foreigner who had come to run her hands across the surfaces of these draughty, uninhabited spaces, everywhere fastening and closing, like a pallid lawyer come to seal the house and the failure of its contract with history.

She paused finally in the hall, looking back at the broad staircase and the smoky ancestral oils that ran up the wall beside it. Then she went out, pulled the door closed behind her, and hurried down the stone steps where a few days earlier the master of the house had been prodded by a bewildered gendarme.

At the end of the drive, she was moved by some final tidying instinct to open the letter box. Inside were half a dozen letters, one of them addressed to her. Her feet on the ground either side of the bicycle, she tore it open. In the light of the torch she saw Levade's handwriting. 'Dear Madame . . . '

She set off with stinging eyes. She would have to find him and tell him what Julien had done. If she could resolve the misunderstanding between Julien and Levade, she might come to see in a purer light the presumed betrayal that had fallen between her and her own father.

This, it was suddenly clear to Charlotte, was her hope of salvation. She would endure the agony of having to abandon her search for Gregory if she could heal these harsh familial wounds. This, in fact, was the way she would make herself worthy of her lover.

★ ★ ★

Julien was in a solitary cell inside the monastery. At the back of the building, beneath the kitchens, it was the space in which the boilers would shortly be installed. He paced up and down on the new cement floor, admiring the solid, level finish the builders had achieved in readiness for the giant cylinders, which stood outside in wooden crates.

I should be praying, he thought, in this dank space hallowed by the prayers of so many devout, unhappy men. I am about to kill a man and I should be praying for my soul, and his.

Against the wall he had leaned the German soldier's rifle. A dozen times now he had cleaned it, pulling an oily rag through the barrel; he had laid the butt against his shoulder, balanced the cool mass in the palm of his left hand, squinted down the sights; he had done all

449

but fire the gun in his desire to be prepared.

He shivered in the cell. Days had passed already, and although he was sure that Dominique would have moved the boys from Sylvie Cariteau's house, he should act before Benech, so well informed about the welfare of the young, discovered their new home.

He stamped up and down the floor, looking at his watch. It was almost dark. In just four hours' time he would risk going into Lavaurette to find Benech; he thought he knew where to look. He wore the battered leather jacket that had accompanied him on so many night-time errands, but still the cold was sinking into him. He had made a bed from the lagging that would be used to insulate the boilers and now he took a strip of it from the floor to wrap round his shoulders.

Outside he could hear the builders packing up for the day. At least that meant he could go above ground and have a change of scene. He had let himself into the fenced-off site with his own key, then made a deal with the foreman, who agreed to say nothing provided Julien stayed out of the view of the other workmen.

He heard the shovels being thrown into metal barrows, the weary calls of farewell, and at last the padlock rebounding off the metal gatepost and rattling briefly against the chain-link fence. Julien opened the door of the cell and climbed the stairs. Outside, he watched as the lorry's tail lights vanished and the red glow from the last bicycle lamp shrank into the January mist. He wandered down the cloister to the abbot's office, which had its own bathroom attached.

Relieved but still shivering, he lit a candle and looked down the bookshelves, whose contents had still not been packed up. He pulled out a copy of Pascal's *Pensées* and began to flick through it, hoping for some consolation. Much of it seemed to be about Abraham or the Jews or to concern Pascal's own reactions to Montaigne. '*Sound opinions of the people,*' Julien read.

'The greatest of evils is civil war . . . '

He moved on through the pages. He lifted the book to his face and sniffed the yellow dusty paper. 'Imagine a number of men in chains, all under sentence of death, some of whom are clearly murdered in the sight of the others; those remaining see their own condition in that of their fellows, and looking at each other with grief and despair await their turn. This is an image of the human condition.' He remembered this melodramatic passage from his school days.

He carried the volume over to the desk. What he wanted was some sort of confirmation that a greater good could excuse an apparent evil. In war, presumably, killing was permitted, if it was a just or holy war, as when priests had come to bless his father at Verdun. What if the war was not declared, what if the war was internal? All Pascal seemed to offer was that 'the greatest of evils is civil war.' Perhaps the words '*Sound opinions of the people*' were in italics to show that the view expressed was second-hand or null, like an entry in Bouvard and Pécuchet's Dictionary of Received Ideas.

Thought 526 read: 'Evil is easy; it has countless forms, while good is almost unique. But a certain sort of evil is as hard to find as what is called good, and this particular evil is often on that account passed off as good. Indeed, it takes as much extraordinary greatness of soul to attain such evil, as to attain good.'

Was that 'greatness of soul' his or Benech's? Neither, he suddenly saw. It was Pétain's.

When it was time to go, Julien walked back down the icy cloister, obliquely admired the new stone fountain they had installed in the middle of the quadrangle, and went down to the cell to retrieve the rifle and his bicycle. He tore off some lagging and stuffed it down inside his jacket to keep out the wind, slung the rifle across his chest by its webbing, then wheeled the bicycle to the gate, let himself out, relocked the site and set off for Lavaurette.

It took twenty minutes before he arrived at the silent factory on the outskirts of the village, where he turned down a narrow side road and left his bicycle. He felt absurdly conspicuous with the rifle, even in the unlit streets. Luckily, the cold was serious enough to deter people from leaving their houses. Julien hoped it would not have been too much for Benech.

As well as the aching in his face and hands he was aware of the pain of hunger in his stomach. It was almost two days since he had eaten, buying eggs and some ham from a remote smallholder who supplied wood for the fires in his apartment building. As he approached the square which held the Café du Centre, he went down a path to the back, where an untidy yard, full of boxes, dustbins and bits of defunct agricultural machinery, was faintly illuminated by a light from the steamy kitchen. He laid his rifle down against a wall, crept across the open space and peered into the wooden crates. From one of them he pulled out a tin, and, looking furtively round, slipped it into his pocket. Just next to the back door was a crate of lumpy objects he thought could be vegetables. The mud of the courtyard was frozen hard beneath his feet as he edged forward; a thin piece of ice on a puddle cracked beneath his step. He could make out the sound of a wireless playing inside as he inched up to the building. With his eyes fixed on the glass of the back door, he lowered his hand into the crate and pulled out what felt like a potato, then made his way quietly back across the yard to his rifle and went out into the dark path that led back to the street.

He squatted on the ground and stuck his torch between his teeth to examine his stolen dinner. It was a potato, with diamonds of frost in its muddy skin; the tin had no label on it. When he had peeled the potato with his pocket knife, he sat on the grass verge and, by hammering the knife with a stone, was able to open the tin far enough to pull out part of the contents. He stuck a piece in his mouth. It was a sliced pear. The starch on the surface of the peeled potato stung the soft inside of his lips and he pushed another piece of pear into his mouth to counteract it. In this way he crunched through the freezing potato and the sleepy grey pear.

The front windows of the Café du Centre gave on to the square, but the side of the bar overlooked a narrow street that led up to the main part of Lavaurette. It was here that Julien made his way. He laid his rifle on the ground by the outside wall of the bar and looked cautiously in.

How strange his peering, unshaven face would look to anyone inside, he thought. He could make out the bar and could see Gayral himself polishing a glass, his mournful moustaches bent to the repetitive task. There were two figures at the bar, one of whom, he was fairly sure from the back view, was Benech. He wondered what he could be drinking, now that alcohol was almost impossible to obtain. It was so quiet in the bar that Julien could make out some of the words of the wireless broadcast. The announcer introduced a government minister, Monsieur Darquier de Pellepoix, the head of the General Council of Jewish Questions, whose ranting voice was quickly subdued by Gayral's hand. Julien could still make out the phrases: 'Killed by London, Washington, Moscow, and Jerusalem . . . England, the hereditary enemy . . . the ideological war desired by Israel . . . Allied Victory would mean more of what we have already seen in North Africa: the return to power of the Jews and Freemasons . . . who for half a century lived on the backs of the settlers and natives until the Marshal cleared them away.'

The Marshal's name always made Julien think first

453

not of Vichy but of Verdun, the glorious context in which, when he was a child, it seemed to have been for ever fixed. He remembered the soft awe of his father when he spoke the name, then thought again with a shiver of Pascal's words: ' . . . It takes as much extraordinary greatness of soul to achieve such evil.'

Then he saw Benech. He turned to offer his cup to Gayral to refill — a cup, not a glass, Julien noticed, as Benech's features came for a moment into his view: perhaps, for lack of wine, he was drinking Viandox or some meat-drink substitute. He must value the social aspect of his visits to the bar very highly to think it worth the cold walk from wherever it was he lived.

Julien had to move quickly into the shadows, down the side of the building, when he heard footsteps on the street coming from the village, but he was back at his place by the window in time to see Benech put on his coat and hat and make his way towards the front door of the café. Julien pulled back into the darkness and waited. It was almost certain that Benech would come past him to go up to the centre of Lavaurette. His only concern was that he would be on a bicycle, but he had seen none left outside the front of the café. After a few moments, he heard footsteps and saw Benech's figure, his shoulders hunched against the cold, his hands thrust down inside his coat, go swiftly past him up the hill. Julien picked up the rifle and followed. If he went too close, Benech might hear him; but if he hung too far back, Benech might vanish down an unlit street. He tried to conceal the rifle from anyone who might be looking from their window by holding it upright between his side and his arm.

The shutters of Lavaurette were all closed. His and Benech's were the only footsteps on the street. Julien walked as soundlessly as he could manage,

454

once pulling back into a doorway when he thought Benech was about to stop. When he peered out, it was to see Benech turning off the main street, and he had to run to the junction. Benech was a short way down the road and was feeling in his pocket, presumably for a key. Julien moved as swiftly as he could along the walls of the houses until he was only a few paces away. Benech pushed the door open and reached inside for the light. Julien ran the short distance to the door, where Benech turned in alarm at the sound of footsteps. In the light of the electric bulb in the hallway he looked into Julien's face with a terrified recognition.

He tried to slam the door, but Julien had stuck his foot in the way. The door rebounded, shuddering on its hinges.

Julien raised his finger to his lips, then showed Benech the rifle. He mouthed the words, 'Where's your apartment?'

Benech breathed in, as though to shout for help, but Julien stuck the muzzle of the gun beneath his jaw and once more raised his finger to his lips. Benech turned to lead the way through the hall.

It was a house divided into rooms rather than an apartment block. Julien noticed a light beneath the door on his right on the ground floor. There could be four or five separate flats, he thought.

On the bare-boarded landing Benech took another key and let them into his apartment. The sitting room was large and tidy, the comfortable home of a professional man, but seemed to be unheated.

'What do you want?' said Benech.

Julien held the rifle pointing at his chest. He looked at Benech's face, the grey and floury skin, the features regular and almost handsome in their way, but made plain by his fear.

'You said something to me the other night. I want you to explain. You said, 'I'm a schoolmaster. It's my business to know the whereabouts of children.' What did you mean?'

Benech turned his back on Julien, walked over to a table and sat down. When he turned round he was smiling.

'You know very well what I mean. I know about you and your father. I know about the English servant-girl, the mistress you share with him. I know about your little escapades at night. People like you can't understand what's in front of them.' He gave a short, derisive laugh. 'You're like the children I teach. Time and again you explain some simple fact, but they're incapable of understanding.'

'Who else have you told about the boys? Did you tell that man Pichon?'

'Never you mind. My organisation can have you arrested any time I like. I'm working for the Government.' He put his hand into the drawer of the table and pulled out a piece of paper. 'My membership of the Milice. Look.'

As Julien moved over to the table to take the paper, Benech put his hand in the drawer again and pulled out his revolver. Julien threw himself to the floor.

The noise of the shot was so loud that it took Julien a moment to realise he had not been hit. The sound and recoil of the gun seemed momentarily to have stunned Benech as well. He was staring at the thing in his hand as though it had somehow fired itself. Julien stood up and rammed the butt of his rifle into Benech's mouth, knocking him backwards off the chair, then wrenched back the rifle and ran out of the apartment. The door of the ground floor flat was opening in the hall as he went past, causing him to step aside. With his back to the wall he looked up to the landing above him, where Benech was standing, leaning on the banister rail, blood dripping from his mouth. Julien raised his rifle and shot him through the heart, causing the revolver to drop from Benech's hand as his body folded at the waist and fell over the rail, a dead weight slamming down and shaking the insubstantial wooden staircase below.

★ ★ ★

Charlotte reached the address Julien had given her late in the afternoon. It was a street in a medium-sized town, and the house appeared to be unoccupied. She returned at hourly intervals until, at about eight o'clock, a light came on.

With the memory of Antoinette in the back of her mind, she had been expecting that 'Zozo' would be a woman. The door was in fact opened by a corpulent man in braces. They went through the formalities swiftly and Zozo ushered her into the hall.

'I expect you'd like some dinner,' he smiled.

'What a wonderful idea.'

'Bring your bicycle in.'

There appeared to be no Madame Zozo, and after a dinner of soup and some noodles, Zozo said; 'Do you want me to send a message? I have a scheduled transmission tomorrow.'

'No,' said Charlotte. 'Not yet. I want you to find me somewhere to stay.'

Zozo nodded. 'I can manage that. At your own risk, of course.'

'Then I need to borrow your telephone.'

'And that's all?'

'For the time being.'

Zozo's plump face split into a smile. 'You're very easy to accommodate, Madame. The telephone's through there.'

Sylvie's voice answered almost at once. Charlotte was excited.

457

'Hello? Hello? Sylvie? Can you talk? Have you heard from our friend? And he's all right? I have a message. He must find out where his father is and leave the answer with you. Do you understand? It's vital. Tell him it's a matter of life and death. I'll call again.'

It would be difficult for Julien to make contact with people, but she knew that he had ways of finding things out: friends, contacts, even Communists. In the meantime, she would wait.

★ ★ ★

Peter Gregory was sitting in a borrowed dressing gown, enjoying a cup of what tasted quite like coffee. He had his feet up on a stool in front of him and was looking down through the window to the narrow street below.

On the other side of the room sat Nancy, her half-moon glasses stuck below the bridge of her nose, inspecting the newspaper with occasional murmurs of dismay.

The telephone began to ring on a table in the corner and Nancy went over, paper in hand, to answer it.

Gregory found French in Nancy's Pennsylvanian accent considerably easier to understand than any of the other regional variants he had encountered, though on this occasion she said very little as she scribbled a note on the margin of her paper while the voice at the other end dictated.

Gregory now felt impatient to be on his way. It was as though his fatal weariness had been purged; the feeling that replaced it was a cold and energetic hope. When he thought about Charlotte he felt sure that what had held him back was fear. He was scared of her clarity of mind and the intensity of her feeling for him; it had taken him time to see that she could love him as he was — that the peculiar shapes and deformities of his

458

personality were not just entrancing but necessary to her. Again he felt blessed by a prodigally generous fate that this should be the case. To be worthy of her he had needed to do just one thing: to want to live. And having accomplished that, he thought with a smile, I have one other small task: to get back.

'That was an Italian friend on the telephone,' said Nancy, sitting down in her chair and resetting her glasses. 'Looks like there's a chance of a little action at last.' She spoke quietly, with her head slightly averted. She said, 'Ever heard of a felucca?'

'Is sounds like a blister on your feet.'

'It's like a Portuguese sardine boat. Kind of uncomfortable, I guess, but you won't be going far.'

'What's this Italian friend got to do with it?'

'East of the Rhône, France is occupied by the Italians. You knew that? Well, this guy, this friend of mine, Gianluca, he's gonna help you. He'll go with you. I'm not sure at this moment exactly what his plan is, but he's never let us down before.'

'But if we cross the Rhône, won't we run into Italian soldiers?'

'I'm not so sure about that, Peter.' When she approached a topic of real urgency, Nancy sometimes had a way of becoming oblique, like a college professor who is still quietly thrilled by the complexity of something she is about to reveal to her students.

'As I understand it, there's some give and take with the Italians. Ask yourself what looks like the easy way out for them. I guess it's been the same with the French, hasn't it? We're all scared of the Vichy police, but it's not all like that, is it?'

Gregory thought of his old couple in the farmyard. 'Not at all.'

'You're supposed to go on Thursday, but it's a movable feast.'

2

Levade arrived in the concentration camp at Drancy
at ten minutes past four on a Monday afternoon, and
for a few moments he felt nothing but relief. To be
in the open air was a benediction to his lungs, which
were seething from the atmosphere of the closed railway
truck. The brief bus journey from the station had
offered no respite, and he sucked down the freezing air
until he began to cough in long, rib-stretching spasms
that made him double over.

When he could stand up, he found himself among
a crowd of bewildered, dirty people staring at the
unfinished housing complex that lay in front of them.
It was in the shape of a rectangle, more than a hundred
yards long and about two thirds that distance in width,
with buildings of four storeys on three sides. The fourth
side was open, though fenced with barbed wire into
which was cut a gate at the bottom right-hand corner.
There were raised guard posts at either end of this
open side, where gendarmes stood with machine guns
pointed over the courtyard enclosed by the rectangle.
Levade could see a tower to one side, the construction
of which seemed to have been abandoned.

His relief passed, as gendarmes pushed among them,
shouting orders; it became, as it had been throughout
the journey, an effort of will to confront the fatigue
that weighed him down.

All round were surly, muttering voices, recalcitrant
in different languages — German, Yiddish, Polish, or
French spoken with a variety of foreign accents. The
gendarmes worked them through the gate, funnelling
them into the narrow opening, so they were once
more forced into the bodily contact that repelled

them. Levade half-walked and was half-carried among the slow tide of people being prodded and marshalled down the length of the rectangle. For a moment he raised his eyes and saw faces pressed against the windows all round the the yard, their gazes wide and expressionless as they swept over the figures of the latest convoy.

At the far end was a wooden barracks, set in from the main buildings, outside which a queue was forming. Levade clutched the handle of his suitcase and leaned against a pillar which supported a shallow flat roof that ran round the three sides of the rectangle to provide shelter above the walkway beside the buildings.

Pushed by the baton of a gendarme, Levade stumbled into the gloom of the barracks where long trestle tables were set up in the bleary light of hurricane lamps. A German officer was sitting at one of these, with a French policeman to his right; but most of the work in the barracks was being done by local gendarmes, who were making the prisoners empty their luggage on to the tables while removing anything that was forbidden by their rules. They threw what was confiscated over their shoulders, where shabby creatures wearing white armbands collected it into piles.

The gendarme opposite Levade unrolled the canvas Charlotte had packed, glanced at it briefly and hurled it behind him. He searched Levade all over, tearing off his jacket and shirt in his hurry to get done; he wrinkled up his nose as his fingers touched the purple scar on Levade's shoulder. He emptied the suitcase on the table, chucked some of the contents over his shoulder, and thrust the rest into Levade's arms. 'Move,' he said. At the doorway, Levade was given a piece of yellow cloth in the shape of a star.

'Read this.' The gendarme pressed a notice against Levade's face. 'Any internee seen within camp bounds not wearing the insignia of the star will be imprisoned

461

and automatically included in the next transport.

'The same sanction will be taken against any internee found on the women's staircases. Only those issued with a white armband are allowed on those staircases.

'The orderlies are responsible for seeing that these orders are carried out.'

Beneath these words was another proclamation, signed by the Commissioner of Police, which detailed the imminent punishment of two people who had breached the rules; despite being married to 'Aryans', they were to be deported at once.

Levade felt his wrist taken by a young man wearing a white armband. They walked along the side of the building among a small group of stumbling new arrivals, some of them weeping with fatigue and fear.

Levade found himself climbing a stairway — with difficulty, as he was finding it hard to breathe, and people were jostling him from behind. Then he was in a large room, filled with panic and loud voices. He sat down on the floor, sweating into his shirt despite the cold, and leaned his back against the wall, clutching his few spared clothes to his chest.

Eventually, a hand rested on his shoulder and he opened his eyes to see the face of a man of about forty, clean-shaven, looking earnestly at him.

'Are you all right?' The man spoke French in a native, educated accent.

Levade smiled and nodded.

'I'm the head of your staircase. I'll try to help you, but it's always chaos when people first arrive. Have you got a knife and fork, or a bowl? No? All right, I'll see you get them.'

Levade looked round. It had grown dark outside, and the room was lit by naked bulbs hung from the ceiling. He saw rows of makeshift wooden beds piled one on top of another to make bunks. From many of these hung coats, shirts, jackets, saucepans and bags that had escaped the search in the barracks.

'My name's Hartmann,' said the man, still kneeling by Levade. 'You can stay sitting here if you like. I'll get the head of the room to find you a bed.' He smiled for a moment. 'We're very bureaucratic here — head of this, head of that. There'll be some soup later. Make sure you get some.'

Levade nodded and tried to thank the man, but his mouth and throat were too dry for words to pass.

He closed his eyes again and thought of the Domaine. He had struggled there with the limits of himself, pressing against the restrictions of what was left to him by age and temperament. He had considered himself unhappy. Yet he could see now that in the north light of that studio, disappointing though the results may have been, there had been a certain pleasure in his work. And the presence of the English woman — that too had been a comfort.

In the time since he left the Domaine the smell of excrement and unwashed bodies had never left him. At the first camp, Beaune-la-Rolande, it was bad; but here, in this place, the air was almost as rank as in the train. It was hard to love your fellow-man in these circumstances.

'Do you want a bed? Come with me.' Levade was addressed in French by a plump, grey-haired man with an accent that sounded Polish or Hungarian. He took Levade by the arm to the corner of the room.

'You'll have to climb up. Let me take the clothes.'

He helped Levade up to a bed that was in the middle of a rack of three. 'Sorry about the crush. The room's only supposed to have fifty people and we've got over a hundred. By the way, you're not allowed to smoke.'

Levade lay down and turned his face to the wall. There were thick electric cables that had not been plastered over but hung loosely from the grey cement; further down the wall was a cavity in which he could see a number of unconnected pipes and other signs of aborted plumbing. On the other side of the room, a long sheet of zinc had been attached to the wall to act as a wash basin, fed by half a dozen tapless pipes.

The window, a foot or so from Levade's face, had for some reason been painted blue — perhaps to stop them looking on to the world outside, he thought. It was of the type that slides along metal runners, and although it had been nailed shut, it did not fit flush with the frame. Levade was grateful for the slim icy draught because it helped against the smell of people in the room. He pulled the pile of his clothes on top of him and huddled down to sleep.

Later, a voice tried to interest him in soup, but Levade shook his head and pulled the clothes higher up over his shoulders. He heard the sound of a whistle and sensed the lights being extinguished.

Then, at last, for the first time for many years, Levade dreamed — rich, sensuous narratives expanded at beguiling length; visual revelations of remembered places; a total habitation of other fully realised worlds.

When he awoke in the morning, he found it impossible to believe that he was back in the room at Drancy. Surely the more powerful existence in which his dreams had so ravishingly placed him should have prevailed over this reduced reality.

It was seven o'clock and one of the orderlies with white armbands had brought a pail of coffee into the room. People crowded round him with their mugs outstretched while the head of the room tried in vain to make them form a line.

Levade stirred beneath the pile of clothes. He could feel an intense irritation in the skin of his chest and legs. It was a familiar sensation that for a moment he struggled to place. Then it came back to him: lice. He had not felt this tormenting itch since he burned his service shirt in Paris after being demobilised in 1918.

He struggled from the bed and asked the head of the room where the lavatory was.

'You have to wait. Our turn in the Red Castle is in five minutes. Wait here.'

Men were washing in the cold water that gushed from the pipes above the zinc trough. Some stood naked and performed their intimate ablutions with unhurried care; some furtively splashed and dabbed, revealing as little of themselves as they could. A father, a religious man, agonisingly hid his nakedness from his son. Levade found that Charlotte had put a toothbrush and some paste in the pocket of his jacket and he waited his turn to use them.

The Red Castle was a block of latrines made from a temporary barracks set near the main gates. When his room was detailed to use them, Levade went down with his fellow-men, herded by the orderly. In the courtyard, they had to keep to the edge of the buildings; they were not allowed to step into the open space, but had to huddle back like shadows on the wall. The latrines were inadequate for the numbers; the paper in the cubicles had been used by previous rooms, and when Levade pulled his plug there was no water in the cistern. The smell and the filth were not new to him; everything reminded him of the earlier war, when he had lived in such conditions. In those days, they had been told there was a reason: the glory and the honour of the country were at stake, and their sacrifices would be honoured when they returned from the front. This time, Levade did not think he would be going home.

The inhabitants of all the staircases in due course assembled in the cinder-covered courtyard for the roll call. Levade marvelled at the variety of his fellow-prisoners. There were sleek and shaven men in heavy overcoats who might have stepped out of an important business meeting for a quiet cigar; there were vagrant people in whose faces the grime was long ingrained; there were bare-legged women fussing over families, trying to keep threads of order; and there were children, large numbers of dark-eyed, lethargic infants, some barely able to stand from fatigue, some with their mothers but most of them isolated and stunned, beyond speech.

The roll call of the thousands gathered there took an hour and a half. Levade leaned on his young neighbour for support and, when it was over, went trembling back to his bed where he coughed until he thought his ribs would crack. A noisy argument was taking place between a group of Frenchmen and some Poles. The French were blaming the Poles for their own plight in being rounded up by the police, while the Poles complained that the French were given privileges by the police who ran the camp. After all, they argued, are we not all Jews?

'Yes,' a Parisian accent turbulently shouted back, 'but we're not all French.'

At eleven in the morning some bread was brought to the room, where it was divided into portions of one seventh of a loaf to each man. The head of the room was scrupulous in his division, as it was carelessness in this task that had once led to two men being immediately deported.

Levade had no appetite, but kept his piece of bread and gave it to the young man on whose shoulder he had leaned at roll call. At midday, the pail that had earlier brought up coffee arrived with what was described as soup — a broth of cabbage shavings and hot water, which was hungrily received by the other inmates.

'Don't you want your soup?' It was Hartmann, the head of the staircase, who had helped Levade when he arrived.

Levade shook his head.

'You don't look well.'

'It's my chest. I haven't been well for a few weeks.

I don't think the conditions are a help.'

Hartmann smiled. 'I'll see if I can get the nurses to look at you. We had a doctor on this staircase but he was deported.'

'These deportations,' said Levade. 'Where do they go?'

'Pitchipoï. That's what we tell the children. It's a name they made up in the infirmary. They go to Poland.'

'And what happens there?'

Hartmann raised his shoulders and spread his hands a little. Levade looked into his face: his eyes, Levade noticed, were of a remarkable deep brown with a thin bar of light at the centre. 'In theory,' Hartmann said, 'they work. In fact . . . In fact, I don't really know. But there are rumours, there are stories you'll hear in the camp.'

'And what do they say, these rumours?'

Hartmann shook his head slowly. 'I don't think it matters. I think we'll find out, you and I.'

Levade was lying on his bed, with Hartmann standing next to him. Levade said, 'Why are you here? What was your crime?'

'My crime . . . aah. So many crimes. As far as they were concerned, the problem was that I wasn't wearing a star. I lived in a little town in Brittany, in the Occupied Zone, and someone informed the local police that I was a Jew and was refusing to wear the star.'

Levade smiled. 'Like me. My papers weren't stamped with the right word.'

'My mother's family isn't Jewish anyway,' said Hartmann. 'My father was an atheist. But they needed people to make up numbers. I've been here six months now. That's how I got appointed to this elevated position, and because I'm a lawyer. The authorities like lawyers for some reason. I suppose they think we're intelligent. Or honest, perhaps.' He laughed.

'Who was it that chose you?'

'The gendarmes. They run the camp really. Officially, the national police are in charge, and it's their commissioner who's the commander of the camp. But they keep at arm's length, they feel happier that way, being the guardians of public order, doing the bidding of the Government but allowing the gendarmes to do the dirty work.'

'And these people with the armbands. Who are they?'

'There's a sort of Jewish administration, too. The gendarmes get us to run the place as much as possible. These people are orderlies. It's the same principle as the Germans using the French police. But if you're the head of a staircase, you can do some good, you're not just working for the enemy. You can help people, you can try to keep their spirits up. We have times of bad morale. Before a deportation there are a lot of suicides. People throw themselves from the windows.'

Levade closed his eyes. Perhaps it was illness as much as religious stoicism that was keeping him at a distance from the circumstances he was in; or perhaps they were simply too strange to be fully apprehended.

He said, 'How long do people stay here before they're deported?'

'Not long,' said Hartmann. 'We had a lull during the winter when no trains seemed to leave, but now it's starting up again. It's a few weeks for most people, and for some just a few days.'

'And who chooses the people?'

'To some extent the Jewish authorities choose. They try to send foreigners before the French, and they try to keep back veterans of the war. But the police can throw in anyone they like, and so can the Germans. In the end it's a matter of chance.'

'And the children?'

468

'Yes, they can go, too. Once they were ruled out, but not any more.'

'I see. And are you a veteran of the war?'

'Yes, but only at the end, from 1917. I was too young to go in before. And you?'

'Yes. Four years. Verdun. The smell here — '

'I know,' said Hartmann. 'It takes you back.'

Levade had closed his eyes again. He felt the other man's hand on his wrist. He said, 'I'll get someone to come and examine you. Perhaps you should sleep now.'

But Levade was already dreaming.

* * *

Sylvie Cariteau took her bicycle from the square and set off into the countryside. The post office was closed on Wednesday afternoon, so she had plenty of time, but she wanted to be back before it was dark.

It took her an hour to reach the farm where the boys were being kept. She felt unsure of her reception as she pedalled down the muddy track; she never really knew if they regarded her as their saviour or their gaoler, and André had become sensitive and strange in the course of the long months without his parents.

André turned out to be in his best mood, skipping and talking incessantly, eager to share with Sylvie the marvels of his new home. He was, or could be, the most delightful child, she thought, and little Jacob never complained, but just tagged along in his own time.

Anne-Marie's mother was in the kitchen, a woman of the same generation as Sylvie Cariteau's own mother, and of a similarly reticent character. She was not pleased at having two extra mouths to feed, but her husband had told her it would work out for them in the long run. He had given Sylvie a mysterious and conspiratorial look.

In the course of the afternoon, Anne-Marie herself came back from work in her café and joined in the games Sylvie was playing with the boys. Then she set to work to make a large omelette with eggs she sent André to gather from the hen coop. She even had butter to set foaming in the blackened skillet she put on the stove.

They were half way through the meal when Anne-Marie suddenly raised her finger to her lips. 'Ssh. I can hear a car. Quick. Upstairs. Quick!'

André and Jacob scrambled up the ladder while Anne-Marie gathered their plates into the sink.

'It's not your father's van?' said Sylvie.

'No. He has no petrol. Wait here.'

Anne-Marie, a slight woman beneath her lumpy winter clothes, went to the door and stood with her hands on her hips.

Coming into the yard was an open-topped German military vehicle with four men in it, their rifles pointing skyward from between their knees.

Anne-Marie stayed where she was as they climbed out and crossed the muddy farmyard.

The tallest of the four men stepped forward. 'You have Jews here,' he said in French. 'We take them. Jewish boys.'

'I don't know what you're talking about. There are no boys here. Just my mother and me. And a friend.'

'Move.' The German sergeant pushed past her, followed by the corporal and the private who had been at the Domaine, and another private who was part of the detachment at Lavaurette.

The sergeant shouted an order to the other three, who began to move about the kitchen, turning over the furniture, opening cupboards.

'What do you want?' said Anne-Marie's mother.

The sergeant stopped at the door to the next room.

'The French police say there are Jews here. Two boys. We take them.'

A cry from one of the privates brought the other three over to his corner of the room. He was pointing to a padlocked door that led into a back store-room.

'Where's the key?' said the sergeant.

Anne-Marie shrugged. 'No key.'

The sergeant hammered at the lock with the butt of his rifle until he broke the housing off the door frame.

While all four men were in the back room the women looked at each other. Sylvie Cariteau held her hand across her mouth. Anne-Marie's eyes darted back and forth between the other two, her lips set resolutely together.

The soldiers returned. 'Where are they?' The sergeant grabbed Anne-Marie by the lapels of her thick woollen jacket and Anne-Marie spat in his face. He pushed her back on the table, ripping the cloth of her coat and the dress beneath, half baring the breasts she had for so long exposed to Levade.

He paused for a moment, then seemed to recollect himself. He pointed to the ladder in the corner of the room and gave another order. The three others climbed up, and Sylvie Cariteau watched their boots disappear into the gloom above. She heard their footsteps overhead and wondered how well the boys were hidden.

The sergeant turned away from Anne-Marie and began to look round the kitchen again.

Anne-Marie leaned over and whispered in Sylvie's ear, 'If you and I can detain them, perhaps Maman can get the boys out at the back, through the window.'

She said the word 'detain' in a way that made its meaning clear to Sylvie Cariteau, who hesitated for a moment, then mournfully nodded.

Anne-Marie whispered to her mother, who pursed her lips.

'What's this?' The German sergeant was holding up a book he had found on the floor by the sink. It was the story of the crocodile who lost her egg.

He raised his eyebrows as he advanced once more towards Anne-Marie. He spoke softly this time. 'Where are they?'

'There's no one,' said Anne-Marie, though her voice had begun to tremble.

The two privates and the corporal came back down the ladder.

The corporal shrugged and spoke briefly in German. The sergeant smiled sceptically and shook his head, too, as he held up the book.

The private who had been overpowered by Julien at the Domaine stepped forward and grabbed Sylvie Cariteau by the hair, twisting her head. She screamed in pain as she turned her body round in the chair.

She pulled herself free from his grasp and stood up. She glanced for a second at Anne-Marie, as though for confirmation, and then, to the private's visible amazement, embraced him.

He pushed her back, but then seemed to think again, as though it was not so much what was offered as the way in which it was being made available that displeased him. He muttered to the corporal, who took Sylvie Cariteau by the arms while the private wrenched at the waistband of her skirt. As it tore, he began to shout at her and slap her in the face.

The sergeant watched indifferently as her clothes were ripped. Beneath the skirt there was a pair of silk drawers with a satin edge of daisies and forget-me-nots.

The sergeant turned back to Anne-Marie and said something to the other private, who held her arms while the sergeant pulled away the clothes from her chest. His movements were slow and quite deliberate, unlike those of the corporal, who was slapping Sylvie Cariteau in a frenzy. Both had loosened their belts and were fumbling with the fastenings of their trousers, pushing the women back against the kitchen table, while the other two men held them down.

Anne-Marie's mother was screaming. 'Stop it, stop it, stop it, you pigs. They're upstairs. I'll show you. Stop it.' She battered the sergeant's shoulder with her small fists. 'The boys. I'll show you. Come, come.' She grabbed his arm and began to drag him across the room.

The sergeant reluctantly buckled his belt and went with her. As he passed the corporal he shouted at him to stop what he was doing, as though unwilling to allow his junior what he himself had given up.

Sylvie and Anne-Marie rearranged their clothes beneath the sullen eyes of the German soldiers. From upstairs they heard a roar, then the sound of childish screams.

André and Jacob were pushed, slithering, down the ladder, followed more slowly by the sergeant and Anne-Marie's mother.

The sergeant smiled thinly at the two private soldiers and jerked his head towards the door. The men dragged the boys out into the dark afternoon.

Anne-Marie's mother stood by the kitchen table, staring first at her daughter, then at the sergeant, her face scarlet with peasant defiance. There was a moment's silence; then the sergeant gestured to the corporal, turned on his heel and left the house. Outside, an engine started up.

★ ★ ★

Zozo moved his charge to a bare room above a chemist's at the other end of town. The shop was

473

owned by his sister, a tall woman in a white coat with grey hair, who looked at Charlotte disapprovingly over the rims of her glasses when she made her way daily through the pharmacy at the back, past the shelves of pills and lotions. She never spoke, as Charlotte went through the door and up the small back staircase. The room had a bed with a blanket, a washing bowl and a jug. It overlooked an untended yard at the back, and beyond that a row of small houses.

Every evening from Zozo's house Charlotte rang Sylvie Cariteau in Lavaurette, but there was never any news. The days went by. She borrowed books from Zozo to pass the time. In her cold room she felt the depth of her loneliness, but she would not give in to it. The value of all that she was and all she might become depended on whether she could see Levade and explain to him what Julien had done. If she failed, then the broken ends of her own life would never be joined.

On the eighth day, Sylvie Cariteau said she had a message, delivered by César. Octave had sent him to say that all was well and that the name of the place was Drancy, near Paris. The word meant nothing to Charlotte.

She asked if there was news of the boys, and Sylvie broke down in tears.

Charlotte went upstairs to Zozo's bedroom, where he was draping the aerial wire of his transmitter over the top of a wardrobe before making a transmission.

'What's the excitement?'

'Zozo, can you find me someone in Paris? Someone who can get me home?'

'Paris. My God. You want to be careful.'

'I know. But do you have a name?'

'No. But I can probably get one.'

'How soon?'

Zozo looked at her curiously. 'I'll see what I can do.'

When she was back in her cold room above the pharmacy, Charlotte said a prayer for André and Jacob.

3

In the morning, the internee whose job it was to clean the room would sprinkle water on the floor from an empty jam tin in which small holes had been pierced. A brush was provided, but for the dustpan he had to use a piece of card, from which the sweepings would then be thrown into a pail by the door. There were only two buckets for the use of the hundred or so occupants of the room; the other one was for food.

Levade was told by the head of the room that he would be on fatigues like everyone else. The most likely task would be the peeling of vegetables, which took place every morning in a room on the ground floor, not far from the main gate. It was tedious work, the man explained, but some people liked it because they could supplement their rations by secretly eating the potato peel when the gendarmes were not looking.

Levade felt lucky that illness had robbed him of his appetite. He heard the complaints of empty stomachs all day long, and witnessed a desperate bartering of half-carrots or small slices of bread for cigarettes. Since no communication was permitted with the outside world, the main source of tobacco — the only hard currency in Drancy — was the gendarmes.

A doctor on another staircase had advised those in a developed state of hunger and weakness that they could best conserve energy by lying all day on their beds. Word of this advice had reached Levade's room, and many of those not on fatigues would pass the long hours between roll calls immobile on their wooden bunks.

The doctor himself, it was noted, had been seen by the gendarmes rooting through a dustbin near the Red Castle, looking for scraps of potato peel from which he would scrupulously clean the cindery dust of the courtyard and other waste or slime before furtively consuming them. He had been a gynaecologist with a large practice in the Opéra district of Paris, but this made no impression on the camp authorities, who decided that his scavenging should be punished by deportation on the next transport.

Hartmann managed to find a German paediatrician called Levi, who came to visit Levade one afternoon as it was growing dark. Levade was asleep when he arrived and was roused by his touch. He looked up to see two men staring down with concerned expressions, Levi and Hartmann, one on either side of the bunk.

Levi spoke good French, though with the pronounced accent of his own country. With no instruments, it was hard for him to diagnose Levade with any accuracy: he felt his forehead, took his pulse and inspected his throat; then he put his ear against his chest and made him cough into a cloth, where he examined what he brought up. He asked him how long he had been ill, how much weight he had lost and when he had last eaten.

'You must at least try to drink,' Levi said. 'You have a cup? Get someone to bring you water from the pipe — there's nothing wrong with it. I'm going to see if I can find a place for you in the infirmary. It's difficult because there's dysentery at the moment among the little ones. But you need to be in bed.'

'What's the matter with me?'

'I think you have pneumonia. Your lungs are very full.'

'And what happens?'

'Nothing. Normally there's a crisis, a big fever, and then either you survive or not. There's no certain cure, even in the proper world.'

Levade looked at the German's serious face, its dark features shadowed by fatigue. Clearly, he had not had the strength to pretend. Levade put his hand on the doctor's. 'Did you fight in the war?'

'Not this one,' said Levi. 'The last one.'

'That's what I meant.'

'We were considered proper Germans then. I resisted for as long as possible. I was making my way as a children's doctor in Hamburg. In the end I had to go. I was in France for two years. My brother Joseph was killed in a tunnel just before the end. But I survived. And you?'

Levade was smiling. 'I was there.' He squeezed Levi's hand. 'We're old enemies.'

Hartmann said, 'When did you come to France?'

'In 1940,' said Levi. 'My wife and children left for the United States, but I stayed to work in the hospital for as long as possible. Then I went to Paris, where I was safe for a time, until that big round-up in July. I managed to get down to Toulouse, but I was arrested there and sent to a camp. I was brought up here a month ago.'

'And now?' said Levade.

'And now . . . When the trains start again, I'll go where everyone goes.'

Hartmann said, 'The wireless in London has said there's no work at the other end. They say we just get killed. Exterminated by the thousand.'

'I don't believe that,' said Levi with a twitch of German pride. 'There are always such rumours.'

'And do you believe it?' said Levade.

Hartmann shrugged. 'Yes, I think I do. I've been told the trains are starting again any day. They're making a list now.'

Levade began to cough and the other two men pulled over him such covers as there were.

Late that night Levade was awoken by the sound of screaming. A woman had thrown herself from a fourth floor window and had landed on the narrow flat roof that sheltered the walkway along the inside of the rectangle. She had learned that her name was on the list of those due to be deported when the transports resumed on Thursday.

'Stupid bitch,' said the man in the next bed to Levade. 'Now someone else'll have to go instead.'

There was no sympathy for the dead woman or for the two men who died in the same way the next day.

That evening, at roll call, Levade leaned as usual for support on his neighbour, a young Rumanian who felt himself lucky to double his daily food ration in return for this slight service.

After an hour in the freezing evening Levade began to feel light-headed. He was aware of a Parisian accent barking names, but his connection with reality seemed slender. He could see that the lights had come on in the rooms inside the buildings, and they reminded him of the lit houses he used to see when, on winter evenings in the small suburban town where he had grown up, his father Max Rutkowski brought him home from school on the handlebars of his bicycle.

The air was so cold that he could barely breathe it in, yet he felt that what made him faint was not so much the thinness of the atmosphere as the thinness of time, as though he was at a great altitude — not of space, but of exhausted years.

He slumped down into the arms of the Rumanian, who laid him on the ground as gently as he could. He answered Levade's name for him, and, when roll call was finally over, promised half his extra share of bread to a friend if he would help him carry the old man up to the room.

Later that night, before the lights were turned out, Hartmann brought Levade some soup he had saved and forced him to drink it. A dribble of the cold broth ran through the grey stubble of his chin. Hartmann kept a distance while Levade gurgled and spat, as though he did not wish to stand close to a man who, after all, had been too ill to wash for several weeks.

Hartmann took the empty cup and said, 'I've got some news for you. They've put up the list of names for Thursday's transport and they've also put up a list of reserves. They always do this. It's about fifty extra names, in case of suicide or last minute changes, or in case they find more room. I'm sorry to tell you that your name's on the reserve list.'

Levade, for all his feverish detachment, felt the cells of his body violently protest.

Hartmann said, 'If I can get you to the infirmary, they'll probably take you off the list.'

Levade was still fighting what felt like waves of freezing vertigo. When he could speak again he said, 'It makes no difference. Leave my name on.'

★ ★ ★

Charlotte was once more on a train. Her bundle of French francs was now almost at an end, but G Section's generous forethought would be enough to see her through at least until she made contact with the name in the rue Villaret de Joyeuse in Paris that Zozo had given her. She had not had time to re-dye her hair before leaving, and there were traces of her own colour showing through at the roots. There was just enough dye left in the bottle Antoinette had given her in Ussel, and that night she would for the last time eliminate the gold and strawberry and barley shades that for the moment were concealed beneath Dominique's felt hat.

Quite how she would manage to find and speak to Levade, she was not sure. Presumably detention camps had facilities for visitors: she would simply go to the entrance and make her request. Doubtless, there would be some form-filling and delay. It was likely there would

480

be set times to visit, or even particular days of the week, but since even criminals in prison were allowed to be visited, she could not imagine that an innocent man would be denied such a modest favour.

Charlotte took out of her suitcase a sandwich made with fresh gooseliver paté that Zozo had pressed on her as she left.

When the war was over, she would return and she would visit all the people who had so unquestioningly helped her — Antoinette, Sylvie Cariteau, Zozo and little Anne-Marie.

And Julien, of course. For the rest of their lives, when each was mired in slack middle-age, they would make the inconvenient journey to the other's country, despite the protests of their respective children. They would continue to laugh at one another and to indulge their love of what they had fought to protect. Their spouses would know nothing of the night they had spent together and they themselves would not refer to it, because it meant little compared to the joy of their companionship.

Her destiny was still with Peter Gregory. Nothing that had happened in her life had changed that conviction. For herself, she had no doubts: it depended only on him, on whether he had changed, on whether he still loved her and, most of all, she reluctantly conceded, on whether he was still alive.

She believed he was; or at least she would not let herself imagine otherwise. Perhaps, on reflection, it was not quite belief, it was more like faith. The difference, she explained to herself, as the train slowed for its arrival at Tours, was that belief was a logical conviction, while faith, because it admitted doubt, required emotional effort.

It was that effort that made her weary, that took so much of her strength, but the rewards of keeping the faith were high. She had seen the people of Limoges protesting their hatred of the English and the Jews, but she had refused to believe that they were typical, and that same night she had, at the time of the drop, been repaid by the sight of those men stumbling about their dangerous business in the fields. She had seen the eyes of Claude Benech that narrowed as he smirked over the long table in the Domaine, but she had also witnessed Sylvie Cariteau's unquestioning efficiency and César's boyish rapture. It was almost as though it was her faith that kept them going; she could not bear to look away.

Charlotte glanced up as the train came into the station at Tours. She was surprised to find the four other people in the carriage looking at her. Had she been talking to herself out loud? An elderly man opposite with a white moustache and a grey Homburg was staring at her lap, in which lay a piece of waxed paper with the remains of her sandwich. She looked round the carriage and smiled. Now she came to think of it, the aroma of brandy and garlic that had come off the fresh pâté was of a peace-time pungency.

'Excuse me,' Charlotte said, and reached up to her suitcase in the luggage rack, where she took out the paper bag that contained the rest of the picnic Zozo had given her. She had had the best part herself, but there was some brawn, some slices of rye bread and a little jar of potted goose which she offered to her companions. 'My brother's a butcher,' she lied happily, with what she hoped was a charming smile. 'Some people have all the luck.'

Two women were getting off at Tours and declined her offer, but the old man in the hat and a small woman with a headscarf helped themselves with incredulous murmurs of appreciation. It was the fattiness of the goose that obviously appealed to people who had been so long deprived of oil or butter. Julien had told her he knew a man in Lavaurette so desperate he had drunk half a litre of motor oil. To Charlotte's dismay, her two companions felt they should pay for their early supper by making conversation.

Having given herself a butcher as a brother, Charlotte felt a hysterical urge to fabricate more, and more bizarre, relations — a family tree of jazz singers, rich industrialists or institutionalised lunatics. How tired my long, long caution has made me, she thought. But she forced herself, for what she hoped would be the last time, to be reticent: my father . . . my husband . . . since 1940 . . . She heard the words, bland and discouraging, then turned the questions on the others.

As the woman chattered on about her family, Charlotte allowed her mind to wander behind her fixed, indulgent smile. She thought of Gregory, of what her first words to him would be.

She was aware that it was now the man who was speaking, telling her of how regularly he took this train, but her reverie remained unbroken until she heard him say, 'But after we've been through Châteaudun the SS always join the train before Paris. They drive up through Illiers and generally get on at Chartres. It's such a nuisance with all their inspections and — '

'What?' said Charlotte. It was the word Illiers, taking her back to reading Proust's novel in Monsieur Loiseau's garden, that had snagged her daydream, but then she let the earlier words replay in her mind. 'The SS?'

'Yes, always. They're such brutes. They know me perfectly well by now, but still they take me into the corridor and search me.'

'I see.' Charlotte licked her lips, then resumed her lighter manner. 'Well, good luck with them. It won't affect me. I shall be getting off at Châteaudun.'

It was dark and raining when Charlotte left the train and made her way into the centre of the town. In the shadow of the improbably grand castle, there were a dozen narrow streets that crossed at regular right angles. In other circumstances the atmosphere might have felt quaint or reassuring, but Charlotte wanted to be out of the rain. In a street called the rue Lambert-Licors she saw the welcome word 'Hôtel' stuck half way up a building and made her way through the glass front door to a cheap wooden desk beneath the stairs. She rang the bell, and a dark-eyed, unsmiling girl of about eighteen appeared from a door behind the desk. Her haughty manner, Charlotte presumed, derived from her looks rather than the dignity of her office. She inspected Charlotte's damp, untidy figure with the disdain of a northern Irène Galliot.

She took Charlotte to a room on the second floor whose ceiling followed the pitched angle of the roof. Dinner would be served at eight, she said, shutting the door briskly behind her.

Charlotte took off her hat and bedraggled overcoat. From her suitcase she took out her washing things and the bottle of hair dye. It occurred to her that the girl had not told her where the bathroom was, and she went out on to the landing to investigate. All the doors she could find had numbers on them, so perhaps it was on a lower floor. In any case, there was only half an hour to wait till dinner; she would ask then. Back in her room, she inspected the roots of her hair in the mirror on the dressing table. Rather than make a mess of it in the gloomy light of the bedroom, she would wear a scarf to dinner and do her hair properly in the bathroom later. She left the dye by the mirror, took off her skirt and sweater and lay down on the bed.

Tomorrow she would think again about how to complete her journey to Paris. Presumably there were buses as well as trains; perhaps she could buy a bicycle and avoid the SS that way. It would probably take no more than two days to reach the outlying stations of the Métro. She would decide in the morning; in the meantime she would rest and see what Châteaudun could offer for dinner.

★ ★ ★

The dining room had small windows with orange curtains that gave on to the narrow street at the front; with its cheap wooden light fittings and scarlet embroidered tablecloths, the room had a faintly Alpine feel, as though a man in leather shorts might at any moment emerge from the kitchen with a steaming dish of sauerkraut and glistening pink sausages.

Four other tables in the room were occupied by people who murmured greetings as Charlotte took a table by the window. Some complicated bartering of coupons seemed to be taking place with a grey-haired man she took to be the proprietor, and, when he approached her table, Charlotte offered him some tickets, letting him also see the corner of a banknote she had slipped into the ration book.

There was little sense of Tyrolean plenty in the small beetroot salad that eventually materialised, wordlessly presented by the haughty girl from behind the desk, but there was a quarter carafe of thin red wine and a single slice of chalky bread with which to eke it out.

Charlotte took out a novel she had borrowed from Julien's shelves, a romance of the kind Dominique might like, and began to read. After a few pages it was clear that the heroine was in for a difficult time with the saturnine stranger she loved from afar. The character's struggles were completely uninteresting to Charlotte, and she remembered Levade's pointing out how absurd and irritating most people found the romantic travails of others. How different her own dilemma was, how much more serious . . . She smiled and thought of Levade again, and how he had told her

485

that everyone was convinced that their own plight had a particular poignancy, a special unfairness. She was just like all the other young women; her crisis was as perpetual and as comic as theirs. She pushed away the plate. What did it matter how her anguish compared to that of other people? It was only its own intensity that was important — that, and the value she allowed it in the battle for an understanding of her life.

As the weeks had passed in Lavaurette, she had noticed a change in people's attitude towards her. In their manner, in the way they looked at her, there was a respect that was sometimes touched with awe. It made her laugh inside. I'm just a romantic girl who's come to find her lost lover, she thought, but they look at me as though I were a woman of fierce conviction, a person of unshakeable dedication in the fight for freedom.

And yet, she thought, as she picked through the food the waitress had brought, perhaps there was something in the attitude of Julien, Sylvie and César. Perhaps there truly was something they had seen. A market is made at the price that someone will pay; to some extent you are what other people think you are. Why then did she feel in some way provisional, almost fraudulent, as though she had always to apologise for herself or justify her existence?

She looked up as the waitress took her plate, and saw the door from the hall being pushed open by the proprietor. On his face was an expression both obsequious and scared as he stood aside for a tall, broad-shouldered man of about forty-five dressed in the shining boots and grey uniform of the German army.

There were further muttered greetings from the other diners as the distinguished visitor sat down, and the manager scurried across with a basket of bread and a full bottle of wine, from which he poured a genteel amount for the German to taste.

Charlotte's fearful inclination was to go up to her room at once, but she felt, since the dessert had not yet been brought, that it might look suspicious if she abandoned her dinner. There was no sign of dessert; service to all other tables came to a halt while the German was plied with the best the hotel had to offer. A smiling woman who was presumably the manager's wife fluttered in from the hall to pour him some more wine, and the waitress brought various dishes of hors d'oeuvre from the kitchen. Charlotte was delighted to see that the Irène Galliot of Châteaudun was completely unaffected by the presence of the German, but dumped down his food with wordless contempt. Equality, thought Charlotte, liberty, fraternity. The Republic is not dead.

Some of the other tables became restive as the German's banquet wore on, but when he had reached his dessert they were allowed to have theirs too. Finally, there was a general clearing of the room, and, in the pushing back of chairs, doors held politely open, Charlotte found herself addressed by the German. In French that was barely comprehensible he was offering her a drink in the small dark sitting room on the other side of the hall.

Charlotte's mouth felt dry, not only from the ersatz coffee she had drunk, as she forced herself across the floor. The proprietor switched on a light in the dingy room, placed a bottle of brandy and two glasses on the low table, then, with ostentatious tact, withdrew.

The German in his way was rather charming, Charlotte thought. He seemed diffident, almost shy in his courtship, hampered no doubt by his stumbling French, for which he several times apologised.

Charlotte concentrated on being Dominique, and her fear made her plausibly abashed. Even within the role of modest married woman, however, there were choices she could make in how to deal with her situation.

Dominique might well be so terrified that she would do anything the man suggested; Charlotte had to find a response that was both realistic and discouraging.

Initially, she kept bringing her husband into every answer, to stress her unavailable state, but then found the German politely inquiring more and more about the work and life of this ever-present man. Charlotte eventually had to plead that it was too painful for her to talk about him. She asked the German about his home and what he was doing in Châteaudun. He did not understand the question about home, or perhaps affected not to, and only shrugged and muttered briefly about his orders.

The peculiar thing about him, Charlotte thought, was that he seemed to be quite unaware of the fact that he was the enemy, the armed occupant of her presumed country. The only word she could think of to describe his attitude was 'friendly', and from this she could only deduce that his motives were improper. After twenty minutes of laboured conversation, Charlotte began to yawn.

'Excuse me. I'm very tired.' She held her hand over her glass as he made to pour more brandy. 'I think I must be off to bed. Thank you very much for the drink.'

The German stood up stiffly, and a trace of displeasure came into his heavy, handsome face. He stood back to let Charlotte pass into the hall, where the proprietor was waiting nervously at the desk. He opened the front door for the officer, but the German looked only briefly into the night, where it had begun to rain, and shook his head. He pointed upstairs.

'Let me see the rooms,' he said. 'For my men. To sleep.'

His manner was now less charming; it was as though the memory of his military duty had made him cold. The manager fumbled with the room keys that hung on a little perforated board behind him; in the dim wattage of the overhead bulb Charlotte saw the bubbles of sweat on his upper lip. He began to climb the stairs, with the German officer behind him. Charlotte hesitated for a moment, then followed.

On the first floor the manager began opening the flimsy doors of the rooms that were not occupied, allowing the German a brief glance inside.

'Good night,' said Charlotte loudly, as she began to climb towards her room on the second floor. 'Goodbye.'

Neither man answered.

Charlotte closed the door of her room and listened. She heard more doors being opened and closed, then she heard heavy footsteps coming up the stairs. There was a jangling and a thudding along the landing, though no sound of voices. The noise came closer to her room. She heard the German speak, briefly, something that sounded like an order, and there was the noise of one man's footsteps departing down the stairs.

Charlotte stood with her ear to the door. There was no sound. She was certain he was still there, so he must be standing in the corridor. He must have seen all he needed to see; surely now he would have to go.

There came the reverberation of boots on floorboards and a violent knocking on her door. Charlotte sprang back into the room and tried to compose herself.

She said nothing, but the knocking came again. She went over and opened the door a little. The space was filled with grey uniform. Charlotte met the German's eyes and gave what she hoped was a smile of surprise, mixed with modesty. She tried to look friendly, but as though she did not wish to be disturbed.

'May I come in?' He had resumed his more diffident manner.

'I was just going to bed.'

'Just for a moment. It's not that I . . . ' His French seemed to fail him.

'It's very late,' said Charlotte.

'Just for a moment.' His foot was in the door.

Once inside the bedroom his manner became nervous. He walked round the room, his eyes constantly moving, as though he did not want to let them rest on some feminine intimacy.

'I want to say that I am sorry if I am not proper.' He had picked up Charlotte's room key and was flipping it back and forth absently in his hand. 'Many difficult things arrive in wars,' he went on. 'We do not do what we want.'

'Of course.' Charlotte had no idea what he was trying to say. She had kept the door open to increase the impression that this was no more than a final word.

The German put down the key on the dressing table and picked up the bottle of hair dye. He tossed it from one hand to another as he walked round the room.

'I have friends, I have brothers who are like me.' He turned his eyes, now large with sincerity, on to Charlotte, but her appalled gaze was fixed on the bottle of hair dye. As it spun back and forth through the air she could plainly make out the label, which stated that it was dye and was decorated with a picture of a freshly coiffed female head. There were only the dregs of the dark fluid inside, but it was of a colour and consistency that the German could not possibly mistake for anything else.

'I have my wife at home. It is difficult for all of us, and to be righteous is my last hope.'

The bottle flew in its highest arc yet, from left hand to right, the brunette liquid slapping up the sides. Suddenly Charlotte thought: it is not his lack of French that is making him incoherent: he's shy — he's frightened of making a fool of himself.

'I fully understand,' she said. 'It's been a pleasure.'

'Yes.' He looked down at the bottle in his hand.

'And one day soon the war will be over.' Smiling brightly, Charlotte extended her hand, as though this was the honourable conclusion to an entirely successful piece of social intercourse. She stepped back a little as she did so, to reveal the beckoning escape of the half-open door.

'Yes, yes.' The German held out his hand to Charlotte, switching the bottle to his left hand as he did so.

'Good night,' said Charlotte.

'Yes. Good night.'

She had backed him into the doorway.

He stood for a moment, unmoving.

'Please.' Charlotte held out her hand and pointed to the bottle.

'Excuse me,' he said. 'I don't know.'

'Thank you.' With the last remnants of Dominique's determined propriety, Charlotte narrowed her eyes into an expression of polite but incontrovertible farewell. 'Goodbye.'

The German nodded, stepped out of the room and made off down the stairs. Charlotte held the bottle in both hands, close to her bosom. Her heart was thudding so hard that it was making her palms tingle. Good God, she thought, what have I become that even German officers are scared of me?

She went out on to the landing and ran to a window that overlooked the rue Lambert-Licors. She saw the street splashed by a rectangle of light as the front door of the hotel opened, then heard the rumble of a military vehicle being started in the rain.

4

A series of country buses brought Charlotte to the outskirts of Paris. At the first sight of the fancy ironwork sign above the steps, she descended, bag in hand, into the Métro.

Within moments she was assailed by a smell as familiar and as loaded with memory as a child's first sensuous impression involuntarily recovered after decades of loss. She had forgotten this extraordinary atmosphere and how, as a teenage girl, it had struck her on her very first descent as something that was already deeply familiar and suggestive, as though she had been there before in a dream or in an earlier life. No one had been able to identify it for her; presumably it had some prosaic mechanical origin, but people talked of tarred hemp rope, of tobacco, garlic or sub-soil in vain attempts to explain this essence of the city.

Charlotte was for a moment so moved by it, and by its persistence, that she did not notice how much other things had changed. There were many more people than usual, queuing in the tunnels to get down to the pneumatic scarlet gates at the end of the platform. Among the austere clothes of the Parisians were flashes of grey uniform, though the Germans democratically awaited their turn among the French. Charlotte noticed that her clothes and her suitcase were not out of place among the Parisians, most of whom seemed to have abandoned their habitual chic.

She squeezed through the barriers as they were closing and clambered on to the last carriage of the train. She put down her case and looked round. Something was strange. All the people were staring at her with dark, distrustful eyes. All of them were

492

wearing a star of yellow cloth pinned to their lapels. The man standing next to Charlotte muttered, 'Jews only', and pushed her out on to the platform.

In the next carriage, Charlotte was offered a seat by a young Parisian as the train clanked off into the tunnel. This was not her normal experience of the Métro, where people had to be reminded by statutory notices to give up their seats to the war-wounded or to pregnant women. There seemed to be a contest of politeness between the French and the Germans, as the soldiers in their pressed uniforms and shining belts made way for shabby matrons, and young Frenchmen, not to be outdone by Wehrmacht charm, mounted a counter-offensive of Gallic courtesy.

Charlotte wanted to have one look at Paris before boarding the suburban train, and she left the Métro at Odéon with the idea of walking up past the restaurant in the rue de Tournon where Monsieur Loiseau had taken her as a girl. On the Boulevard St Germain the green and white municipal buses moved with unchallenged ease, the only other traffic being licensed bicycles, many ridden by wobbling citizens long past their cycling peak.

The Métro might have kept its pungency, but the streets of the sixth arrondissement had become odourless and pale, with no sudden gust of coffee or fresh bread from open doorways, no morning freshness from the water-sprinkled pavements. It was quiet and anaemic in the rue de Tournon, as though proper circulation had been strangled by the Nazi flag that draped the Senate House. The restaurant had shut down.

In the Jardin du Luxembourg Charlotte walked the dusty paths she so acutely remembered and stopped before the statues that had puzzled or entranced her: Watteau being adored by a décolletée creature from one of his own paintings, the Comtesse de Ségur,

493

née Rostopchino (1799–1874) and a bearded man of bronzed self-importance called José Maria de Heredia, whose claim to a plinth in this moody garden was his membership of the Académie Française. By the wooden summer-houses, beneath the scabby plane trees, there were a handful of children, mufflered and wrapped against the winds from the Boulevard St Michel, but their games seemed, to Charlotte's searching eye, inhibited, and their voices thin and scratchy in the winter air.

She took herself off to make what she assumed would be almost her final rail journey before her return to England. On the suburban train she thought of Levade, picturing him in some tidy, if ascetic, little room, surrounded by his few possessions, with his painting hung above the bed.

At Le Bourget-Drancy station she asked the way to Drancy in a glass-fronted café by the road, and the proprietor directed her across the large bridge that spanned the tracks. Beneath her in a siding as she crossed was an idle express, the wooden destination board slid into the side of the carriage proclaiming PARIS NORD and, upside down, AMIENS.

She remembered her father talking of Amiens as a place where British soldiers went on leave during the Great War. Its great cathedral was sandbagged to the level of the stained-glass windows — a big cold barn, he had called it, a frightening place, and an unforgiving town despite its inhabitants' claims for the dazzling cathedral and charming water-gardens.

The long, broad road that led Charlotte down to Drancy had streets of all the usual names: those of Alsace-Lorraine, always among the first places to be claimed by any French municipality, and of Jean Jaurès, the martyred president. There was a spacious, unkempt park on the left, though the town seemed hardly inhabited enough to need such recreational

494

space. The houses were in a variety of urban styles, one of the most popular of which was stone and cement with wooden gables, like the holiday villas just back from the front at Deauville.

Nothing was strange about Drancy, Charlotte thought, nothing was less than typical. Quite what she expected to see, she could not say, but surely if she was so close to a place of such despair there should be some sign of stress or concealment.

The camp itself was visible enough. Its abandoned towers were several storeys higher than any building in the area, and an elderly woman Charlotte stopped to ask the way pointed to it with an exhalation of distaste. The road went past the southern, open side of the rectangle of the camp, and an area of broken ground lay between the street and the barbed wire fence.

Charlotte stopped. In the raised observation posts were gendarmes with what appeared to be machine guns. While the housing complex looked civilian, even hospitable in a bleak way, there was something wrong about the barbed wire and the guns. She could see the wooden gate that had been set into the wire fencing, but at the thought of simply going up and asking to see her friend, she faltered.

On the other side of the road, looking across at the camp, was a café, and Charlotte went inside to ask advice.

'Excuse me,' she said to the proprietress, 'I have a friend in this place here and I wondered how — '

'You want a room?' said the the woman quickly. 'We've got one spare at the moment. Binoculars are extra.'

Charlotte was taken aback by the speed of the response. 'You have people staying here in order to look, to — '

'You'd better hurry if you want the room. There's more coming every day.'

'I really just wanted to see this friend, to pay a visit.'

The woman laughed. 'Are you out of your mind? They're not allowed to see anyone. They're only allowed out for the roll call. That's when you need the binoculars, to see if they're still there.'

Charlotte looked at the woman's rapacious eyes. Inside her skirt pocket her hand closed on the last of her francs.

'Do you ever manage to get word to people? Can you ever get messages in?'

The woman ran her eyes up and down Charlotte's cheap clothes. 'There's a gendarme who comes over for a drink, but I don't think someone like you could — '

'How much?'

'You take the room and I'll have a word this evening.'

★ ★ ★

The room was little more than a cubicle, recently partitioned from a larger space to increase the guest capacity, but it had a bed and it overlooked the camp. For the room and the binoculars Charlotte was asked to pay three times what she had been charged in Châteaudun. In the afternoon she drafted a message that would as briefly as possible tell Levade what had happened. Several times in the course of the evening she went down to see if the pliable gendarme had called, but each time she was disappointed. She had fallen asleep over her romantic story when she was woken by a sharp knocking.

The proprietress put her head round the door. 'He's here. Come now if you want to see him.'

Charlotte slid off the bed, straightened her skirt and pressed her feet back into her shoes. She followed the woman down a narrow passage to a small sitting room, where a uniformed gendarme was standing with his back to the door.

'Here she is,' said the woman, and left the room.

When the gendarme turned round, Charlotte saw a pale man, probably not more than thirty, but heavily jowled and unathletic with a moustache in which grey hairs were already sprouting.

He said nothing, and Charlotte guessed he would prefer her to take the initiative.

'I have a friend. I need to get a message to him. Can you help me?'

The gendarme wordlessly inclined his head.

'His name is Auguste Levade. He's French. He's been here only a few days. And I need to hear a message back. I need to know he's understood.'

The gendarme nodded again.

'How much?' said Charlotte.

The man took a piece of paper from his pocket on which he had already scribbled a figure.

It was slightly less than Charlotte had expected: presumably most people who required this service were refugees, or French whose businesses had been closed down by the Government.

She handed him the note she had written to Levade.

The gendarme spoke for the first time. 'I can't take that.' His voice was unexpectedly high and nervy. 'Just tell me.'

'It's complicated,' said Charlotte.

The gendarme shrugged.

'All right, let me try. My name's Dominique. Can you remember that?'

'Yes.'

'Tell him . . . Julien was acting, to save two children. Say 'at the Domaine' as well. 'At the Domaine Julien was acting to save two children.' From Dominique.

497

Can you remember? Say it to me.'

Like an overweight schoolboy, he repeated the words.

Charlotte produced the banknotes from her pocket. 'And I'll see you back here tomorrow night?'

The gendarme nodded once more as he left the room, and Charlotte felt the rising of elation. She was almost there.

★ ★ ★

In the morning, the young Rumanian and his friend carried Levade down to the infirmary, a series of five rooms in the north-west corner of the rectangle with seventy-five sheetless beds.

Some of the patients had been ill on their arrival at Drancy. There were old men who had been transferred from Jewish hospices in Paris, and lifetime inhabitants of psychiatric wards removed from their hospitals by gendarmes to make up the numbers demanded by the deportation programme. There were also those who had grown sick since arriving at the camp, women giving birth to babies conceived at liberty and many young children whose soft skin was covered with scabs and sores caused by malnutrition and the bites of vermin. From the lips of these children there rose a permanent, bewildered wailing against which the other inmates tried to stop their ears.

Levade was given a bed with two others stacked on top of it. A Jewish nurse brought him a glass of water, but his hand was trembling too much to hold it. His whole body had begun to shiver. He tried to calm the quivering muscles of his arms and legs, but even his neck and head were shaking with the spasms of cold.

The nurse brought him the only spare blanket she could find, but his rage for warmth could not have been satisfied by all the coverings of his life-time piled on top of him. 'Cold . . . cold,' he muttered to the nurse, the words broken up by the rattling of his teeth.

She took him in her arms and tried to warm him, but she could not contain the jerking movements of his body. A young Jewish doctor came and cast an eye on the violently trembling figure. He wiped some blood from Levade where his teeth had pierced his lip, then passed on to other patients.

After an hour or so, the temperature of Levade's body began to rise. The shivering died down and for a moment his body was relaxed. He looked about him and saw the bare cement walls, the Red Cross nurses and their co-opted Jewish sisters, the frightened gaze of the powerless Jewish doctors. A crisis, he remembered the other doctor, Levi, saying: a crisis through which you may or may not pass . . .

By this time he was starting to sweat, so he pushed back the blanket. Soon, the skin of his face was flushed purple with heat and he had to keep licking his lips. Everything seemed to be moving very quickly; his thoughts started to become disarrayed: it was like being carried on some machine of colossal momentum over which he had no control. He tried with his conscious mind to calm his thoughts, but he had no sense of time any more; it had collapsed on him.

A gendarme was leaning over his bed and speaking. For a moment Levade re-established contact with the world. The man was giving him a message. Julien . . . two children . . . But what did it matter? Julien, the dear boy, his only son, how much he loved him . . . How dearly, dearly . . .

But the gendarme was not there. When had be been? An hour ago? A day? Had he been yet? Had he come?

'A priest . . . I want a priest.'

A passing nurse looked at him in surprise. 'A rabbi, don't you mean?'

A minute later, or perhaps two hours, a doctor came to his bed. 'Those on the Reserve list have to go to the other corner of the courtyard. Block One. Staircase Two. We need your bed.'

The man helped Levade to the door, then turned back into the infirmary.

Outside, Levade leaned against the side of the building, beneath the shallow roof. It was dark.

He knelt down on the ground, then laid his cheek against the cold stone. Some stirring of childhood memory came to him at the touch of it; some recollection of the crawling world of the infant who is intimate with floors and surfaces.

He closed his eyes to spare his mind the images of the night and felt time rushing up suddenly in him. Once more he was at a thin altitude of years; but as the final wave built up, it was not with the memory of war, not with thoughts of women he had loved, not with the touch of the God he had worshipped or the pained awareness of the nights when dreams had fled from him.

It came in sounds of elsewhere, of other people's lives. He heard a baby cry, he heard the sound of a bird; there was a motor lorry backfiring in the quiet street and then a woman's voice; he heard a jangling bell.

Then all the years rose up and swallowed him in one rapid, sweet unravelling.

5

'This is Gianluca Soracci. Peter Gregory.' Nancy made the introduction and the two men shook hands.

'I'm sorry it take me so long,' said Soracci in English. 'Is difficult. I have much work to do.'

'That's all right,' said Gregory. 'I understand.'

'What's the plan, Gianluca?' said Nancy.

'First I have a cigarette.' Soracci took an onyx lighter from Nancy's table and lit up shakily. After a deep inhalation he sat down and smiled. He was a delicate man, with small hands and feet, brown, candid eyes and a slight plumpness round the belt.

'Are you taking him in the felucca?' said Nancy.

'No, no, we do different. I take him to Italy. We go to Genoa. Then he take a ship to North Africa. Is easy.'

'Any particular part of North Africa?' said Gregory.

'We see. I think soon you go where you like. Anywhere is yours. The Germans soon finished.'

'Rommel?'

'*Si*.' Soracci nodded quickly and pulled a shred of tobacco from his lower lip.

'Isn't it going to be dangerous for an Englishman in Italy, getting over the border and so on?'

'No. I fix it. I know many people. Soon all Italy is on your side. You see.'

'I think he's right,' said Nancy. 'There's no enthusiasm for the Germans. Especially now they're losing.'

'What kind of boat?' said Gregory.

'A big boat. Goes quick.' Soracci laughed. 'Then you see your old friends. The boys in blue. They take you home.'

'That sounds good.'

'You can trust Gianluca,' said Nancy. 'He knows what he's doing.'

'All right,' said Gregory. 'When do we leave?'

'We leave tomorrow. I come for you in the morning. I don't know how long you wait in Genoa, but not long I think. Is the best way.'

They shook hands, and Soracci disappeared.

There was a silence after he had gone. Nancy coughed and began to speak in an artificial way, as though talking to a schoolboy. 'The Italians have been useful in France,' she said. 'They've stopped Vichy sending all the Jews from east of the Rhône up for deportation.'

She began to tidy the living room in a distracted way. As she was making a pile of some newspapers, she turned to Gregory and said abruptly, 'Now why don't you go and pack your case?'

'I don't have a case, Nancy.'

'I'll lend you one.'

'When'll I give it back?'

'When I come and see you in London. After the war.'

'Do you promise you'll come?'

'What are war-time promises?'

'It would mean a lot to me.'

'Go and pack,' said Nancy softly. 'Just go and pack.'

★ ★ ★

All day Charlotte fretted about her gendarme and whether he would be able to repeat her message to Levade. With nothing to do to pass the time, she walked round the perimeter of the camp. A narrow road ran along the eastern flank of the building, where there was a further line of barbed wire. In the north-eastern corner there was a small entry into the camp, not large enough for a vehicle, guarded by a gendarme. The windows in the long eastern side were painted over blue, and the inhabitants behind them were invisible.

For all that she tried to imagine the hardships inside, the place and the surrounding area retained an extraordinarily normal atmosphere. This suburb was not a wealthy one, but people came and went along the street with shopping bags; bicycles rang their bells and dogs barked as they sniffed along the pavement. Life went on, and no one seemed concerned.

In the afternoon, Charlotte went back to her room and looked through the binoculars. Between roll calls, the courtyard was almost deserted. Sometimes she could see inmates slinking round against the inner wall, presumably on their way to work in the kitchens or the repair shops.

It was dark when the evening roll call began, and she could not make out the faces of the multitude who grudgingly assembled in the cold air. She went downstairs to find something to eat. While she was sitting at a table by the door, her gendarme came in.

There were about a dozen other people in the café: some workers on their way home, and four or five people staying upstairs, hoping for news of their families. Charlotte said nothing to the gendarme, but allowed him time to have a drink at the bar. He caught her eye as he looked round the room and she walked slowly past him, up the stairs, and waited on the landing. The sound of his boots was not long in coming, and he gestured with his head down the corridor towards the little sitting room.

Charlotte went softly after him and closed the door behind her.

'Did you find him?'

The gendarme nodded. 'He's dead.'

'When?'

'This evening.'

'Did you give him the message?'

'Yes.'

'Was he all right when you told him? Did he understand?'

The gendarme had taken off his cap and was moving it slowly round in his hands. He licked his lips and swallowed, 'Yes. He understood.'

'And did he have a message for me?'

The gendarme looked down at his boots. There was a soft silence in the room. Then he nodded violently, twice. 'He said, 'Thank you.' '

'I see.' Charlotte breathed in. 'And thank you, Monsieur. Thank you for — '

But the gendarme brushed past her in his hurry to be gone. Charlotte heard him thundering down the stairs. She sat down suddenly on the edge of an armchair.

★ ★ ★

André Duguay could not see out of the windows of the bus as it drew into the courtyard; it was packed with children and their suitcases and bundles of belongings. He was jolted back and forth between Jacob and a girl of about the same age, whom the motion of the bus had made vomit on the floor.

When the doors were finally opened, the smaller ones were helped down off the platform by gendarmes. André stood blinking in the large cindered courtyard of Drancy, Jacob's hand clenched in his.

Some women were hovering at the edge of the group of children, and André instinctively went towards one of them. She did not look like his mother: she was fatter, and she spoke with a strange accent.

'My God, the smell. Where have you come from?'

André shrugged. In the jostling of people he heard the question repeated and the word 'Compiègne.' Was that where he and Jacob had been? It had been a filthy place.

Holding Jacob, he went with a group of children, following two women down the courtyard. They were in a room where they were made to take their clothes off. André had been able to keep himself clean, but Jacob's shorts were caked with excrement. The women held their hands across their faces as they tried to clean the children in the showers. Some of them were covered with sores where the acid of their waste had eaten into their skin. Other women tried to wash the clothes, while the children were pushed into another room where two or three soaking cloths were used as towels. One woman who was drying them wept at their pitiful state, but another one looked at her sternly. 'Don't worry,' she said, patting André's bare chest, 'you're going to find your parents again.'

A doctor, who painted purple liquid on their sores before their damp clothes were returned to them, looked at her with a quizzical stare. She shrugged and pouted, as though to say, What else can I tell them?

André was in another building. A gendarme was asking his name. He wrote it on a wooden tag and hung it round André's neck. Some of the children did not know what they were called. The girl behind André, a child of about three, stared up, uncomprehending, into the big face of the gendarme. Some of the children swapped name tags.

Out in the courtyard again, André stood unsure of what to do. He saw some other children following a grown-up man with a white band round his arm, and assumed he might be someone in authority. He pulled Jacob along with him.

They entered a staircase, but the steps were too high for some of the smaller children, who were carried by their brothers and sisters, panting and heaving to the floor above. Here, on the bare concrete landing, another man told them to keep climbing. Dragging themselves and their squawling burdens, they came to the third floor where they were shown into an empty room.

André and the other children stood beneath the single, blue light bulb for some time, uncertainly, before they eventually sat down on the mattresses that were soaked in the filth of previous children. A bucket was placed at the doorway for those too small to make the long climb down to the courtyard, but it soon overflowed.

André, who never remembered either to take his bag of books and shoes to school in Lavaurette or to bring it home at night, had left his suitcase on the bus.

'I must go and find it,' he said. 'It's Madame Cariteau's case, the one we did tobogganing with. She'll be cross if we lose it.' Anne-Marie had delivered the suitcase to Bernard, the gendarme, who had passed it to them through the window of the departing train at Lavaurette. André had been delighted.

Outside again, he went over to where the bus was now leaving the compound. Three more buses had been and gone in the meantime, and André found a number of children of his age wandering among the hundreds of forgotten bundles and bags, looking for some identifying mark. One boy sat cross-legged on the cinders, his head between his knees. André noticed the scabs and sores on the back of his hands, which were clamped round his neck. The boy appeared to be immobilised; it was as though he had found the point beyond which he could not go. André saw the fair hairs on his neck, matted together with filth.

André wanted Madame Cariteau's case with a fierce desire. There was a sweater for Jacob, who was shivering after his shower, and, more than this, there were the tin soldiers and the adjustable spanner. Suddenly, he caught sight of the brass locks and the name CARITEAU on a case half-hidden beneath a pile of other bags and he pulled it out. Bumping it across the courtyard with both hands on the grip, he found he had forgotten which was his staircase: there were so many similar doors on the ground floor, each of them opening on to identical stone steps.

With great politeness he asked for the help of a man who seemed to be directing traffic and who reminded him a little of his father. 'Monsieur, I've lost my brother. I'm afraid I've forgotten which room he's in and I'm worried he may be afraid without me. He doesn't like the dark.'

André hoped God would forgive him this lie; it was he who was so scared of the night, not Jacob, who was always willing to go into a darkened room on any errand André asked him.

The man smiled. 'Don't worry. We'll find him.' He took André's hand.

'Are you a policeman?'

'Good God, no.' The man laughed. 'I'm in charge of this staircase. My name's Hartmann. You won't remember that, will you? It doesn't matter. I can see what your name is from your tag.'

Up and down the dim stairwells the kindly man led André until they found the room where Jacob was lying, huddled on a mattress. He gave a little cry when André came across the room, stood up and kissed him, with terrible tenderness, on the face.

There was a solid wailing in the room as though the children's nerve had given way in a collective wave of despair. The older ones could no longer be of comfort to the younger, and even the women who tried to help them were in tears. Jacob clutched André, his arms round his neck like a monkey clinging to its mother, and André held on tight for his own sake too.

A pail of cabbage soup came up in the evening, and the children clustered round with what cups they had found or been given. One of the women warned them that it would make their diarrhoea worse, but they drank it and shared it out among themselves with ravening hands.

Later André saw the kind man from the courtyard, who came back into the room with a second man in whose concerned expression even André could see exhaustion. He went from one soaked mattress to another, tapping the chests of the children with his long fingers, feeling their wrists, and laying his hand across their foreheads. Some of them seemed better for his touch.

★ ★ ★

'Dysentery,' said Levi to Hartmann when he had finished his futile round.

'Where did they come from?'

'Some came from the camp in Compiègne and some from a children's home in Louveciennes.'

'We've never really got rid of the dysentery here, anyway,' said Levi. 'Some of these children should be in the infirmary, but there isn't any room.'

Hartmann walked with him to the end of the corridor. 'I don't think it matters very much,' he said. 'I doubt whether they'll be here more than two days.'

They heard the scream of a whistle signalling that the lights should be turned out. In their fouled bed, André and Jacob heard it too.

'It's very dark,' said André, as the glow of the blue bulb was extinguished.

'Don't worry,' said Jacob, close in his arms. 'I'm not frightened of the dark.'

★ ★ ★

Through her binoculars Charlotte watched the morning roll call. Now that the children she had seen arrive the

508

day before were standing still in rows, she had a chance to scan their faces.

Towards the back she could see two small boys she thought she recognised. The distance was too great for her to be certain, but there was something about the way the elder one's hair stood on end, something, too, about the pliant attitude of the smaller one, his hand lightly resting on his brother's forearm.

She did not know what she could do to help them. Perhaps she could send some words of encouragement. What she wanted to do was take them in her arms and kiss them as a mother might. She no longer had enough money left to bribe the gendarme; the only thing she could think to do was to walk along the outside of the camp to where she had seen the second, smaller entry, and try to persuade someone to bring the boys over to her.

Later in the morning, she walked up the street to the north-east corner of the camp. A gendarme was standing guard over the entrance; it was not promising. Throughout the day, Charlotte watched the narrow gateway in the hope that it would for a moment be unguarded. All that happened was that, in the afternoon, a second gendarme came and smoked a cigarette with the first before taking over his position. Charlotte looked up to the long lines of blue-painted windows in the eastern side of the building. If one should open just a crack she might be able to shout up a message.

The afternoon turned to early darkness. Charlotte felt hungry, and stupefied by the anxious tedium of her wait. It was no good. She had done what she first came to do: she had enabled Levade to die in peace of mind. The comforting of André and Jacob was a secondary consideration, and the truth was that a brief meeting with her would make very little difference. What they wanted was their mother, and nothing Charlotte could do would affect whether or not that joy would ever come to them again.

With the greatest reluctance, she would have to leave them. All her maternal feelings cried out against it; she hated the thought that she of all people should be abandoning the boys. It troubled her that she had been unable to finish her self-imposed task, but she saw that there was nothing more that she could do for them. After one more night in the café she would return to Paris.

* * *

The evening before a transport was the time Hartmann feared. An atmosphere of nervous dread seeped through the bare concrete and straw mattresses of Drancy. These people, driven and starved, were made to contemplate a new uncertainty: while few of them believed the foul gossip of gas and crematoria, none of them could look with equanimity on their departure.

Word came to Hartmann in his room that an an extra wagon had been added to the train. In view of the poor condition of the new arrivals, it was suggested by the French police authorities that the wagon should be filled with children. The Jewish committee had protested that many of the children were French nationals, and that there were Poles and Rumanians to spare, but in the random logic of the concentration camp the children were selected. The specificity of the typed lists, with their details of family names and dates of birth, concealed the haphazard nature of the selection, but once the carbon copies rolled off the platen the list was unalterable.

Hartmann went up the stone treads of his staircase with aching steps. Going into the room at all was hard enough, with its faecal stench and background of permanent wailing. He would have to tell them that they were going to rejoin their parents; such a lie was not only forgivable, it was obligatory if they were to get through the next few hours.

He carried a sheet of paper in his hand.

★ ★ ★

André looked up from his bed. He was pleased to see the man who looked like his father. This was what they needed — someone from the old days, someone from before the world went wrong, a man with a handsome face and deep voice who would take them back to their house and let their lives start up again.

'Very early in the morning you'll be leaving. You're going on a train.'

Hartmann did not get far before children began to jabber and shout. 'Pitchipoi!' an older one called out in excitement. Some of the others were encouraged by the childish word and began a chant. The younger ones looked bewildered.

Hartmann's own expression was unconvincing. 'You are advised to make sure your bags are labelled clearly. I will ask some grown-ups to come and help you. You can take a blanket and any little bits of food you may have.' He looked down at the piece of paper. 'Any larger items of baggage will be transported separately.'

'Where are we going?'

'The train goes to Poland.'

'Will we see our parents again?'

'I . . . think so. I can't promise, but I think you probably will.'

'Yes!' Jacob squeezed André hard in his delight.

Hartmann managed a smile. 'I must warn you that the journey is long and uncomfortable. You must be brave. All of you must be brave.'

André noticed that the kind man's voice had gone

peculiar. He was starting to cough.

'Later in the evening, you will move to the departure staircase in the corner of the courtyard near the main gate. Please make sure all your bags are packed and labelled. I'll be back later.'

Hartmann left quickly, ignoring the volley of questions that followed him.

André at once pulled out Madame Cariteau's suitcase and began to arrange his possessions inside it. He took the sweater Jacob was wearing and folded it carefully on top of the book about the crocodile. There was nothing else to put in; all their possessions were already safely stowed. André closed the lid of the case to make sure everything fitted. Then he clicked the brass locks open and straightened the contents all over again.

An hour or so later, two gendarmes came into the room and ordered the children downstairs. Those who did not understand or who were too numbed to obey were prodded out by truncheons. André pulled Jacob by the wrist and hurried into the safety of the mass that was descending. Outside, it was still daylight, and André saw a line of people of all ages waiting to be shaved by the camp barbers. Half a dozen of them attacked the women's hair with long scissors, then ran clippers over their shorn scalps; the men's faces and heads they shaved with razors. Then it was the children's turn. André shuffled up along the queue, frightened of what his mother would say if she saw him with a shaved head. He remembered the feeling of her hand as she stroked his skull, allowing the soft, dark hair to trickle out over the webbing of her fingers. Would she recognise him shorn?

The wind coming in through the open end of the camp lifted tufts of fallen hair, mixed with the cinders of the courtyard, and carried them high on to the inner roof and even up to the windows of the rooms, where they made small drifts of grey and black and blonde and brown.

When they were back in their room, some women came with paper luggage labels and some pencils. André, shaven-headed, wrote his name with lip-scouring care, but had to ask the help of one of the women to tie the label on. Then they were ready.

After the cabbage soup, towards nine o'clock, Hartmann came back into the room, accompanied by two Jewish orderlies.

He stood in the doorway and swallowed hard. 'All right,' he said. 'It's time to go.'

There was no movement in the room. The children were suddenly reluctant.

Hartmann spoke very gently into the silence. 'We have no choice in this. We must go quietly. I cannot promise you that you will find your parents at the end of the journey, but I think there's a chance. There is hope. Make your parents proud of you now. Be brave and be hopeful.'

One of the elder children, a boy of about fourteen, stood up and turned to face the younger ones. 'We must trust Monsieur Hartmann. Let's go.'

Many of the children did not speak French, but something of the boy's manner convinced them, as though the adult world had been mediated to them by one of their own. Slowly, the fetid bunks emptied and the children trailed their bags out on to the concrete landing.

Down in the freezing courtyard, the orderlies led them to the search barracks. Inside were long trestle tables manned by gendarmes under the supervision of two officers of the Inquiry and Control Section, formerly the Police for Jewish Affairs.

André and Jacob shuffled up in the queue until they came to the table. A gendarme took the case from André and opened it on the table. He took out the adjustable spanner and threw it over his shoulder. He picked up the book and laughed.

'Won't be needing that where you're going.'

This was a phrase they heard repeated along the line of tables as the book fluttered like a broken-winged bird into the the corner of the barracks. When the case was returned to André it contained only Jacob's sweater, a shirt and a dirty pair of shorts. Then the gendarmes searched their bodies, smacking their bony ribs and running their hands up inside their thighs.

'Got some money sewn in there, have you?' said the man, feeling the fabric of Jacob's shirt. 'God, you smell horrible.'

The gendarme next to Jacob tore the earrings from a little dark-haired girl. 'Won't be needing jewellery where you're going!'

'All right, then, get out of it, move along. Go on.'

At the door of the barracks a gendarme marked their backs with a chalk cross.

'Wait here.'

Jacob had started to weep. He put his hand in André's, which already held a lone tin soldier he had managed to smuggle through.

From a carbon copy of the irreversible list their names were read in alphabetical order, and they were marched off to the south-east corner of the camp, next to the main gate. This section had been separated from the rest of the courtyard by rolls of barbed wire strung between hastily erected wooden posts.

At the foot of Staircase Two stood a gendarme and a Jewish orderly, who ticked their names off another copy of the list as they went through the door.

On the first floor, they were shown into an empty room. There were no beds, no mattresses, no tables; beneath the single light bulb and between the unplastered concrete walls there was only a scattering of straw and two empty buckets. There were more than a hundred children in the room, and the contents of the bucket rapidly overflowed and trickled down the steps.

André turned his head against the wall. He could read the names and messages written there by others on the eve of their departure. 'Léon Reich'. 'Last convoy. We will be back.' And next to his head: 'Natalie Stern. Still in good heart.'

He broke down and fell to the floor.

★ ★ ★

Through a window on the other side of the courtyard, Hartmann and Levi were able to watch the people entering the departure staircase in the path of the searchlight fixed on the corner of the courtyard.

Levi said, 'In the war, did you ever take part in an attack?'

'Once.'

'Do you remember the night before?'

The two men looked at each other.

Hartmann said, 'When time collapses.'

Levi nodded. 'I wish I had faith.'

'You're here because of your faith.'

'My father's faith.'

Neither spoke for a long time as they watched the last of the deportees going in. He was a man of about their age and they could hear his violent protestations. 'I'm a Frenchman! I was decorated at Verdun! You cannot do this to me!'

'You're a filthy Jew like all the others.'

The door to the staircase was closed.

Hartmann looked at his watch. 'About five hours to go.'

From the deportation staircase they could hear the beginnings of the Marseillaise, followed by a boy scout song, 'It's only a short goodbye.'

Hartmann said, 'You believe me now, don't you?'

'About the destination?'

'Yes.'

'All logic is against it.'

'But you feel it, don't you?'

'I'm a German. I'm a reasonable man.' Levi stared into the darkness where the gendarme had turned off the searchlight. 'I cannot permit myself such beliefs.'

★ ★ ★

André was lying on the floor when a Jewish orderly came with postcards on which the deportees might write a final message. He advised them to leave them at the station or throw them from the train as camp orders forbade access to the post. Two or three pencils that had survived the barracks search were passed round among the people in the room. Some wrote with sobbing passion, some with punctilious care, as though their safety, or at least the way in which they were remembered, depended upon their choice of words.

A woman came with a sandwich for each child to take on the journey. She also had a pail of water, round which they clustered, holding out sardine cans they passed from one to another. One of the older boys embraced her in his gratitude, but the bucket was soon empty.

When she was gone, there were only the small hours of the night to go through. André was lying on the straw, the soft bloom of his cheek laid, uncaring, in the dung. Jacob's limbs were intertwined with his for warmth.

The adults in the room sat slumped against the walls, wakeful and talking in lowered voices. Somehow, the children were spared the last hours of the wait by their ability to fall asleep where they lay, to dream of other places.

It was still the low part of the night when Hartmann and the head of another staircase came into the room with coffee. Many of the adults refused to drink because they knew it meant breakfast, and therefore the departure. The children were at the deepest moments of their sleep.

Those who drank from the half dozen cups that circulated drank in silence. Then there went through the room a sudden ripple, a quickening of muscle and nerve as a sound came to them from below: it was the noise of an engine — a familiar sound to many of them, the homely thudding of a Parisian bus.

At once the gendarmes were in the room, moving quickly and violently, as though anxious to have them gone. Cowering, the adults clasped their cases and bundles and stumbled down the dark stairs out into the courtyard, where the sudden heat of searchlights flared up from the guard posts.

Five white-and-green municipal buses had come in through the main entrance, and now stood trembling in the wired-off corner of the yard. At a long table in front of the Red Castle, the commandant of the camp himself sat with a list of names that another policeman was calling out in alphabetical order. In the place where its suburban destination was normally signalled, each bus carried the number of a wagon on the eastbound train.

Many of the children were too deeply asleep to be roused, and those who were awake refused to come down when the gendarmes were sent up to fetch them. In the filthy straw they dug in their heels and screamed. They clung to walls and floors and bits of plumbing; they held on to one another and gripped the cold steps as they were dragged out beneath the thrashing truncheons. For every sound of wood cracking on bone they screamed more loudly in their frenzy not to leave.

The gendarmes staggered down with their arms full of children, blood on their truncheons, out into the sweeping light. Some of them were sobbing as they hurled their living bundles on to the ground and turned back into the building. In the glare of the hurricane lamps at his table, the police commandant's face was drawn with impatient anguish.

André heard his name and moved with Jacob towards the bus. From the other side of the courtyard, from windows open on the dawn, a shower of food was thrown towards them by women wailing and calling out their names, though none of the scraps reached as far as the enclosure.

André looked up, and in a chance angle of light he saw a woman's face in which the eyes were fixed with terrible ferocity on a child beside him. Why did she stare as though she hated him? Then it came to André that she was not looking in hatred, but had kept her eyes so intensely open in order to fix the picture of her child in her mind. She was looking to remember, for ever.

He held on hard to Jacob as they mounted the platform of the bus. Some of the children were too small to manage the step up and had to be helped on by gendarmes, or pulled in by grown-ups already on board.

André's bus was given the signal to depart, but was delayed. A baby of a few weeks was being lifted on to the back, and the gendarme needed time to work the wooden crib over the passenger rail and into the crammed interior.

Eventually, the bus roared as the driver engaged the gear and bumped slowly out through the entrance, the headlights for a moment lighting up the café opposite before the driver turned the wheel and headed for the station.

When the last bus had gone, it was daylight and the

cleaners went into the departure staircase, wearing clogs with high soles.

★ ★ ★

There were people going early to work or taking their dogs to the park on the straight road to the station. They looked curiously on the small convoy of buses that rumbled past, down the broad, empty street. They saw faces pressed against glass and, where the destination should have been, a number.

At Le Bourget-Drancy station there were German soldiers as well as gendarmes. In the milling turbulence of the platform, André Duguay held on hard to his brother and the suitcase which for once he had remembered.

The soldiers prodded the throng down to a siding, where there was a line of boxcars normally used for the transportation of horses. With a screaming of German words, they pushed and herded the sullen mass towards the doors.

Commuters on the main platform looked on, while the gendarmes, who had relinquished their charges to the German soldiers, shuffled from foot to foot and looked away from the local travellers' puzzled gaze.

Jacob could not manage the height of the boxcar and had to be lifted by an adult. The inside of the wagon was crammed with standing people of all ages. There were two buckets, one of which held water and a cup.

As André clambered up, a German soldier took his case and threw it down the platform, where it joined a pile of bags and bundles that the soldiers told them they would not be needing. A woman in the wagon who spoke German translated to the others.

André and Jacob stood among the taller people, their vision blocked by coats and legs and bulky adult hips.

Then a German soldier heaved the sliding door along its runners and bolted it.

It was by now a bright morning, and André could still see a little patch of cloud through an opening in the wagon. Then, from outside, came the noise of hammering, and the last glimpse of French sky was suddenly obliterated.

★ ★ ★

'What was all that noise in the night?' said Charlotte to the proprietress as she settled her bill.

'The buses. Another load of them.' The woman counted the notes carefully on the zinc-topped bar and slid them into the cash till.

'I see. Where do they take them?'

'To the station.'

Charlotte squared her shoulders and breathed in deeply as she stepped out into the winter morning. She walked a short distance to a large crossroads, where she saw people waiting for a bus. A few minutes later they were on their way, the big engine throbbing, the destination clearly marked.

Charlotte had slept late, and it was almost eleven o'clock by the time the bus crossed the railway bridge and deposited the passengers at the top of the slope down to the station. The next train into Paris was not for half an hour, and she had time to telephone 'Félix' on the number she had memorised.

She had no idea what sort of street the rue Villaret de Joyeuse was, though, being in the seventeenth arrondissement, on the western outskirts, it was likely to be filled with large semi-suburban apartment blocks rather than small cafés and cobbled yards. Félix agreed to be there at four in the afternoon to meet her, and Charlotte strolled out through the booking hall and on to the platform.

As she walked up and down, she glanced over to a siding, where she noticed a large number of apparently abandoned suitcases and bundles. After checking to see if anyone was watching her, she walked over to inspect them.

The contents of the bags had spilled on to the platform. They were mostly old clothes, filthy or torn, odd shoes and the occasional child's toy. Charlotte wondered if they had been rejected by their owners on some hygienic grounds: perhaps this was a rubbish dump waiting to be cleared. Then her eye was caught by something white that stuck out from under a grey woollen jacket. It was a bundle of unposted letters and cards.

Making sure once more that no one was watching her, Charlotte stooped down on the platform and picked them up.

Some were composed and thoughtful. Some were mere scribbles: 'My dear parents, they're taking us to work in Germany. I hope I will see you again soon'; 'To whoever finds this card. Please, please post it to the right address, to my old Mayor who can save me.'

Others seemed heavy with knowledge. 'We are being taken to the east. I embrace you, dear parents, with all my heart. Goodbye for ever.'

Charlotte put the little bundle in her pocket and stood up. Towards the end of the pile was a small suitcase with brass locks, canted over to one side, its mouth gaping. Inside was a soiled pair of boy's shorts. Between the locks, on the front, a leather label that was glued to the case bore the word 'CARITEAU'.

★ ★ ★

On the train, Charlotte found a compartment to herself, in which she looked at the letters. She did not like to read their contents too closely, but there was one she returned to twice, despite herself.

It was written in a sloping, educated hand, in blotted pale blue ink, with no crossings-out or corrections. It was the letter of a man to his daughter. The handwriting suggested someone in middle age, and the girl must have been in her late teens or older, to judge from the tone her father had chosen.

'My dearest little Gisèle,

They allowed us some post last week and I was delighted to receive your card and to know that you and Maman are in good health. I too am extremely well and in excellent spirits. Alas, I am to be deported in the morning by train to a destination as yet unknown. I am going with plenty of old friends from Paris and I am very much hoping that I'll find Charles and Léonore at the other end.

Please look after yourself, my little squirrel. That is the best thing you can do for me today and every day. Don't worry about me, think only of yourself: eat well — as well as you can! — keep your clothes clean, make yourself pretty and work hard for Maman and for yourself. The sweetest joy of my life was buying little things for you when you were younger. How I loved your solemn face, the way, when you were tired, your laughter hovered on the brink of tears; above all, the way you loved me as only a little girl can, with no resentment or fear of me and such trust.

I will return in good health, quite soon, I think. Even if this letter does not reach you — the orderly was unsure of the facilities for posting — I hope my previous letter has got there. Please keep the photograph of me as a souvenir until such time as you see me again.

Look after yourself, my darling little girl. I am not lost; I will return. I embrace you with all my heart.

Charlotte put down the letter. 'No resentment or fear of me.' Were fear and resentment the normal emotions between a daughter and her father? 'Such trust . . . ' She was touched by the unknown man's tenderness. She had not imagined fathers to feel such vulnerability or to rely on their daughters for comfort.

★ ★ ★

From the Métro station Argentine, Charlotte emerged into the wide spaces of the Avenue de la Grande Armée. It was only a few steps to a triangle of street-ends, from which the rue Villaret de Joyeuse led gently downhill.

The door of the building was open, and Charlotte proceeded cautiously over the scarlet carpet of the hall. In front of her was a lift, with broad stone stairs to the left. She needed only to climb half a flight to reach a glass door with the name of a company printed in black. She pressed the lower bell, as instructed, and a few seconds later the door was opened by a plump, fair-haired man with a brightly coloured cravat. He ushered her across a gloomy vestibule and through the front door of a dark apartment with low ceilings. He showed her to a hard, upholstered chair in the sitting room, then went down the corridor and returned with a bottle of brandy and two glasses.

'Chin-chin, Danièle.' He sounded English.

'Yes . . . Chin-chin.'

A white Persian cat slunk into the room and rubbed itself against Félix's legs.

'So. How did you manage to get up here?'

'Trains. Buses. I've done a lot of travelling. Are you English?'

'Yes, but my dear Mama was French. I have a little shop in the Place des Ternes. It's a perfect front.'

'And can you help with transport?'

'Stop it, Marat! He's scratched all the furniture and

523

it's not my flat. As a matter of fact, you're in luck. On Wednesday night, weather permitting, a Lysander is leaving from a field near Rouen. I've been in touch and they've got room for a small one.'

'How will I get there?'

'I can arrange everything. You look awfully tired.'

'Tired? Do I?'

'Yes. A lot of people who pass through here look the same way. They've been active for several weeks and I think they've got used to being short of sleep. I notice these things, though.'

Charlotte thought guiltily of her late start that morning, and how she had missed the departure of the buses from Drancy. Yet Félix was right. Now that she sat in this domestic room, each spare surface of which was covered with small ornaments, she felt an ache in her arms and back, while her legs felt almost boneless with fatigue.

Félix stood up and pushed the cat away. 'I expect you'd like a rest. Then this evening I'll find you some nice dinner. You're hungry, I expect, aren't you?'

Charlotte nodded. Speech seemed suddenly beyond her. Félix led her down a dark corridor, and opened a door on the left. It was a large shadowy room with a huge oak desk, a narrow window hung with net curtains and a low bed with a tasselled cover. 'Will you please take care of these?' she said, handing him the bundle of letters and cards from the train. 'Perhaps you could post them.'

'I'll call you later,' said Félix as he shut the door, the letters in his hand. Charlotte lay down and closed her eyes.

★ ★ ★

André Duguay was standing in the darkness. Three hours in the truck, and still the train had not moved.

Some people were still talking; an old woman was moaning her prayers.

The wheels ground suddenly on the track, and they were thrown against one another. The full pail of water had been drunk, and the empty one was already full of waste, which slopped beneath their feet as the train jerked forward.

Jacob had slumped to the wooden plank floor, through whose narrow gaps he could see slivers of French ground.

The hours would not pass. High up there was a small slit in the wall of the boxcar. A tall man stood by it and told them what he could see. 'Epernay,' he said, when the train had pulled into a station, and another man began to weep, as though with longing for the lost associations of the name.

Although it was winter outside, the air was rank. When it grew dark the train stood motionless for many hours. The slit man said there was no light. They seemed lost in a night without direction.

André had fallen against other children. They leaned on one another, half sleeping, with no room to lie down. A man near him was thrusting himself at a woman. She had lifted her skirt and moaned when he pushed.

The old woman was still muttering in Hebrew; sometimes she sang with a wailing voice that sounded to André very foreign, from a strange, far-off land.

I will see Maman, thought André; when I get there, I will see Maman.

'Metz,' said the slit man. Each time the train stopped, there was a beat of hope. A destination, any place on earth, was better than being lost in the bottomless night. The doors were thrown back and they saw a snowy countryside. A German soldier was shouting at them and a woman translated.

'If anyone tries to escape he will be shot. If anyone has died, throw out the body.'

They begged him for water. Even a handful of snow.

The old woman was almost mad. The doors were closed again. The stretched hours would not amount to days; there was no sense of time passing, though by now it was the second night. Someone had died in their wagon, and the others were edging away from the body.

André held Jacob in his arms.

There was another stop. The slit man said they were at a station with a German name. 'There are ordinary people. It's morning. They're going to work. They're staring at our train.'

They moved on again into another day. André held tight to hope. His life had been ordered properly: bad things did not happen. If he could believe strongly enough in the normal world that he inhabited, it would return.

The stench of the boxcar was making him feel sick. He had almost forgotten the darkness. They went through fatigue and its boundaries so many times that they were beyond exhaustion.

It was deep night. The train stopped.

The slit man said, 'There's no town, only fields. This is it. We're there.'

There was elation: at last they had arrived. Then some smoke came through the slit, a pungent smoke.

'There's a long platform. Hundreds of people. German soldiers. There are dogs. It's very bright, there are searchlights. There are people in striped uniforms. They must be the workers. They're unpacking the wagons. Hey!' In German, the slit man called out, 'What happens here?'

'What do they say, what do they say?'

A sweep of light came through the narrow grille as the slit man turned back into the packed wagon. 'One went like this.' He ran his index finger like a knife across his throat. 'And one went like this.' He made a twisting gesture with his fingers that, to André, conjured rising smoke.

With a scream of metal runners, the doors were pulled back and the wagon was filled with light. ''*Raus, 'raus, alles 'raus!*' There were men shouting. There were dogs howling.

André held Jacob as they stumbled forward. Two dead men were on the step. Someone helped the boys down.

'Say you're older than you are.'

'Say you're younger than you are.'

A huge dog was tearing at its chain. It was the closest thing André could see to a world he had lost. He forgot his parents' firm instructions and made to stroke it.

He was pushed away by a man in stripes. His wooden clogs went clacking up and down the ramp. The striped men were hunched and hurrying; they would not look at you. Their faces were tight on their bones.

André saw a tall woman with fair hair. She was like his mother: he would follow her. 'Come on, Jacob.'

Up ahead, from a remote, high building, they saw flames pouring into the black sky, and there was this burning, melting smell. Was it the rails, hot beneath the iron wheels? It seemed too rich.

Shuffling up the platform, André made his effort of belief. From his memories of being alive, from the trust of normality and in his parents' world, he tried to dredge up faith. That certainty was invincible; no hell could overcome it. He would see his mother.

The people were dividing. The fair-haired woman was pushed one way, and André saw her child steered into another line. The woman screamed at the man in uniform. He merely shrugged and pushed her, too, into the line of children. André was pleased. He would be with her.

The dogs were leaping at him, but he held Jacob

527

hard. They were coming to a tall man who stood on the platform with a stick, like a man doing music.

He moved his baton gently, inclined his head, gazing with wise eyes on those in front of him, directing them this way or that. He was like the doctor in Drancy, who tapped the children's chests and made them better with his touch.

André had trust in the man; but when their time came he barely glanced at the Duguay boys.

Now they were in a line of children and old people. They were climbing into lorries.

André was at the back. They went past a long ditch in which ragged flames were rising. From a tipped lorry, what looked to André like giant dolls with broken limbs were being poured into the trench.

They stopped at two whitewashed farmhouses with thatched roofs. The lorry's headlights showed up pretty fruit trees.

Now they were naked. It was very cold in this room. Jacob took André's hand and found that there was already something in it — a tin soldier.

André kissed Jacob's shorn head, the stubble tender on his lips.

There was another room, another door, with bolts and rubber seals, over whose threshold the two boys, among many others, went through icy air, and disappeared.

6

From the car which took her from the airfield into London, Charlotte noticed signs of early spring among the hedgerows. It was noticeably warmer than in Lavaurette or Paris; there were buds and scents the Highlands would not see for weeks.

She thought of the house where she had spent her childhood, of the bursting pink and white blossom on the chestnut trees, the daisy-covered lawn on which she walked out one May morning and saw inlaid with a fantastic marquetry of violets. The house outside Edinburgh, where her parents now lived, held no interest for her by comparison: it was a solid building, ample and spacious, but neither its view over the hills nor its square, chilly rooms were inviting to her.

Yet it was to this house that she found her thoughts turning as the black Wolseley entered the London suburbs. She must not only contact her parents, she must go to see them as soon as she was free. Such a visit seemed less of a duty than usual; she found that she was anxious to see them again and to reassure them.

The FANY driving the car asked if she wanted to be dropped anywhere, or if she should go straight to G Section headquarters. Charlotte thought of her narrow room in Daisy's flat and wondered who was living there now. Presumably G Section would help find her somewhere for the time being.

'Straight to the office, please,' she said. She was the only passenger in the car, and was enjoying the comfort of it. There had been four of them in the Lysander, which was one more than the usual load. One man had been on the floor, one on the shelf, and Charlotte had shared the seat with a third man, who politely arched himself away from physical contact with her. Charlotte felt she should be similarly delicate, with the result that her hip developed periodic spasms of cramp.

The fat leather bench-seat of the Wolseley felt luxurious, and she sat back to watch the big buildings of Whitehall as the car waited for a group of men with briefcases to hurry across the street. There was hardly any traffic as they moved smoothly up towards Trafalgar Square.

Charlotte thought of the gaping suitcase on the platform at Le Bourget-Drancy. CARITEAU. The single word had removed all doubt. Until then, she had felt that the camp at Drancy was perhaps not as bad as people feared. Levade had died from illness, from whatever problem his chest had developed at the Domaine, and the camp had not affected the outcome of his disease. And André and Jacob, they were refugees, like hundreds of thousands in Europe; it was a hard fate for children, but they would survive being moved around, as others had survived. Then the cases and bundles, contemptuously hurled down the platform, had in an instant crushed that easy hope — Cariteau: the simple name from an old village, cast aside.

It occurred to Charlotte that she was too tired to register exactly what she felt about the death of Levade and the deportation of the boys. She suspected, as she sometimes had when tormenting herself with thoughts that Peter Gregory was dead, that her emotions could not encompass the complexity of feeling that the circumstances seemed to demand. It was beyond her; the pressure of sadness would eventually find its own expression. Meanwhile, there were times when you merely had to go to your next appointment, go through the day and hope for sleep at the end of it.

The car pulled up some way from the flat in

Marylebone, and the FANY asked Charlotte if she could remember the way.

'It's just a final precaution. You know Mr Jackson.' The woman smiled.

'Thank you. I can manage from here.'

The door was opened by the butlerish figure Charlotte remembered from the day of her departure, and she felt drab in Dominique's clothes beneath his appraising eye. He gave no sign of recognition as he showed her to an empty bedroom in which to wait. Charlotte sat on the bed with her case on her knees. She did not feel anxious about what Mr Jackson might think of her extended stay; or, at least, she felt she had the answer to any reprimand, because she was happy to resign from G Section at once.

'This way, Miss.'

She followed the butler to the door of Mr Jackson's office, where he knocked discreetly.

'Ah, Danièle. Thank you, Philips, you can leave us now.'

Jackson stood up and came round the desk, his froggy face split open by a huge smile. Charlotte held out her hand, but to her surprise he kissed her on the cheek.

'Welcome home, Danièle, welcome home. You poor thing, you've had a rough time, haven't you?'

'No, I . . . I think it went quite well, really. I was able to do what I went there to do.'

'Absolutely. Transmissions from Ussel have been with us loud and clear since August. You seem to have inspired the local operator.'

Charlotte smiled as she thought of Antoinette with the wireless aerial draped round the furniture of her bedroom.

'I saw Yves a month or so ago on a return visit. He spoke very well of you. Said your French was absolutely tip-top.'

'That's very kind of him, though I'm not quite sure

he'd be the best judge of that.'

'Quite, quite. Anyway, Violinist has been performing well. We managed to get a lot of stores in, thanks to you and your Frenchman.'

'Are you still doing drops there?'

'Not there, no. It's too dangerous. Since Mirabel, alas, disappeared. But there's another drop zone not far away. What they're doing now is helping train the troops. They're getting a lot of volunteers, thanks to the Germans.'

'What do you mean?'

'Haven't you heard of the Statutory Work Order? Ah, well, Monsieur Laval has been our best recruiting sergeant. He's decreed that all young men have to go and work in Germany for a time, a sort of national service. He's achieved what General de Gaulle and even we have so far not quite managed, which is to drive large numbers of young men into the Resistance.' Mr Jackson paused and coughed. 'Of course, the fact that the Allies are now manifestly winning the war may have been a further incentive.'

'That's good news.'

'It's very good. Now, tell me, Danièle, what was going on in Paris? I'm glad you were able to make contact with Félix, he's an excellent chap. But, to be frank, we had rather expected to pick you up from somewhere near Limoges. A long time ago. Last summer, to be precise.'

'It was important that I stay.' Various fabricated and implausible stories suggested themselves to Charlotte, but in the end she thought she might as well tell the truth. All Jackson could do was dismiss her from the service, and, now that she had been to France, she had no desire to stay in it. Her encounter with Mirabel had not shaken her conviction about the morality of the war, but it had lessened her loyalty to G Section. It had also frightened her; and, for fear of incriminating herself or others, she thought it best to say nothing of it to Mr Jackson.

Meanwhile she did her best to explain to him about her feeling for the country and her conviction that it had been necessary for her to remain there. The wireless operator had, after all, been able to reassure them that she was safe and useful. Both Mirabel and Octave had said they needed more people. As for being in Paris, she told Jackson about the night they took Levade from the Domaine; she talked of her sense of responsibility to him and to the Duguay boys. And if Julien was a key part of the G Section network, whether he admitted it or not, then she was presumably entitled to pursue his interests.

Jackson gave a little laugh. 'I'm quite used to our people popping up in the most unexpected places, don't worry about that. They have carte blanche to travel where they like. But those are agents, and not, if I may say so, couriers. I had heard from Mirabel that you were still there and I was happy for you to stay on for a time, but you must understand that a woman is more at risk than a man. The other thing, which I'm sure you know, is that every time you travel and use people and addresses, the more you expose them to danger. It's really a matter — to borrow an expression — of 'Is your journey really necessary?' '

'I do understand,' said Charlotte. 'It seemed necessary to me, that's all I can say. And perhaps you haven't had first-hand accounts of these camps and trains before.'

'No, indeed. That could be useful. It's not really my pigeon, but I certainly know who would be interested.'

'Anyway,' said Charlotte, 'if you'd like me to resign, I quite understand.'

'Good God, no! My dear Danièle, you're a first-class asset. I wouldn't dream of letting you go. There are one or two people in this organisation who doubt your utter dependability. I think I recall hearing the phrase 'loose cannon' used by one of them. We may find you a slightly more . . . domestic role at first. But as far as I'm concerned you'll jolly well stay with G Section until the hostilities are satisfactorily concluded.'

'I don't know. I think I've really done all I can do, and — '

'Excuse me, Danièle. Will you please stop talking such utter rot? I presume this is just a way of teasing me into buying you lunch. Very well. If you'd like to go to the bedroom at the end of the corridor, I'll get Valerie to bring your old clothes back. You can smarten up a bit and we'll pop out in half an hour. How does that suit you?'

'It sounds fine. There's just one thing.' From her handbag Charlotte took out an empty bottle of hair dye and placed it on Jackson's desk. 'I was fortunate enough to be given this.'

'Fortunate?' said Jackson. 'It was only your decision to stay on that made it necessary. Surely Valerie had already organised everything here.'

'Not quite everything.'

'Why are you smiling, Danièle?'

'I don't think she foresaw the possibility of my taking a bath — in a public bath house.'

'I'm not with you.'

'Certain . . . inconsistencies of colouring.'

'What do you — oh my God, I see what you mean. Yes, yes, indeed.' Jackson stammered for a moment, then regained his composure. 'Well, I think you've certainly caught us with our trousers down, if you'll forgive the expression.'

'Gladly.'

'I'll make a note about the dye for future use. Now. Lunch. Do you like fish?'

'Yes, I still like fish.'

534

It seemed that what Jackson had in mind was a job training agents. Charlotte would help with their language and pass on various tips and information from her own experience. He mentioned one of the holding schools in Suffolk. There would have to be a full-scale debriefing in London first, and in the meantime he could offer a bed in one of the FANY hostels.

Charlotte felt oddly ill at ease in her old clothes. The skirt was loose, and the stockings, after months of Dominique's, felt draughty when she walked. After lunch she sat on Jackson's desk, swinging her legs back and forth, and making telephone calls. It was a delight to speak English.

Her mother wanted her to come to Scotland at once, but Charlotte said there were things she had to attend to in London. Roderick, her mother told her, was in Tunisia and doing well when they had last heard. Then Charlotte telephoned Daisy at the Red Cross. Daisy let out a long theatrical scream of delight, and, when she had regained coherence, arranged to meet that evening.

Finally she telephoned Squadron Leader Allan Wetherby.

She did not really expect to be able to talk to him, but after various delays and protective enquiries she heard the man himself say, 'Wetherby.'

'You very kindly wrote to me a few months ago about a friend of mine, Peter Gregory. I'm sure this is most irregular, but I just wondered if you had had any news.'

Charlotte found that the combination of trying not to sound too eager and of speaking English for the first time for six months made her sound, in her own ears, almost regal.

Wetherby appeared unimpressed.

'It's just that since you wrote to me, I thought you wouldn't mind having an unofficial word,' said Charlotte.

Wetherby coughed. 'I tell you what, Miss Gray. I have heard reports — and I must stress that these are very, very unofficial reports — of one of our chaps making touch with various local people, who belong to . . . to a different organisation. With whom we're co-operating.'

'These unofficial reports, they're just rumours, are they?'

'No, they're better than that. The dates and the places just about tally. Except . . . '

'Except, what?'

'Except I don't know how he ended up in Marseille.'

Charlotte thought of Gregory's French. 'He could have ended up anywhere.'

'I suppose so. At any rate, someone's trying hard to make his way back. Whether it's Gregory or not I can't say for sure.'

'How can I find out more?'

'I don't know if you can. Unless you try your luck with . . . the other organisation.'

'All right. Thank you.'

The trouble was, she did not trust herself to ask Jackson if he knew anything without giving away her interest. By the time he knocked before re-entering his own office, she had been through, and abandoned, various ruses concerning the brother of a friend, the fiancé of a neighbour and so on. She would have to think of a better lie.

Meanwhile, Gregory was on his way. No, that was a foolish thing to think; she would not allow herself to believe it. But the more she struggled to suppress her springing hope, the more it animated her.

★ ★ ★

536

'My God, Charlotte, what happened to your hair?'

'Oh, I just felt like a change of colour.'

Daisy let Charlotte out of her fierce, welcoming grip. 'Come in, come in. I've arranged a bit of a party later on. Let's have a look at you.'

Charlotte went into the sitting room, where Daisy stood back and inspected her. 'I think you've lost weight. Apart from that, you look gorgeous. Why didn't you write, though? We were worried sick.'

'I couldn't really write. It was all — '

'All very hush-hush, I know. You can't have your old room back, I'm afraid. We've got a new girl. Alison.'

'What's she like?'

'Delightful. You'll meet her later on. Little bit of a prude, but otherwise terrific fun. Which reminds me, have you heard anything? About . . . '

'Peter? Not exactly. But I spoke to the squadron leader this afternoon and he sounded quite hopeful. Apparently there's someone stumbling around there, trying to get back. They just don't know if it's him.'

'It must be awful not knowing.'

'I'd rather not know than know the worst.'

'Of course.' Daisy looked a little doubtful. 'Sally's got a new boyfriend. They're engaged. She's absolutely dotty about him.'

'What happened to Terence?'

'She found out he was being unfaithful to her.'

'What, with his wife?'

'No, with another woman.'

'Oh dear. Poor Sally. You wouldn't think, looking at Terence, that — '

'She's well out of it if you ask me. This new chap's a bit of a stuffed shirt, but at least he's single. You can sleep on the sofa, by the way, if you haven't got anywhere else.'

'It's all right, thanks. They've found me a room in a funny little block in Riding House Street.'

'You can always come back, Charlotte. When Sally leaves. Listen. I think that's Michael.'

Daisy went to the window and looked down into the narrow street where Michael Waterslow was hooting the horn of his car.

'Yes, come on, let's go down. Lazy so-and-so. He never comes up.'

Michael drove them to a pub in Maida Vale, a huge building with engraved Victorian glass and a gleaming mahogany bar. To Michael's disappointment there was a blackboard outside with a mournful drawing of a long-nosed character, new to Charlotte, and the words, 'Wot, no beer.'

'We'll just have to drink gin instead,' said Michael.

As the evening progressed, they were joined first by Ralph, at whose flat in the Fulham Road Charlotte had met Gregory for the second time, then by his drunk friend, Miles.

Michael, with his neatly pressed suit and punctilious manner, was a generous host and kept a steady tide of drinks coming to the table. At one point he turned to Charlotte and said, 'Don't worry about Greg. I know it's a long time, but he'll be back. He's got the luck of the devil. That's the whole point about Greg.'

Charlotte nodded and smiled. Gregory seemed more real to her since she had been with people who knew him — even people as marginal as these now seemed to her. It was no longer her willpower alone that was keeping him alive.

The party swelled in numbers as the evening went on. There were people Charlotte recognised from the Melrose literary party and others she had never seen before. Primed by Daisy and Michael, they all bought drinks and toasted her safe return. In the smoky racket of the pub, Charlotte became aware that she had drunk too much. She went outside for a moment into the night and walked up and down, breathing in the cold air. She thought for a moment of Julien, hiding out on some freezing hillside. She thought of Levade, and of the gaping suitcase.

Then she went back into the noisy warmth and accepted the full glass that was pressed into her hand.

★ ★ ★

The next day, in a bare room in Whitehall, while she sat describing her French experiences to three men behind a table, she found that parts of the night before came back to her, bit by bit, unexpectedly.

There had been another pub, in St John's Wood, and then a group visit to an ABC café. Then there was a club somewhere in the West End. She noticed how close Daisy and Michael were dancing. When Daisy returned to the candle-lit table, Charlotte asked her, 'Are you and Michael . . . '

'Yes, darling, I'm afraid so. He's awfully sweet, you know.'

Charlotte had begun to laugh in a feeble, defenceless way, that she later recognised was close to tears.

The three men in Whitehall dismissed her. They had been interested in what she told them and would pass it on, though it was not really their pigeon either. Next there was a full debriefing in the flat in Marylebone with Mr Jackson and two senior colleagues. Charlotte had to keep asking for glasses of water.

★ ★ ★

A week later, she sat on the train to Edinburgh. She placed a suitcase, her own at last, not Dominique's, in the luggage rack and sat down by the window.

Until York she was alone in the compartment. She read a book for an hour, then gazed at the English

539

fields. Nothing about their tracks and barns, the clumps of elm and ash, the mess of farming with its rusted tractors and dung-smeared animals was, on the surface, any different from what she had seen from the windows of numerous trains in France.

She stood up to go to the buffet car and caught sight of her reflection in the small, rectangular mirror with its bevelled edges above the seats opposite. The hairdresser to whom she went in Bond Street could see enough of her hair's natural colours to give him an idea of how he should re-dye the Ussel brown. The result was so close to how she had looked on the train coming down a year before that even Charlotte could barely see the difference.

Her face was perhaps a little thinner, though the change was not obvious. Were there black marks beneath her eyes? Not really: her skin was still so young that it was incapable of showing weariness in lines or shadows. The dozen dark brown freckles over the bridge of her nose and beneath her eyes remained the same, and she remembered how Gregory used to touch them with the tip of his tongue, claiming they had a taste of their own. Yet even if her skin denied it, she was not the same person who had gone down the swaying corridors with Cannerley and Morris.

After the second pub, after the night-club, when they had gone back to the flat and drunk coffee, Daisy, in a moment of extreme alcoholic candour, had said something like, 'When you first arrived from Scotland, darling, I thought you were a bit of a shop-window mannequin, with all your clothes and your self-control. But you're not, are you?' Daisy had leaned forward and placed her hand on Charlotte's thigh. 'You're . . . God, I don't know. You're a rum one, aren't you?'

Charlotte pulled back the door of the compartment and stepped out. Levade had told her one day that there was no such thing as a coherent human personality.

When you are forty you have no cell in your body that you had at eighteen. It was the same, he said, with your character. Memory is the only thing that binds you to earlier selves; for the rest, you become an entirely different being every decade or so, sloughing off the old persona, renewing and moving on. You are not who you were, he told her, nor who you will be.

★ ★ ★

Amelia Gray was waiting at Waverley station. She signalled cheerily to Charlotte from the barrier and grappled with her briefly in a botched, powdery kiss.

Charlotte abandoned herself to her mother's control. She sat in the passenger seat of the car and responded happily to Amelia Gray's anxious questions. However much Charlotte had been disappointed and irritated by her over the years, she had always been fond of her, and there was a self-indulgent pleasure in allowing herself to be mothered.

'Your father'll be back at about seven. He's got a meeting at the hospital, but he's so much looking forward to seeing you.'

'Good. I'm sorry I couldn't keep in touch more. It was impossible.'

'Just so long as you're safe and well now, that's what matters.'

In her absence, Charlotte's parents had acquired a small terrier called Angus. For some reason this struck her as peculiar. Were they lonely? Was it a substitute for their children? What future did they envisage for themselves and the dog?

Amelia Gray had kept bedrooms for both her children in the spacious house, even though neither of them had lived there for some time. On the bookshelves in Charlotte's room were various tales of witches and ponies she had had as a child; the bed was the same one she had had in their old house in the Highlands.

She unpacked her case, in which she had put enough things to last four or five days. In the chest of drawers were old clothes of hers, wrapped in tissue paper and mothballs by her mother. They looked slightly less ravishing than she had imagined in the draper's shop in Limoges.

The disjunction between what had happened to her in France and the life, both past and present, suggested by her bedroom in her parents' home was very strange. She could not reconcile the different experiences at all, and trying to do so made her feel unreal, as though she was still drunk from her return party.

She went downstairs to the sitting room where her mother poured her a glass of sherry. Half an hour later they heard the front door open.

★ ★ ★

William Gray was not sixty years old, but he had not worn well since his return from the Western Front. He seemed to move straight from youth to late middle age, without passing through the vigorous part of his life; then, in the twenty-five years that followed, he had rapidly aged. His mental curiosity and his wiry body gave him a certain energetic presence, but it was that of a springy old man who is fit for his years. His hair was white, and his eyes were sunk deep in his head, with heavy pouches underneath. His skin felt dry and cracked where Charlotte kissed him on the cheek.

There was an awkwardness between them that never changed. As Gray tried to express his delight at seeing her again, Charlotte recoiled; when she gave him her most candid and affectionate look, he would make some dry remark. Amelia Gray watched, powerless to help, as she fluttered between them.

Charlotte was aware of the way she reacted to

her father, and knew that it was different from her behaviour with other people. One of the reasons she had so much valued the company of friends as a child was that, with them, she felt liberated and at ease, while at home she felt reduced. As the evening progressed, she was disappointed to find herself going down familiar paths, becoming evasive and discouraging in her answers to her parents' questions. She was not like this with Julien, or Daisy, or Levade and, least of all, with Gregory. She did not like herself for it.

At dinner, Gray opened a bottle of wine he had long been saving and drank to his daughter's safe return. He was encouraged and amused by how much of it Charlotte drank, and went to fetch another from the cellar. She told him of a man she had known in France, who could drink huge quantities with no apparent effect, and said it must have been from him she had learned. For a time they talked of French customs and habits, of Paris and the provinces, and everything went well. Amelia Gray served out plates of gooseberry tart, made with fruit she had bottled from the garden.

Afterwards, they sat round the fire in the sitting room, and Gray poured brandy from an old ship's decanter on the sideboard.

'And will you be going back to France?' he said.

'I doubt it. Things are changing rapidly. It's becoming more of an open war. They need men and guns more than interpreters and so on.'

'I see,' said Charlotte's mother. 'And the work you did, what — '

'Don't tell us,' said Gray forcefully. 'We don't need to know.'

'All right,' said Charlotte. 'I won't.'

A silence descended. It seemed that their combined mental resources were unable to conjure a single conversational topic beyond the one that had been brought so abruptly to an end. Eventually, Amelia Gray managed to achieve utterance by addressing the dog and telling him it was time for bed. With the help of some business with the coffee cups she was able to restore some sense of geniality.

Charlotte expected that her mother would return to say good night, and that she herself would take the opportunity to go up to bed at the same time. After ten minutes or so, it became clear that Amelia Gray was not coming back, and that Charlotte would have to negotiate her own departure.

She could not pretend to be tired when she felt so alert; and, although she found the conversation with her father awkward, she was aware of an urge, perhaps inspired by the wine, to communicate in some way. She felt the weight of many unassimilated experiences pressing her for some expression.

With an effort, she said, 'I met another interesting man in France, a painter. We had lots of long talks together. I was a lodger in his house for a time.'

'Oh yes. What sort of painter?' Gray was lighting a pipe. 'One of those daub and splash merchants, or the real thing?'

'Oh, the real thing. I think he was famous once, but he says he lost his way. He lost his inspiration.'

'I suppose that can happen.'

'He said it was because he had stopped dreaming.'

Gray laughed. 'Sounds a wee bit like an excuse to me.'

'Perhaps.' Charlotte did not know why she wanted to talk about Levade, but was reluctant to let the subject go. 'He was in the war, you know. Your war. He told me some terrible stories.'

'Aye, well, they were terrible times. Best forgotten.'

Charlotte felt she was close to something. It was vital to keep the conversation going. With a greater effort this time, she said, 'Don't you think you ought to talk

544

about it? To get it out? Isn't that what you tell your patients?'

Gray laughed drily. 'Well, you never forget. It's always with you. Just now, when I told you not to tell us what you'd been doing, I know you thought I was being rude and uninterested. No, wait, Charlotte, let me finish. It wasn't that.'

'I'm sorry.'

'No, no. It's just that when you've commanded a battalion for three years you understand about war. Security, intelligence and so on. You have people's lives in your hands, so you do understand.'

'Of course you do. I'm sorry if I seemed . . . '

Gray suddenly stood up and went to the fireplace. With his back to Charlotte, he said, 'My dear girl, I'm very proud of you.'

Charlotte could say nothing.

Gray turned round. 'So very proud of you. Now, will we be friends?'

'Friends . . . friends?'

'Please, Charlotte. I know I've failed you as a father. But it was difficult, after the war. It was very difficult. I tried to keep a balance, but I was troubled by memories. And dreams.'

Charlotte still said nothing, too frightened to confront what Gray seemed to be suggesting. Was he asking her forgiveness for what had once happened between them? If so, could she trust her memory of what had taken place?

Gray said, 'Do you remember, I told you once of how some men in another company took some German prisoners and then, instead of handing them over, took them into a wood and shot them?'

'Yes, I remember.'

'We were very tired,' said Gray. 'We'd been under shellfire for days, and the men were not themselves. There'd been a hit in our part of the trench, and terrible casualties. It was raining and we were supposed to walk for almost five miles with these Boches. I couldn't get my men to do it. I couldn't make them. I think they might have shot me if I'd pushed them any harder.'

'So it was your company?'

'You can't possibly understand what it was like. Three years of this. They'd seen all their friends slaughtered. We stopped at a little copse and I said, "I'm going to speak to the officer in the village. I leave the prisoners to your disposal." I knew perfectly well what they'd do. And they knew I knew.'

Gray's voice was flat and without remorse.

'Is that what you dreamed of?'

'No. The dreams were of my men's faces. The look of incomprehension, the look of terror when I told them we were ordered to attack at dawn. On the Somme. In daylight. At walking pace. Night after night I saw those young men's faces. Boys younger than you are now. They looked at me and they knew. We all knew what was coming.'

Somehow Gray had remained calm. Charlotte murmured some soothing words.

'Now, Charlotte, you must try to forgive my shortcomings. Or at least describe them to me, so perhaps I can explain or understand.'

'I . . . I don't think I can.'

There was a silence for a moment; then they heard rain beginning against the windows.

In a voice of desperation, Gray said, 'What did I do wrong?' When his self-control gave way, it went completely. A great sob rose up in his chest and made him double over. 'For God's sake, Charlotte, please tell me what I did wrong.'

Gray held out his hand to her, but Charlotte would not take it.

'My dear girl,' he sobbed, 'whatever it was, can you not forgive me?'

546

Confronted at last with the outline of the thing that had lain for so long unrealised in her mind, Charlotte was too terrified to look.

'No,' she said. 'No, I can't.'

★ ★ ★

In the days that followed, Charlotte tried never to be alone with her father. When he returned from work at six o'clock, she made sure she went upstairs for her bath, then helped her mother in the kitchen until it was time for dinner.

In the afternoons, she went for long walks in the hills and tried to understand herself. She could not but be impressed by her father's anguish. If he had done something terrible to her, how would he have been able to beg her to explain it to him? He had always been an honest man; he would not only have thought dissimulation to have been immoral in such circumstances, but would also have been incapable of acting.

Yet, if he truly had no idea of what had passed between them, it must mean that she had imagined it, or somehow misremembered. This she could not accept, or force herself to believe. In some physical and cruel way, he had destroyed her innocence; and while the fallible functions of memory would not tell her exactly how, she was as certain of that simple fact as she could be, with an instinctive conviction that had never before let her down.

Still it seemed vital to her to establish what had really happened, and she felt agonisingly close to doing so. She thought of what her father had told her about the war, about his dreams and subsequent sufferings. For some reason, she remembered, too, the letter from father to daughter she had found at Le Bourget-Drancy station. She strained at the memory of her own childhood, at the sense of some rapture lost. Yet it all remained like some frozen sea: great blocks of ice, submerged, but static, and beyond the melting capacity of her conscious will.

As she strode over the damp hills and turned for home, she felt torn between guilt that her father stood in some way wrongly accused by her and an absolute knowledge that her memory had, if not in detail, then at least in essence recorded what had happened.

At tea-time on the third day of her visit she returned from her walk and went to the kitchen, where her mother was taking a tray of scones from the oven.

Amelia Gray gave her usual friendly, slightly startled smile of welcome. 'You're just in time,' she said, as she poured tea from the pot on the scrubbed table. 'Let's have it in here, shall we, as it's just the two of us?'

Perhaps her mother could help, thought Charlotte; perhaps this was the time to enlist her confidence. Somehow, the very thought of it was discouraging to Charlotte: her mother would turn her face from intimacy of this kind, she would run for some domestic cover.

In her state of heightened introspection this, too, seemed suggestive to Charlotte. Was this another aspect of the problem? Or was she now turning in such tight circles that she could no longer distinguish between the trivial and the significant?

She put her elbows on the table and sighed, holding her face between her hands, the restored colours of her hair tumbling down over her fingers.

Amelia Gray was looking at her daughter with anxious concern when the telephone rang.

'Oh, drat,' she said. 'Who can that be?'

She went into the sitting room to answer it. 'Charlotte,' she called out a few moments later. 'It's for you.'

'For me?' Charlotte was dragged out of her reverie. 'Who is it?'

'He didn't say,' said her mother, as she came back into the kitchen.

In the sitting room Charlotte picked up the big receiver from the polished occasional table where it lay on its side.

'Hello?'

'Is that Charlotte?'

'Yes, it is.'

'Charlotte, you may not remember me. It's a voice from long ago. This is Peter Gregory.'

'Oh, my God. Oh, my God.'

'Charlotte?'

'Oh, my God.'

★ ★ ★

At the end of their conversation, Gregory had to inhale deeply. He was sitting in the office of the convalescent home near Godalming, to which he had been sent on his return from North Africa. There had been a wait of two days before Daisy could contact her mother to find out the telephone number of Charlotte's parents, and he feared that she might already be on her way back to London by the time he got through.

Gregory was not by nature a timorous man, but on board the ship from Genoa he had run this conversation through his mind several times. At various points he had convinced himself that he should not contact Charlotte. He could not offer her what she was worth; all he could bring was this absurd passion that he had conceived for her almost in the moment of their separation, then kept doggedly alive in the months of his absence. He knew that it was this feeling alone that had brought him through the agony of his untended injuries and through the pain of his reconnection with the world.

He valued it accordingly, but was not convinced it was worth offering.

Only when he heard her stunned and gasping reaction to his voice did he fully register the depth of his passion for her. There was such struggle and humility in her tone, the sense of something so long and terribly desired, that he felt crushed by it. But for the first time since he had known Charlotte he no longer felt intimidated, and he understood that the complexity of her feelings was not for her the source of any sense of superiority but, on the contrary, the cause of awful anguish. For the first time he believed that his own life, however tarnished in his eyes, was what was necessary for the redemption of hers.

★ ★ ★

Charlotte put down the telephone and walked out of the house, down to the end of the garden. She sat on a wooden bench in an area of lawn surrounded by rhododendron bushes and tried to control her feelings. She could not at first think of Gregory as a person, as a man with a voice and hands and things of his own to say; his return seemed only a disembodied vindication of her long and solitary refusal to give up hope. She felt stunned by gratitude, because that hope had never amounted to belief.

In the evening, over dinner with her parents, her trance-like incredulity began to be penetrated by the first movements of joy. What would he look like? What would he say?

'You're in a world of your own tonight, Charlotte,' said her father.

'I'm sorry.' She smiled at him.

She tried to hold his eye and in some way to encourage him. She felt the return of Gregory had a bearing on her father, too, and that there might yet be some way out of their impasse.

That night, sleeping deeply beneath her old quilted eiderdown, she had a sequence of dreams. They were mostly of the intensely realised but inconsequential kind that her father's friend had characterised as 'neural waste'. She dreamed she was a nurse at war, and that Levade came to her with the wound on his shoulder gaping. She was on a ship, and had to organise interminable games among unruly children who would not listen to her orders. Finally, she dreamed she was herself a child. She was on the deck of the ship, surrounded by her dolls and by her books, and, from a door down to a lower deck, her father emerged.

Instinctively, she recoiled as he came and knelt beside her. He opened his arms and hugged her, hard, against his chest, then laid his face on her shoulder. Looking down, expecting to see his cruelty or rage, she saw instead that he was weeping. She brushed away the tears with her fingers; she soothed him and stroked his white hair.

★ ★ ★

All the next morning she paced round the house and garden. She had the feeling that the blocks of frozen memory were melting, that movement was coming back into these long-locked regions. There was nothing she could do to speed it up or clarify it, but she felt that physical activity would in some way help.

After lunch, she went for another walk, and, as she sat on a hill looking back towards the city of Edinburgh, she began to think of Levade's death. The rooms of the Domaine — her bedroom and, in particular, his studio — seemed very clear in her mind: she could smell the lime wood of the back staircase, the oil paints, the dusty air.

She mourned her dead friend at last, thinking of his undignified death in that half-built place among strangers. She cried for his lonely end and for his defeated struggle, and she cried, if she was honest, a little for herself as well, and a suspicion that, whatever the degree of anxiety in which she had lived those days in the Domaine, she might never again exist at such a level of intensity.

Later, when she was walking home, she felt an uplifting gratitude towards Levade. Perhaps a dozen times in his life he had painted pictures in which he had been able to pierce the deceptive layer of appearances that clothed the world, to go beyond it and re-imagine a deeper existence that lay beneath. Then he had become a prisoner of his sensual desires, and of his mind's refusal to unlock itself, with the result that the last ten years of his life had passed with a vain hammering at the gates of his memory. Yet, Charlotte thought, as her quickening steps carried her toward the lights of the village below, that dreaming process he had so passionately desired had worked instead for her: what had long imprisoned him had set her free.

★ ★ ★

The next day was a Saturday, the last but one of Charlotte's intended visit. Her mother went into Edinburgh to do some shopping. Charlotte said she would stay and cook lunch for her father. Both her parents looked surprised, and her mother talked temptingly of Princes Street and new clothes.

Charlotte remained firm and, when they had had lunch and cleared the plates away, forced herself to confront her father once more.

'You know what we were saying the other night? About . . . you and me, being a father and so on.'

'Yes.' Gray sounded uneasy.

They were in the sitting room, either side of the fire, on which he now self-consciously threw another log.

Charlotte folded her hands in her lap. 'I've been thinking. I think I must apologise.'

'Oh, yes?' Gray was at his most discouraging. His tone suggested that not only was what Charlotte was trying to say intrusively personal, but that it was also likely to be misguided.

Very slowly, and picking the words she felt were as gentle as possible while still being truthful, Charlotte said, 'All my life I've believed that when I was young, perhaps seven or eight, you did something to me. You hurt me. I've never known exactly how. All I knew for sure was the result. I felt as though my childhood had ended. As though something had been prematurely and cruelly taken from me.'

Gray looked appalled. 'What did I do?'

Still speaking with slow precision, despite a constricting pressure in her lungs, Charlotte said, 'My memory is of some physical contact that went too far. Later on, I came to believe that it might have been something sexual. I don't believe that now, but only something like that could have explained the depth of the wound you inflicted.' She found her cheeks and forehead were burning.

Gray swallowed. For a moment his devastation at what his daughter had said appeared to overwhelm him; then some professional curiosity steadied him. 'I'm glad you've told me, I'm glad it's out at last.'

His shattered voice sounded anything but glad, but Charlotte was reassured by his response. There was no trace of guilty recollection, and his attitude meant she might now carry on.

'Since I've been here, in these last few days,' she said, 'I feel as though I've somehow come to grips with it. This thing, this terrible thing that has been in my mind all my life . . . ' She began to sob, then

553

controlled herself. 'By a complicated process, too much to explain, I think I may have understood.'

Gray was nodding, but did not speak.

'Do you remember anything?' said Charlotte. 'Any incident?'

Gray stood up. 'Before you tell me what you think, would it help if I told you what I had thought? Then if we think the same, at least you won't think I'm just agreeing with you to bring it all to a close?'

'All right.'

Gray chose his words with equal care. 'What you must understand first is that you were a miracle to me. At that time of war. To return from the scenes I'd witnessed, and to see this girl child . . . To look at my hands, know what they had done, what my eyes had seen and then to think that from inside my own body I had created this female flesh . . . '

He shook his head and breathed in tightly for a moment. 'That's what a father feels about a girl — this otherness, this innocence, when I myself felt so terribly old and filthy and corrupted by experience. And as a little girl you did love me. Then I was aware that something was wrong. You weren't an easy child, Charlotte.'

'I know.'

'You turned into such a bluestocking. You were so ferocious with your studies, so good at them. But I felt I couldn't reach you. And then those awful depressions. I felt powerless. This was my profession, and I couldn't help you. Of course, I strongly suspected that I was the problem, or part of it. It was agonising to watch. Can you imagine? Because, still, for me you were the hope of life and femininity.'

'I can imagine.'

'Your mother was . . . a wonderful woman, but she was not comforting in any physical sense. I don't mean like that, but — '

'I understand.'

'Perhaps there was a time, a particular incident.' Gray spoke very slowly. 'Perhaps there was. I can honestly say I don't remember, but perhaps at some level I was determined not to. And this cruelty I forced on you. Do you know what it was?'

'I think so,' said Charlotte, very softly. 'War. The memory of war.'

There was a long silence in the room. Eventually, Gray said, 'Better men than I were destroyed by it.'

'I'm sorry I was no comfort to you.'

'I must have asked too much. I asked a child to bear the weight of those unspeakable things, a weight that drove grown men mad.'

'And do you think there was a time, an incident?'

Gray breathed in deeply. 'I do remember crying once. I was suddenly caught by this frightening emotion I had so long held in check. I remember it was triggered by something trivial, then it came up out of me with these terrible noises, a sort of primeval howling. I think you came to me. Perhaps you were worried by the noise. Perhaps I shouted at you to go away because I didn't want you to stay.'

'No. You did want me to stay. You held me, and you held me so hard it almost crushed me. But I don't think it was that pain that remained with me. It was the sight and the sound of your grief. Somehow you must have conveyed to me the horror of what you had seen. You told me about it. The millions of dead.'

Gray's voice was scarcely audible. 'I was so alone.'

'And is it possible that I would remember it as physical pain?'

'It's possible.' He lifted his head. 'Your memory may have been trying to protect you. To lay a screen across something worse. A child would find it easier to think of being hurt in some way, crushed or beaten, than to look on the misery I had somehow opened up to you.'

Charlotte was very calm. 'I think that's right, I think that may be right.'

Her father, meanwhile, was distraught. 'But my dear Charlotte, to think that I did this to you. That I couldn't face it on my own. That I had to take away all your poor childish innocence to help me bear it.' He began to weep. 'The faces of those young men at dawn . . . All that joy that should have been yours.'

Charlotte stood up and went to her father. She held out her arms.

Gray came into her embrace and laid his head on her shoulder. He was howling. 'All that innocence. From my own daughter.'

'It doesn't matter,' said Charlotte, as she held her father in her arms and stroked his face. She felt love erupt in her. 'It doesn't matter now, it doesn't matter any more.'

7

By the time Charlotte returned to London, Peter Gregory had been moved from the convalescent home and sent to an airfield in Suffolk to be debriefed by the RAF. Both of them used Daisy's flat as a place to leave messages, but there followed a frustrating three days' delay before he would be free to come back to the capital.

Charlotte returned to her room in Riding House Street, but it was only for a short time, as a place in the flat was shortly to become vacant again.

'The invitations went out while you were in Edinburgh,' said Daisy. 'There's one here for you. Shall I read it out?'

'Go on.' Charlotte was on the telephone in the hall of the hostel.

'Colonel and Mrs Michael Ridley invite you to the marriage of their daughter Sally to Mr Robin Morris on 3 June 1943 at St Andrew's Church, etcetera, etcetera, and afterwards at the White House, Crookham End. Isn't it marvellous? What are you going to wear?'

Charlotte laughed. 'God knows. Is this Robin Morris the stuffed shirt?'

'Yes, that's right.'

'I think I met him once. On a train. Does he work in the Foreign Office or something like that?'

'That's right. Sally's in seventh heaven, as you can imagine. Anyway, you can have your old room back if you like. Alison can move into Sally's.'

'I think I'd rather have Sally's if you don't mind.'

'I thought your old room would have sentimental memories.'

'Yes, it does. But it's a bit small, to be honest, Daisy.

And we don't want to inconvenience Alison, do we?'

'Not very romantic, are you, Charlotte?'

'Oh, I wouldn't say that.'

Later in the day Charlotte went into the offices of G Section in Marylebone, where Mr Jackson told her she could have a further week's leave before her new posting came through.

She walked up Marylebone High Street and over into Regent's Park. It was a warm spring day. Mothers were pushing children along the paths; there was a certain lightness in their step and in their called greetings. Charlotte passed the coffee stall where she had bought a leaden bun one day in her lunch break from Dr Wolf's consulting rooms. She could still recall the feeling of intense separation from the world that meeting Gregory had induced in her. She had never really believed that it would work out happily; she had hoped, but she had not believed. Before she left Edinburgh, her father had warned her that it was dangerous ever to think that one had solved buried problems of memory and fear. The human desire for neatness, he said, would always ultimately be defeated by the chaos of the mind's own truths.

Charlotte resented this dour note at the moment of her joy and freedom, but recognised that he was probably right. She would never really know what had happened, but between them they had come close enough to the truth. It would suffice, she knew, because in the days that followed, the feeling of relaxation continued. As she walked through Regent's Park, she felt that a long-broken circle had finally been closed: as a grown woman she had re-established contact with her childhood self, and there was now a continuous line through her life.

★ ★ ★

558

Peter Gregory arranged to meet Charlotte the next evening in Daisy's flat. Daisy said she could organise for all three tenants to be out until at least ten o'clock, so they would have plenty of time to themselves.

Gregory took a train to London in the morning. He had booked a table for dinner at a restaurant near the flat, and somehow had to pass the day. In the afternoon, he went to a cinema in Leicester Square, but found it impossible to concentrate on the film, a patriotic naval adventure, full of improbably stoical sailors. The expectation of seeing Charlotte was so intense that he felt as though his skin was going to burst beneath the pressure.

He walked out of the film and down to the river. What would he say to her? What physical reaction was going to take place? Would his wounded leg give way? Would he shake so much that he would have to sit down? Later, he went to a pub in Chelsea, where he sat in the window and drank beer. He thought of Forster and all the others he had flown with. Those few, hot weeks had burned themselves into his memory and into the flesh of who he was, but in the turmoil of his nervous anguish he no longer felt that by continuing to live he was in some way unfaithful to them.

He bought some flowers from a barrow on the Brompton Road as he walked north in the early evening. His leg was beginning to hurt, and he hailed a taxi to take him the rest of the way. He had concealed the champagne in a briefcase with an evening paper, so that when she opened the door all she would see were the flowers. It was not too presumptuous.

He was talking to himself in the back of the cab. He was more frightened than he had ever been in flying. What terrified him was the thought of some hideous physical collapse, of his bones and blood breaking.

He was trembling as he went up the steps and rang the doorbell. He stared hard at the painted wood

559

of the door as he waited. He could not picture Charlotte's face.

The door opened, revealing at first shadow and space, then all at once a young woman in a summer dress with a cardigan draped over her shoulders.

Gregory stepped inside and wordlessly held out the flowers. Charlotte took them from him, then dropped them on top of the briefcase as she opened her arms and gathered him in, pressing her cheek against his. He smelled the lily of the valley on her neck and burst into tears.

* * *

Later, in the restaurant, he told her about Jacques and Béatrice, how they had cared for him and how he was determined to revisit them. When he came to the part of the story that took place in the Mayor's front room, he noticed that Charlotte had stopped eating and was holding her knife and fork in mid-air. He described his journey to Marseille, but left out the more adventurous episodes, deterred by some residual airman's code against what the men called shooting a line. He talked a little of the crash and his injuries, and spoke of Nancy and of Gianluca, who had been as good as his improbable word.

All the time Gregory talked, he felt compassion emanate from Charlotte, not some passive sympathy, but a radiant force that seemed to soothe his wounds and make past unhappiness appear something insubstantial, hard even to remember.

Then Charlotte told him how she had been to visit Monsieur Chollet in Clermont Ferrand, and of her despair when he said he had had no word. She described her friendship with Julien and Levade, and told him how Levade had died.

Her story was more complicated than his, and

towards the end she gave up. She held out her hand across the table and took Gregory's. She sat for a long time staring into his eyes, holding his hand in hers.

When they went back to Daisy's flat, Gregory opened the champagne and they drank to Jacques and Béatrice; to Monsieur Chollet in his oily garage; to Gianluca and Nancy; to Levade and Julien; to Sylvie Cariteau and little Anne-Marie. Charlotte could not bring herself to mention André and Jacob.

'I'll have to go soon,' said Gregory.

'You don't have to go just because the others are coming back.'

'I don't think I could face Daisy tonight.'

'You'll have to soon. When you come to Sally's wedding.'

'Am I invited?'

'You will be.'

Gregory looked round the sitting room. He said, 'Do you remember the first time we came back here after lunch in that awful hotel in Streatley? You were so shy.'

'I had a good deal to be shy about.'

'And now?'

'Now . . . ' Charlotte sighed. 'Now I feel so many things. I feel exhausted by happiness.'

'Not sad?'

'Well, there are never just the broad sunlit uplands.'

Gregory also sighed. He took out a cigarette, keeping himself in control, not wishing to force anything.

Charlotte suddenly turned and unleashed her most unguarded, intimate smile. 'And what do you feel?'

Gregory put down the cigarette. 'For the time being I feel that I would like it if, just for a moment, just for a second, you would wrap your arms round me and let me feel your skin on mine. That's all I ask.'

Charlotte came towards him. He looked into her face

and saw that there there was a power of acquired self-knowledge that had steadied her eyes' once prodigally sensitive and unsettled gaze. He stretched out his hands, hesitantly, and touched the bare flesh of her forearms.

'That's all you ask,' she said in her humorous, forgiving voice, as she held him hard against her. 'My darling, that's all there is.'

★ ★ ★

But he came back in the middle of the night, bribed his way past the night watchman of her block in Riding House Street and knocked softly on her door.

'Oh my darling, my darling,' she said.

She told him everything this time, about her father and her lost childhood, about Julien and the boys and Levade, and, as she saw the anguish in his tearful eyes, Charlotte had for the first time in her life the exquisite exhilaration of being understood.

He made love to her in the narrow bed and covered all of her with his hands and his lips. She had no modesty or inhibition; she looked at herself through his dazed eyes and felt powerful with the desperation she ignited in him. When they made love again, she thought for a moment of Levade. She felt he would have approved, and she laughed for a moment, not without sympathy for the man who had died, but because she was alive.

It was growing light outside when she could leave him alone long enough to sleep. She could see smoky rain pattering on the roof tiles.

8

A week later, Charlotte went in to G Section headquarters to receive details of her posting to Suffolk. Before she left, Mr Jackson handed her a letter.

'This was brought back by one of our chaps yesterday. I've given him the most tremendous ticking off, as you can imagine. If he'd been found with this on him they'd have known at once what sort of game he was in. That's the trouble with agents. Once they're out there, some of them seem to feel invincible.' He gave her a knowing look. 'Anyway, I hope it's good news.'

Charlotte recognised the handwriting before she opened the letter and saw the signature: 'Octave'. She took the letter up to Regent's Park and walked up to a semi-circle of chairs arranged in front of the bandstand.

My dear Danièle,

I doubt whether you will ever read this letter, but I want to write to you anyway, to set out my thoughts. And who knows, perhaps some Englishman will bring it back to London. You know how reckless these English are.

I am in a very cosy little farm in the hills, quite a long way now from our own town. (I'll be at least prudent enough not to mention actual names). I'm with César, who is a splendid young man, and half a dozen others in their twenties who have come to escape the Statutory Work Order. We have enough arms for the time being and are receiving more volunteers all the time. Monsieur Laval's perpetual desire to please the Germans has rebounded greatly to our advantage.

I have heard no news from my father, but I'm hopeful that the worst rumours about camps and so on are not true. C. told me that, alas, the boys were taken. I pray for their safety. C. travels a lot and brings news as in some way he has managed to keep up good appearances as a model citizen.

I, on the other hand, am not so well respected in the town and must keep my head down. The death of a certain person has not been connected in any way with me as far as C. has been able to discover. I can say no more about this in any detail. However, following scenes at which you were present (or later scenes at which you can guess), our friends in grey do not like me.

I will wait until the war is over. Things will be forgotten if we win. In fact, history is already being rewritten. C. tells me that since the war has turned, many of the Marshal's oldest supporters are saying they never trusted him and that the General was always the best bet. Some of the most dedicated Pétainists are already beginning to talk about 'our Anglo-Saxon friends' and 'the noble Tartar'!

We will win; somehow we will win. And we have kept alive something of France to make the victory worthwhile. That is the achievement of the dark days.

How long it will take, I don't know, because it's very complicated. Within an hour or so of here I know of three different resistance groups. One of them detests the other more than it detests the Occupant! This is a civil war as well as a national war; it is a fight for influence and for possession of history. It is squalid, Danièle, it is mean and horrible, and the only way our group keeps going is to remember its clear objective: to defeat the invader.

I expect you're safe at home now. Perhaps you're even back with your lover. Dear Danièle, your friendship was a wonderful thing to me at that time of greatest darkness. Being a man, an awful base creature, I do also treasure the memory of the night of the drop, and I will never forget it. But I know that it was not the most important thing, and I do know that your future is elsewhere.

As for me, I'm very excited by what we can do. Despite the squalor and the shame and the bloodshed that will come, I feel great hope. We will be free, and we will have a true government again. I will return to Paris and I will see my old boss Monsieur Weil restored and in his pomp, ordering oysters from the big restaurants on the Boulevard de Montparnasse.

Will you come down for the opening of the hotel? What a party we'll have. And I'll come to visit you as well, many times in the years to come. Thank you for everything, Danièle, my friend, my dear, dear friend. A thousand kisses, 'Octave'.

The day of Sally's wedding dawned hot and clear. Charlotte awoke in the bed in Sally's old room, having come down from her holding school in Suffolk the night before. Sally was with her parents, but Daisy and Alison kept the bathroom occupied for the first two hours of the morning. Charlotte was still in her dressing gown when they heard Michael Waterslow's imperative hooting in the street below.

Daisy pulled up the window and shouted that he and Gregory should come upstairs. Charlotte dressed in her bedroom and hurriedly put on her make-up in the finally vacated bathroom. When she went into the sitting room, she found Peter Gregory and Michael Waterslow drinking bottled beer, while Daisy and Alison completed their preparations.

Michael was in a morning suit, Gregory was in

uniform, his unusually neat appearance spoiled by a small speck of blood on the collar of his shirt. Charlotte kissed his smooth cheek.

'Must you have that stick?' she said.

'I thought it made me look distinguished.'

'Just as you like.' She straightened his lapels and smiled.

All of them were ready: they stood in a circle inspecting each other's appearance. Alison, a slender, dark-haired woman, was in a pre-war Hardy Amies suit; she indignantly pointed out that Charlotte's dress had too many pleats in the skirt and that both the collar and belt were wider than wartime restrictions allowed. Daisy was wearing a floral print dress with a turban and sunglasses.

After almost an hour in the car, as they approached rural Surrey, Gregory asked Michael if he would mind making a short detour. He had made an arrangement to meet someone, he said, some time after midday. In a village with some Tudor and more mock-Tudor houses with pots of geraniums outside their doors, Gregory directed Michael to a pub called the Rose and Crown. The bar was cool and dark after the hot June sunshine outside.

'Greg! I never thought you'd make it!'

Borowski loomed out of a shadowy corner and took Gregory's hand. 'You remember Leslie, don't you?'

'Still alive, Brind?' said Gregory.

Leslie Brind touched the wood of the bar before shaking hands with Gregory, who introduced the others.

Charlotte watched the delight the men took in each other's company as they poured drinks into one another and competed in their mocking rudeness. Gregory was persuaded by Borowski to stay for just one more, and then by Brind for just one more on top of that, but they were still in good time for lunch at the town nearest to the wedding. It was market day, and many of the stallholders were packing up and going off in search of food and drink. Michael swung the car beneath an arch in the high street, into a lane that ran down beside the White Hart Hotel and to a car park behind.

Inside the hotel they followed a carpeted corridor to the lounge bar, which was full of local people from the market as well as others in uniform or morning dress who were on their way to the wedding. The women sat at a table while Michael and Gregory pushed their way to the bar.

The bell on the till was ringing in a continuous monotone as a barmaid from the public bar was summoned to help. A tray of drinks was held high above the throng, with tall mugs of beer, glasses of fizzy drinks with slices of cucumber and orange, smaller glasses with cherries on sticks and pink gin. Gregory arrived with an oval plate of sandwiches, hastily cut by the harassed barmaid, but full of fat ham and mustard that, Charlotte thought, would have caused a riot in Lavaurette.

Charlotte found herself swept up in the air of slightly frantic joy. There was no point in resisting it, she thought, as she raised her glass and drank to Sally's health for the third time that morning.

She looked across at Gregory, who was in earnest conversation with Alison. In all the long months she had forgotten how much she enjoyed his company — the simple pleasure of being with him. And, as he put his head on one side, the better to listen to something Alison was saying, she thought how she had also forgotten how beautiful he was, how very beautiful.

When they reached the churchyard at last, Charlotte saw Dick Cannerley and Robin Morris in anxious conversation. Morris went inside the church, while Cannerley stood for a moment with a pile of service sheets. He divided them between two other young men in morning dress, then followed Morris inside. Cannerley had aged, Charlotte thought.

She stood by the lych gate where Michael had dropped them while he went off to find somewhere to park along the crowded verge. She inhaled the smell of cow parsley from the bank as she looked over the gently swelling tumuli of grassy graves that led up to the church.

There was Peter Gregory, leaning on his stick half way up the path, talking to Sally's mother, who was looking nervous beneath a wide-brimmed hat.

In Charlotte's mind, Gregory belonged to the category of dreams and traumas. The possibility of happiness he had once held out, and that she had briefly tasted, was of an intensity so great that even at the time it had seemed already to belong to the past. The power of such feelings, it seemed to her, lay in their promise of transcendence. People followed them and believed in them because they offered not only a paradise of sensation but the promise of meaning, too; like the miracle of art, they held out an explanation of all the other faltering lights by which people were more momentarily guided.

By their nature, however, these feelings were unreliable. Sometimes, they seemed to be remembered before they were even experienced, and they could leave in those who felt them a fear that only what had been forgotten, what stayed beyond the reach of recollection, was capable of truly transcending the limits of their sad incorporation in the flesh, and of their death.

To believe otherwise remained an act of faith, but it was one that Charlotte felt prepared to make. She walked up the path of the churchyard and took Gregory lightly by the arm. They went between the grey, lichen-covered headstones, and turned for the final few yards towards the door of the Norman church. As they came near to it, Charlotte slipped her hand into Gregory's and found that it already contained something — the handle of his stick.

She held on tight to his arm, nevertheless, as they walked through the porch, stepped over the stone threshold, worn smooth and low by many centuries of people passing through. They crossed into the cold interior of the church, heavy with the scent of cut flowers and the murmuring of the organ, into the soft air, and disappeared.

Author's Note

Although this is a work of fiction, I have tried to represent the historical background as it actually was. For this purpose I have relied only on books that were based on first-hand documentary evidence, or on such documents themselves. G Section is an invention, but its techniques are modelled on those of actual organisations. Pichon is a fictional character, but the Enquiry and Control Section and the Police for Jewish Affairs acted as described. The Milice oath and the quotation from the broadcast by the Commissioner for Jewish Affairs are verbatim.

Drancy came under German command in July 1943. There are survivors' accounts of both French and German régimes.

I should like to thank the large number of people in England and France who helped me with aspects of the background of this novel.

S.F. Toulouse-London 1995 – 1998.

Other titles in the
Charnwood Library Series:

LEGACIES
Janet Dailey

The sequel to THE PROUD AND THE FREE. It is twenty years since the feud within his family began, but Lije Stuart, son of the Cherokee chief The Blade, had never forgotten the killing of his grandfather. Now, a promising legal career beckons, and also the love of his childhood sweetheart, Diane Parmalee, the daughter of a US Army officer. Yet as it reawakens, their love is beset by the beginning of civil war.

'L' IS FOR LAWLESS
Sue Grafton

World War II fighter pilot Johnny Lee had died and his grandson was trying to claim military funeral benefits, but none of the authorities have any record of Fighter J. Lee. Was the old man once a US spy? When PI Kinsey Millhone is asked to straighten things out, she finds herself pursued by a psychopath bearing a forty-year-old grudge . . .

BLOOD LINES
Ruth Rendell

This is a collection of long and short stories by Ruth Rendell that will linger in the mind.

THE SUN IN GLORY
Harriet Hudson

When industrialist William Potts sets himself to build a flying machine, his adopted daughter, Rosie, works through the years as his mechanic. In 1906 Pegasus is almost ready, and onto the scene comes Jake Smith, a man who has as deep a love of the air as Rosie herself. But Jake sparks off a deadly rivalry, and the triumph of flight twists into tragedy.

A WOMAN SCORNED
M. R. O'Donnell

Five years after the tragedy that ruined her fifteenth birthday, Judith Carty returns to Castle Moore and resumes her flirtation with its heir, Rick Bellingham. The tragic events of the past forge a special bond between the young couple, but there are those who have a vested interest in the failure of the romance.

PLAINER STILL
Catherine Cookson

Following the success of her previous collection of essays and poems, LET ME MAKE MYSELF PLAIN, Catherine Cookson has compiled a further selection of thoughts, recollections, and observations on life — and death — together with another collection of the poems she prefers to describe as 'prose on short lines'.

THE LOST WORLD
Michael Crichton

The successor to JURASSIC PARK.

It is now six years since the secret disaster of Jurassic Park, when that extraordinary dream of science and imagination came to a crashing end — the dinosaurs destroyed, and the park dismantled. There are rumours that something has survived . . .

MORNING, NOON & NIGHT
Sidney Sheldon

When Harry Stanford, one of the wealthiest men in the world, mysteriously drowns, it sets off a chain of events that reverberates around the globe. At the family gathering following the funeral, a beautiful young woman appears, claiming to be Harry's daughter. Is she genuine, or is she an impostor?

FACING THE MUSIC
Jayne Torvill and Christopher Dean

The world's most successful and popular skating couple tell their own story, from their working-class childhoods in Nottingham to world stardom. Finally, they describe how they created their own show, FACE THE MUSIC, with a superb corps of international ice dancers.

ORANGES AND LEMONS
Jeanne Whitmee

When Shirley Rayner is evacuated from London's East End, she finds herself billeted with the theatre's most romantic couple, Tony and Leonie Darrent. She becomes firm friends with their daughter, Imogen, and the two girls dream of making their names on the stage. But they have forgotten the very different backgrounds from which they come.

HALF HIDDEN
Emma Blair

Holly Morgan, a nurse in a hospital on Nazi-occupied Jersey, falls in love with a young German doctor, Peter Schmidt, and is racked by guilt. Can their love survive the future together or will the war destroy all their hopes and dreams?

THE GREAT TRAIN ROBBERY
Michael Crichton

In Victorian London, where lavish wealth and appalling poverty exist side by side, one man navigates both worlds with ease. Rich, handsome and ingenious, Edward Pierce preys on the most prominent of the well-to-do as he cunningly orchestrates the crime of his century.

THIS CHILD IS MINE
Henry Denker

Lori Adams, a young, unmarried actress, gives up her baby boy for adoption with great reluctance. She feels that she and the baby's father, Brett, are not in a position to provide their child with all he deserves. But when, two years later, life has improved dramatically for Lori and Brett, they want their child returned . . .

THE LOST DAUGHTERS
Jeanne Whitmee

At school, Cathy and Rosalind have one thing in common: each is the child of a single parent. For them both, the transition to adulthood is far from easy — until their unexpected reunion. Working together, the two friends take a bold step that will help them to become independent women.

THE DEVIL YOU KNOW
Josephine Cox

When Sonny Fareham overhears a private conversation between her lover and his wife, she realises she is in great danger. Shocked and afraid, she flees to the north of England to make a new life — but never far away is the one person who wants to destroy everything that she now holds dear.

A LETHAL INVOLVEMENT
Clive Egleton

When Captain Simon Oakham of the Royal Army pay Corps goes A.W.O.L. immediately after a suspicious interview with the security service, Peter Ashton is asked to track him down. The key to it all is an embittered woman whose unsuspecting knowledge of a lethal involvement makes her especially vulnerable.

THE WAY WE WERE
Marie Joseph

This is a collection of some of Marie Joseph's most outstanding short stories, and is the companion volume to WHEN LOVE WAS LIKE THAT. With compassion, insight and humour, these stories explore the themes of love — its hopes, joys, disappointments and reconciliations.

EXTREME DENIAL
David Morrell

When CIA agent Stephen Decker is sent on a sensitive mission to Italy, his partner is Brian McKittrick, the incompetent and embittered son of the former chairman of the National Security Council. Disobeying orders throughout the mission, McKittrick makes one final mistake: sleeping with the enemy.

THE WOOD BEYOND
Reginald Hill

Seeing the wood for the trees is a problem shared by Andy Dalziel and Edgar Wield, the latter in his investigations into bones found at a pharmaceutical research centre, and the former in his dangerous involvement with animal rights activist Amanda Marvell.

RAGE OF THE INNOCENT
Frederick E. Smith

The first of a trilogy.
Young Harry Miles clashes with Michael Chadwick, son of a wealthy landowner, and sows the seeds of a lifetime's conflict. When the 1914 – 18 war breaks out, Harry is driven into volunteering and finds himself under Chadwick's command. Taking his revenge, Chadwick makes Harry a machine gunner . . .

MOTHER OF GOD
David Ambrose

Tessa Lambert has just created the first viable artificial intelligence programme — a discovery so controversial that she must keep it a secret even from her colleagues at Oxford University. But soon there is to be a hacker stalking her on the Internet: a serial killer who is about to give her invention its own terrifying and completely malevolent life . . .

THE ANDROMEDA STRAIN
Michael Crichton

When *Project Scoop* sends satellites into outerspace to 'collect organisms and dust for study', one of them crashes into the town of Piedmont, Arizona. Soon after, all but two of the inhabitants are found dead from a strange disease. The scientists must trace what is causing the horrifying virus before it spreads . . .

TO WAR WITH WHITAKER
Countess of Ranfurly

When World War II broke out, Dan Ranfurly was dispatched to the Middle East with his faithful valet, Whitaker. These are the diaries of his young wife, Hermione, who, defying the War Office, raced off in hot pursuit of her husband. When Dan was taken prisoner, Hermione vowed never to return home until they were reunited.

IN PRESENCE OF MY FOES
Frederick E. Smith

Sequel to RAGE OF THE INNOCENT.
Harry Miles is now recovered from his war wounds, but a mysterious and compelling urge drives him back to the Front. He faces the menace of Michael Chadwick, his commanding officer and life-long rival, and the fearsome German offensive of March 1918.

YEARS OF THE FURY
Frederick E. Smith

The third volume of the trilogy which began with RAGE OF THE INNOCENT and continued with IN PRESENCE OF MY FOES.
The First World War has ended and, with Harry Miles back from France, he and Mary are hoping to settle down to their married life at last. But they have not taken account of their two unrelenting enemies.

FAMILY TREES
Kate Alexander

Catherine Carew fills her life with good works and is a pillar of the community. But in her distant university days she was a very different person. One night's indiscretion leaves her with a burden of guilt and regret that overshadows her later years — until a stranger appears on her doorstep . . .

INDIAN SUMMER
James Mitchell

Mixed blood courses through Veronica Higgins' veins, resulting in an exotic beauty. But to the expatriates in India at the height of the British Raj she is just another 'bloody chee-chee'. When her Aunt Poppy falls in love with an English industrialist, the three set off for his homeland. The arrival of one of England's richest men with two exquisitely beautiful women causes a flurry of excitement . . .

VANISHING POINT
Morris West

When Carl Strassberger, the son of an old New York banking family, renounces his position in the business to become an artist, his place is taken by his brother-in-law, Larry Lucas. But when Larry disappears, Carl must put himself at risk as he investigates those who live 'on the dangerous edge of things'.

THE RUNAWAY JURY
John Grisham

In Biloxi, Mississippi, a landmark trial begins routinely, then swerves mysteriously off course. The jury is behaving strangely, and at least one juror is convinced that he is being watched. Is the jury somehow being manipulated or even controlled? If so, by whom? And, more importantly, why?

SHADOWS OF THE PAST
Palma Harcourt

When Christopher Grayson, a young Oxford don, decides to trace his family history, he learns that during the Second World War the de Mourvilles were condemned as Nazi sympathisers. Even worse, his grandfather was accused of crimes against humanity. But someone is on Christopher's trail, willing to kill in order to keep a tragic secret.

YEAR OF THE TIGER
Jack Higgins
When Paul Chavasse looks out of his window on a November evening, he is unaware that the figure standing opposite knows a great deal about his past. Back in 1961, Chavasse — now chief of a little-known section of British Intelligence — had been captured by the Chinese. When he had at last escaped he knew that he could be taking with him the means of his betrayal.

THAT CAMDEN SUMMER
LaVyrle Spencer
It is 1916 and Roberta Jewett has returned to the town where she was raised. But in Camden, Maine, a woman divorced is a woman shunned. Only Gabriel Farley treats her with respect. Although the chemistry between them is undeniable, they fight it. Then, a brutal act of violence forces them to aknowledge the powerful feelings that have grown between them.

PASSIONATE TIMES
Emma Blair
When Corporal Reith Douglas was injured during the Second World War, he lost his memory. But once he returns to his wife, Irene, in Glasgow, he gradually recalls the joy of his early married life, and the pain he suffered when Irene declared her love for a renowned villain. Little does he realise that he could well recapture the passionate times of his past.

NOT JUST A SOLDIER'S WAR
Betty Burton

For Lu Wilmott, the call to Spain is irresistible. Signing up as a driver, she breaks the last link with her past and becomes Eve. Her work takes her close to figures of many nationalities, but it is the country and its people in the struggle against Franco that have the greatest effect on her.

THE WITCH OF EXMOOR
Margaret Drabble

The Palmer family and their children are coming to the end of an enjoyable meal. As usual, their conversation is brought back to their eccentric mother, Frieda, who has abandoned them and gone off to live alone on Exmoor. She has always been a monster mother with a mysterious past. What is she plotting against them now?

LEWIN'S MEAD
E. V. Thompson

The sequel to the bestselling novel BECKY
When artist Fergus Vincent forsakes the Bristol slums of Lewin's Mead he leaves behind him Becky, the street urchin whom he loved and married. After Becky is struck down in a cholera epidemic, she is cared for by Simon McAllister, a blind musician. But she never gives up hope that one day Fergus will return.

ENDPEACE
Jon Cleary

When Detective Inspector Scobie Malone's host, the wealthy Sydney newspaper magnate Sir Harry Huxwood, is shot dead in his own bed, it is Malone's job to name the killer. He uncovers the stuff of headlines, including a family dogfight over millions of dollars.

TO THE HILT
Dick Francis

Artist Alexander Kinloch's peaceful existence on a remote Scottish mountain is shattered when he returns home one day to find a group of strangers waiting for him. The days that follow contain more danger than he could ever have imagined.

WISH LIST
Fern Michaels

Hollywood actress Ariel Hart has become tired of the empty glamour, so she returns to the place where she was once truly happy — where she was plain Aggie Bixby, in love with a dark-eyed boy named Felix. Then she comes across wealthy rancher Lex Sanders, and there is something familiar about those smouldering eyes . . .